SUPERIOR SATURDAY

Garth Nix

Illustrated by Tim Stevens

GALAXY PLUS

First published in the USA in 2008
by Scholastic Inc
First published in Great Britain in 2008
by HarperCollins Children's Books
This Large Print edition published by
BBC Audiobooks
by arrangement with
HarperCollins Children's Books 2009

ISBN: 978 1405 663519

British Library Cataloguing in Publication Data available

Printed and bound in Great Britain by
CPI Antony Rowe, Chippenham and Eastbourne

To all the patient readers and publishing folk who have been waiting for me to finish this book. And, as always, to Anna, Thomas and Edward, and all my family and friends.

PROLOGUE

Saturday, self-styled Superior Sorcerer of the House, stood in her private viewing chamber at the very apex of her dominion, atop the tower that she had been building for almost ten thousand years. This clear crystal-walled room was always at the top, the builders lifting it higher and higher as new levels were slotted in below.

Saturday looked down through the rain-washed glass, at the multitude of fuzzy green spots of light below. It looked like the tower, which was thousands of feet high, had suffered a vast, vertical infestation of green glow-worms, but the spots of light actually came from the green-shaded lamps that sat on every desk in the Upper House, in exactly the same position, just as each desk was set exactly in the middle of an open cube of wrought red iron, with a grille floor and no ceiling.

These cubes—the basic building blocks of Saturday's tower—ran on vertical and horizontal rails, ascending, descending or moving sideways according to the merits of the Denizens who worked at the desks.

Each cube was dragged into place by a series of chains that were driven by mighty steam engines, deep below the tower. The actual work of building the rails and fuelling the engines was done by bronze automatons and a small number of luckless Denizens who had failed Saturday in some way. Even lower in status were the grease monkeys, Piper's children who oiled and maintained the miles and miles of dangerous, fast-moving machinery.

Superior Saturday looked down upon her domain, but the sight of her mighty tower and the tens of thousands of sorcerers within it did not quicken her pulse. Eventually, though she fought against the urge, she stopped looking down and started looking up.

At first she saw only cloud, but then came a glimmer of green light, a darker, more mysterious green than the glow of her lamps. The clouds parted slightly to show the emerald ceiling of the Upper House, which was also the floor of the Incomparable Gardens. Saturday grimaced, an ugly look on her otherwise extraordinarily beautiful face. For ten thousand years she had been building her tower in order to reach and invade the Incomparable Gardens. Yet no matter how high she built, the Gardens moved further away, and Lord Sunday taunted her by making sure she was the only one to see it. If any of her Denizens looked up, the clouds would close again.

Saturday curled her lip and looked away, but her new view offered no solace. Far off, on the edge of the Upper House, there was a dark, vertical shadow that stretched from the ground to the clouds. Close up, it too would shine green, for it was a vast tree, one of the four Drasil trees that supported the Incomparable Gardens above.

The Drasil trees were the reason Saturday could never build her tower high enough, because the trees grew faster than she could build, and lifted the Gardens as they grew.

She had tried to destroy or stunt the Drasils with sorcery, poison and brute force, but none of her schemes had affected the trees in the slightest. She had sent Artful Loungers and Sorcerous Supernumeraries to climb the trunks and infiltrate the domain of Lord Sunday, but they had never made it further than halfway up, defeated by the huge defensive insects that lived in tunnels within the bark of the great trees. Even flying was out of the question. High above the clouds, the Drasils' branches spread everywhere, and the trees' limbs were predatory, vicious and very fast.

This had been the situation for millennia, with Saturday building, the Drasils growing, and Sunday remaining aloof and mighty above, secure in the Incomparable Gardens.

But all that had changed with a sneeze on the surface of a distant dead star. The Architect's Will had finally been released and had selected a Rightful Heir. Now that Heir was gathering the Keys from the disloyal Trustees. Arthur, his name was—a mortal whose success and speed had surprised not only Saturday.

Not that Arthur's triumphs mattered too much

to Saturday, given that she had been planning for the execution of the Will and the arrival of an Heir almost since the moment the Architect disappeared. She was not just a Trustee, with the power the Architect's Key gave her; she was also an enormously powerful and learned sorcerer in her own right. Apart from the Old One and the Architect, she was the most ancient entity in the Universe. Therein lay the canker in her heart. She was the first Denizen the Architect had made and she felt she should have been supreme over all others, including the Architect's children (an experiment she had decried at the time). It was not Sunday who should dwell in the Incomparable Gardens, but Saturday. Everything she did was directed to remedying this injustice.

A muffled cough behind her recalled Saturday to present events. She turned, her cloak of starshine and moonshade billowing up around her shapely legs. Apart from the cloak, which was an ancient thing of sorcery, Saturday wore a robe of spun gold scattered with tiny sapphires, and high-heeled shoes that were made of steel and had vicious points. Her long electric-blue hair was loose on her shoulders and restrained at the brow by a gold circlet on which sorcerous words looped and writhed, spelled out in shifting diamonds.

'I beg your pardon, Majesty,' said a tall, impeccably-dressed Denizen. He knelt as she turned around, his swallow-tailed coat falling on his impossibly shiny boot heels.

'You are the candidate to be my new Dusk,' said Saturday.

The Denizen bowed his head still lower, indicating agreement.

4

'The former Dusk was your brother? Turned out of the same mould?'

'Yes, Majesty, the elder of us by a moment.'

'Good,' said Saturday. 'He served me well, and was at least partially successful in his last assignment, though he met his end. Has Noon acquainted you with all the matters at hand?'

'I believe so, Majesty,' said the new Saturday's Dusk.

Saturday flicked a finger and her Dusk stood up. Though he was easily seven feet tall, his mistress was at least a foot taller, even without her steel shoes. In any case, he kept his head bowed, not daring to look her in the eye.

'Tell me then,' she said. 'Do all my enterprises conjoin for the final victory?'

'We believe so,' said Dusk. 'Though the House does not crumble as swiftly as was hoped at one time, it does fall, and our new offensive should accelerate matters. At present our reports show that Nothing has impinged greatly into the Far Reaches and across large areas of the Border Sea, and though it is not related to our activities, there has been some considerable damage to the mountain defences of the Great Maze. It is now almost certainly beyond the power of Dame Primus, as the Will calls itself, and its cat's-paw, Arthur, to prevent the destruction.'

'Good,' said Saturday. 'What of the effect upon the trees?'

'As the Nothing spreads, the deeper roots of the Drasil are severed. This has already slowed their growth by some six per cent. However, they still lift the Gardens faster than we can build. Projections indicate that when the entirety of the Far Reaches

5

and the Lower House has been devoured by Nothing, we will be able to build faster than the trees can grow and can reach the target position in days. If more of the House falls, it will be a matter of hours.'

'Excellent!' cried Saturday, a smile rippling across her shining, blue-painted lips. 'I trust the Front Door remains closed and the elevators secured? I want no interference from Primus or the Piper.'

'The Front Door remains shut, though the Lieutenant Keeper has petitioned the Court of Days for it to be reopened. So if Lord Sunday—'

'Sunday immures himself in the Gardens,' Saturday interrupted. 'He cares not for anything else. He will not interfere—at least not until it is too late for him to do anything.'

'As you say, Majesty,' said Dusk diplomatically. 'All elevator entrances into the Upper House have been sealed and are guarded, but it is believed that renegade operators have opened some services in other parts of the House.'

'Let them run about the ruins,' said Saturday. 'The sorceries against the Improbable Stair and the Fifth Key remain constant?'

'Four shifts of nine hundred sorcerers each maintain the wards. Twenty-eight hundred executive-level sorcerers wait at ready desks, should they need to counter any workings of the Keys held by the Pretender or a sorcerous attack from the Piper.'

'The Piper!' Saturday spat. 'If only I had managed to finish him centuries ago! At least he blames his brother. What is the latest news of the Piper? Have we got rid of his blasted Rats?'

6

Dusk proceeded with caution. 'We are not absolutely clear on what the Piper is doing. His forces have withdrawn from the Great Maze, presumably to the worldlet he made for his New Nithlings. But we have not yet located that worldlet, nor do we know if he masses his forces there against us or against Dame Primus.'

'Our defences will hold as well against the Piper as they will against the Pretender,' Saturday stated confidently. 'They cannot enter via elevator, Stair, Front Door or by use of the Fifth Key. There is no other way.'

Saturday's Dusk did not speak, but the faintest frown line appeared on his forehead, just for a moment, before he smoothed it away.

'And the Rats?' prompted Saturday.

'None has been spotted in five days. We have lost fourteen lower-level clerks and some Piper's children to the Rat-catcher automatons, and there have been requests that they be recalled.'

'No,' said Saturday. 'Keep them at it. I do not want those creatures sneaking about here.'

'Speaking of Piper's children, we employ a large number of them as grease monkeys and chain-hands, but there was a report that some of Sir Thursday's Piper's children were turned against him by the Piper. We would not want our Piper's children to be similarly turned against us.'

'Yes,' said Saturday. 'He has power over his creations and they must answer to his pipe. It is not an eventuality that should arise, if he is kept out of the Upper House, and we need those children to maintain our building speed. However, we should be prepared. Tell Noon to detail a suitable number of Sorcerous Supernumeraries to

7

shadow the Piper's children—and slay them, if I so command.'

'Very good, Majesty,' said Dusk. 'There is one other matter . . .'

'Yes?'

'The Pretender, this Arthur Penhaligon. We have just had a report that he has returned to the Secondary Realms, to Earth. Do we implement the contingency plan?'

Saturday smiled.

'Yes, at once. Do we know if he has a Key with him?'

'We do not know, Majesty, but circumstance suggests he has at least the Fifth Key.'

'I wonder if that will protect him? It will be interesting to see. Tell Pravuil to act at once.'

'Ahem . . .' Dusk coughed. 'I regret to say that it is not yet Saturday on Earth, Majesty. It is some forty minutes short of Friday's midnight, and the House and that Secondary Realm are in close temporal step.'

Saturday hesitated, weighing up the situation. The Accord between the Trustees was effectively broken, but the Treaty still existed and there could be sorcerous implications if she or her agents acted outside their allotted span of power in the Secondary Realms.

'Then Pravuil must strike as the twelfth chime of midnight fades,' she instructed. 'In the first second of Saturday. No later. See to it at once.'

'Yes, Majesty,' replied the new Dusk. After an elegant bow, he retreated to the silver spiral stair that led down to the desk cube immediately beneath the viewing chamber.

As soon as he was gone, Superior Saturday's

gaze was once again drawn to the sky, the parting clouds, and another infuriating but tantalising glimpse of the underside of the Incomparable Gardens.

CHAPTER ONE

It was dark outside the small private hospital, the street lights out and the houses across the road shut up tight. Only the faintest glowing lines around some windows indicated that there were probably people inside and that the city still had power. There were other lights in the sky, but these were the navigation lights of helicopters, tiny pinprick red dots circling high above. Occasionally a searchlight flickered down from one of the helicopters, closely followed by the harsh clatter of machine-gun fire.

Inside the hospital, a flash of light suddenly lit up the empty swimming pool, accompanied by a thunderclap that rattled every window and drowned the distant sounds of the choppers and gunfire. As the light from the flash slowly faded, a slow, regular drumbeat echoed through the halls.

In the front office, a tired woman clad in a

crumpled blue hospital uniform looked away from the videoscreen that was carrying the latest very bad news and jumped up to flick on the corridor lights. Then she grabbed her mop and bucket and ran. The thunderclap and drumming announced the arrival of Doctor Friday, and Doctor Friday always wanted the floors cleaned ahead of her, so she could see her reflection in the glossy surface of the freshly-washed linoleum.

The cleaner ran through the wards, turning on lights as she passed. Just before the pool room, she glanced at her watch. It was 11:15 on Friday night. Doctor Friday had never come so late before, but her servants sometimes did. In any case, the cleaner was not allowed to leave until the day was completely done. Not that there was anywhere to go, with the new quarantine in force and helicopters shooting anyone who ventured out on to the streets. The news was now also full of talk of a 'last-resort solution' to the 'plague nexus' that existed in the city.

Outside the pool room, the cleaner stopped to take a deep breath. Then she bent her head, dipped her mop and pushed it and the bucket through the doors, reaching up to flick the light switch without looking, as she had done so many times, on so many Fridays past. She had learned long ago not to look up, because then she might meet Friday's gaze or be dazzled by her mirror.

But it wasn't Friday or her minions who were emerging from the dark portal in the empty swimming pool and climbing up the ramp.

The cleaner stared at their bare feet and the blue hospital nightgowns. She dropped her mop, looked up and screamed.

'They're coming back! But they never come back!'

The sleepers that she had seen enter the pool only that morning, led by Doctor Friday herself, were shambling their way up, arms outstretched in front of them in the classic pose of sleepwalkers seen so often in films and television.

But this time Doctor Friday wasn't there, and neither were any of her ridiculously tall and good-looking assistants.

Then the cleaner saw the girl, the one who had been awake that morning. She was shepherding the very first sleeper, a woman at the head of the line, steering her to the centre of the ramp. The sleepers weren't as obedient as they had been going out, or as deeply asleep.

'Hi!' called the girl. 'Remember me?'

The cleaner nodded dumbly.

'My name's Leaf. What's yours?'

'Vess,' whispered the cleaner.

'Give us a hand then, Vess! We've got to get everyone into bed, at least for tonight.'

'What . . . what about Doctor Friday?'

'She's gone,' said Leaf. 'Defeated by Arthur!'

She gestured behind her and the cleaner saw a handsome young boy of a similar age to Leaf. His skin was almost glowing with good health, his hair was shiny and his teeth were very white. But that was not the most striking thing about him. He held a light in his hand, a brilliant star that the cleaner recognised as Friday's mirror.

'Sir!' said the cleaner, and she went down on one knee and bent her head. Leaf frowned and looked back at Arthur, and in that moment saw him anew.

'What?' asked Arthur. 'Hey, keep them walking

13

or we'll get a pile-up back here.'

'Sorry,' said Leaf. She hastily pulled the leading sleeper—her own Aunt Mango—out of the line and held on to her arm. 'It's . . . well, I just realised you look . . . you don't look the same as you used to.'

Arthur looked down at himself and then up again, his face showing puzzlement.

'You used to be a bit shorter than me,' said Leaf. 'You've grown at least three or four inches and got . . . um . . . better looking.'

'Have I?' muttered Arthur. Only a few weeks ago he would have been delighted to hear he was getting taller. Now it sent an unpleasant shiver through him. He glanced at the crocodile ring on his finger, the one that indicated just how far his blood and bone had been contaminated by sorcery. But before he could gauge how much of the ring had turned from silver to gold, he forced himself to look away. He didn't want to confirm right then and there if his transformation into a Denizen had gone beyond the point of no return. In his heart, he knew the answer without even looking at the ring.

'Never mind that now,' continued Arthur. 'We'd better get everyone settled down. What's your name again? Vess, we'll need your help getting all these sleepers back into bed, please. There's about two thousand of them, and we've only got Martine and Harrison to help.'

'Martine and Harrison?' yelped Vess. 'I haven't seen them in . . . I thought they were dead!'

'Martine and Harrison have been . . . looking after sleepers at Lady Friday's retreat,' Arthur reported. 'Hey! Leaf, they're running into the door!'

Leaf gently spun her aunt around to face the wall and sprinted ahead to guide the leading sleepers through the door, pressing down the catch to keep it open. Then she took a small silver cone from her belt and held it to her mouth. The cone was one of the tools Friday's servants used to direct the sleepers. It amplified and changed Leaf's speech, and Vess shivered as she caught the echo of Lady Friday's voice.

'Walk to an empty bed and stand next to it,' ordered Leaf. 'Walk to an empty bed and stand next to it.'

The sleepers obeyed, though they tended to bunch at a bed and bump against one another before one firmly established himself or herself next to the bedhead. Only then would the others shamble off. Leaf ran back to her aunt, who was turning in circles trying to obey the command to find a bed.

Arthur stayed back at the pool, repeating Leaf's instruction to the sleepers as they came through. He didn't need a silver cone to be obeyed, probably because he held the Fifth Key, or because the sleepers responded to the power in his voice, feeling the authority of his position as the Rightful Heir of the Architect.

In outward appearance he looked just like a boy, but Arthur had wrested five Keys from five of the faithless Trustees. Now he ruled over the majority of the House, the epicentre of the Universe. In the process he felt he had grown much older, even if little time had actually passed. He also knew that he was becoming less human.

The sleepers kept coming through, emerging out

15

of the dark floor of the pool that was in fact a passage to another Secondary Realm, the secret retreat of Lady Friday, where she had been stealing humans' memories, leaving them as mindless husks. The sleepers who were being returned had narrowly avoided that fate. They would wake in due course, knowing nothing of their ordeal.

Martine, one of Lady Friday's human staff, emerged and nodded at Arthur before starting up the ramp. She had an expression on her face that Arthur guessed was equal parts fear and excitement. Martine had been forced to stay and work in Friday's retreat for more than thirty years.

She would find the contemporary world a very strange place, Arthur thought. A world that was getting stranger by the day—not least because the appearance of Denizens and Nithlings from the House had a bad effect upon the Secondary Realms like Earth, disrupting the environment on many different levels, including the spontaneous generation of new and deadly viruses.

Arthur thought about that as he watched the sleepers march, occasionally intervening to keep them moving. His presence now with the Fifth Key would undoubtedly destabilise something on Earth, maybe even create something really bad like the Sleepy Plague. He would not be able to linger, and perhaps should not even stay long enough to go home and check up on his family. But he desperately wanted to see if his sister Michaeli and brother Eric were all right, and also to find some clue to where his mother Emily might be or who might have taken her, if Sneezer was correct and she was no longer on Earth at all.

A ringing phone interrupted his thoughts. It got louder and louder, closer and closer. Arthur scowled. He didn't have a mobile phone, but the old-fashioned ring tone was coming from the pocket of his paper suit . . .

He sighed, put the Fifth Key in his pocket and rummaged around to see what else was in there. When his fingers closed on a small cold tube he knew hadn't been there before, he pulled it out and found a full-sized, antique candlestick-style phone with a separate earpiece that could neither have fitted into his pocket in the first place or come out of it if it had. It was, in other words, a perfectly normal manifestation of a House telephone, behaving according to its own magical rules.

'Yes?' said Arthur.

'Stand by,' said a voice that sounded much more like a human telephone operator than a Denizen. 'Thru-connecting now, sir.'

'Who's that?' asked someone else. A familiar, masculine voice—again not a Denizen.

'Erazmuz!?' asked Arthur in surprise. Erazmuz was his oldest half-brother, a major in the army. How could he be calling on a House telephone?

'Arthur? How come the screen's off? Never mind. Is Emily home?'

'Uh, no,' said Arthur. 'I'm not—'

'Eric? Michaeli?'

Erazmuz was talking really fast, not letting Arthur get a word in, so he couldn't tell him that he wasn't home, even if it was the number that Erazmuz had dialled.

'No, they're not—'

'That's . . .'

Erazmuz's voice trailed away for a second, then he came back, talking faster than ever.

'OK . . . you've got to grab any bottled water and food, like tins or packaged stuff, and an opener, get warm clothes and head down to the cellar as soon as you can, but no more than ten minutes from now. Ten minutes maximum, OK? Shut it up tight and stay down there. Do you know where Emily and the others are?'

'No! What's going on?'

'General Pravuil has just flown in and he's ordered the launch of four micronukes at what's left of East Area Hospital at 12:01. If you get to the cellar, you should be OK, just don't come out till I get there. I'll be with the clean-up—'

'What!' exclaimed Arthur. 'Nukes! I can't believe you—the army—is going to nuke part of the city? There must be thousands of people—'

'Arthur! I shouldn't even be talking to you! Don't waste time!'

There was a clear sound of desperation in Erazmuz's voice.

'We can't stop it; the general's got every clearance—the hospital's been declared a viral plague nexus under the Creighton Act. Get water and food and some blankets and get down to the cellar *now!*'

The line went dead. The phone started to fade in Arthur's hand, becoming insubstantial, its sharp edges turning foggy and cold.

'Hold on,' ordered Arthur. He tightened his grip. 'I want to make a call.'

The telephone solidified again. There was a sound like a distant choir singing, followed by some indistinct shouting. Then a light, silvery voice

18

said, 'Oh, get off, do. This is our exchange—we don't care what Saturday says. Operator here.'

'This is Lord Arthur. I need to speak to Dr Scamandros urgently, please. I'm not sure where he is—probably the Lower House.'

'Ooh, Lord Arthur. It's a bit tricky right now. I'll do my best. Please hold.'

Arthur lowered the phone for a second and looked around. He couldn't see a clock and he had no idea what time of day it was. Nor did he know how close this private hospital was to the big East Area Hospital—it could be next door for all he knew. Leaf, Martine and Vess were in the other rooms, settling down sleepers, so there wasn't anyone to ask. Many more of the old folk continued to shamble past.

Arthur ran up the ramp, narrowly missing slowly-swinging elbows and widely-planted feet. He kept the earpiece to his head, but he couldn't hear anything now, not even the shouting in the background.

'Leaf! Leaf! What time is it?' he shouted in the general direction of the door. Then he raised the telephone and, hardly lowering his voice, insisted, 'I *must* speak to Dr Scamandros! Quickly, please!'

CHAPTER TWO

Leaf came running back as Arthur ran forward and the two nearly collided at the door. In recovering, they turned several sleepers around. It took a moment to get them sorted out, with Arthur still trying to hold the phone.

'What time is it?' Arthur asked again.

'Time? I wouldn't have a clue,' puffed Leaf. 'It's night-time outside.'

'Ask Vess, quickly. The army is going to nuke East Area Hospital at 12:01 Saturday morning!'

'What!?' shrieked Leaf.

'I can probably do something,' said Arthur hastily. 'I have to check with Dr Scamandros. Find out how close to East Area we are!'

Leaf turned and ran. Arthur pressed his ear harder against the phone, thinking he heard something. But the only sound was the shuffle of the sleepers as they slowly passed by him. The telephone itself was silent.

'Come on, come on,' whispered Arthur anxiously, half into the telephone, half out into the air. He had an idea about something he could do, but he needed to check with Scamandros about exactly how to do it and what could go wrong.

No answer came from the phone, but Leaf came running back.

'It's ten minutes to midnight on Friday night!' she shouted. 'We're less than half a mile away from East Area. This even used to be part of the big hospital years ago!'

She skidded to a halt next to Arthur and gulped down several panicked breaths.

'What are you going to do? We've only got ten minutes!'

'Hello!' Arthur shouted into the telephone. 'Hello! I have to speak to Dr Scamandros *now*!'

There was no answer. Arthur gripped the phone even tighter, willing it to connect, but that didn't help.

'Probably nine minutes now,' said Leaf. 'You've got to do something, Arthur!'

Arthur glanced at the crocodile ring very quickly. Leaf saw him look.

'Maybe Scamandros is wrong about the sorcerous contamination,' she said. 'Or the ring doesn't measure very well.'

'It's OK, Leaf,' said Arthur slowly. 'I've been thinking about all that anyway. You know why the Will chose me to be the Rightful Heir, how it tricked Mister Monday? I was going to die . . . but getting the First Key saved me—'

'Sure, I remember,' said Leaf hastily. 'Now we're all going to die unless you do something!'

21

'I am going to do something,' said Arthur. 'That's what I'm explaining to you. I've worked out that I was going to die anyway, so everything I've done—everything I do from now on—is a kind of bonus anyway. Even if I turn into a Denizen, I'll still be alive and at least I can help other people—'

'Arthur, I understand!' Leaf interrupted. 'Just do something, please! We can talk afterwards!'

'OK,' said Arthur. He dropped the telephone. As it fell, it turned into a shower of tiny motes of light that faded and were gone before they hit the floor.

Arthur took a deep breath and for a moment marvelled at just how deeply he could breathe now, his asthma gone with his old human self, all earthly frailties being left behind in his transition to a new immortal form. Then he took the mirror that was the Fifth Key out of his pocket and held it up in front of his face. An intense light shone around it in a fierce corona, but Arthur looked directly at the mirror without difficulty, seeing only the reflection of his own changing face, his more regular nose, his whiter teeth and his silkier hair.

Leaf shielded her eyes with her arm, and even the sleepwalkers turned their heads away and screwed their eyes shut tighter as they kept shuffling forward.

I really hope this works, thought Arthur. *It has to work. Only I wish I could have checked with Dr Scamandros, because I don't really know what . . .*

Arthur grimaced, banished his fearful inner voice and focused on what he wanted the Fifth Key to do. Because it seemed easier and somehow made it sound more like it would happen, he spoke aloud to the Key.

'Fifth Key of the Architect! I, Arthur Penhaligon, Rightful Heir of the Architect, um . . . I desire you to shield this city inside a bubble that keeps it separate from the Earth, a bubble that will protect the city and keep everyone in it safe from all harm, and . . . well . . . that's it . . . thanks.'

The mirror flashed and this time Arthur did have to blink. When he opened his eyes, he felt momentarily unsteady on his feet and had to raise his arms like a tightrope-walker to regain his balance. In that instant he saw that everyone else had stopped moving. Leaf and the line of sleepers were still, as if they had been snap-frozen. Many of the sleepers had one foot slightly off the ground, a position that no one could possibly keep up in normal circumstances.

It was also newly quiet. Arthur couldn't hear the helicopters or gunfire or any other noise. It was like being in a waxwork museum after closing time, surrounded by posed statues.

Arthur slipped the mirror into his pocket and ran his fingers through his hair—which had got considerably longer than he cared for, though it somehow stayed out of his face.

'Leaf?' he said tentatively, walking over to tap his friend lightly on the shoulder. 'Leaf? Are you OK?'

Leaf didn't move. Arthur looked at her face. Her eyes were open but her pupils didn't move when he waved his finger back and forth. He couldn't even tell if she was breathing.

Arthur felt a sudden panic rise in him.

I've killed them, he thought. *I was trying to save them, but I killed them . . .*

He touched Leaf on the shoulder again, and

though a faint nimbus of red light sprang up around his fingers, she still didn't move or react in any way.

Arthur stepped back and looked around. There was a faint red glow around each of the sleepers too, and when he walked over and touched them, this light also grew momentarily brighter. Arthur didn't know what the glow meant, but he found it slightly comforting, as it suggested some sorcerous effect was active and he hadn't just killed everyone.

But I don't even know if I have protected us from the nukes, Arthur thought. *What time is it?*

He turned and ran down the hall, through the next two wards and out into the lobby. From there it took him a minute to find the office and a clock. It had stopped at exactly 11:57, the second hand quivering on the twelve. The clock also had a faint red sheen, and there were ghostly scarlet shadows behind the second and hour hands.

Arthur ran outside. The front doors slammed shut behind him with a sound all too like the trump of doom. He slid to a halt just before he fell down the wheelchair ramp, because everywhere he looked was tinted red. It was like looking at the world through red sunglasses on an overcast day, because the night sky had been replaced by a solid red that was buzzing and shifting and hard to look at, like a traffic light viewed far too close.

'I guess I've done *something*,' Arthur said to himself. 'I just don't know exactly what . . .'

He walked a little further, out into the car park. Something caught his eye, up in the sky, a small silhouette. He peered at it for a few seconds before he worked out that it was a helicopter gunship. But it wasn't moving. It was like a model stuck on a piece of wire, just hanging there in the red-washed sky.

Stuck in a moment of time.

That's why everyone is frozen in place, Arthur thought. *I've stopped time . . . that's how the Key is keeping everyone in the city safe . . .*

If time was only frozen or slowed inside a bubble around the city, it could start again, or be started again by some other power. Which meant that the nuclear strike on East Area Hospital would still happen. He hadn't saved the city from the attack. He'd just postponed it . . .

'If it isn't one thing, it's another,' whispered Arthur. He looked along the empty street, all strange and red-hued, and wondered if he should run over to his home and see if his family was all right. Maybe he could carry them down into the cellar . . . but if he did that, he might be wasting time better spent in learning how to protect everyone else. He couldn't carry everyone in danger to safety.

He'd gained a breathing space for the city, and he could extend it by going back to the House. If he left now, he should be able to return to almost exactly the same time, even if he spent days or even weeks in the House.

Should is not the same as definitely, thought Arthur grimly. *I wish I understood the time relativities better. I wish I knew more about how to use the Keys. I wish I'd never, ever got involved in all—*

Arthur stopped himself.

'If I wasn't involved, I'd be dead,' he said aloud. 'I just have to get on with it.'

Getting on with it, Arthur thought, included facing up to things. He held his hand up close to his face and looked at the crocodile ring. Even in the weird red light he could see it clearly. The diamond eyes of the crocodile looked baleful, as dark as dried black blood rather then their usual pink. The ten marked sections of its body, each inscribed with a roman numeral, recorded the degree of sorcerous contamination in his blood and bone. If more than six sections had turned from silver to gold, Arthur would be permanently tainted with sorcery and irretrievably destined to become a Denizen.

Arthur slowly turned the ring around, to see how far the gold transformation had progressed, counting in his head. One, two, three, four, five . . . he knew it had gone that far already. He turned the ring again, and saw the gold had completely filled the fifth segment and had flooded over, almost completely across the sixth segment.

I am . . . I am going to be a Denizen.

Arthur took a deep, shuddering breath and looked again, but there was no change in the ring. It was six parts gold. He was sixty per cent immortal.

'No turning back now,' said Arthur to the red world around him. 'Time to get back to work.'

He looked away from the ring and lowered his hand. Bending his head for a moment, he drew out the Fifth Key from his pocket and raised it high. According to Dame Primus, the mirror of Lady Friday could take him to anywhere he had previously seen within the House, if there was a reflective surface there.

Arthur pictured the throne room in the Lower

House, the big audience chamber where he had met Dame Primus and everyone before he was drafted into the Army of the Architect. It was the place he could most easily visualise in Monday's Dayroom, because it didn't have much detail and was so over the top in decoration—including floors of reflective marble.

'Fifth Key, take me to the throne room in Monday's Dayroom.'

The Fifth Key shivered in Arthur's hand and a beam of white light sprang from it, banishing the red. The light formed a perfect, upright rectangle, exactly like a door.

Arthur walked into the rectangle of light and disappeared from his own city, from his Earth, perhaps never to return.

CHAPTER THREE

The throne room was empty. Otherwise it looked the same as it had when Arthur had last been there: like one enormous, ritzy, poorly-conceived hotel bathroom. It was about as large as a big city theatre, and the walls, floor and ceiling were all lined with gold-veined white marble that was polished to a highly reflective sheen.

The vast, red-iron round table was still in the middle of the chamber, with the hundred tall-backed white chairs around it. On the other side, Arthur's own high throne of gilded iron sat next to the rainbow chair of Dame Primus.

'Hello!' Arthur called out. 'Anyone here?'

His voice filled the empty space and the echoes were the only answer. Arthur sighed and strode over to the door, his footsteps setting up another echo behind him, so it sounded like he was being followed by many small, close companions.

The corridor outside was still crowded with thousands of bundles of paper, each tied with a red ribbon and stacked like bricks. Unlike last time, there were no Commissionaire Sergeants standing at attention in the gaps between the piles of paperwork.

'Hello!' Arthur shouted again. He ran down the corridor, pausing several times to see if there were doors leading out. Eventually he came to the end of the corridor, where he found a door propped half open and partially covered in bundles of paper. He could only see it because one of the piles had collapsed.

There were still no Denizens. Arthur rushed through the half-open door and along another empty corridor, pushing doors open as he passed them without encountering anyone else.

'Hello! Anyone here!' he shouted every few yards, but no answer came.

Finally he came to a pair of tall, arched doors of dark oak. They were barred, but he easily lifted the bar—not even pausing to marvel that he had grown so strong that he could move a piece of timber that must weigh several hundred pounds. Once the bar was up, the door was easily pushed open.

This particular door led outside. Arthur had expected to see the lake and the rim of the crater that surrounded the Dayroom, and the ceiling of the Lower House above. Instead he saw a vast, arching wave of Nothing that rose way above him, a wave that had already eaten up everything but the small villa behind him. He felt like he was on a small hilltop, the last piece of dry land ahead of a tsunami—but the wave was coming, climbing high, and it would soon crash down to destroy even this last refuge.

Arthur turned to run, his heart suddenly hammering in fear, his mouth dry as dust. But after that first panicked step, he stopped and turned back. The wave of Nothing was coming down and he didn't have time to run. He doubted the Fifth Key could protect him from such a vast influx of Nothing. At least not unless he actively directed its power.

I have to do something, thought Arthur, and he acted with the speed of that thought.

Even as the wave of Nothing crashed down upon him, he raised the mirror and held it high, pushing it towards the dark, falling sky.

'Stop!' he shouted, his voice raw with power, every part of his mind focused on stopping the tsunami of Nothing. 'Stop! By the Keys I hold, I order the Nothing to stop! House, you must hold against the Void!'

Blinding light shone from the mirror, hot white beams that set the air on fire as they shot out and up, striking the onrush of Nothing, splashing across the face of the darkness, small marks of brilliance upon the Void.

Arthur felt a terrible pain blossom in his heart. The pain spread, racing down his arms and legs. Awful cracking sounds came from his joints, and he had to screw his eyes shut and scream as his teeth rearranged themselves into a more perfect order in his jaw. Then his jaw itself moved and he felt the plates of bone in his skull shift and change.

But still he kept holding the mirror up above his head, even as he fell to his knees. He used the pain, channelling it to fuel his concentration, directing his will against the rush of Nothing.

Finally it was too much. Arthur could neither bear the pain nor continue the effort. He fell forwards on his face, his screams becoming dull sobs. His strength used up, he dropped the Fifth Key on the narrow band of grass that was all that remained of the lawns that had once surrounded the Dayroom villa.

He lay there, partially stunned, awaiting annihilation, knowing that he had failed and that when he died, the rest of the Universe would follow. All he loved would be destroyed, back on Earth, in the House and in the worlds beyond.

A minute passed, and then another, and the annihilation didn't happen. As the pain in his bones ebbed, Arthur groaned and rolled over. He would face the Nothing, rather than be snuffed out by it while he lay defeated upon the grass.

The first thing he saw was not incipient destruction, but a delicate tracery of glowing golden lines, like a web or a mesh net of light thrown against the sky. It was holding back the great mass of threatening darkness, but Arthur could feel the pressure of the Nothing, could feel the infinite Void pushing against his restraints. He knew that it would soon overcome his net of light and once again advance.

Arthur picked up the mirror and staggered to his feet. The ground felt further away than normal and he lost his balance for a moment, swaying on the spot. The sensation passed as he shook his head and he ran back to the open doors. There was a telephone in the library, he knew, and he needed to call and find out where in the House was safe, instead of going somewhere that might have already succumbed to Nothing. He didn't want to think about what would happen if he used the Fifth Key to take him straight into the Void, though it probably would have the advantage of being quick . . .

Or maybe the Key would protect me for a little while, Arthur thought with sudden nausea. *Long enough to feel the Nothing dissolve my flesh . . .*

He hurried along the main corridor until he saw a door he recognised. Darting through it, he leaped up the steps four at a time, bouncing off the walls as he tried to take the turns in the staircase too fast.

At the top, he sprinted down another long corridor, this one also narrowed by piles of records, many of them written on papyrus or cured hides instead of paper. Pausing to shift a six-foot-high stone tablet that had fallen and blocked the way, Arthur didn't bother with the handle of the door at the end, but kicked it open and stumbled into the library beyond.

The room was empty, and not just of Denizens. The books were gone from the shelves, as were the comfortable leather armchairs and the carpet. Even the scarlet bell rope that Sneezer had pulled to reveal the heptagonal room which housed the grandfather clocks of Seven Dials was missing, though the room was presumably still there, behind the bookcase.

The telephone that had stood on a side table was also missing.

Arthur's shoulder slumped. He could feel the pressure outside, like a sinus pain across his forehead. He knew it was the weight of Nothing striving to break the bonds he had placed upon it.

The weight was there in his mind, making him weary, almost too weary to think straight.

'Telephone,' mumbled Arthur, holding out his right hand, while he cradled the Fifth Key in his left. 'I need a telephone, please. Now.'

Without further ado, a telephone appeared in his hand. Arthur set it down on the floor and sat next to it, lifting the earpiece and bending to speak into the receiver. He could hear crackling and buzzing, and in the distance someone was singing something that sounded rather like 'Raindrops keep falling on my head', but the words were 'Line-drops are lining up tonight'.

'Hello, it's Lord Arthur. I need to speak to Dame Primus. Or Sneezer. Or anyone really.'

The singing abruptly stopped, replaced by a thin, soft voice that sounded like paper rustling.

'Ah, where are you calling from? This line doesn't appear to be technically, um, attached to anything.'

'The Lower House,' said Arthur. 'Please, I think I'm about to be engulfed by Nothing and I need to work out where to go.'

'Easier said than done,' replied the voice. 'Have you ever tried connecting a non-existent line to a switchboard that isn't there any more?'

'No,' said Arthur. Somewhere outside he heard a twanging sound, like a guitar string snapping. He felt it too, a sudden lurch in his stomach. His net, his defence against the Void, was breaking. 'Please hurry!'

'I can get Dr Scamandros—will he do?' asked the operator. 'You wanted him before, it says here—'

'Where is he?' gabbled Arthur.

'The Deep Coal Cellar, which is kind of odd,' said the operator. 'Since nothing else in the Lower House is still connected . . . but metaphysical diversion was never my strong suit. Shall I put you through? Hello . . . hello . . . are you there, Lord Arthur?'

Arthur dropped the phone and stood up, not waiting to hear more. He raised the mirror that was the Fifth Key and concentrated upon it, desiring to see out of the reflective surface of a pool of water in the Deep Coal Cellar—if there was such a pool of water, and a source of light.

He was distracted for an instant by the sight of his own face, which was both familiar and strange. Familiar, because it was in essence much the same as it had been at any other time he'd looked in a mirror, and strange because there were numerous small changes. His cheekbones had become a little more pronounced, the shape of his head was a bit different, his ears had got smaller . . .

'The Deep Coal Cellar!' snapped Arthur at the mirror, both to distract himself and get on with his urgent task: finding somewhere to escape to before Nothing destroyed Monday's Dayroom.

His image wavered and was replaced by a badly-lit scene that showed an oil lamp perched on a very thick, leather-bound book the size of several house bricks, which was set atop a somewhat collapsed pyramid made from small pieces of coal. The lamplight was dim, but Arthur could perceive someone on the far side of the pyramid who was raising a fishing pole over his head, ready to cast. Arthur saw only the caster's hands and two mustard yellow cuffs, which he immediately recognised.

'Fifth Key,' Arthur commanded, 'take me to the Deep Coal Cellar, next to Dr Scamandros.'

As before, a door of pure white light appeared. As Arthur stepped through it, he felt his defensive net tear asunder behind him and the onrush of the great wave of Nothing.

A scant few seconds after his escape, the last surviving remnants of the Lower House ceased to exist.

CHAPTER FOUR

Arthur appeared next to a pyramid of coal, stepping out of the air and frightening the life out of a short, bald Denizen in a yellow greatcoat, who dropped his fishing pole, jumped back, and pulled a smoking bronze ball that looked like a medieval hand grenade out of one of his voluminous pockets.

'Dr Scamandros!' exclaimed Arthur. 'It's me!'

'Lord Arthur!'

The tattooed trumpets on Dr Scamandros's forehead blew apart into clouds of confetti. He tried to pinch out the fuse on the smoking ball, but a flame ran around his fingers and continued on its way. Even more smoke boiled out of the infernal device.

'Scamand—' Arthur started to say, but Scamandros interrupted him, lobbing the ball behind a particularly large pyramid of coal some thirty feet distant.

'One moment, Lord Arthur.'

There was a deafening crack and a fierce rush of air, closely followed by a great gout of smoke and coal dust that spiralled up into the air. Moments later, a hail of coal came down, some fist-sized pieces striking the ground uncomfortably close to the sorcerer and the boy.

'I do beg your pardon, Lord Arthur,' said Dr Scamandros. Puffing slightly, he went down on one knee, clouds of disturbed coal dust billowing up almost as high as his shoulders. 'Welcome.'

'Please, do get up,' said Arthur. He leaned forward and helped the Denizen rise. Dr Scamandros was amazingly heavy, or possibly all the things he had in the pockets of his yellow greatcoat were amazingly heavy.

'What's going on?' Arthur asked. 'I came back to Monday's Dayroom but there was this . . . this huge wave of Nothing! I only just managed to hold it off long enough to escape.'

'I fear that I lack exact knowledge of what has occurred,' replied Scamandros. The tattoos on his face became a herd of confused donkeys that ran in a circle from his chin to the bridge of his nose and back again, and kicked their heels at each other. 'I have been here since we parted company at Lady Friday's retreat, a matter of some days. Dame Primus wished me to investigate some unusual phenomena, including the sudden growth of flowers and a powerful aroma of rose oil. It has been quite a restful interlude in some ways, though I have to say that attar of roses is no longer . . .'

The Denizen noticed Arthur's frown and got back to the question.

'Ahem, that is to say, just under an hour ago, I felt a tremor underfoot, followed a moment later by a sudden onslaught of Nothing that annihilated at least a third of the Cellar before its advance slowed. Fortunately it was not the third I happened to be located in at the time. I immediately attempted to telephone Dame Primus at the Citadel, but found all lines severed. Similarly, I was unable to summon an elevator. The few short experiments I have conducted suggest the following.'

He held out three blackened fingers, closing them into his fist one by one.

'Item One. The defences against the Void in the Far Reaches must have suddenly collapsed, allowing a huge surge of Nothing to smash through.

'Item Two. If you encountered a wave of Nothing as high as Monday's Dayroom, then it is likely that the entire Far Reaches and all of the Lower House have been destroyed. But there is a brighter note, which I shall label as Item Three.

'Item Three. If you got an operator on the line, the bulwark between the Lower and Middle House must have held. Or be holding, though everything below it has been lost.'

'Everything? But here . . . where we are right now,' said Arthur. 'This is part of the Lower House, how come it's not . . . uh . . . gone?'

'The Old One's prison is very strong,' said Scamandros. He pointed to his left. Arthur looked and saw in the distance the faint sheen of blue light that he knew came from the clock face where the Old One was chained. 'The Architect had to make it particularly resistant, to keep the Old One in check. Being of such adamant stuff, it has held against the initial inrush of Nothing. But now it is but a small islet, lost in the Void. We are entirely surrounded and totally cut off from the rest of the House. It is very interesting, but I have to confess I'm relieved you're here, Lord Arthur. Without you, I fear that—'

Scamandros paused. The tattooed donkeys hung their heads and slowly became tumbledown stone cairns, memorial markers for the fallen.

'I fear that I would find the current situation, interesting as it is, likely to be fatal in a relatively short space of time, given that Nothing is eating this small refuge at a rate of approximately a yard an hour.'

'What? You were just saying this area is adamant and strong and all that!' protested Arthur. He peered into the darkness, but he couldn't tell whether he was looking at advancing Nothing or just couldn't see very far because the only immediate light came from the feeble lantern on the coal pile.

'Oh, the area *immediately* adjacent to the clock is doubtless proof against the Void,' said Scamandros. 'But before your arrival I was weighing up the relative ... er ... benefits of being throttled by the Old One as opposed to being dissolved by Nothing.'

'The Old One wouldn't throttle you ... oh ... I guess he might,' said Arthur. 'He does hate Denizens ...' Arthur stopped talking and looked over at the blue glow, thoughts of his very first encounter with the Old One going through his mind. He could well remember the feel of the prison chain around his neck. 'I hope he'll still talk to me. Since I'm here, I want to ask him some questions.'

Dr Scamandros peered owlishly at Arthur, with his half-moon spectacles glinting on his forehead, helping him focus his invisible third and fourth eyes.

'It is true that the Old One has a fondness for mortals. But I think you are no longer mortal. What does my . . . your ring indicate?'

Arthur looked. The gold had washed well into the seventh segment.

'About seventy-five per cent contaminated,' he said quietly. 'I hope the Old One can recognise the quarter-part of humanity inside me.'

'Perhaps it would be best to simply depart,' said Scamandros nervously. 'Though I should say that the ring has a margin—'

'I do need to at least try to get some answers from him,' said Arthur distractedly. 'If I keep my distance it should be OK. Then we'd better get up to the Citadel and find out what's happening from Dame Primus. Oh, and I need to ask you about something I've done back on Earth . . .'

Quickly Arthur described what he'd done with the Key, and the strangely red-lit environment of what appeared to be a town frozen in time.

'I cannot be entirely sure, Lord Arthur, without proper investigation,' said Scamandros. 'But as you suspected, you may have separated your entire world from the general procession of time in the Secondary Realms, or have temporally dislocated just a portion of it, around your town. In either case, the cessation will slowly erode. In due course the march of time will resume its normal beat, and everything that was to happen will occur unless you return and prevent it before the erosion of the cessation, which you should be able to do given the elasticity of time between the House and the Secondary Realms. I'm sure Sneezer could tell you more, using the Seven Dials.'

'But the Seven Dials must have been destroyed,' said Arthur. 'With Monday's Dayroom.' He stopped and slapped the side of his head. 'And all the records stored in the Lower House. They must have been destroyed too! Doesn't that mean that whatever those records were about in the Secondary Realms will also be destroyed? My record was there!'

Scamandros shook his head.

'The Seven Dials will have moved to safety of its own accord, hopefully to some part of the House we control. As for the records, only dead observations are held in the Lower House. Admittedly their destruction will create holes in the past, but that is of no great concern. Monday must have been given your record temporarily, I presume by the Will, but it would normally have been held in the Upper House, as an active record.'

'Sneezer gave it to me after I defeated Monday, but I left it behind,' said Arthur. 'So Dame Primus has probably got it.'

'Unless it has returned to the Upper House. Such documents cannot be long held out of their proper place.'

'But then Saturday can change my record and that would change me!' exclaimed Arthur. 'She could destroy it . . . me . . . both!'

Scamandros shook his head again. A tattoo of a red-capped judge with a beaked nose appeared on his left cheek and also shook his head.

'No—even if Saturday knows where it is, she could not change or destroy it. Not once you had even a single Key.'

'I feel like my head is going to explode.' Arthur massaged his temples with his knuckles and sighed. 'There's just too much . . . What are you doing?'

Scamandros paused in the act of removing a very large hand-drill from inside his coat and a shining ten-inch-long drill bit from an external pocket.

'If I bore a hole in your skull just here,' said Scamandros, tapping the side of his forehead, 'it will relieve the pressure. I expect it is a side effect of your transformation into a higher Denizen—'

'I didn't mean my head was *actually* going to explode,' said Arthur. 'So you can put that drill away. I meant that I have too much to do, too much information to deal with. Too many problems!'

'Perhaps I can assist in some other fashion?' asked Scamandros as he stowed his tools away.

'No,' sighed Arthur. 'Wait here. I'm going to talk to the Old One.'

'Um, Lord Arthur, I trust that I can move a little in that direction?' Scamandros pointed at a pile of coal a few yards away and added, 'As I observe that the front half of yonder pyramid has ceased to exist . . .'

'Of course you can move!' snapped Arthur. He felt a peculiar rage rising in him, something he'd never felt before, an irritation at having to deal with lesser Denizens and inferior beings. For a moment he even felt like striking Scamandros, or forcing the Denizen to prostrate himself and beg forgiveness.

Then the feeling was past, replaced by a deep sense of mortification and shame. Arthur liked Scamandros and he did not like the way he had just felt towards the sorcerer, the proud anger that had fizzed up inside him, like a shaken bottle of pop ready to explode. He stopped and took a deep breath and reminded himself that he was just a boy who had a very tough job to do, and that he would need all the help he could get, from willing friends, not fearful servants.

I'm not going to become like one of the Trustees, thought Arthur firmly. At the back of his head, another little thought lay under that. *Or like Dame Primus . . .*

'Sorry, I'm sorry, Dr Scamandros. I didn't mean to shout. I just . . . I'm a bit . . . um . . . anyway, do whatever you need to do to keep away from the Nothing. We'll get out of here soon.'

Dr Scamandros bowed low as Arthur walked away, and another baseball-sized grenade fell out of an inner pocket and immediately began to smoke. The Denizen tut-tutted, pinched the burning fuse out and slipped it up his sleeve, which did not look like a secure place for it go. However, it did not immediately fall out.

Arthur walked on, weaving between the pyramids of coal and splashing through the puddles of dirty coal-dust-tainted water. He remembered that he had been very cold when he'd last visited the Deep Coal Cellar, but it felt quite pleasant now to him, almost warm. Perhaps a side effect of the Nothing that now surrounded the place, he thought.

There were other changes too. As he drew closer to the blue illumination spread by the clock,

43

Arthur noticed that many of the pyramids now sprouted flowers. Climbing roses twined up through the coal, and between the puddles there were clumps of bluebells.

The bluebells spread as the ground climbed a little higher and got drier, the flowers now growing out of stone slates rather than a bed of coal dust, which was equally impossible, but did not bother Arthur. He was fairly used to the House. Flowers growing out of coal and stone were far from the strangest things he had seen.

At the last pyramid he stopped, as he had done all that time ago, when he had first cautiously approached the Old One's prison. The shimmering blue light was less annoying that it had been then and he could see more clearly this time, even without calling on the Fifth Key to shed some kinder illumination.

Arthur saw a markedly different landscape from what it had been. Between him and the clock-prison was a solid carpet of bluebells, interspersed with clumps of tall yellow-green stalks that burst out at the top in profuse, pale white flowers that were shaped a little like very elongated daffodils, but at the same time looked too alien to have come from the Earth he knew.

The raised circular platform of stone, the clock face, was significantly smaller, as if it had been shrunk. It had been at least sixty feet in diameter, the length of the drive at Arthur's own home. Now it was half that, and the Roman numerals that had stood upright around the rim were smaller and tarnished, much of their blue glow gone. Some of them were bent over at forty-five degrees or more, and the numbers and most of the rim were

44

wreathed in climbing red and pink roses.

The metal hands had shrunk with the clock face, to remain in proportion. Long, shining blue-steel chains still ran from the ends of the hands back through the central pivot, fastened at the other end to the manacles locked on the wrists of the Old One.

The Old One himself was not as Arthur had last seen him. He still looked like a giant barbarian hero, eight feet tall and heavily-muscled, but his formerly old, almost-translucent skin was now sun-dark and supple. His once-stubbled head now sported a fine crop of clean white hair that was tied back behind his neck. He no longer wore just a loincloth, but had on a sleeveless leather jerkin and a pair of scarlet leggings that came down to just below his knees.

Where he once looked like a fallen, fading ancient of eighty or ninety, the Old One now looked like a super-fit sixty-year-old hero who could easily take on and defeat any number of lesser, younger foes.

The giant was sitting on the rim of the clock between the numbers three and four, slowly plucking the petals from a rose. He was half-turned away from Arthur, so the boy couldn't see the Old One's eyes—or, if it was soon after they had been torn from their sockets by the puppets within the clock, the empty, oozing sockets.

Thinking that was something he definitely did not want to see, Arthur craned his neck to check the position of the clock hands. The hour hand was at nine and the minute hand at five, which relieved him on three counts. The Old One's eyes would have had plenty of time to grow back and his chains would be fairly tight, keeping him close to the clock. Perhaps most importantly, it also meant the torturer puppets would not be emerging for several hours.

Arthur stepped out and crossed the field of bluebells. Chains rattled as he approached and the Old One stood to watch him. Arthur stopped thirty or forty feet from the clock. While the face had shrunk, he couldn't be sure the chains had as well, so he erred on the side of caution.

'Greetings, Old One!' he called.

'Greetings, boy,' rumbled the Old One. 'Or perhaps I can call you boy no longer. Arthur is your name, is it not?'

'Yes.'

'Come sit with me. We will drink wine and talk.'

'Do you promise you won't hurt me?' asked Arthur.

'You will be safe from all harm for the space of a quarter hour, as measured by this clock,' replied the Old One. 'You are mortal enough that I would not slay you like a wandering cockroach, or a Denizen of the House.'

'Thanks,' said Arthur. 'I think.'

He approached cautiously, but the Old One sat down again and, doubling over his chain, swept a space next to him clear of the thorny roses, to make a seat for Arthur.

Arthur perched gingerly next to him.

'Wine,' said the Old One, holding out his hand.

A small stoneware jug flew up out of the ground without parting the bluebells. He caught it and tipped it up above his mouth, pouring out a long draught of resin-scented wine. Arthur could smell it very strongly, and once again it made him feel slightly ill.

'You called the wine with a poem last time,' Arthur said hesitantly. He was thinking of the questions he wanted to ask, and wasn't sure how to start.

'It is the power of my will that shapes Nothing,' replied the Old One. 'It is true that many lesser beings need to sharpen their thoughts with speech or song when they deal with Nothing. I do not *need* to do so, though on occasion it may amuse me to essay some rhyme or poesy.'

'I wanted to ask you some questions,' said Arthur. 'And to tell you something.'

'Ask away,' said the Old One. 'I shall answer if I choose. As for the telling, if I do not like what I hear, it shall not make me stray from my promise. Whatever your speech, you may still have safe passage hence. If you do not overstay your allotted time.'

He wiped his mouth with the back of his hand and proffered the jug. Arthur quickly shook his head, so the ancient drank again.

'You probably know more than anyone about the Architect,' said Arthur. 'So I wanted to ask you what happened to her? And what is the Will exactly, and what is it . . . she . . . going to do? I mean, I'm supposed to be the Rightful Heir and all, and I thought that meant that I was going to end up in charge of everything, whether I wanted to or not. Only now I'm not so sure.'

'I knew the Architect long ago,' said the Old One slowly. He drank a series of smaller mouthfuls before speaking again. 'Yet not so well as I thought or I would not have suffered here so long. I do not know what happened to her, save that it must have been at least in part of her own choosing. As for the Will, it is an expression of her power, set up to achieve some end. If you are the Rightful Heir, I would suggest the question you need ask is this: what exactly are you to inherit and from whom?'

Arthur frowned.

'I don't want to be the Heir. I just want to get my old life back and make sure everyone is safe,' he said. 'But I can't get everything sorted out without using the Keys, and that's turning me into a Denizen. Scamandros made me a ring that says I'm six . . . more than six parts in ten . . . sorcerously contaminated, and it's irreversible. So I *will* become a Denizen, right?'

'Your body is assuming an immortal form—that is evident,' said the Old One. 'But not everything of immortal flesh is a Denizen. Remember, the Architect did not make the mortals of Earth. She made the stuff of life and sowed it across all creation. You mortals arose from the possibility she made, and though she always liked to think so, are consequently not of her direct design. There is more to you, and all mortals, than the simple flesh you inhabit.'

'But can I become a normal boy again?'

'I do not know.' The Old One drained the last of the wine from the jug, then threw it far past the light of the clock. The sound of its shattering came faint and distant from the darkness, reassurance that there was still solid ground out there—at least for a little while longer. 'In general, one cannot go back. But in going forward, you may achieve some of what you desired of the past. If you can survive, anything may happen.' The Old One plucked another rose, careless of its thorns, and held it beneath his nose. 'Perhaps you will even be given flowers. The clock ticks, Arthur. Your time is almost sped.'

'I have so many questions,' said Arthur. 'Can you give me another ten—'

The Old One put down his rose and looked at the boy with his fierce blue eyes, a gaze that would make the most superior Denizen quail and tremble.

'Never mind,' gulped Arthur. 'I just wanted to tell you that if I do end up in charge of everything, I'll do my best to set you free. It isn't right that the puppets should torture you.'

The Old One blinked and took up the rose again.

'I honour you for that. But look—the puppets are no more. As the House has weakened, I have grown stronger. An hour ago the clock shivered and I felt Nothing draw close. The puppets felt it too and, as is their duty, came forth before their time, to prevent a rescue or an attempted escape. I fought with them, broke them and cast them down.

'I am still chained, but as the House falls, my strength will grow and my prison will weaken. In time, I will be free, or so these flowers promise me. I have been stripping the petals to throw upon my enemies. The puppets do not like it, for they know the flowers are a harbinger of change. Go, I grant you the time to look upon them!'

Arthur stood up nervously and looked across the clock face, but he didn't move. He didn't really want to go anywhere near the trapdoors on either side of the central pivot of the clock.

'Hurry,' urged the Old One.

Arthur walked closer. The trapdoors were

smashed in, splintered stubs of timber hanging from the thick iron hinges. Something rustled from inside and Arthur looked down into a deep narrow chamber that was piled high with rose petals. The puppet woodchopper was there, still with its green cap on, the feather bent in half. But its limbs were broken and all it could do was wriggle on the rose petals, gnash its teeth and hiss.

Arthur shuddered and retreated to the rim, almost backing into the Old One.

'I hope . . . I hope we will not be enemies,' said Arthur.

The Old One inclined his head, but did not speak. Arthur jumped down from the clock face and hurried away, his mind churning with fears and facts and suppositions. He had hoped the Old One could help him make sense of his situation, make matters clearer.

But he had only made it worse.

CHAPTER FIVE

'Lord Arthur, I am vastly relieved to see you,' called out Scamandros as he saw Arthur hurrying back. 'I trust the Old One answered your questions?'

'Not exactly,' said Arthur. 'Not even close really. Is the Nothing still advancing?'

In answer, Scamandros cast out a lure with his fishing rod. The lure, a lobster-like crustacean four or five inches long, disappeared into darkness. Scamandros wound the line back in, counting marks on the woven thread as he did so. There was no lure on the end.

'Six . . . seven . . . eight. The speed of encroachment has increased, Lord Arthur.'

'Where was Dame Primus when you last were in touch? And Suzy?'

'They were both in the Citadel,' said

Scamandros. 'It has become the general headquarters of your forces throughout the House, Lord Arthur.'

'Could be tricky to get there,' said Arthur. 'Using the Fifth Key, I mean, since they secured the Citadel against Lady Friday. I suppose we could take the Improbable Stair—' Scamandros began to shake his head and Arthur stopped himself. 'Oh yeah, you can't go on the Stair. Oh well . . . there was a mirror in Sir Thursday's . . . in my quarters. I guess I can try that, and if it doesn't work then we'll have to think of somewhere else, in the Middle House or wherever, and try to take an elevator from there.'

He took out the Fifth Key and held it up for a moment in front of his face, then dropped it to his side.

'Uh, if I can make a door, how do I take you with me?'

Dr Scamandros held up his hand and wiggled his fingers.

'If you allow me to hold on to your coat-tails, I shall be carried through, Lord Arthur.'

'Hold on then,' said Arthur. 'We'll give it a try.'

He looked into the mirror and tried to remember what his quarters in Thursday's Citadel had looked like. He remembered the big four-poster bed with the carved battle scenes on the posts, and then there was the wardrobe, the chair he'd been shaved in and, yes, there was a tall, bronze-framed mirror in the corner. If he thought of that mirror like a window, then looking through it he would be able to see the bed, and the door, and the painting on the wall . . .

Slowly he began to see the room, though much

of it was clouded and fuzzy. It took him a few seconds to work out that the bronze mirror was partially covered with a cloth. But he could see enough of the chamber, he was sure, for the Key to open a door there.

'Fifth Key, take me . . . us . . . to my room in the Citadel of the Great Maze!'

It was not so easy to go through the door of white light this time, nor was the transfer so immediate. Arthur felt himself held back not just by his coat-tails, but by a force that pushed against his entire body and tried to throw him back. He struggled against it, with mind and body, but it was like walking against a very powerful wind. Then all of a sudden it was gone. He fell into his room in the Citadel and Dr Scamandros fell over his legs. Both of them tumbled across the floor and Arthur hit his head against the carved battle scenes on the left-hand post of the huge bed.

'Ow!' he exclaimed. He felt his head, but there was no blood, and after a moment the sharp pain reduced to a dull ache.

'I do beg your pardon, Lord Arthur,' said Dr Scamandros as he got to his feet. 'Most clumsy of me. That was fascinating—quite a different experience than a Transfer Plate. I am enormously grateful to you for saving me from the Deep Coal Cellar.'

Arthur stood, using the bedpost to haul himself upright. As he did so, the sleeves of his paper coat rode up. He slid them back down and for the first time noticed that they finished well short of his wrists. His trousers were also now ridiculously short, real ankle-freezers.

'I'd better get changed,' Arthur said. He started

towards the walk-in wardrobe, hesitated, and went back to the door, throwing it open to shout, 'Sentry!'

A startled Denizen in the uniform of a Horde Troop Sergeant hurtled into the room and stood quivering at attention, his lightning tulwar crackling as he saluted with it. Arthur heard the crash of at least a dozen boots out of sight down the corridor, evidence of more troopers suddenly coming from rest to parade-ground attention.

'Lord Arthur! Guard present, sir!'

Arthur was already in the wardrobe, taking off his paper clothes and quickly putting on the plainest uniform he could find, which happened to be the sand-coloured tunic and matching pale yellow leather breeches of a Borderer on desert duty, though this particular tunic had gold braid stitched across the shoulders and the leather breeches had gold stripes down each leg. Both tunic and breeches were much softer and more comfortable than anything a regular Borderer would ever be lucky enough to wear. They fitted perfectly after a moment, shifting and altering themselves from Sir Thursday's size to Arthur's new height and musculature.

'Thank you!' Arthur called out to the sergeant. 'We'll go down to the operations room in a minute. Is Dame Primus here? And Suzy Turquoise Blue?

'Dame Primus is in the operations room, sir!' boomed the Troop Sergeant. He appeared to be under the impression that Arthur was either deaf or much further away than he actually was. 'General Turquoise Blue is somewhere in the Citadel.'

'General Turquoise Blue?' asked Arthur. 'I

didn't make Suzy a general, did I? I remember her talking about it, but I don't remember actually . . .'

'She probably just put on the uniform,' said Dr Scamandros. 'No one would question her.'

Arthur frowned, but the frown quickly gave way to laughter.

'That sounds like Suzy,' he said. 'I bet she did it to get a better grade of tea or something. Or to annoy Dame Primus.'

He picked up a pair of armoured sandals, looked at them for a moment, then dropped them back on the shelf and chose a pair of plain, but glossy black boots instead.

'It's good to have you back, sir,' said the Troop Sergeant as Arthur strode out of the wardrobe.

'Thank you again, sergeant,' said Arthur. 'Let's get to the operations room. I need to find out exactly what's going on.'

There were at least twenty guards in the corridor, who formed up around Arthur as soon as he appeared. As they all marched together to the operations room, Arthur asked the guard commander to also send a messenger to find Suzy.

The operations room had grown larger in the few days of House time that had passed since Arthur had been there last. It was still a large domed chamber, but the walls had been pushed back to make it twice the size it had been before. It was now as big as his school gym, and in addition to all the soldiers in the various uniforms of the Regiment, the Horde, the Legion, the Moderately Honourable Artillery Company and the Borderers, there were also numerous Denizens in civilian attire, many of them with their coats off and the sleeves of their white shirts covered with green ink-protectors up to the elbow.

Besides the central map table, which was also much longer and broader than it had been, there were now rows and rows of narrow, student-style desks for the civilians, who were all busy talking on old-fashioned phones or scribbling down messages. Every few seconds one would push his or her chair back and race across the room with a message slip, going either to Marshals Dawn, Noon or Dusk, or to Dame Primus, who loomed over the map table, looking intently at various details, while many Denizens babbled out messages around her, often at the same time.

Dame Primus was taller than ever, perhaps eight and a half feet from toe to crown. She was wearing an armoured hauberk of golden scales that clattered as she moved. The whole outfit looked decidedly uncomfortable, and dangerous for others, as it was ornamented with spiked pauldrons made to look like gripping claws. Even though the points of the claws gripped her shoulders, they also had spurs and flanges poking out in all directions.

The gauntlets that comprised the Second Key were folded through Dame Primus's broad leather belt, next to the buckle. The clock-hand sword of the First Key hung scabbarded at her left hip. The small trident that was the Third Key sat in its holster on her right hip, and she held the marshal's baton that was the Fourth Key, occasionally gesturing with it.

The cacophony of shouted messages, ringing telephones, scraping chairs and clattering, hob-nailed or leather-soled Denizens suddenly ceased as Arthur's presence was announced. Then the noise redoubled as everyone in the room leaped from their chairs or pushed themselves off a wall, turned to the door and came to attention.

'Carry on!' called Arthur immediately. There was just a moment's more silence and then the room erupted into motion once more. The telephone earpieces rattled on their candlestick bodies as the old bells inside clattered more than rang, the messengers ran across the room and the officers resumed talking all at once.

But the messengers did not get to deliver their hastily-scrawled message forms to Dame Primus. She held up one hand and waved them back, striding across the room to greet Arthur, with Marshals Dawn, Noon and Dusk close behind her.

'Lord Arthur, a most timely arrival. I trust you have learned not to accept gifts from strange visitors?'

It took Arthur a moment to work out that Dame Primus was referring to the package he'd taken from Friday's servant Emelena, which had contained a Transfer Plate that had immediately activated, taking him to the Middle House. He had forgotten that he hadn't seen Dame Primus since then, or not all of her at least. He'd found Part Five, whom he quite liked and had hoped would round out the character of the Will, adding some much-needed common sense. Part Five had been assimilated, judging by what he had first assumed was a half-cloak on the back of Dame Primus, but now saw were in fact delicate, semi-transparent grey wings that were very similar to those that had been on the bat-beast that had lurked in the Inner Darkness of the Middle House.

'I'll know better next time,' he said. 'What I need

to know now is what's happening. Is the Lower House really destroyed?'

'Apart from the Deep Coal Cellar, the Lower House is entirely lost,' Dame Primus confirmed. 'As are the Far Reaches, and Nothing continues to surge against our defences. Only the Keys can strengthen the fabric of the House and we are threatened on too many fronts for me to deal with everything by myself. If you take the Fifth Key to the Middle House and reinforce the bulwark there, I will go to the Border Mountains here and build them up—'

'Hold on,' interrupted Arthur. 'How did this happen in the first place? And where is the Piper's Army? Are we still fighting Newniths here?'

'Really, Lord Arthur, there is no time to waste,' said Dame Primus. 'The Piper's Army has withdrawn and is no longer of immediate importance. Shoring up the foundations of the House is, and only you and I can do anything about that—'

'What about Superior Saturday?' asked Arthur. 'What is she up to? Why does she want the House to fall and what are we going to do about her? I'm not going anywhere until you, or someone, tells me everything I want to know!'

Dame Primus loomed over him. Though he had got taller, she was far taller still, and her eyes were narrowed and her mouth was tight with displeasure. Arthur felt a strong urge to step back, even to kneel in awe of her terrible beauty and power. Instead he forced himself to take a step forward and look at her straight in her strange eyes, their pink irises surrounding pupils of intense darkness. She was every inch the embodiment of the Architect's Will, and Arthur knew that if he gave in to her now, he would never have the chance to make his own decisions ever again.

'I am the Rightful Heir, aren't I?' he said. 'I want to know *exactly* what the situation is. Then *I* will decide what we are going to do.'

Dame Primus met his gaze for a full second, then slowly inclined her head.

'Very well, Lord Arthur,' she said. 'As you command, so it shall be.'

'Right then,' said Arthur. 'First things first. What actually happened to the Lower House? Did Nothing break through in the Far Reaches?'

'I will show you, through the eyes of someone who was there.' Dame Primus gestured with the baton and all the lamps in the room suddenly dimmed. 'Mr Skerrikim, I trust you still have the survivor?'

A Denizen in a dark frock coat, black cravat and embroidered silver skull-cap answered in the affirmative from the back of the room and made his way over to Dame Primus, lugging a large and rather battered leather suitcase fastened with three straps.

'An elevator operator was just closing his doors when it happened,' said Dame Primus to Arthur. 'He managed to get most of the way out of the Far Reaches before the Nothing caught him. By holding on to the ceiling light of the elevator with his teeth, his head and a small remnant of the elevator actually arrived here. Fortunately Mr Skerrikim was just in time to prevent his total dissolution.'

Mr Skerrikim, who Arthur had never seen before, laid the suitcase down on the floor, undid the straps and opened it up. The case was full of rose petals, and in the middle of the petals lay a disembodied head swathed from temple to chin in clean white bandages, like an old-fashioned treatment for a toothache. The head had its eyes shut.

Mr Skerrikim picked up the head by the ears and propped it against the open lid so it faced Arthur and Dame Primus. Then he took a small bottle of Activated Ink out of his pocket, dipped a quill pen into it and wrote something in extraordinarily tiny letters on the forehead of the survivor.

'Wake up, Marson!' instructed Mr Skerrikim cheerfully.

Arthur started as the head's eyes flicked open. Dr Scamandros, who was a step or two behind the boy, muttered something that did not sound very friendly.

'What is it?' Marson's head asked grumpily. 'It's hard work growing a new body. Not to mention painful! I need all my rest.'

'You shall have plenty of rest!' declared Mr Skerrikim. 'We're just going to have another look at what happened down that pit, near the dam wall.'

'Must you?' asked Marson. The head's mouth quivered and tears formed in the corners of his eyes. 'I just can't relive it again—the pain of the Nothing as it ate away my limbs—'

'This is entirely unnecessary!' protested Dr Scamandros as he pushed past several interested officers to stand next to Arthur. The tattoos on his face were of painted savages dancing around a bonfire, under the direction of a witch doctor in a ludicrous feathered headdress. 'This poor chap need not *feel* his immediate past merely for us to see it! I see also that you, sir, have used a quite discredited spell for the preservation of a head, and I must ask you to relinquish care of this individual to someone who knows what they are doing!'

'Mr Skerrikim is quite adequately trained,' said Dame Primus smoothly. She did not look at Dr Scamandros, but spoke to Arthur. 'As Sir Thursday's Chief Questioner, Skerrikim has conducted many showings from Denizens' minds, and as you know, Arthur, Denizens do not really feel much pain. Marson will be well rewarded when his new body grows.'

'I thought Dr Scamandros was the only sorcerer not in Saturday's service,' said Arthur.

'Mister Skerrikim is not exactly a sorcerer,' Dame Primus clarified. 'It is true he is a practitioner of House sorcery, but his field of specialisation is quite narrow.'

'Jackal,' hissed Scamandros quietly.

'Blow-hard,' retorted Skerrikim, not so quietly.

Arthur hesitated. He wanted to see what Marson had experienced, but he didn't want the dismembered Denizen to suffer.

'Scamandros, can you show us what we need to see without hurting him?'

'Indeed I can, sir,' said Scamandros, puffing out his chest.

'Skerrikim is an expert,' said Dame Primus. 'Far better to let him—'

'No,' Arthur said quietly. 'Scamandros will do it. That will be all, thank you, Mister Skerrikim.'

Skerrikim looked at Dame Primus. She did not move or give any signal that Arthur could see, but the skull-capped Denizen bowed and withdrew.

Scamandros knelt by the side of the suitcase and used a red velvet cloth to wipe off whatever Skerrikim had written on Marson's head. Then he took out his own bottle of Activated Ink and a peacock-plumed pen and wrote something else.

'Move aside,' Scamandros instructed several officers. 'The vision will form where you're standing. I trust you feel no pain, Marson?'

'Not a thing,' Marson reported. ' 'Cept an itch in the foot I don't have any more.'

'Excellent,' said Dr Scamandros. 'Open your eyes a little wider, a touch more . . . very good . . . hold them open there . . . Let me get these matchsticks in place and we will commence.'

The sorcerer stood back and spoke a word. Arthur could almost see the letters of it, see the way the air rippled away from Scamandros's mouth as he spoke. He felt the power of the spell as a tingle in his joints, and some small part of him knew that once, long ago, he would have felt pain. Now his body was accustomed to sorcery and used to power.

Two tiny pinpricks of light grew in Marson's eyes, and then two fierce beams shot forth, splaying out and gaining colour, dancing around madly as if a crazed and manic artist was painting with streams of light.

An image formed in the air by the table, an image projected from Marson's propped-open eyes. A broad, cinematic view some twelve feet wide and eight feet high, it showed a part of the floor of the Pit in the Far Reaches, the great, deep hole that Grim Tuesday had dug in order to mine more and more Nothing, no matter how dangerous it was, and no matter how much it weakened the very foundations of the House.

Arthur leaned forward, intent on the scene. Even though what he was to see had already happened, he felt very tense, as if he was actually there . . .

CHAPTER SIX

'The memory is blurred,' said Dame Primus. 'We should have had Skerrikim do it.'

'Merely a matter of focus, milady,' said Scamandros. He bent down and adjusted Marson's eyelids, the shadows of his fingers walking across the lit scene like tall, dark, walking trees. 'There we are.'

The picture became sharp and sound came in as well. They were seeing what Marson had seen. The Denizen was looking out through the door of his elevator, his finger ready to press one of the bronze buttons that would take it up. Beyond the door, there was a rubble-strewn plain, lit here and there by an oil lamp hanging from an iron post. Some fifty yards away, a group of Denizens had gathered at the base of a great wall, a vast expanse of light grey concrete that had rods of shimmering iron protruding from it at regular intervals.

'Hey, that's the part I fixed up!' exclaimed Arthur. 'With Immaterial-reinforced concrete.'

The Denizens were looking at something. All of a sudden they backed away and one of them turned to call to someone out of sight.

'Sir! There's some sort of curious drill here! It's boring a hole all by itself! It's—'

Her words were cut off by a sudden, silent spray of Nothing that jetted out of the base of the wall. All the Denizens were cut down by it, instantly dissolved. Then more Nothing spewed out and there was a terrible rumbling sound. Cracks suddenly ran from the ground up through the wall, cracks that began to bubble with dark Nothing.

A bell began to clang insistently and a steam whistle sounded a frantic scream.

Marson's finger jabbed a button. The doors began to close, even as a rolling wave of Nothing came straight at the elevator. His voice came through, loud and strange, heard through his own ears.

'No, no, no!'

He kept jabbing buttons. The doors shut and the elevator rocketed upwards. Marson's fingers fumbled in his coat pocket, withdrawing a key that he used to quickly open a small hatch under the button panel. Inside was a red handle marked EMERGENCY RISE. Marson pulled it, a silk thread and wax seal snapping. The elevator gained speed and he fell to his knees, but even the emergency rise was not fast enough. The floor of the elevator suddenly became as holed as a piece of Swiss cheese, blots of darkness eating it away.

Marson leaped up and grabbed the chandelier in the ceiling, hauling himself up even as the lower half of the elevator disappeared. He was screaming and shrieking now, looking down at himself, where his legs had just ceased to exist—

'Stop!' said Arthur. 'We've seen enough.'

Scamandros snapped his fingers. The light from Marson's eyes faded. As the sorcerer bent down and removed the matchsticks, the disembodied head spoke.

'That weren't so bad.'

'Thank you, Marson,' said Arthur. He looked at Dame Primus. 'I am sure you will be well looked after.'

'As you see, Lord Arthur,' said Dame Primus, 'some kind of sabotage device of considerable power was used to breach the dam wall. It is likely that many other devices were employed at the same time, because almost the entire length of the dam wall fell at the same time. This allowed entry to a titanic surge of Nothing, which annihilated the Far Reaches in four or five minutes.

'Fortunately the bulwark between the Far Reaches and the Lower House held for several hours, allowing enough time for the evacuation of important records and items, and a fair number of Denizens. Complete destruction of the Lower House followed, with the final remnants succumbing an hour ago. Nothing now presses directly against the lower bulwark of the Middle House.

'In a possibly unrelated complication, when the Piper's army withdrew, he covered his retreat with an explosion of Nothing that has weakened the barrier mountains here in the Great Maze and, as always, there is Nothing leeching into the Border Sea. That is why we are both needed. We *must* use the power of the Keys to delay the destruction of the House.'

'*Delay* the destruction?' asked Arthur. 'Can't we stop it?'

'I doubt it. But we must hold off the Void long enough for you to claim the last two Keys. Then matters can be arranged in an orderly fashion.'

'You mean that no matter what we do, the House—and the whole universe beyond—is doomed?' asked Arthur. 'It's only a matter of time?'

'I didn't say that, Lord Arthur.' Dame Primus glanced away as she spoke, as if something had caught her eye. 'You misunderstood me. Once we have stabilised the House, you can gain the Keys, and then we will be in a position to assess the damage and see what can be done.'

'But I thought you said—'

'You misunderstood me,' Dame Primus repeated smoothly. She looked back at Arthur again and met his gaze. Even more than usual he felt like a small animal caught in the glare of the headlights of a rapidly approaching truck, but he didn't look away. 'Now, where do you wish to commence work? Here, with the mountains, or in the Middle House?'

'Neither,' said Arthur. 'Someone put those drills to work, and that someone pretty much has to be Superior Saturday, doesn't it? Or Lord Sunday, working with her, I suppose, though that bit of paper poor old Ugham had suggests otherwise.'

'What paper?' Dame Primus asked suspiciously.

'The one signed just with an 'S', that said 'I do

not wish to intervene or interfere' or whatever. It's in my old coat, I think.'

'Signed merely with a single 'S'? That is Lord Sunday's mark. Superior Saturday, as she calls herself, would not be so humble as to use a single letter.'

'OK, that pretty much confirms Sunday's out of it—for now at least. So we need to make sure that Saturday can't do anything else. I mean, it's all very well shoring up the defences, but what if she's undermining the House somewhere else we don't even know about?'

The three Marshals nodded in approval. Attack was the best method of defence as far as they were concerned.

'I agree that Saturday must be dealt with,' said Dame Primus, 'but our first priority must be to reinforce the House! It is not supposed to fall like this. I cannot be in two places at once, so you have to do some of the work. When what we hold of the House is secure, then we can talk about freeing Part Six of myself and confronting Saturday. Not before!'

'You can't be in two places at once,' said Arthur thoughtfully, almost to himself.

'I beg your pardon?' Dame Primus bent forward a little, as if to hear Arthur better.

'You can't be in two places at once,' Arthur repeated loudly. 'Yet we have five Keys between us, and once you were five separate beings. Is it possible for you to become two?'

Dame Primus frowned even more.

'I mean two of you, with an equal mix of all parts of the Will,' Arthur added hurriedly. Most of the individual parts of the Will were quite unbalanced, some of them dangerously so. He didn't want the snaky, judgmental Part Four off on its own, for example.

'It . . . is . . . possible,' said Dame Primus. 'But not at all recommended. We would do much better—'

'And you can join back together again?' Arthur was not giving up on the idea so easily.

Dame Primus nodded stiffly.

'OK, then you can split into two, and each half of you can take two Keys and go and fix up whatever needs fixing up,' said Arthur. 'Or, hey, you could split into four and take a Key each—'

'I will *not* divide myself so much!' said Dame Primus furiously. 'It would merely offer a target for Saturday or even the Piper, who might well overcome such a fraction of myself and wrest the Keys from our control.'

'Two then,' said Arthur. 'Dame Primus and Dame . . . uh . . . Two?'

'Secundus,' whispered Scamandros.

'This is not a good idea, Arthur,' said Dame Primus. 'To lessen my power by half is foolish in the extreme. And if you think this will allow you to return to your Secondary Realm then you have failed to consider your own transformation and the effect you will have—'

'I'm not going back home,' Arthur interrupted coldly. 'At least not yet. Like I said, we need to deal with Superior Saturday. That means freeing Part Six of the Will to start with, so please tell me—do you know where it is? I know you can sense the other parts of yourself.'

Dame Primus straightened up.

'Part Six of myself is definitely somewhere within

the Upper House. I do not know where exactly and I have no means of finding out. The Upper House has been closed to us by means of sorcery. No elevators go there now, there are no telephone connections and the Front Door remains firmly shut. So once again, even if it was in our best interests for you to go there, it is not possible, and you would do better to help me and not make foolish—that is to say, *naive*—suggestions about me dividing myself.'

'There's no way there at all?' asked Arthur. 'What about the Improbable—no, I'd have to have visited there before. Same for the Fifth Key . . .'

'As I said, there is no way,' Dame Primus insisted. 'Once again illustrating that I know best, Arthur. You must remember that although you are the Rightful Heir, you were just a mortal boy not so long ago. No one can expect you to have the wisdom—'

Arthur ignored her. Another plan had just occurred to him. 'There might be a way,' he said. 'I'll have to go and check it out.'

'What?' asked Dame Primus, indignant. 'What way? Even if you *could* get to the Upper House, you must remember that Saturday has thousands of sorcerers, perhaps even tens of thousands. Acting in concert and directed by her, they could easily overcome you, take you prisoner—'

'I'm not just going to charge in,' said Arthur. He was getting increasingly tired of Dame Primus's objections. 'In fact, if I can get there the way I'm thinking, it will be a very sneaky approach. Anyway, we're wasting time. You need to split into two, Dame Primus, and get to work. I have to head over to the Border Sea.'

'This is all too hasty!' protested Dame Primus. 'What can you possibly want in the Border Sea?'

'The Raised Rats.'

Dame Primus took in an outraged breath and her frown got so deep her eyebrows almost met in a huddle above her nose.

'The Raised Rats are agents of the Piper! Like the Piper's children, they are not to be trusted! They are to be hunted down and exterminated!'

'Old Primey got her undergarments in a twist again,' said a voice behind Arthur. He turned and smiled as he saw his friend Suzy Turquoise Blue expertly slide between two Denizens to stand next to him.

'Suzy! What on earth are you wearing?'

'M'uniform,' said Suzy. She raised her battered top hat, which now had two oversized gold epaulettes sewn to the back like a sun-cape, and bowed. The half dozen probably unearned medals on her red regimental coat (that had the sleeves cut off to show her yellow shirt) jangled as she made a bow, and the leg she thrust forward creaked, since she was also wearing the same kind of leather breeches as Arthur, which he had thought were exclusive to Sir Thursday. Her boots were red and did not resemble those in any uniform that Arthur had learned about in his recruit training. Neither did the iridescent green-scaled belt she wore, though the savage-sword at her side was in a regulation sheath.

Arthur blinked, not least because there were several other Piper's children clad in similar strange combinations standing behind Suzy.

'Suzy's Raiders,' Suzy said, seeing him look.

'Irregulars. Marshal Dusk signed off on it. Told 'im it was your idea.'

'My idea,' Arthur started to say, but he bit off his words as he saw Suzy wiggling her eyebrows at him.

'On account of the Piper's children bein' under a cloud, so to speak,' added Suzy. 'Better to to 'ave us all in one lot. Easier to watch that way. If Old Prim—I mean, if Dame Primus wants to knock us off.'

'It's not a personal matter, Miss Blue,' said Dame Primus with a sniff. 'I am merely doing whatever is necessary to ensure Lord Arthur's eventual triumph. You yourself have fallen under the spell of the Piper's music once. Ensuring that it doesn't happen again is simply common sense.'

'You don't have to kill us,' said Suzy, bristling. She rummaged in her pockets and produced two ugly grey stumps of candle-wax. 'We can just stick this 'ere wax in our ears and we won't be able to hear the pipe! Besides, it's General Turquoise Blue now!'

Dame Primus snorted and was about to speak when Arthur held up his hand.

'I've already given orders that no Piper's children are to be harmed,' he said. 'Neither are the Raised Rats, provided they do not act against us. Now I *am* going to see the Rats. They owe me a question and I owe them an answer, so I'm sure they will at least negotiate. Dame Primus, Marshals, everyone, please carry on as we have discussed. Dr Scamandros, would you mind coming with me?'

'Certainly, Lord Arthur, certainly,' puffed Dr Scamandros. 'Ah, do you intend to use the Fifth

Key again?'

'It's the quickest way,' said Arthur. 'I can go straight to the *Rattus Navis IV*. I can probably see out of the reflection of the silver jug they had. What, Suzy?'

Suzy was tugging at his sleeve.

'I'm coming too, right? To see the Rats and then sort out Saturday?'

'You probably should stay and look after the Piper's child—'

'Stay! Just because you've got taller than's sensible and your teeth all shined up doesn't mean you can do without me! Who's saved your bacon a mort of times?'

'I perhaps should advise you, Lord Arthur, that I felt quite a level of resistance when we travelled here,' said Scamandros. 'Indeed, I was almost hurled back. It might be more prudent to take the elevator to Port Wednesday and send for the Raised Rats.'

'There isn't time,' said Arthur. 'But I think I will need you, so if you can bear it—'

'I will attend you,' said Scamandros. 'I will hold on more tightly this time, though you now lack coat-tails. If I may take your arm?'

'What about me?' Suzy demanded.

'Yes, you can come too,' Arthur told her. 'At least to talk to the Rats.'

Arthur offered one arm to Dr Scamandros and the other to Suzy, though this made it difficult to hold up the Fifth Key. He was about to gaze into it when he hesitated and looked across at Dame Primus. She had gone back to the map table and was studying it, giving no sign that she was about to split in two and do as he asked.

Arthur had also remembered something else.

'Dame Primus!' he called out. 'Before you do split into two, I would like *The Compleat Atlas of the House* back again. I expect it will also be very useful.'

Dame Primus kept looking at the table and did not turn her head to speak.

'The Atlas has a mind of its own,' she said. 'I believe it was last seen in the Middle House, probably getting a new binding put on without visible assistance. I expect it will return here in due course, or it will find you wherever you are. I suggest that you check any bookshelves you happen to be near.'

'Oh,' said Arthur, and then it struck him.

She's lying to me, he thought. *Or avoiding the truth. I wonder why she doesn't want me to have the Atlas? It could be very useful. But she can't look me in the eye and lie—*

Marshal Dawn erupted from her desk and rushed across the room, brandishing a message slip and calling, 'Dame Primus! There is a small geyser of Nothing reported near Letterer's Lark!'

Dame Primus took the slip.

'You see, Arthur! Well, if you will not go, then I must do as you ask. Marshal Dawn, prepare an escort and the private elevator!'

Dawn saluted and rushed away. There was a hush in the room as everyone watched Dame Primus, a hush that immediately dissipated as she looked about her, a deep frown on her face. Frenetic activity resumed everywhere, apart from a quiet space around Dame Primus and another around Arthur, Suzy and Scamandros.

'Reckon this'll be worth seeing,' muttered Suzy.

'Think she'll split in half and wriggle like a worm?'

Arthur shook his head. That would be too undignified for Dame Primus.

As they watched, she took a step forward, and as she did so, she blurred and diminished, as if she'd walked into a hole in the ground. Then a smaller version of herself walked ahead, leaving a second smaller version behind, so that there were two seven-foot-tall Dame Primuses standing in a line, instead of one eight-foot-plus version. They looked identical and were dressed exactly the same, but one had the clock-sword of the First Key and the trident of the Third Key and the other had the gauntlets of the Second Key and the baton of the Fourth.

The two embodiments of the Will turned to each other and curtsied.

'Dame Quarto,' said the one who had the sword and the gauntlets.

'Dame Septum,' said the one who had the trident and the baton.

'Hmmph,' whispered Scamandros. 'Self-aggrandisement. They've added one and three and two and five. Trying to make the sum of the whole greater, I suppose.'

Quarto and Septum turned and curtsied to Arthur.

'Lord Arthur,' they chorused.

'Hello,' said Arthur. 'Thank you for splitting. I guess we'd all better get on with it.'

'Indeed,' said Dame Quarto.

'We had,' added Dame Septum. She raised her hand and dramatically announced, 'I shall attend to the Middle House!'

'And I to the mountains!' declared Dame

Quarto, and both strode from the room.

'And I to . . . sorting out Superior Saturday,' said Arthur. Somehow it didn't sound the same. He raised the mirror and concentrated on looking through it and out of the reflection in the silver jug in the stern cabin of the *Rattus Navis IV*. He would soon find himself wherever the ship might be upon the strange waters of the Border Sea.

CHAPTER SEVEN

It was much harder going through the doorway with two people hanging on and for a fearful moment Arthur thought all three of them would be thrown back, and not to the safety of the Citadel, but somewhere else not of his choosing. The ground swayed unsteadily beneath his feet, the light dazzled his eyes, and Suzy and Scamandros felt like enormous lead weights dragging his arms back and down. But he kept pushing forwards, his total concentration on reaching his goal. He could half-see the table and chairs in the big cabin on the *Rattus Navis IV*. Even though it looked just a step away, it was almost impossible to reach.

Then, with a Herculean effort that left Arthur sweating and gasping, they fell out on to the tilted-over floor of the ship and slid across the floorboards into the starboard hull. Then, as the ship rolled back the other way and pitched forwards, they slid diagonally across to the port side, smacked into the table and sent the silver jug clanging on to the deck.

As they got up and grabbed hold of whatever they could to stay upright, the door burst open and a Newnith soldier gaped in the doorway.

'Boarders!' he shouted as he drew a sparking dagger from the sheath at his belt. 'The enemy!'

Scamandros reached into his sleeve and came out with a tiny cocktail fork with a pickled onion on it, which he didn't expect and hurriedly replaced.

Suzy drew her savage-sword at the same time, but the Newnith was quicker and had his sea legs. He rushed at Arthur, who instinctively raised his arm to protect himself, even though an arm would be no real protection from a long dagger that was spewing out white-hot sparks.

But it was his right arm, and in his right hand Arthur held the Fifth Key. Before the Newnith could fully complete his downward cut at the boy, there was a brilliant flash of light, a sudden, strange chemical stench, a stifled scream and then just a pair of smoking boots on the deck where the Newnith had been.

Arthur felt a surge of irritation and annoyance.

How dare these pathetic creatures attack me? he thought. *How dare they! I shall walk among them and wreak havoc . . .*

Arthur shook his head and took a breath, forcing this arrogant temper tantrum back to wherever it had come from. He was frightened by it, frightened that he could get so angry and that his immediate response was to attack.

As the rage lessened, he became aware that his arm hurt quite a lot.

'Ouch!' he exclaimed. The point of the Newnith's dagger had made contact with him after all. He rolled his arm over to get a better look and saw that it had done more than just scratch the skin. There was a six-inch-long incision in his forearm and it looked cut to the bone. Yet even as he looked, the cut closed up, leaving only a very faint white scar. Arthur wiped off what little blood there was with his left hand, and tried not to notice that it was neither red like a normal human's nor blue like a Denizen's. It was golden, like a deep, rich honey, and that was almost more painful to him than the cut itself. Whatever he was becoming was very strange indeed.

'There's nothing left of 'im,' said Suzy with satisfaction, turning over the vaporised Newnith's smoking boots with the point of her sword.

'I didn't mean to do it,' said Arthur sadly. 'It was the Key.'

'We'd best get ready.' Suzy tugged on the table, to drag it to the door, but it was bolted to the deck and she only succeeded in staggering into Scamandros when she lost her grip. Still unsteady, both of them went backwards into one of the well-upholstered chairs. Suzy was up again in a moment, while Scamandros struggled like a beetle thrown upon its back.

'Won't just be one Newnith on board,' Suzy warned. 'They'll be charging in any moment.'

'They might not have heard,' said Arthur. It *was* noisy, the constant rhythmic thud of the ship's steam engine mixed with the groan and creak of the rigging above, as well as the regular crash and jolt as the ship plunged through what had to be fairly sizeable waves.

'They heard orright,' said Suzy. She spat on her hands and gripped her sword more tightly. 'I expect your Key can burn up a passel of 'em though.'

'I don't want to burn them up,' Arthur protested. 'I just want to talk to the Raised Rats!'

'We are very glad to hear that,' said a voice from under the table.

Suzy swore and ducked down to have a look.

'A trapdoor,' she exclaimed in admiration. 'Sneaky!'

A four-foot-tall rat, clad in white breeches and a blue coat with a single gold epaulette on his left shoulder, clambered out from under the table and saluted Arthur, his long mouth open in a smile that revealed two shiny, gold-capped front teeth. He had a cutlass at his side, but it was sheathed. A Napoleonic hat perched at a jaunty angle on his head.

'Lord Arthur, I presume? I am Lieutenant Goldbite, recently appointed to command this vessel following Captain Longtayle's promotion and transfer. I didn't have the pleasure of meeting you before, but I am acquainted with your past dealings with us. Perhaps you and your companions would like to sit?'

He gestured at the armchairs.

'Do we have a truce?' asked Arthur, still standing. 'And do you speak for all aboard?'

'I am the captain,' said Goldbite. 'I say truce for all of us, Newniths and Raised Rats.'

'The Piper's not 'ere, is he?' asked Suzy. She

hadn't sat down either, though Scamandros had settled back down only moments after finally managing to get up.

'The Piper is not aboard this ship,' said Goldbite. 'And though we owe him a considerable debt and so will carry his troops and so forth, the Raised Rats have chosen to be non-combatants in the Piper's wars and should not be considered in the same light as the Newniths. Speaking of them, if you wouldn't mind sitting down, I shall just pop out and stand down both my own folk and the Newniths.'

'I'm sorry about the one . . . the one I killed,' said Arthur. He was very aware that the Newniths, though they felt obliged to serve the Piper, actually just wanted to be farmers. Arthur felt they were much more like humans than Denizens. 'He attacked me, and the Key . . .'

Goldbite nodded. 'I will tell them. He was not the first, nor will he be the last. But I trust there will be no more fighting between us on the *Rattus Navis IV*. Please do help yourself to biscuits from that tin there, and there is more cranberry juice in the keg.'

'Might as well,' said Arthur as the Raised Rat left via the door. He picked up the silver jug and refilled it from the keg, while Suzy got out the biscuits, tapping them on the table to make the weevils fall out. She offered them around, but Arthur and Scamandros passed, the latter taking a slightly crushed ham and watercress sandwich on a red chequered china plate out of one of his inner pockets.

'I'm curious to know why there are Newniths on board,' said Arthur quietly. 'I hope the Piper isn't

81

going to attack us here in the Border Sea.'

'Port Wednesday is well defended,' said Dr Scamandros. 'The Triangle would be more at risk, if none of the regular vessels are there to protect it. But there would be little to gain from taking that, since it has no elevators or anything very useful. But of course the Rats could be taking the Newniths elsewhere by way of the Border Sea, out into the Secondary Realms—'

'Ssshhh,' Arthur hushed. 'Goldbite's coming back.'

Goldbite knocked and then poked his long nose around the door.

'All settled in?' he asked before coming in. 'Very good. I'm afraid my First Lieutenant can't join us, as she has the watch, but my Acting Third Lieutenant will do so. I believe you have already met.'

The Raised Rat behind Goldbite stepped out and saluted. Though his whiskers had been trimmed and he wore a blue coat, Arthur recognised him immediately.

'Watkingle! You've been promoted!'

'Yes, sir,' said Watkingle. 'And it was for hitting you on the head, sir, and averting a disastrosphe or cataster, whichever you like. That was a good hit for me, if you don't mind me saying so, sir.'

'I don't mind—it was needed at the time.' Arthur got up and shook Watkingle's paw. 'Feverfew would have had me otherwise.'

'You're looking . . . uh . . . well, sir,' said Watkingle. 'Taller.'

'Yes,' replied Arthur, not very happily. He sat back down. Watkingle lounged back against the hull, bracing his paws so that he was not thrown off balance by the pitch and roll of the ship.

'I take it you have come to ask your third question?' said Goldbite, after the ensuing silence started to feel uncomfortable.

'Well, both a question and a request for aid,' Arthur replied. 'I hear that Superior Saturday has completely cut off the Upper House and that there is no way to get there. But I bet you Rats know a way. In fact, I know you must, because a Raised Rat managed to get out with a piece of paper. I want to find out what that way is, and I want you to help me get there.'

'And me!' added Suzy.

'Hmmm,' said Goldbite. 'I shall have to send a message to Commodore Monckton—'

Arthur shook his head.

'There's no time. I presume you know that the Nothing defences in the Far Reaches were sabotaged and the dam wall was destroyed. The Lower House has also been destroyed. I have to stop Saturday before she manages to destroy the entire House.'

Goldbite wrinkled his nose in agitation.

'We had news of a disaster, but did not know it was so extreme,' he said. 'But to answer your question I must reveal secrets. I've not been in command of this vessel long, nor am I very senior . . .'

'I have already ordered the Raised Rats to be left alone unless they act against my forces,' said Arthur. 'I'm happy to do anything I can for you, and to answer any number of questions, if you can tell me how to get into the Upper House.' He paused and then corrected, 'How to get into the Upper House without being noticed, that is.'

'As you have guessed, Lord Arthur, there *is* a way,' said Goldbite slowly. He looked at Watkingle, who shrugged. 'All things considered, I believe I must assist you. But you must agree to a price to be set by Commodore Monckton and those Rats senior to me, in addition to the answer you already owe us.'

'That's a pig in a poke,' said Suzy. 'You Rats really take the biscuit.'

'Why, thank you,' said Watkingle. He leaned forward and took a biscuit.

'That's not what I meant!' protested Suzy. 'Why should Arthur agree to—'

'It's OK, Suzy,' said Arthur. 'I do agree.'

If I don't agree, it soon won't matter, he figured. And a small voice inside him, a deep and nasty part of his mind, added, *Besides, I can go back on my word. They're only rats . . .*

'I must also ask you to keep this secret, Lord Arthur,' continued Goldbite. 'All of you must keep it secret.'

Arthur nodded, as did Suzy, though he had a suspicion she'd crossed her fingers behind her back.

'Always happy to keep a secret,' said Scamandros. 'Got hundreds of them already, locked up here.'

The sorcerer tapped his forehead and a tattoo of a keyhole appeared there, a key went in and turned, and then both transformed into a spray of question marks that danced over his temples to his ears.

'Very well,' said Goldbite. 'Lord Arthur, you know about our Simultaneous Bottles, how something put in one bottle of a matched pair will appear in the other bottle?'

'Yes. For messages and so on. But Monckton told me they only work in the Border Sea!'

'That is true for most of them. But we do have a small number of very special Simultaneous Bottles, or, to be accurate, Simultaneous Nebuchadnezzars that not only work outside the Border Sea—'

'What's a Nebuchadnezzar?' asked Suzy.

'Size of bottle,' said Scamandros. Eight bottles of increasing size appeared on his left cheek and spread across to his right cheek. The smallest was about half an inch high; the largest began at his chin and went to the top of his ear. 'Big one. There's your ordinary bottle. Then comes a Magnum—that's two bottles worth. Then a Jeroboam—that holds the same as four of the regular size. And so forth: Rehoboam, six bottles; Methuselah, eight; Salmanazar, twelve; Balthazar, sixteen; Nebuchadnezzar, twenty!'

He started to rummage inside his coat and added, 'Got a Jeroboam of quite a nice little sparkling wine here somewhere, a gift from poor old Captain Catapillow—'

'Yes, yes,' broke in Goldbite. 'The Simultaneous Nebuchadnezzars are very large bottles that we have twinned in various locations about the House, including one in the Upper House. Their size is important because they are large enough to allow the transfer of one of us. But not, I hasten to say, someone of your size, Lord Arthur.'

'I thought it might be something like that,' said Arthur. 'That's where you come in, Dr Scamandros. I want you to turn me into a Raised Rat. Temporarily, that is.'

'And me,' said Suzy.

85

'It is not an easy thing to do,' Dr Scamandros warned. 'It is true I once created illusions for you, to give you the appearance of Rats. Actually reshaping you, even for a limited time—I don't know. You could do it yourself with the Key, Arthur.'

Arthur nodded. 'I probably could. But I would be worried about turning back again. But if you do it, it will wear off, won't it?'

'I should expect so,' said Scamandros. 'But I cannot be sure how any spell will effect you, Lord Arthur. It is possible the Key might perceive such a spell as an attack and do the same thing to me that it did to that Newnith.'

'I'm sure it wouldn't if I was concentrating on wanting to turn into a Raised Rat,' said Arthur. 'Anyway, let's give it a try.'

Goldbite coughed and raised a paw.

'The Simultaneous Nebuchadnezzar that is twinned with the one we have secreted in the Upper House is not aboard this vessel. Should you wish to try it, upon the terms I have outlined, we must rendezvous with the *Rattus Navis II*. If I send a message and she steams towards us, and we to her, it should only be a matter of half an hour. We have been travelling in convoy.'

'Convoy?' asked Arthur. 'With loads of Newniths aboard? I hope you're not planning to attack Port Wednesday after all?'

'I do not know the ultimate destination of the Newnith force,' answered Goldbite. 'But I can tell you that we took them aboard in the Secondary Realms, and so I expect we shall disembark them in another.'

'OK, good,' said Arthur. 'I think. What can they

be up to? I wish the Piper would just stay out of everything. I suppose I could ask one of the Newniths—'

'Please!' interrupted Goldbite. 'As I said, the Raised Rats seek to be non-combatants. At present the Newniths have agreed to the polite fiction that one of their number was lost in an accident at sea. They will not come below to seek you out, but should you make yourself known, then they will feel compelled to fight. I expect you would win, Lord Arthur, but your companions could be killed and certainly many Newniths would die. Please stay here, drink cranberry juice, and when we have made our rendezvous, we will transfer you to the other ship as quickly and quietly as is possible.'

'All right.' Once again Arthur had to fight back the urge to stride out upon the deck and order the Newniths to bow before him. And if they would not, then he would blast them to cinders and let wind and wave blow them away . . .

No, thought Arthur. *Stop! I will do this my way. No matter what I look like on the outside, I am not going to change who I truly am. I am human and I know how to love, and be kind, and be compassionate to those who are weaker than me. Just because I have power doesn't mean I have to use it!*

'I am going to need some things,' announced Dr Scamandros, who was rummaging in his pockets. 'Hmm . . . freshly-cut Rat hair . . . four paw prints in jelly or plaster or sand, at a pinch . . . grey or brown paint, a bigger brush than this one . . . I think I have everything else.'

'Watkingle can organise those items for you,'

said Goldbite.

'Whose fresh-cut Rat hair, sir?' asked Watkingle. 'I aint due for a haircut—'

'Someone will need one,' said Goldbite. 'See to it at once.'

'Aye, aye,' grumbled Watkingle. He left the cabin, mumbling to himself, 'Hair, plaster, grey or brown paint . . .'

'Let me see,' continued Dr Scamandros. He set a green crystal bottle stoppered with a lead seal on the table. 'The large bottle of Activated Ink . . . might be best to read up a little. There's that piece in *Xamanader's Xenographical Xactions* . . . sure I had a copy somewhere . . .'

'Where is the other Nebuchadnezzar? The one in the Upper House?' asked Arthur, though as always he was fascinated by the amount and size of the stuff Scamandros could keep in his coat. 'And are there Rats who might be able to help me there?'

'I don't know much,' replied Goldbite. 'I believe it is in the very lowest levels of the Upper House, by the steam engines that drive the chains. We do have some agents in place. And, of course, the Piper's children there who help us would probably assist you too.'

'Piper's children?' asked Suzy. 'I never knew there was a bunch of us lot in the Upper House.'

At the same time, Arthur asked, 'Steam engines? Chains?'

Goldbite explained what little he could, with Scamandros interrupting a little, in between cataloguing items he needed and re-sorting strange things that had come out of his coat. As it happened, the sorcerer could add little to

Goldbite's explanations. Scamandros had been expelled from the Upper House several thousand years previously and back then Superior Saturday had used more conventional means to build her tower, and there had been other buildings too, not just one enormous, sprawling construction of iron cubes.

'It sounds like some sort of giant toy construction set,' said Arthur. 'And all the cubes get moved along rails by steam-driven chains?'

'So I am told,' said Goldbite.

'Reckon that'll be worth looking at,' said Suzy happily. 'Nothin' like a nice cloud of honest steam and a bit of sooty coal smoke to invigilate the lungs.'

'Vigorate,' said Scamandros absently. 'In-vig-o-rate. The other's to do with exams and looking into matters. Cause of my downfall.'

'I'm sure it will look interesting enough,' said Arthur. 'But we have to remember it's the fortress of our enemy. If you do come, Suzy, you have to stay out of sight and be sneaky. I don't want to have to fight thousands of sorcerers. Or Saturday, for that matter—not in her own demesne with the Sixth Key. We'll just go in, find Part Six of the Will, get it and get out. Get it?'

'Got it,' said Suzy.

'Good,' said Arthur. At that moment, a fleeting memory of his father, Bob, flashed through his head, of him watching one of his favourite Danny Kaye films and laughing fit to burst. But then it was gone and Arthur couldn't think why it had come to mind. He wished he could have held on to it longer. His father and his family felt so distant. Even a brief memory of them made him feel not so much alone.

CHAPTER EIGHT

They were taken in a ship's boat from the *Rattus Navis IV* to the *Rattus Navis II*. Rowed by eight salty Rats with blue ribbons trailing from their straw hats who kept in time to Watkingle's hoarse roars of 'Pull! Pull!' the boat made a quick passage across the few hundred yards of open sea that separated the ships.

Arthur sat with his back against the bow, looking at the *Rattus Navis IV* and the ranks of Newniths on the deck. They were all facing the other way, studiously ignoring the departure of their brief fellow passengers. He was thinking about them, and where they might be going, and also thinking about where he was going, when a great spray of cold seawater splashed across his shoulders. He turned around just in time to cop the last of it in his open mouth, and saw that they were plunging down the face of a wave, having just cut through the crest of it, in the process taking on perhaps a third of a bucket of water. It would have been much more, save for Watkingle's skill in steering the boat.

In that small amount of water, which had mostly fallen over Arthur, there was something else, which now lay wet and sodden in his lap. It was a fluffy yellow elephant—his toy elephant, which he'd already found once in the Border Sea, home of lost things, only to lose it again somewhere between the Sea and the Great Maze.

'Elephant,' he said dumbly, and clutched it to his chest, as tightly as he'd ever held it as a small child. Then he remembered who and where he was, and slowly lowered the toy back into his lap.

'You need to careful with that,' said Dr Scamandros, looking at him over the top of his open copy of *Xamanader's Xenographical Xactions*, a small scarlet-coloured book that looked too slim to have much sorcerous wisdom in it. 'Childhood totems are very potent. Someone could make a Cocigrue from it, like the Skinless Boy, or perhaps a Sympathetic Needle to bring you pain.'

'I won't lose Elephant again,' said Arthur. He put the small toy inside his tunic and made sure it couldn't fall out. It made rather a strange lump, but he didn't care.

'I 'ad a toy when I was a little,' said Suzy. She frowned for a moment, then added, 'Can't remember what it was. It moved and made me laugh . . .'

'Ahoy the boat! Come alongside!'

Suzy's recollections were left behind as they scrambled up the rope ladder to the deck of the

91

Rattus Navis II, where they were met by a nattily-dressed Raised Rat whose uniform was much finer and considerably more decorative than any other Arthur had seen. Even the basic blue material of his coat had a swirling, silken pattern that caught the light.

'Greetings, Lord Arthur! I am Lieutenant Finewhisker, commander of this vessel. Please, come below. We have our own small contingent of Newniths aboard, senior officers for the most part, who have been kind enough to foregather in the bow and take tea while you . . . ahem . . . visit.'

'Thank you,' said Arthur.

'Follow me, please.' Finewhisker moved quickly to the aft companionway and ushered them down to the captain's great cabin. It was similar to the cabin in the *Rattus Navis IV*, but was much more elaborately decorated. There were red velvet curtains on the windows, and the chairs were upholstered in a bright patterned cloth that looked almost like a tartan.

Arthur hardly noticed the decorations. The cabin was dominated by an enormous green glass bottle that sat in a wooden cradle that was lashed to the deck. The bottle was at least eight feet long and five feet in diameter, and if it wasn't for the neck being only as thick as his leg, he could have easily got inside *without* being turned into a Rat first.

The green glass was cloudy, but not entirely opaque, and something that looked like smoke or fog was swirling about inside, prevented from issuing out into the cabin by the Simultaneous Nebuchadnezzar's huge, wire-wrapped, steel-bonneted cork.

'Everything is prepared,' said Finewhisker. 'You need only enter the bottle, whenever you are . . . ah . . . made ready to do so. May I offer you a refreshing cordial, Lord Arthur, while your sorcerer prepares his spell?'

'No, thank you,' said Arthur. 'How long will it take you, Dr Scamandros?'

Scamandros was sorting out his various supplies on the bench. He glanced over at Arthur, blinked several times at the Nebuchadnezzar and coughed.

'Perhaps thirty minutes, Lord Arthur. If I may prevail upon someone to fetch me a large piece of cheese with the rind on, I would be grateful. I thought I had a slab of Old Chewsome, but I can't lay my hand on it.'

'I will have the cook deliver some,' Finewhisker said. 'Please make yourselves comfortable. I must go on deck for a few minutes, but I will be back in plenty of time to open the Nebuchadnezzar. Quite a specialised technique is required, so please do not attempt the cork yourselves. I should also warn you not to touch the glass. The exterior of the bottle is often very, very cold, and occasionally very, very hot. As neither the heat nor cold radiates, it can be a very unpleasant shock.'

'Doesn't radiate?' muttered Scamandros. 'How very interesting.'

He turned away from the plaster Rat footprints he had been holding and took a step towards the Nebuchadnezzar, then threw his hands up and turned back, the tattoo of a spinning ship's wheel on his forehead indicating that he had recalled his immediate task.

'So we go through this 'ere bottle,' said Suzy thoughtfully, 'then we find Part Six of the Will, right?'

'Yes,' said Arthur.

''Ow exactly do we do that?' asked Suzy. 'Reckon it might turn up like Part One and jump in me gob?'

'I wish it would,' said Arthur. 'But it will be trapped somehow. I'm hoping that I'll be able to feel its presence—I can kind of sense the Parts of the Will now. Or maybe it will be able to speak into my mind, as the other Parts did when I got close enough.'

'I get a stomach ache when Dame Primus is around,' said Suzy. 'Maybe that'll help.'

'Anything might help. We'll have to be very careful. Presuming we can find and free Part Six, we'll use the Fifth Key to head straight back to the Citadel—'

'Oh, no, no, no,' interrupted Scamandros. 'You daren't do that! Didn't I explain? There's always a working of sorcerers watching for sorcery in the Upper House. I dare say there's even more of them than ever, these days. As soon as you start to use a Key, they'll hit you with a confinement or encyst you—'

'They will not dare cast a spell against the Rightful Heir, wielder of the Fifth Key!' pronounced Arthur in stentorian tones. He stood up and thumped his chest. 'They are mere Denizens; it is I who—'

He stopped, wiped his suddenly sweating forehead and sat down.

'Sorry,' he said, in his normal voice. 'The Keys . . . they're working on me. So how do we get out once we have Part Six, Doctor?'

'I don't know, Lord Arthur,' said Scamandros. 'I

94

am not much of a strategiser . . . all I know is that if you use a Key, you will have only moments before they act against you. If you are very swift, you might be able to get out before they land a spell on you. And it is possible you might be too strong, even for hundreds or thousands of Saturday's sorcerers. But if they can hold you for a few minutes, that would be enough for Saturday herself to join the working.'

'And the Sixth Key is strongest in its own demesne,' said Arthur. 'What does getting encysted mean, by the way?'

Scamandros shuddered and his tattoos turned a sickly green.

'You get turned inside out and trapped inside a . . . kind of bag . . . made out of your own bodily fluids . . . which are then vitrified, like glass.'

'That's awful! If that happened, wouldn't I be dead?'

'Not if you're a Denizen. They can survive being encysted for a few months, maybe a year. Saturday used to have the cysts hung up here and there, as a warning. It was quite a rare punishment in my day.'

'Sounds better than a hanging,' said Suzy brightly. Then she frowned and added, 'Only I can't remember any hangings. We used to go to them and my mum'd take our nuncheon wrapped up in a white cloth . . .'

Her voice trailed off as she tried to recall her long-ago human life.

'I will also have to give you something to wrap the Fifth Key in,' Scamandros continued. 'To hide its sorcerous emanations. I have just the thing somewhere . . . but first I must finish constructing this spell. If you would both be so kind as to remain totally silent and look the other way for a few minutes, I need complete concentration.'

Arthur and Suzy complied. Arthur twitched one of the fine curtains aside and looked out at the rolling sea. The waves came almost to the window, and spray splashed across every time the ship heeled over. But it was a tight window and didn't leak. Arthur found it quite hypnotic just watching the mass of moving grey-green water topped with white. For a few minutes he could empty his mind of all his troubles and just watch the endless sea . . .

'Done!' exclaimed Scamandros.

Arthur and Suzy turned back. The plaster footprints and the Rat hair had disappeared and the bottle of Activated Ink was empty. Scamandros was holding the tin of grey paint in one hand and the large brush in the other.

'Right, clothes off. I've got to get you painted up.'

Suzy took off her battered hat and started unbuttoning her coat.

'Hang on, uh, wait a moment.' Arthur's cheeks coloured with embarrassment. He'd got used to mixed washrooms in the Glorious Army of the Architect, though they never really got completely undressed. But that was with Denizens. Suzy, though he could forget about it most of the time, was practically a normal human girl. 'Why do we have to take our clothes off?'

'The paint is transformative—it will prepare you to become a Raised Rat,' Scamandros answered. 'The activation I shall write upon the rind of the cheese, and then when you eat it, you will become a Raised Rat. I think.'

'OK,' muttered Arthur. He turned back to look out of the window and hesitantly undressed.

'Least there aint no Bibliophages wanting to have a nibble on any writing like,' said Suzy. 'You had writing all over your other clothes, Arthur. Is that what they do back home these days?'

'Yes,' said Arthur. He took a deep breath and slipped off his underwear. 'Start painting, Scamandros.'

' 'E's painting me,' said Suzy. 'You'll 'ave to wait. Youch, that's cold paint!'

Arthur bit back an order to hurry up and focused on the view out of the window. He didn't know what to do with his hands. Putting them on his hips seemed ridiculous when naked, but so did just letting them hang. Finally he folded them at the front, even though he thought that probably didn't look too good either.

'Right, Lord Arthur, here we go,' said Scamandros. The next second Arthur felt a slap of cold fluid on his back and flinched.

'Steady!' instructed Scamandros. 'Haven't any to waste.'

Arthur gritted his teeth and stood very still as Scamandros quickly brushed paint from his head to his heels.

'Very good, Lord Arthur. Turn about, if you please.'

Arthur shut his eyes and slowly turned around. He heard a knock at the door at the same time and a Raised Rat called out, 'Got that cheese for you, sir. I'll just put it here.'

'Arms up, Lord Arthur,' said Scamandros cheerily.

Arthur screwed his eyes shut even tighter and

quickly raised his arms. He couldn't help flinching as the paint went on some delicate areas.

'You're done!' said Scamandros.

Arthur opened his eyes and looked down. He'd been expecting to see grey paint on himself, but instead he saw a fine coat of grey-black fur that covered him from ankle to wrist like a hairy wetsuit.

Though the fur went some way to preserving his modesty, Arthur quickly sat down, crossed his legs and draped his coat across his lap.

'You won't have tails,' said Scamandros sadly. 'Couldn't do it. But quite a few of the Rats go without, having lost them in sea fights and the like.'

He picked up the slab of cheese, broke it into two equal parts and started writing with a peacock-feather pen he dipped in a tiny bottle of Activated Ink no larger than Arthur's little fingernail.

'I could get used to fur,' said Suzy. 'Save washin' and changin' clothes.'

Arthur raised his eyebrows.

'I do wash 'em,' Suzy protested. 'And change 'em. Lot of Denizen clothes clean themselves, you know. And change to fit. I wonder if this fur gets all manky in the rain . . .'

'The cheese is ready,' said Dr Scamandros. He held up the two pieces, each roughly triangular and about ten inches long.

'Do we have to eat it all?' Arthur didn't sound excited by the prospect.

'Um, perhaps not.' Scamandros hesitated. 'About two-thirds should do the trick . . . but it would be best to err on the side of completion.'

'Right,' said Arthur. 'All we need now is

Lieutenant Finewhisker to open the Nebuchadnezzar—oh, I almost forgot. You were going to give me something to hide the Key's thingummies—'

Dr Scamandros nodded and fossicked about inside his coat for a few moments before bringing out a crumpled piece of glittering metallic cloth that looked rather like a crushed tinfoil hat. He smoothed it out and pushed the edges apart, revealing that it was a small rectangular bag.

'Put the Key in there and they won't sniff it out,' he said, handing it over. 'At least, not unless they're very close and looking for it.'

Arthur took the mirror-shaped Fifth Key and put it in the bag. He pulled its drawstring tight, then opened it again, to put Elephant inside as well. Then after almost closing it, he added the Mariner's medallion that he'd been wearing on a makeshift dental-floss chain around his neck. With all three items safely in the bag, he finally drew the drawstring tight and tied the cord securely around his left wrist.

'The cheese will complete your transformation,' said Scamandros.

'Except the Raised Rats usually wear clothes, so we'll need some too,' said Arthur. 'We should get some of the sailors' breeches or *something*. Is there anything in that chest over there?'

No one moved.

'Have a look, please, Suzy,' Arthur said.

Finally Suzy wandered over, threw open the chest and rummaged about, retrieving several very fine uniforms which must have belonged to Lieutenant Finewhisker. Suzy threw a pair of breeches and a white shirt over to Arthur, and put on a similar set herself. She looked longingly at a long, swallow-tailed coat with its swirling azure patterns before reluctantly returning it to the chest.

'Keep track of my gear, Doc,' she said to Scamandros.'I'll be wanting it, by and by.'

'I guess we're good to go,' said Arthur. He looked across at Suzy and raised his cheese. She raised her lump back, as if making a toast.

'Let's eat!' said Arthur, and he bit his cheese.

It wasn't very tasty cheese. Arthur swallowed another huge mouthful and felt suddenly quite sick, the cabin spinning as it never had before. He started to say something about seasickness and the change in the swell, but stopped. He was dizzy because he was shrinking and his eyes were moving in his head. His field of vision was changing—the things in front of him were harder to see, but he could see far more to the sides. The cabin was brighter than it had been too.

'Excellent!' exclaimed Scamandros. A tattooed torrent of Rats ran out from under his neckcloth and up the side of his face. 'It works.'

'Yes,' said Arthur. He looked down at his odd, foreshortened arms and saw they ended in pink paws. 'I'm a Raised Rat.'

His voice was higher-pitched and husky. He raised one paw to check that the bag with the Key and Elephant was still there. It felt much heavier than it had before, but it was securely fastened.

Arthur slowly began to get dressed, his paws fumbling till he got used to them, and to his different vision. He'd just finished doing up his trouser buttons when Lieutenant Finewhisker knocked and entered the cabin without waiting for a reply. He saluted Arthur, who inclined his snout in greeting.

'Ready for the Nebuchadnezzar, Lord Arthur?' Finewhisker asked.

'Yes,' Arthur replied.

'Very nice clothes you have on, if I may say so,' said Finewhisker cheerily. 'Excellent taste. Now a twist here, a twist on the other side . . .'

He deftly removed the wire cage that held the cork in place, and then gently turned the huge cork, easing it out. It made a screeching, fingernails-on-the-blackboard noise as it slowly revolved out, and then a surprisingly small *pop* as it came free and Finewhisker staggered back with it in his arms.

A thin waft of smoke billowed out of the neck of the bottle—black, choking coal smoke.

'You need to jump straight through the neck,' Finewhisker instructed. 'A good strong jump with your paws forward. Avoid touching the glass if you can.'

'Thank you, Finewhisker,' said Arthur. 'Thank you too, Dr Scamandros. I will see you at the Citadel, I hope.'

'Good luck, Lord Arthur,' said the sorcerer. He bowed and added, 'The spell will last a few hours, I should think.'

'Come on, Arthur!' said Suzy. She hopped over to the bottle and tensed, ready to jump at the neck. 'Last one in is a stinking ra . . . um . . . rabbit.'

Arthur pulled her back by the scruff of her neck.

'Not this time, Suzy,' he said. 'I go first.'

Suzy wriggled, but didn't really resist as he moved her aside. Even as a Raised Rat, he was unnaturally strong, though it didn't occur to him that he shouldn't be able to pick up someone who weighed as much as he did, using only a paw.

With Suzy out of the way, Arthur took a few practice hops across the cabin. Then he stretched his paws and backed up to stand in the open cabin doorway, facing the open neck of the Simultanous Nebuchadnezzar. Smoke was still wafting out of it, and the interior was dark and cloudy.

Bravery and stupidity can be quite closely related, Arthur thought. *I wonder which this is going to be . . .*

He bent his legs, rushed forward and dived straight at the open neck of the bottle.

He was in mid-air when a terrible last-minute thought slipped into his head:

What if the Raised Rats are lying? What if this bottle takes me somewhere entirely unexpected?

CHAPTER NINE

Arthur had expected to land inside the huge green glass bottle, at least for a few seconds before he was transferred, but instead he found himself diving *out* of the neck of a completely different Nebuchadnezzar, one made of sparkling blue glass. He landed heavily on a floor made of lozenge-patterned iron mesh, which hurt and left an imprint of itself on his fur.

Arthur rolled to a stop and immediately got up. He hardly had a moment to look round before a Raised Rat he only barely recognised as Suzy crashed into him and they both went sprawling on the iron floor again. They were disentangling themselves when a harsh, low voice spoke.

'Quickly now! Help me move the bottle! They'll be on to us in a minute or two.'

Arthur jumped up and looked around. The blue

Nebuchadnezzar was on a lashed-together wooden trolley with uneven wheels, and pushing it was the strangest, ugliest Piper's child that Arthur had ever seen. He wore a black cloak and a broad-brimmed hat with a feather, but even under the shadow of the brim, Arthur could see that the boy had a lumpy face and a ridiculously large nose.

The Nebuchadnezzar, Arthur, Suzy and the ugly Piper's child were all on a broad metal walkway suspended from the ceiling by bronze rods every few yards. Though it was twelve feet wide, it had no rails, and was wreathed in smoke and steam.

Arthur gingerly peered over the edge. There was nothing beneath the walkway, no sign of solid ground. All he could see was a thick cloud of roiling black smoke. He could hear the *whoosh*, hiss and deep bass beat of big steam engines somewhere down below, but he couldn't see any sign of them.

Then the smoke currents whorled and shifted and he caught a glimpse of the upper half of a huge bronze wheel as big as a house. It was turning very slowly, but before Arthur could see what it was connected to or what its purpose was, more smoke billowed across and obscured it again.

Closer to the walkway, a black cloud parted to reveal the end of a huge, rusted iron beam that was as long as three school buses joined together. The beam rose up through the smoke like a whale breaching, then descended into the depths with a gargling *whoosh*, and the industrial fog closed up again.

The metal mesh under Arthur's feet was vibrating in time to the beat of the engines below, and the bronze supporting rods hummed at

Arthur's touch. The rods were tarnished, Arthur noted with concern, and their connection to the ceiling looked none too secure, though it was hard to see exactly how the thirty-foot-long rods were joined to the stone above. Judging by the occasional clean patches, the ceiling was a solid, pale rock, but most of it was so stained with soot it resembled a dirty carpet of the blackest plush.

'Hurry! Help me push!' cried the Piper's child. He was struggling to get the bottle moving.

Arthur cautiously ran round the right-hand side of the bottle, while Suzy ran round the left. They put their shoulders to the base of the Nebuchadnezzar and heaved. The trolley creaked and rumbled forward, slowly gathering speed. It had a tendency to veer dangerously off towards the edge, so all three pushers needed to be constantly vigilant.

'Got to get it back to the lubricant store,' wheezed the Piper's child. 'Fill it up with oil again and make ourselves scarce. You'll need disguises too.'

Arthur glanced across at the boy and did a double-take. It wasn't a Piper's child at all under the broad-brimmed hat with the scarlet feather, but a Raised Rat wearing a papier-mâché mask painted to look like a human face. The ridiculous nose covered the rat's own snout.

'Lord Arthur, I presume,' husked the Rat. 'Dartbristle, at your service.'

'Good to meet you,' said Arthur. 'This is my friend Suzy.'

'General Suzy Turquoise Blue if you don't mind,' sniffed Suzy.

'Welcome to the Upper House, General,' said

Dartbristle. 'Up ahead, we need to heave her around to the left. Hurry now.'

The walkway met another broader walkway at a T-junction. Manhandling the trolley without it—or them—falling off the edge was no easy task, but they got it turned and were able to push the Nebuchadnezzar faster once they were in the clear.

Dartbristle kept looking behind them, so Arthur looked too, but all he could see was the thick grey smoke, with occasional eddies of thicker blacker smoke coiling up through it. He was no longer surprised that the smoke had no effect upon him. In fact, he even quite liked the smell, though he knew that his old human lungs would have quickly failed in the toxic atmosphere.

'What are you looking for?' Arthur asked after they had pushed the bottle several hundred feet and there was nothing to see ahead or behind except more of the platform and more of the smoke.

'Rat-catcher automatons,' said Dartbristle. 'The sorcerers know when the Nebuchadnezzar fires up—least they know there's serious sorcery afoot—but it takes 'em a minute or two to plot where it occurred. Since we're under the floor, they don't come down here themselves. They send Rat-catchers. But I reckon we might have got away fast enough. Lubricant Store's just ahead, in the bulwark rock.'

'We're under the floor of the Upper House?' asked Arthur.

'Yep.' Dartbristle moved around to the front of the bottle and slowed it down as they came up to a sheer and apparently solid rock face of grimy yellow stone that was shot through with barely visible veins of a glowing purple metal. 'We're in the bulwark between the Middle and the Upper House. Saturday had a bit of the top part of it burrowed out to put in all her steam engines, chain-gear and so on. Where is that bell push?'

The Rat began pressing different protuberances of rock, but none of them moved in the slightest.

'Curse the thing, always moving around. You'd think it was made by a practical joker!' Dartbristle griped.

'There's something behind us,' said Suzy. 'I saw something go under the walkway.'

'Rat-catcher!' hissed Dartbristle. He reached under the Nebuchadnezzar and drew out three long, curved knives from the trolley, handing one to Suzy and one to Arthur. 'They're armoured, so you need to get them in the red glowing bit right on the front of their head. I suppose it's an eye or something like it. But watch out for its nippers. And the feelers—they're like the tentacles of a Blackwater squid.'

He spoke quickly and unhooked the mask off his face so it dangled under his mouth, allowing him to see better. His deep black eyes moved rapidly from side to side and his nose twitched as he tried to smell out the approaching enemy. Suddenly he started forward and raised his knife.

'Where is—' Suzy started to say, when all of a sudden the Rat-catcher automaton sprang out from under the walkway. Darting forward in a flash of steely plates and accompanied by a sound like the soft chink of coins in a leather purse, the twelve-foot-long, two-foot-wide, metallic preying mantis opened its huge claws and nipped at Dartbristle. At the same time, its impossibly long,

107

razor-edged feelers whipped at Arthur and Suzy.

Dartbristle ducked under and around one set of pincers and heaved on the joint, pushing the automaton's left claw into its right, whereupon they gripped each other tightly. Suzy jumped back from a feeler. It cut her across the chest and tried to wrap itself round her neck to cut her head off, but she blocked it with her knife and slid under the Nebuchadnezzar trolley.

Arthur instinctively parried with his knife and twisted it to trap the feeler. Then, without thinking, he grabbed it and heaved. The razor-edges cut his paw, which hurt, but he also managed to pull the feeler entirely out of the Rat-catcher's head, which caused a great fizz of sparks to jet out like a firework.

'Get the red eye!' shouted Dartbristle. 'While the claws are locked!'

Arthur ran forward. The automaton's remaining feeler whipped at his legs, but he jumped over it, leaping so high that he landed on the Rat-catcher's back. The automaton immediately threw itself backwards, but he gripped it around its triangular head and plunged his knife deep into the red orb at the head's centre. The little bag that held the Fifth Key knocked against the Rat-catcher's overlapping metal plates as Arthur stabbed the automaton several more times, before at last it gave a high-pitched, almost electronic squeal and slowly collapsed to the walkway, its rear legs hanging over the edge.

Arthur carefully climbed down, anxious not to overbalance the defunct automaton and send both of them down into the smoky depths. As soon as the boy stood safe on his own feet, Dartbristle began to push the Rat-catcher over the side.

'They can track these too,' he said. 'More come to find the remains, whenever one is slain.'

Arthur helped him push, and Suzy slid out and gave the Rat-catcher a not very helpful but certainly satisfying kick just as it tumbled over.

'Right—I'll get that door open,' said Dartbristle. He looked admiringly at Arthur and added, 'Well fought, Lord Arthur.'

'Thanks,' said Arthur absently. He looked at his paw and saw that it was already almost healed, the gold blood disappearing as it dried. Belatedly he remembered that Suzy had been hurt.

'Suzy, that feeler cut you! Are you all right?'

Suzy, who had been looking over the side, turned round. Her shirt was cut through and gaped open, and there was a line of blood across her furry stomach, blood that was neither the blue of a Denizen nor entirely the red of a human, but something in between.

'Nah, I've had worse,' Suzy said dismissively. 'If I'd 'ad my old coat on, it would never 'ave even broken the skin. Give it a day or two to scab up and I'll be right as rain.'

'Found it!' declared Dartbristle. He pushed energetically on a slight knob of rock that was at the level of his knee. His push was answered by a rumble inside the stone. Slowly a great rock slab door as wide as the walkway pivoted open.

'In with the bottle,' ordered Dartbristle. He started pushing the trolley and Arthur quickly joined him. Suzy moved more slowly to help, and Arthur noticed she grimaced as she set her shoulder to the Nebuchadnezzar and began to push.

Beyond the door—which creaked shut behind them—was a rough-hewn stone chamber the size of a small auditorium, with a very high ceiling. Huge glass bottles as large or larger than the Simultaneous Nebuchadnezzar were lined up against the walls, and in front of them were stacked many smaller bottles, jars, jugs, urns and other containers of glass, metal or stoneware.

There was an open space on one wall, between an amber bottle full of a dark viscous fluid and a nine-foot-tall clear glass bottle filled with what looked like light green olive oil. Dartbristle pointed at this gap and they manoeuvred the Nebuchadnezzar to the space, untied it from the trolley and began to lift it up.

'Hold it at an angle and lean it on that pot there,' Dartbristle instructed. 'Got to put some oil in it, so it doesn't look out of place. The purloined letter, you know.'

'The what?' Arthur asked as Dartbristle picked up a jeroboam-sized bottle and with great difficulty poured a stream of purple-black oil into the Nebuchadnezzar.

'Oh yes, heard that one before,' said Suzy. She left Arthur holding up the Simultaneous Bottle and wandered over to look at a small, narrow door on the other side of the chamber.

'Hide a letter by putting it in plain sight, where it will be considered ordinary,' explained Dartbristle. 'Good idea. Right, got to slap the cork in and then we'll be off.'

'Off where exactly?' asked Arthur. 'We need to get some clothes for when we stop being Raised Rats. This gear we have on won't fit.'

'Exactly!' said Dartbristle. 'Half a mo.'

He took off his hat, tipped it over and took out a very small bottle, the kind that might hold perfume, and what Arthur at first thought was a cigarette packet. Dartbristle took a tiny rolled up scroll out of the packet, checked what was written on the outside of it, unstoppered the bottle and thrust the scroll in. He then replaced the stopper and put everything back into his hat, which he pulled firmly down upon his head, before also replacing his mask.

'Smallest Simultaneous Bottle there is,' he said. He pointed to the Nebuchadnezzar. 'One hundred and twentieth the size of that. Just had to report your arrival. Saturday's lot can't track the small bottle—it's sorcery on a scale too tiny for them to contemplate. Come on.'

'I asked where we're going to,' said Arthur frostily.

Really, these inferior creatures are galling. They should learn instant obedience—

Arthur shook his head and touched the bag at his wrist, feeling for Elephant.

I am not an angry, puffed-up Superior Denizen, he thought sternly. *I am human. I am polite. I care about other people.*

'Up to the floor,' said Dartbristle. 'To join a Chain Gang. When you're back in normal shape, you'll fit right in with the Piper's children. They're a good bunch; they'll take you on without too many questions. And they'll have clothes for you too.'

'Very good,' said Arthur. 'How do we get there?'

'Service chain-haul. To shift the lubricants. We'll just grab hold and it'll take us up.'

He took a small key from his hatband and

trotted over to the narrow door. For the first time, Arthur noticed that, like himself, Dartbristle was a tailless Raised Rat. But where Arthur didn't have a tail because Scamandros couldn't make one in time, Dartbristle had once had one, as evidenced by the battered stump poking out through an elegantly sewn hole in his black breeches.

The Raised Rat opened the door and pulled it open, revealing a vertical shaft about twelve feet square. In the middle of the shaft a heavy chain hung down. Each of its links was easily two feet tall and made from four-inch-thick dark iron. It wouldn't have been out of place on a battleship, Arthur thought.

'Got to start her up,' said Dartbristle. He leaned precariously into the shaft and grabbed hold of the motionless chain, which was so heavy it barely rattled.

Arthur poked his head in and looked up and down. The chain extended in both directions as far as he could see into the smoke-shrouded shaft.

Dartbristle continued his instruction. 'When she starts, you'd best jump and hold on quick, while she's still slow. Then wait for me to give the word to jump off, and jump. If you wait too long, the chain'll go over the wheel and take you back down again—or mash you up. Stand by the door . . . ready?'

Arthur and Suzy stood shoulder to shoulder in the doorway.

Dartbristle shifted his grip, then swung fully on to the chain. As it took his weight, it fell a few feet, causing a frightful screech and rattle. Then there was a click almost as loud as a gunshot and the chain began to move upwards, taking Dartbristle with it.

Suzy jumped before Arthur could even think of doing so. She landed well and climbed up a few feet to settle below Dartbristle's rear paws.

'I like this!' she exclaimed and was gone, the chain already accelerating.

Arthur gulped and leaped for the chain.

CHAPTER TEN

Arthur hit his snout on the chain, but got a good pawhold, gripping the link he held with remarkable strength. The chain was rising up at a speed that felt like forty or fifty miles an hour, the smoky air whistling past them fast enough to plaster Arthur's long Rat ears against his head.

'Uh oh,' said Suzy.

'What?' Arthur asked. He looked up. Suzy was only holding on with one paw while she wriggled her other paw in the air. 'What are you doing?! Hold on with both hands . . . paws . . . whatever!'

'That's it!' said Suzy. 'I can't. My paw is turning back into a hand and it's not working properly!'

'Hold on with your teeth!' called Dartbristle. He demonstrated with his own front teeth, which were at least five inches long and rather impressive.

'Can't!' said Suzy. 'My mouth has gone weird and wobbly!'

She slithered down the chain towards Arthur. She looked half-Rat and half-human. He climbed up to her, and one human and one Raised Rat foot scraped his head before landing on his shoulders.

'Almost there!' called Dartbristle. 'I'll count. Jump on three—it doesn't matter which direction.'

'Can't . . . hold on!'

Suzy crashed into Arthur. He gripped the chain with his own huge front teeth and one paw and grabbed her with the other paw. He wasn't exactly sure what he was holding on to, because her body was rippling and changing, parts of it Raised Rat and parts human. It looked very disturbing and very painful, and her sailor's clothes were now nothing but rags, ripped and torn by the transformations.

'One!'

Suzy slipped from Arthur's grasp, but he swung his feet out and gripped her with his back paws, which in Rat-shape were almost as dexterous as his front paws.

'Two!'

They shot out of the narrow shaft into a huge, dirty warehouse that was two-thirds full of the same kind of oil containers as the chamber below.

'Three! Jump!' shouted Dartbristle.

Arthur opened his mouth and pushed off from the chain, using all his strength so he took Suzy with him. The two of them landed on the edge of the shaft and he had to scrabble and claw his way to safety, dragging Suzy with his back paws.

Above them, the chain continued up through a broad chimney to some other chamber, and Arthur caught a glimpse of the enormous, fast-spinning driving wheel that had pulled the chain.

'I'm going to kick Scamandros in the shins when I see him next!' growled Suzy. She stood up and then immediately fell down again as her lower half became human and her top half Raised Rat, so she was totally out of proportion and her centre of gravity was all wrong.

'I'm sure it will wear off . . . ugh . . . soon,' said Arthur. He had to pause mid-sentence as a wave of nausea ran through his body. His torso suddenly stretched up several feet, then snapped back again, and his paws turned to four sets of feet.

'It'd better,' said Suzy. 'Thanks, Arthur.'

She crawled away from the shaft and, after a moment's thought, Arthur followed her. The rapid changes to his body might topple him in if he stayed too close to the edge.

'I'll scout out the lay of the land while you're sorting yourselves out,' said Dartbristle. 'The grease monkeys—that's what the Piper's children here call themselves—have a depot across the way, and there's a drain that connects us here. We can't cross outside, because there's a detachment of Sorcerous Supernumeraries watching the depot, but I'll nip through, have a word with the grease monkeys and pick you up some clothes.'

'Don't tell them our real names,' said Arthur. He had an unbearably itchy nose, but he couldn't control his arms enough to be able to scratch it. 'Tell them . . . uh . . . tell them we're Piper's children discharged from the Army and we've just been washed between the ears and can't remember our names or anything yet.'

'Aye, aye,' said Dartbristle. He went over to a

nearby trapdoor and lifted it. As he did, the sound of rushing water—a great deal of rushing water— filled the warehouse.

'Got to wait a few minutes,' he said. 'This is a flood channel—takes an overflow every now and again. Timing is everything, as they say.'

'Quiet!' Arthur suddenly ordered. He sat up as best he could with a rubbery neck and cocked his one Rat ear to listen. Amid the sound of the rushing water, he'd heard a distinctive call, and at the same time he'd felt a familiar twinge inside his head.

'Arthur!'

It was the Will, calling his name. But the voice was distant and fleeting. Even with the others quiet, all he could hear now was running water, the jangle of the moving chain in the shaft and the more distant *thrum* of the subterranean engines.

'Did you hear that?' he asked. 'Someone calling my name?'

'No,' said Suzy. She looked herself again. Even the torn rags of her Rat-breeches and shirt weren't that out of place on her, considering her normal choice in clothes. 'Didn't hear nuthin'.'

'Nor I, I fear,' added Dartbristle. 'And with my ears I have won many a Hearing Contest in the fleet.'

'Never mind,' said Arthur.

It must have been speaking in my head, he thought. *Like the Carp did . . . but from far away. Or perhaps the Will could only escape its bonds for a moment . . .*

The sound of the rushing water died away. Dartbristle waved his hat over his head and jumped down. Arthur and Suzy could hear the splash as he landed in the channel.

'There's a window up there,' said Suzy, pointing to a large, iron-barred window of dirty, rain-flecked glass that was set into the riveted iron walls about twelve feet up. 'If I climb up those bottles and stand on top of that big yellow one, I reckon I could see outside.'

The window let in a subdued greyish light. Looking at it, Arthur realised for the first time that he must have developed better night vision, because he could see quite clearly, even though the warehouse had only one dim lantern hanging from the high ceiling, and the six windows, all on the same wall, did not admit much extra light.

'Suzy, how light is it in here?' he asked.

'In here? If it weren't for the windows and that lantern, it'd be dark as a dog's dinner inside of a dog, and even with the windows and the lantern it's not much better,' answered Suzy, who was starting to climb from one bottle neck to another, stepping across an impromptu stairway to her chosen window. 'But I reckon it is daytime outside, only it's raining.'

'What can you see?' Arthur was now almost himself, apart from his hands, which were still paws and not under his control. They were twitching and wriggling in a very annoying way. He had already slapped himself in the face several times and would have suffered more if he hadn't got control of his arms and neck and twisted away. His clothes were also reduced to shreds, which was probably just as well as they would have been terribly restrictive now that he was back to his full height.

'Rain,' said Suzy. 'And not much else. There's a

very tall building, with lots of green lights.'

'Ow!' said Arthur as his paws turned into hands, but kept twitching, smacking his fingers against the floor. 'That's enough! Stop!'

His hands tingled and stopped. Arthur flexed his fingers and gave a relieved sigh. He was himself again and everything was under control.

Suzy climbed down and both of them went over to look through the trapdoor. There was a rusted iron ladder that led down to an arched passage lined with small red bricks. A thin trickle of water ran down the middle, but from the dampness of the walls it was evident that the water rose nearly as high as the trapdoor when it was in full spate, as it must have been just a few minutes before the Raised Rat went through.

Suzy immediately started to climb down the ladder, but Arthur pulled her back.

'Hold on! Let's wait for Dartbristle. We need proper clothes. Besides, there might be more water flooding through.'

'I was just 'aving a look,' grumbled Suzy.

'How's that cut?' asked Arthur.

Suzy looked down and felt her chest through her ripped rags.

'It's gone!' she exclaimed. 'That was at least a four-day cut, that was!'

'Healed in the transformation, I suppose,' said Arthur.

'Maybe I won't kick old Doc after all,' said Suzy cheerfully.

'I'm glad you're better.' Arthur knelt down and peered into the flood channel. Though it wasn't lit at all, he could see at least thirty or forty feet along it. That made him have a second thought about his eyes, and he sprang back up and looked carefully at Suzy. Her eyes looked the same as ever: dark brown, curious and sharp.

'Suzy,' he said. 'My eyes haven't stayed like a Raised Rat's, have they?'

'Nope. But they've gone bright blue. Wot's called cornflower blue in the inkworks. Only yours is kind of glowing. I reckon it's to do with the Keys turning you into . . . whatever it is they're turning you into.'

'A Denizen,' said Arthur glumly.

'Nah,' said Suzy. 'Not even a Superior Denizen looks like you do. When that Dartbristle gets back, we'd best smear some grease on your face so you'll pass as one of us.'

I can't even be mistaken for a Piper's child any more, thought Arthur with unexpected sadness.

Suzy cocked her head, sensing his mood.

'You'll still be Arthur Penhaligon,' she said. 'Not the brightest, not the bravest, but up for anything. Least, that's how I see you. Kind of like a little brother, only you're taller than me now.'

She paused and frowned. 'I think I had a little brother once. Don't know whether it was here, or back home, or what . . .'

She stopped talking and their eyes met briefly. They both remembered the Improbable Stair and their visit to Suzy's original home back on Earth, back in time, a city in the grip of the bubonic plague. If Suzy had once had a brother, he'd likely died young and long ago, stricken by the disease.

That reminded Arthur of the plagues back home, the modern ones, and the hospital, and the Skinless Boy who had taken his place, and his brother calling about the nuclear strike on East

120

Area Hospital. He felt a tide of anxiety rise up from somewhere in his stomach, almost choking him with responsibilities. He had to find the Will here and defeat Saturday, and get back home in time to do something about the nuclear attack before it happened . . .

'It's not a good idea to stop breathing,' said Suzy, interrupting Arthur's panic attack. She clapped him on the back and he took a sudden intake of breath.

'I know,' he said. 'It's just, it's just—'

'Ahoy there, children!'

Dartbristle climbed out of the flood channel, carrying a large cloth bag marked **LAUNDRY**. He tipped it up and emptied a pile of clothes and boots on to the floor.

'Help yourself,' he said. 'Stuff should resize to fit, if it ain't worn out. I picked up a few sets to be sure.'

The clothes were dirty, off-white overalls that had lots of pockets. Arthur picked a set up, hesitated a moment, then stripped off his rags and put on the overalls as quickly as he could. The overalls immediately resized themselves to fit, and several oil stains moved around as well to get better positions, some bickering before they established their pre-eminence.

'Odd clothes,' said Suzy doubtfully. She put the overalls on, but tore a strip of blue cloth off her old rags and added it as a belt.

'You'll get utility belts at the depot,' said Dartbristle.

'I like a bit of colour,' sniffed Suzy.

'There's boots there,' Dartbristle pointed out. 'You'll need them for the climbing and jumping and whatnot.'

'Climbing and jumping?' asked Arthur. He sat down and pulled on a pair of the boots. They were made of soft leather and had strange soles that were covered in cilia like an anemone. They gripped Arthur's finger when he touched them.

'Everything up past the ground-floor level here is made up of desk units,' said Dartbristle. 'Open iron boxes with a lattice floor, stacked and slotted into a framework of guide rails, and moved up, down and across by shifter chains. The Piper's children here are grease monkeys—they keep the chains oiled, free up obstructions, service the pneumatic message tubes and so on. Requires a lot of climbing, jumping and the like. If you're going to be looking around the Upper House, you'll need to fit in as grease monkeys.'

'Who said we'd be looking around the Upper House?' asked Arthur suspiciously.

Perhaps I should slay this Rat now, came an unbidden thought. *He knows too much and I probably don't need him . . . Stop . . . stop! I don't want these thoughts . . .*

'The message that came through advising me of your arrival,' Dartbristle replied. 'Said you'd be looking for something and to offer you any reasonable assistance.'

'Yes,' said Arthur, keeping a tight lid on the nasty, selfish thoughts that were roiling about in the depths of his head. 'Thank you. We are looking for something. In fact—'

He took a breath and decided to go for it. He had to trust people, even if they happened to be Raised Rats. Or Denizens. Or Piper's children.

'I'm looking for Part Six of the Will of the

122

Architect. It's here somewhere. Trapped or held prisoner. Have you heard anything about it?'

Dartbristle took off his hat and scratched his head. Then he took off his mask and scratched his nose. Then he put both back on and said, 'No, I'm afraid not. The grease monkeys might—'

'Maybe,' said Arthur. 'But I want to check them out first, so keep it secret for now. Remember, we're newly returned from the Army and washed between the ears.'

'Aye, I'll remember,' said Dartbristle. 'We're good with secrets, we Raised Rats. Are you ready to go?'

The question was addressed to Suzy, who was playing with the sole of one of her boots.

'Reckon,' she said, slipping on her footwear. 'Down that tunnel?'

'Yes, we have to avoid the Sorcerous Supernumeraries, as I said,' replied Dartbristle. 'We should have an hour or more before the next flood.'

'How can you tell?' Arthur asked. He looked up at the window. 'Doesn't it depend on the rain?'

'Yes and no,' said Dartbristle as he led the way down the ladder. 'You see, it always rains here, and always at the same, steady rate. Makes traversing the flood channels and storm-water drains very predictable.'

'It always rains?' asked Arthur. 'Why?'

'She likes the rain,' Dartbristle told him. 'Or maybe she likes umbrellas.'

There was no doubt who 'she' was: Superior Saturday, who Arthur was beginning to think more and more must be his ultimate nemesis, and the cause of not only his own troubles, but those of the entire House and the Universe beyond.

Now he was in her demesne. She and her thousands of sorcerers were somewhere up above him. Hopefully in ignorance of his presence, but possibly all too aware that he had come within her reach.

CHAPTER ELEVEN

As Dartbristle had claimed, the flood channel did not suddenly fill with rushing water as Arthur half-feared it might. All the way along he listened carefully for the sound of an approaching deluge, and was ready to race back to the ladder and the warehouse. Then, when he caught sight of a ladder ahead, he had to hold himself back from trampling over the Raised Rat to get to it and climb out.

Maybe all my worries have made me claustrophobic, Arthur thought with some concern. But then he told himself it was perfectly normal to be concerned when walking along what was basically a big underground drain in the middle of a heavy rainstorm. People got drowned all the time doing stupid stuff like that, and as he had thought before in the Border Sea, Arthur was particularly concerned that the Key would keep him sort of alive underwater and he might take a long time to die.

However, he managed to stay calm and didn't streak up the ladder like a rat up a drainpipe. Instead he remembered what Suzy had said about his looks and paused to pick up some mud, which he smeared on his face and front. After that he climbed out slowly, and so had time to adjust to the light and noise that was filtering down the access shaft to the channel.

The chamber above was very different from the warehouse. It was smaller, sixty feet square, and had thick stone walls without any windows and only a single door, which was shut and barred. But it was full of light from the dozens of lanterns that hung from wires of different lengths from the arch-beamed ceiling high above, and it was full of noise, from the thirty or so grease monkeys who were sitting on simple wooden benches at six old oak tables—or not sitting, since a good number of them were jumping over the tables as part of a dozen-person game of tag, or doing cartwheels along them, or playing shuttlecock with improvised shuttles and bats, or constructing curious pieces of machinery. Or completely monopolising a tabletop by lying asleep on it, as one nearby grease monkey was doing.

As Dartbristle helped Suzy out, and she and Arthur stood at the rim of the trapdoor, all this activity ceased. The children stopped their games and activities and turned to look at the new arrivals.

'Wotcher!' said Suzy, and went to tip her hat. She got halfway to her head before she remembered it wasn't there and so had to be satisfied with a wave.

The grease monkeys didn't wave back. They stood there, staring, until the one who was apparently asleep on the table rubbed her eyes and sat up. She looked like a typical Piper's child, with her ragged, self-cut hair, dirty face and oil-stained overalls. But from the way the other grease monkeys' eyes shifted towards her, Arthur could tell she was the boss.

'Mornin',' she said. 'Dartie here says you've been demobbed and sent back, with a washing between the ears behind you.'

'That's right,' said Arthur. 'Uh, I think.'

'I'm Alyse Shifter First Class,' said the girl. 'I'm gang boss of this bunch, the Twenty-seventh Chain and Motivation Maintenance Brigade of the Upper House. What're your names and classifications? Don't tell me your House precedence—we don't bother with that here.'

'Uh . . . I can't quite . . . remember,' said Arthur. 'I think my name's Ray.'

'Got your paperwork?' asked Alyse, holding out her hand.

'Lost it,' muttered Arthur.

'Somewhere,' added Suzy vaguely. 'Think my name's Suze though.'

'Suze and Ray,' said Alyse. 'Well, what's your classification?'

'Uh . . .' Arthur let his voice trail off as he looked around in what he hoped was a gormless manner, till he spotted a long line of coats and other items hanging from coat-hooks down the far wall. Each hook held a duckling yellow peaked rain-cap, a rubberised yellow rain-mantle and a broad leather belt loaded with pouches, tools and a holster that held a long, shining, silver shifting spanner.

'I think I used to do up nuts,' he said. 'For bolts?'

Alyse looked at him.

'You got long enough arms for it,' she said. 'Nut-turner, I guess. Maybe First Class. What about you?'

'Dunno,' said Suzy. 'Forget. Reckon I could turn my hand to anything though.'

Alyse looked her up and down and shrugged.

'Nice under-belt,' she said. 'Blue sky wisher, are you? You must be a Wire-flyer?'

'Maybe,' agreed Suzy guardedly.

'What's a Wire-flyer?' Arthur asked.

'You *did* get scrubbed good and proper,' said Alyse. 'Try and remember! I'm talking installation, not maintenance. A Wire-flyer flies the guidewires up, so as the Rail-risers can put up the rails for the Chain-runners and the Hook-em-ups can slot in the desk unit and the Nut-holders and Bolt-turners make it fast and the Shifter gives the word. Only if we're not building up, the Wire-flyers do odd jobs, help out the Chain-oilers, stuff like that. Coming back to you now?'

'A . . . a bit,' said Arthur. He didn't need to act confused by her explanation.

'Have to see it, I reckon,' said Suzy. 'Picture paints a thousand words. Is that tea over there?'

'It'll come back to you,' declared Alyse, ignoring Suzy's question. She held out her palm, spat in it and offered her hand to Arthur. 'Welcome to the Twenty-seventh Chain and Motivation Maintenance Brigade, or as we like to call it—'

'Alyse's Apes!' roared the assembled grease

128

monkeys.

Arthur shook hands and Alyse spat again. Suzy spat on her own hand and Arthur thought he should have spat on his too, and hoped his recently washed-between-the-ears state would let him be forgiven for this lapse in Piper's child etiquette.

'Tea's in the pot,' said Alyse, pointing to the huge teapot that was simmering on a trivet above a glass spirit burner in the corner. She then pointed to a large and decrepit looking cuckoo clock that had half-fallen off the wall and was slumped just above the floor at an odd angle. Its hands still moved and Arthur could hear the quiet *thock-thock-thock* of its inner workings. It said the time was seventeen minutes to twelve.

'Help yourself. Shift starts at twelve, so get a cup down you while you can. Don't forget to check your gear before noon.'

Alyse yawned and began to lie back down on the tabletop, but one of the other grease monkeys called out, 'Alyse! Which pegs do they get?'

Alyse scowled and sat back up again.

'Never a moment's rest,' she sighed, though Arthur was sure she had been sound asleep when he arrived. She opened one of the pockets on her overall and drew out a thick and well-thumbed notebook. 'Let's see. Yonik was the last one to fall, so his peg's free—that's number thirty-three. Before that was Dotty—'

'But Dotty didn't fall; she just got her leg crushed,' said one of the grease monkeys. 'She'll be back.'

'Not for three months or more,' said Alyse. 'So her peg and her belt are free. Them's the rules.'

'Number twenty,' she added to Suzy, pointing

halfway along the line of coat-hooks. 'You're lucky—Dotty kept her gear very nice. Better than Yonik, which goes to show. He wouldn't have fallen if he'd kept his wings clean.'

'And his nose,' added someone, to general laughter.

'Was he badly hurt?' asked Arthur.

'Hurt?' Alyse laughed. 'When you're working on the tower, as we was, if you fall off and your wings don't work, you don't get hurt. You get dead. Even a Denizen can't survive that fall. Twelve thousand feet, straight down. We were lucky to find his belt and tools, and his spanner had to be replaced. Bent like a crescent, it was.'

Arthur shook his head. He'd always thought Suzy was quite callous, but these Piper's children were even worse.

I suppose when you've lived a very, very long time, you feel differently about dying, he figured. *I wonder if I will feel the same . . . not that I'm likely to live that long . . .*

A tug at his elbow interrupted his thoughts.

'I have to go,' said Dartbristle. 'Got work to do and there's a flood due through right after twelve.'

'Thank you,' said Arthur. 'I really appreciate your help.'

He offered his hand, and bent down close to shake the Raised Rat's paw and whisper in his ear, 'If you hear anything about Part Six of the Will, send word to me.'

'Aye,' said Dartbristle. 'Goodbye, Ray and Suze.'

'Thanks, Dart,' said Suzy with a wave. Once the Raised Rat was gone, she added, 'Come and get yer tea, Ray,' as she searched out two good-sized mugs from the dozens of chipped and damaged

130

porcelain teacups and mugs that lay in disorganised piles around the spirit burner. Several grease monkeys who were gathered there to drink tea started to say hello, and Suzy poured tea with one hand as she spat and shook with the other.

'I'm going to check my stuff,' Arthur called out, which was probably the wrong thing to do. The other grease monkeys went back to their activities and none came to introduce themselves as he went over to his peg.

Arthur put on his rain-mantle, which was like a sleeveless raincoat with a hood that went over his peaked cap. The cap had a buckle to fasten under the chin. Beneath the cap on the peg was a pair of clear goggles, which Arthur tried on and adjusted to fit. In the single large pocket of the rain-mantle there was a folded pair of dirty yellow wings. Arthur took them out, shook them so they expanded to full size, and spent ten minutes plucking out pieces of grit and dirt before folding them back up again.

The utility belt was very heavy. One of the six pouches held several different sizes of nuts and bolts. Another had a mouldy apple core in it, which Arthur removed. The next had a small grease gun, which was leaking until Arthur tightened the nozzle. The fourth pocket contained a pair of light leather fingerless gloves which he put on. The fifth had an apparently unused cleaning cloth, small cleaning brush and a cake of soap that had **BEST QUALITY WATERLESS PERPETUAL SOAP** stamped on it.

The sixth pouch was empty. Arthur tested its strap, then quickly slipped his elephant and the Fifth Key inside.

He looked around to see if anyone had seen him, but it looked like he had managed to be surreptitious. That done, he took the soap back out of the fifth pouch and tried it on an oily patch on his overalls. Part of the stain was erased with surprising ease. Arthur was about to clean it off completely, but paused to look once more at the other grease monkeys, most of whom were now putting on their gear.

All of them had stained overalls, and Alyse's overalls were the most splotched of all, with at least a dozen different-coloured oil stains.

Arthur quietly put the soap back in its pouch and put the belt on. Suzy was putting her belt on too, further down the line. She waved at him and smiled.

Having fun as usual, thought Arthur. *She lives in the moment. I wish I could.*

He smiled a slight smile and waved back, then drew out his shifting spanner and hefted it, slapping the head against his palm. It was very shiny and *very* heavy. The screw-wheel that opened and shut the mouth of the spanner was gritted up, so Arthur quickly cleaned it with the brush and applied a spot of grease from his grease gun, not noticing that Alyse was watching him with approval.

'They can scrub us between the ears,' she said, 'but good workers never forget to look after their gear.'

She climbed up on to one of the tables and waited expectantly. The last of the grease monkeys finished putting on his belt and they all turned around to face their leader. Arthur and Suzy followed a beat behind.

'Are we ready?' asked Alyse.

'Ready!' called the grease monkeys.

'Then let's go!' Alyse jumped off the table and took her place at the head of the line. The grease monkeys did a right turn that would have made Arthur's old drill instructor, Sergeant Helve, start screaming at the informality and slovenliness of it. Completely out of step, they marched to the door.

CHAPTER TWELVE

Alyse unbarred and opened the door. Splashing through the first puddle outside, she led the grease monkeys out on to a rainy, cobble-paved square that was surrounded on three sides by warehouse-style buildings made of riveted iron, and on the fourth side by the sharp corner of a truly vast and massive construction.

There was a bedraggled reception committee waiting outside. A group of a dozen Denizens huddled under black umbrellas, wearing long black coats over grey waistcoats and pale blue shirts, with grey cravats and hats that were like top hats only not so tall. Their white trousers were tucked into green waterproof Wellington boots and they stood in a semi-circular line around the door.

Alyse ignored them, splashing between them

towards the huge building that Arthur figured was the one Suzy had spotted from the window of the warehouse. Now that they were closer, he could see it was a tower that stretched up and out of sight, its great bulk appearing to rise even higher than the pallid, rain-obscured sun that hung off to one side.

Arthur could now also see what he had been told—that this tower was completely made up of box-like office units that had no walls and latticed floors, so you could see a long way up the inside. It was rather like looking into a modern glass skyscraper at night, if that skyscraper also had interior glass walls.

Judging from the closer offices, which Arthur could see into very distinctly, each one of these little boxes was inhabited by a Denizen working at a desk. Each desk had a green-shaded lamp and an umbrella over it. The umbrellas, Arthur noted, were of many different shades and colours, although he couldn't figure out why.

Arthur was second-to-last in the line of grease monkeys. The grease monkey behind him stopped to shut the door behind them, then ran to catch up. He was a good foot shorter than Arthur, had brown hair as badly cut as Alyse's and big sticking-out ears. Instead of marching behind Arthur, he walked next to him, spat on his palm and offered his hand.

'Whrod,' he said. 'Bolt-turner Second Class. We'll probably be working together.'

'Rod?' asked Arthur, remembering to spit this time before he shook.

'Whah-rod,' said Whrod.

'Good to meet you,' Arthur replied, but he was

already looking over Whrod's shoulder at the black-suited umbrella wielders who had begun to follow them in a doleful fashion.

'Don't mind them,' said Whrod, following Arthur's glance. 'Sorcerous Supernumeraries. Detailed to kill us if the Piper shows up and tries to make us do something. Terrible job for them, standing outside in the rain all night, not to mention trying to follow us all day and never quite managing to catch up. Still, they're used to disappointment.'

'Uh, why?' Arthur asked. They certainly *looked* miserable. He'd never seen such mournful-looking Denizens. Even Monday's Midnight Visitors hadn't looked so terminally depressed.

'They're Sorcerous Supernumeraries of course,' said Whrod. 'Failed their exams to become proper sorcerers and can't get a decent post in the Upper House. They've got no chance of moving up higher than the floor . . . it gets them down.'

'Why don't they leave? Go to some other part of the House?'

Whrod looked at Arthur.

'You did get a good washing, didn't you? No one leaves Superior Saturday's service. Unless they get drafted like you did, and then it's only for a hundred years. Besides, I reckon they secretly enjoy being miserable. Gives them a focus in life. Come on, we're lagging behind.'

Whrod walked faster, and Arthur picked up his pace. Behind them, the Sorcerous Supernumeraries followed at a gloomy lope.

Alyse led them into the base of the tower. Arthur thought they would go through a door and a corridor, but instead they just walked into an office, filing past the desk of a Denizen who was watching something in what looked like a shaving mirror. At the same time he was writing on two separate pieces of paper with a quill pen in each hand, occasionally dipping them in a tarnished copper-gilt inkwell. The umbrella that shielded his desk from the rain and the constant rush of water from above was dark brown and rather mouldy, letting in numerous drips that somehow only fell on the Denizen and not on his work.

He didn't look up as the grease monkeys and their shadowing Sorcerous Supernumeraries filed past. Nor did the next one, or the next, or the one after that. By the fiftieth office, Arthur didn't expect them to do anything but look at their mirror and write feverishly.

At the fifty-first office, Alyse held up her hand and everyone halted. She climbed up to one corner of the Denizen's desk and, stretching to her full height, made some adjustment to a six-inch-wide pipe. Now that Arthur's attention was drawn to it, he saw that there was a network of similar pipes that ran through every office and horizontally under the floor of the offices above, with junctions every now and then for vertical pipes that ran up the corners of certain offices, like the one Alyse was in.

'What are those pipes?' Arthur asked Whrod.

The grease monkey gave Arthur another look of disbelief.

'They done a job on you,' he said. 'Practically the village idiot. Those pipe—'

He was cut off as Arthur gripped him by the collar of his overalls and lifted him up, twisting the cloth tight upon his throat.

137

'What did you call me?' he hissed.

'Arghh,' Whrod choked out. His right hand felt for the spanner at his side, but before he could draw it, Arthur grabbed his wrist with his left hand and squeezed.

'Ar—I mean, Ray—drop him!'

Suzy's voice penetrated the total focus of rage that had gripped Arthur. He shivered and let go, and Whrod fell at his feet. Suzy ran up and slid to a halt next to him, immediately holding on to his arm. Arthur wasn't sure if it was a gesture of friendship and solidarity or a preparation to restrain him.

The Sorcerous Supernumeraries, who were spread out through several adjoining offices, glided closer, some of them even forgetting themselves so much as to look directly at what was going on, rather than stare at the ground and take occasional furtive glances when required.

'Sorry,' Arthur whispered. He lifted his head and took a gulp of air and a faceful of water, most of which splashed off his goggles. 'Sorry . . . I think . . . my head's not quite right. I take insults badly.'

Whrod felt his throat, then got up.

'Didn't mean nothing by it,' he said gruffly. 'You're strong—stronger than anyone I ever met.'

'A hundred years in the Army will do that,' said Suzy. 'Come along, Ray.'

'What's the hold-up?' called out Alyse from up the front.

'Nothing! All sorted!' answered Suzy.

'I really am sorry,' said Arthur. He offered his hand to Whrod, who hesitated, then shook it briefly. Neither of them spat and Arthur wondered whether this meant anything. He couldn't tell under the peaked cap and the goggles whether Whrod was looking at him with newly kindled hatred, curiosity or some other emotion.

I'll have to watch my back. It's easy enough to fall if you're pushed, and even I might not survive a thirteen-thousand-foot fall.

'The pipes,' Whrod said carefully, 'are pneumatic message tubes. For sending records and messages around. They're not used much down here, not among the lowest of the low. These clerks just copy stuff, and their papers are taken and delivered by slow messenger.'

'Thanks,' Arthur muttered.

They started walking again, trailing through more offices, mostly in a straight line with an occasional detour, such as one made to avoid an office that was essentially in the midst of a raging waterfall. The sodden Denizen there bravely continued to work on her completely dry papers as water cascaded from her head and shoulders, her stoved-in umbrella at her side.

Around the hundredth office, Arthur noticed a noise coming from somewhere ahead—a deep, rumbling noise that sounded as if there was a very large coffee grinder working away. It got louder as they continued walking, until it was so loud that it drowned out the sound of the rain, the drips and even the *swoosh* of an occasional cascade from above.

The noise came from an open space up ahead, which Arthur could only glimpse through the offices, umbrellas and the grease monkeys ahead of him.

When they got closer, he saw there was a small cleared area the size of several office units, bordered by massive vertical iron beams in each corner, with similar horizontal beams above at the next level of offices, and more beyond that, a square strut of iron box-work that went up and up and up.

In the middle of this shaft, two chains hummed and groaned and rattled. One went up and one went down, through a grilled hole which every few seconds emitted a waft of steam and smoke.

The chains were not like the one Arthur and Suzy had ridden up from the oil warehouse. They were more like bicycle chains—huge bicycle chains, with each link six feet wide and six feet high. In the space in the middle of each link, there were rings welded to the inside wall. Sometimes there were frayed ropes tied to these rings, and sometimes even a welded iron chair or a bench.

Both chains moved at the same rate—about as fast as Arthur could run, he gauged. As soon as he saw them, he knew that this was how the grease monkeys were going to get higher up in the tower.

Alyse stopped and gestured, and the line of grease monkeys spread out to gather around her.

'You know the drill,' she said. 'But we've got two washed-between-the-ears folk with us today, so we'll go over it again. This is the north-east Big Chain that provides the main motivation power for all the north-east Little Chains. Because it's the Big Chain, we can travel two per link. We get on together and we leave together. If you see the link looks oily or has a problem, you shout 'Wait' before your partner gets aboard it and you take the next. Now let's see—'

She took a piece of paper out of a pocket and unfolded it, at the same time hopping to the right to avoid a sudden downsplash.

'We're helping the automatons do a move today. There's someone going up from Level 6995 to Level 61012, and across forty-two offices on the diagonal chain. We'll do the vertical first and make it as quick as we can—we don't want to give this lucky chap's neighbours time to cause trouble. So we get off at 6995. Everyone got that? Suze and Ray?'

'Yes,' said Arthur. Suzy nodded.

'Good,' said Alyse. 'Ray, come over here. You'll jump on the first link with me, and Suze, you jump on the second with Vithan.'

Arthur splashed over to Alyse's side. She held out her hand commandingly and took his, almost dragging him towards the rising chain before he caught up.

'The trick is not to jump, because you'll probably fall,' Alyse cautioned. 'You just sidle up close and then step on to the rising link as it comes up.'

'Whatever you say,' said Arthur.

It wouldn't be so bad if only the chain wasn't going so fast, he thought. *I could get my leg torn off here . . .*

'Come right up to it,' Alyse instructed. They walked closer to the chain, moving around so they faced the open link and were only a step away. Arthur could feel the rush of the chain's movement, too close for comfort if a link swayed out of line. It still looked to be going too fast to simply step on.

'You ready?' asked Alyse.

'Yes,' said Arthur, and he was—until a huge shower of water landed on top of him, so much water that the peak of his cap collapsed into his face and he leaned back and almost went down on one knee. In the middle of it all, he heard Part Six of the Will.

Arthur! You have to come and get me in the—

With a jerk, Alyse pulled him forward. Blinded by his collapsed cap and all the water in his eyes, Arthur had no choice but to step out, not knowing whether he was with her or had fallen that deadly half a step behind that would mean he would miss the inside of the link and instead fall into the grate and be mashed to bits by the next massive piece of the monster chain.

He stretched out and his foot went down . . .

CHAPTER THIRTEEN

Leaf's eyes narrowed and she blinked hard several times. Arthur had vanished in mid-conversation. One second he was there, and then he wasn't.

She looked around and scowled. Not only had Arthur disappeared, but everyone else had become frozen—

The army is going to fire nukes at somewhere very close by, Leaf suddenly remembered. *At one minute past midnight. So why I am standing here with my mouth open like some stupid goldfish?*

'Arthur!' she shouted. Then she started running, out through the ward with its frozen statues of sleepers. 'Arthur!'

No one answered her. Leaf stopped at the end of the ward and looked around. Not only was everyone frozen, but there was also a kind of weird red light around them. Like a faint aura that she could only see when she looked out of the corner of her eyes. That same red glow was around the ward clock, high on the wall, which was stuck at three minutes to twelve.

Or not stuck. As Leaf looked, the red haze vanished. The minute hand sprang forward and simultaneously the ward came alive with shuffling sleepers. Leaf heard someone call out from the office. Not Arthur—a woman's voice. Probably Vess or Martine.

Two minutes! thought Leaf in panic. *There's not enough time to do anything. We're all going to die!*

The clock stopped. The sleepers became petrified once more. The red aura-effect came back.

But Leaf could still hear the woman's voice, and it got louder and louder until Martine burst into the ward.

'What is going on? Where's Lord Arthur?'

'I don't know,' Leaf said. 'Is there anything underneath this hospital? I mean underground levels . . . even a bomb shelter?'

'I haven't been here for twenty years!' exclaimed Martine. 'Ask Vess.'

Leaf looked around then pointed. Vess was standing frozen in a corner of the ward.

'Oh,' Martine said. 'Well, twenty years ago there were operating theatres on B3, and there was a bomb shelter once. I mean this place was built in the fifties, so what do you expect?'

'We have to get everyone down there,' said Leaf firmly. 'You and me. As quickly as we can.'

'But they're like statues . . .'

'We'll wheel them in beds. Two or three to a bed. I wonder if the elevators work? The lights do.'

Leaf saw the hesitation on Martine's face. 'Come on—help me load these two into this bed.'

'I don't understand,' Martine said. 'I thought that once I finally got back home, everything would be all right. But I still don't understand anything. Why are we taking everyone downstairs? Why do we need a bomb shelter?'

'Arthur said the army is going to nuke East Area Hospital at 12:01 because it's a plague nexus. And East Area is only a couple of streets from here. Arthur's done something to stop time, I guess, but it restarted a moment ago. It could restart again in a second, or a minute, who knows! Please, we have to get going!'

'No,' said Martine. 'No.'

She turned and ran away sobbing, crashing through the swing doors and disappearing.

Leaf stared after her for a microsecond, then went and examined the closest hospital bed. It had wheels with brakes on them, which she clicked off. There was already a sleeper in the bed, so she grabbed hold of the rail and pulled the bed out and swung it around. It was harder than she'd expected, possibly because the bed had not been moved in a long time.

'You're number one,' she said to the man asleep in the bed. 'We'll pick up Aunt Mango on the way and that'll be two. After you I'll only have approximately one thousand nine hundred and ninety-eight people to get to safety. In two and a half minutes.'

It took Leaf a lot longer than two minutes to find the elevators and then she was dismayed to find that they weren't working. Clearly, things that stayed the same from one moment to the next—

like lightbulbs—continued to work while things that moved were stuck in place. Luckily there was a map next to the elevator bank which showed where there was a wheelchair ramp to get to the lower floors.

She'd loaded not only her Aunt Mango, but two other people on to the bed. They were the two smallest she could find in the immediate vicinity of her aunt, but even so her back ached from dragging them across the floor and then levering them on to the bed. They actually were like statues to move, though fortunately ones made of flesh and blood, not marble, but even so their rigidity made them difficult to shift and manoeuvre.

There was another wall map near the top of the ramp, but it didn't indicate where the operating theatres used to be, or the old bomb shelter. Leaf would just have to find them through trial and error. As she wheeled the bed along, she noticed a frozen TV at one of the nurses' stations. The corner of the screen said it was 11:57, and a video image of some news was paused mid-sentence. The newscaster's mouth was wide open and a frozen caption across the bottom said only *measures may include drastic*.

Once she got to the bottom floor, Leaf saw it had long been deserted. It was dusty, there were cobwebs trailing from the ceiling and only one in three ceiling light panels worked.

But there was also a faded sign on the wall, and colour-coded trails on the floor, which she could just make out through the dust. The red trail was to the operating theatres and there was a blue trail to something euphemistically called 'Survival Centre' which was almost certainly the bomb shelter.

Leaf pushed the bed into the corridor, then left it to scout out where she should push it to, her running footsteps sending up clouds of dust as she raced along the corridor.

The Survival Centre was a disappointment. It was definitely a bomb shelter, featuring a reinforced door with a hydraulic wheel to open and shut it. But it was way too small and could only ever have sheltered perhaps twenty people standing up. All its pipes and fittings had been removed as well, leaving ugly holes and hanging wires. Leaf thought she might be stuck wherever she was going to be for some time, and she didn't want that place to have no toilet or running water.

She raced on, flinging open doors. Most of the rooms were small and useless, but the operating theatre complex was more promising. Though it had been cleared out, there were four big operating theatres clustered around a large central room that had several sinks with taps that worked, and there was a bathroom with at least one flushing toilet reached from the corridor outside.

Leaf propped the doors open and ran back to get her first bed-load. As she pushed the bed back to the theatre complex, she wondered what on earth she was going to do. There was no way she could bring all the sleepers down here on beds. Even loading them up was very hard for her, given that nearly all of them were bigger than her; some of them weighed at least twice what she did and their rigidity just added to the level of difficulty. She would be exhausted before she transported a dozen of them, even if she could do that before time restarted for everyone else.

I'll just have to pick out the smallest, she thought. *And do my best.*

'What have you got me into now, Arthur?' she said aloud. 'And where have you gone?'

CHAPTER FOURTEEN

Arthur didn't feel a sudden shock of pain as he was mangled by the rising chain, and Alyse was still holding his hand, so he flipped back the peak of his cap and shook his head to get the water out of his eyes.

'Careful!' said Alyse. 'No sudden moves. Grab hold of the ring there.'

They were standing in the chain link that was rapidly rising up through the middle of the stacked office units. Arthur grabbed the ring welded into the link's left inner wall, and Alyse let go of his hand to nonchalantly step over and hold the ring on the other side.

'Good view of one of the Drasils coming up,' Alyse pointed out. 'Or as good a view as you can get with the rain. Level 6222 is always empty, so you can see through it.'

'Why is it empty?' asked Arthur. 'And what's a Drasil?'

He was still wondering what the Will had tried to say, and why it had only spoken to him at that moment, and for such a brief time, so he forgot to put on the vacant, gormless expression of the recently washed-between-the-ears.

Alyse looked at him sharply before answering, but Arthur's mind was still on the Will and he didn't notice.

'Dunno why they're empty. There's empty offices from 6222 to 6300, at 6733 to 6800, and I've heard there's a bunch just below the top as well, whatever the top is now. It's probably near 61700, or something like that.'

'Sixty-one thousand, seven hundred levels?' Arthur was paying attention now. 'But each of the office cubes is about ten feet high, that would make the tower six hundred thousand feet high—'

'Nah, the levels just have a six in front for some reason. They start at sixty-one,' said Alyse. 'Tradition, I suppose. Depending on where the top has got to this week, it'll be about seventeen thousand feet. I'd love to see up there.'

'We don't go up that far?' asked Arthur, somewhat reassured.

'Not yet we haven't,' said Alyse. 'Other gangs do a bit up there. Most of the top construction work is done by automatons. Hey, triple two's coming up. Look that way.'

Arthur stared out at the offices flashing by, blurred images of green lamps and different-coloured umbrellas and Denizens in black or dark grey coats hunched over identical desks.

150

Then that view suddenly disappeared. Arthur could see the skeleton of the tower, empty office units that were just cubes of wrought iron, with exposed horizontal and vertical driving chains here and there, and the network of pneumatic message pipes. The view was broken in places by closed vertical shafts or walled-off rooms, but for the most part he could see through and out of the tower to the rain-swept sky beyond.

Far off in the distance, there was something he thought was another tower—a dark, vertical smudge on the horizon that went up and up until it disappeared into the sky.

'Good view of that Drasil today,' said Alyse. 'I wouldn't mind climbing one of them too, if it weren't for the insects.'

'Insects?' Arthur didn't like the sound of that. He wanted to ask more about what a Drasil was, but he had finally noticed that Alyse was looking at him suspiciously and he was wondering if he had pushed the washed-out memory excuse too far.

'Yes, Sunday's guard insects that patrol the Drasils. And the trees defend themselves too, I've heard. You know, now that you're clean, Ray, you don't look much like a Piper's child.'

'I don't?' asked Arthur. The cascade of water had taken all the mud off his face.

'Nope.' Alyse had her hand on her spanner and her eyes behind her rain-washed goggles were very cold.

Arthur let his hand fall on to his own spanner and he tensed a little, ready to draw.

'I reckon you must be some sort of short Denizen spy for the Big Boss. It's bad enough having the Sorcerous Supernumeraries following us about, without a spy among us. So it's time for you to—'

Arthur blocked her sudden swing at his legs with his own spanner. Sparks flew as the silver tools met. Alyse let go of the ring and struck again, a two-handed blow that would have overcome any normal Piper's child. Arthur met it one-handed, and it was Alyse who reeled back and would have fallen if Arthur hadn't hooked his foot around her ankle just before she went over.

'I'm not a spy!' Arthur shouted. 'Or a Denizen!'

Alyse grabbed hold of the ring again and eyed him warily.

'What are you then?'

'I'm Arthur, the Rightful Heir of the Architect. I've come here to find and free Part Six of the Will.'

'No, you're not!' exclaimed Alyse. 'Arthur's eight foot tall and he's got a pointy beard down to his waist!'

'Those stupid books!' groaned Arthur. Some Denizen (or group of Denizens) somewhere in the House was writing and distributing very much fictionalised accounts of Arthur and his activities in the House. 'Those books are all lies. I really am Arthur.'

'You *are* very strong,' said Alyse. 'And you are more like us than a Denizen . . . no pointy beard, hey?'

'No.'

'If you are Arthur, then you're an enemy of the Big Boss, right?'

'If you mean Superior Saturday, yes I am.'

'Who doesn't trust us any more, on account of the Piper being out and about again.'

'Yes. Neither does Dame Primus—I mean, the Will of the Architect. The parts I've already gathered, that is. But I trust you. I mean I trust Piper's children in general. In fact, I reckon the children are the smartest and most sensible people of anyone in the whole House.'

'That's true,' Alyse easily agreed. 'But speaking for the gang, we don't care for politics. We just want to get our work done.'

'I'm not going to interfere with your work,' Arthur promised. 'Just don't report me. As soon as I can figure out where the Will is, we'll be off.'

'That Suze who's with you—she really *is* a Piper's child, isn't she?'

'Yes.' Out of the corner of his eye, Arthur saw that they had passed the empty office blocks, and the cubes were all full of green lamps and working Denizens again. Only here the umbrellas were all orange.

Alyse looked at Arthur thoughtfully.

'I suppose we could just go along with it for today,' she said. 'I mean, accept you for what you say you are. If there's any trouble, I'll act as surprised as anyone.'

'That'd be great!' exclaimed Arthur. 'I just need some time to track down the Will. I'll stay out of your way.'

'Just do your work,' said Alyse. 'Otherwise it'll look suspicious. You can sneak out of the depot tonight. I want you gone before morning.'

'Very well,' said Arthur. 'Hopefully I'll know where I need to go by then.'

'You don't know where this Will is?'

'No. But the Will can speak inside my mind, tell me how to find it. I've already heard it twice. I

153

heard it just before we got on this chain, when all that water splashed on my head.'

'There's always a lot of splashes,' said Alyse. 'The full sorcerers, up above 61000, they like to play games, weave spell-nets to catch the rain and then let it all go at once on their inferiors below. Can be dangerous. We've lost a few workers washed right out of an office and into a shaft, or even out of one side.'

'It's odd,' said Arthur. 'This constant rain. I mean, the weather was broken in the Middle House, but it must be on purpose here, since Superior Saturday has all her sorcerers to fix it.'

Alyse shrugged.

'It's just the way it's always been,' she said. 'Least for the last ten thousand years. Same as when the Boss started building this tower.'

'Ten thousand years?' asked Arthur. 'It's been raining for ten thousand years in House time? How do you know? Haven't you been washed between the ears?'

'Course I have,' said Alyse. 'That's what the Denizens say. They're always talking about the plan, and building the tower, and how it's been ten thousand years, and if only the tower would reach the Gardens, then the rain will stop and all that. Look, there's the Drasil again—we're going through the seven hundreds.'

'Reach the Gardens?' asked Arthur. 'The Incomparable Gardens? That's what Saturday is trying to do?'

'That's what the sorcerers say. We just do our job. Can't be worrying about all the top-level stuff and plans and that.'

'What is a Drasil?' Arthur looked through the

empty, spare structure of the tower at the distant, vertical line.

'A very, very big tree. There's four Drasils. They hold up the Incomparable Gardens and they're always growing. I don't know how high they are, but everyone says the tower is not even close.'

'Maybe the rain makes them grow,' said Arthur.

'Maybe.'

Arthur kept looking at the Drasil until they passed through the empty section and the view was once more obscured by thousands of offices. Alyse didn't talk, but that suited Arthur. He had a lot to think about.

The rain is important, he thought. *It must be, if it started ten thousand years ago, when the Trustees broke the Will. I wonder if it's Sunday who makes it rain, for the Drasil trees? But that couldn't be right, because Saturday has the Sixth Key, and it would be strongest here . . . only I kind of remember someone saying the Seventh Key was paramount or the strongest overall or something like that . . .*

'We're coming up to the eight hundreds.'

Alyse's voice interrupted Arthur's train of thought. He looked out and wondered how she knew what level they were at. Then he saw green umbrellas everywhere, in many different shades. The sorcerers, or would-be sorcerers, had umbrellas of dark green, bright emerald green and lime green, as well as ones that had graduated washes of green and patterns of green.

'Green umbrellas in the eight hundreds,' said Arthur. 'That's how you know where we are—from the colour change in the umbrellas.'

'Yep,' Alyse confirmed. 'Yellow at nine hundred, then you count. There are numbers on the framework, but they're too small and hard to read from the Big Chains. Now get ready—we'll have to step off in a minute.'

She took his hand again and they shuffled to the edge of the link. The offices were flashing past very swiftly, Arthur thought. Suddenly the umbrellas changed to yellow. He glanced at Alyse and saw her lips moving as she counted. He tried to count too, but couldn't keep up.

'Eighty-five—get ready!' snapped Alyse.

Arthur started counting again in his head.

'Ninety-four! Go!'

They stepped off the link, Alyse dragging Arthur, timing it to perfection so that it felt no more dangerous than stepping down from a high kerb.

'Move!' Alyse snapped again. Arthur followed her, splashing past the desk and its oblivious Denizen under his yellow umbrella.

'Got to make room,' explained Alyse as she led the way through to a neighbouring office. Behind them, two more grease monkeys stepped off the link and quickly moved diagonally through to an adjacent office.

Arthur looked around and noticed that for the first time, the Denizens at their desks were covertly watching the grease monkeys. While most of them were continuing to write with both hands, they all slowed down to get a better sidelong look.

'Why are they watching us?' Arthur whispered to Alyse.

'Because they know we're here to shift someone up or *down*,' said Alyse loudly. She glared at the Denizen behind the desk next to her. He immediately looked back at his shaving-mirror screen and his writing speeded up.

'Right,' said Arthur. More grease monkeys stepped off the chain and one waved as they splashed their way across. It was Suzy, who looked like she was enjoying herself. He waved back and learned that he shouldn't tip his head back when doing so, because a sheet of rain fell on his face.

Alyse had her notebook out again and was studying an entry, her finger moving along the lines. Arthur noticed that all the closer Denizens were watching intently despite Alyse's earlier glaring.

More grease monkeys arrived in pairs and moved through the offices, until the last, Whrod, stepped off alone.

Alyse shut her notebook with a snap and pointed deeper into the tower.

'This way!' she declared.

'Is it a promotion?' asked a Denizen. He had given up all pretence at work and was staring at Alyse, his mouth twisted up in an ugly expression that didn't match his handsome features.

Alyse ignored him. Striding through a waterfall that had just started coming down, she led the gang deeper into the tower, pausing every now and then to check the numbers that were embossed on the red iron posts that made up the framework of the building.

As the grease monkeys marched, Arthur heard the Denizens whispering all around them.

'Promotion . . . it must be . . . promotion . . . who is it . . . promotion . . . anyone see a purple capsule . . . promotion . . . promotion . . .'

'There she is, four offices ahead,' Alyse whispered to Arthur. 'With the saffron checks on the darker yellow. You wait here and join Whrod—he'll tell you what to do. And look out.'

'For what?' asked Arthur.

'The others will throw things as soon as they know it's a promotion. Wait for Whrod now.'

Arthur nodded and stopped where he was. Whrod was close behind, and the other grease monkeys were approaching in an extended line across a dozen offices.

'Go!' shouted Alyse. She ran ahead to the chosen office, jumped on the desk and then from there to a corner of the cube. Holding on to the frame with one hand, she started working on something with a spanner.

The Denizen stood up and folded her yellow umbrella. It turned black as it closed. Then, as she reopened it, a rich purple colour spread in swirls across the fabric like oil in water. She propped the umbrella up then quickly climbed under the desk, calling out as she did so.

'Goodbye, idiots! Long may you labour in vain!'

As the other grease monkeys swarmed over to the office, Arthur ran with Whrod to the lower-left corner. Whrod had his spanner out and started working on a large bolt that fastened the office cube to the framework. Arthur didn't know what he was supposed to do. He drew his spanner but only stood there until Whrod looked up at him angrily.

'Come on! Get the other side!'

The restraining bolt went through the frame and was fastened on the other side with a large hexagonal bronze nut. Arthur got his spanner on to it as Whrod turned the bolt and drew it free.

Arthur caught the nut as it fell, just before it

disappeared through the latticed floor.

'Next one up!' Whrod called out, immediately going to another bolt a foot up from the first. Three other teams of grease monkeys were undoing the bolts in the other corners, and more were working above and around the office, some of them standing on each other's shoulders and some even hanging by their fingers from the latticed floor above, like real monkeys.

'Booklicker!' shouted a nearby Denizen.

'Toady!'

'Slithering sycophant!'

'You stole my promotion!'

All the Denizens in the nearer offices were shouting, waving their umbrellas and becoming very obstreperous.

'Hurry!' snapped Whrod. 'They'll start throwing things in a second.'

As Arthur crouched to get his spanner positioned, something hit him hard in the back and fell at his feet. He looked down and saw it was a broken tea-cup. Then a saucer smashed into pieces in front of his face, the debris falling on Whrod's back.

'Lower East bolts clear!' shouted a grease monkey.

'Lower West bolts clear!'

'Lower North bolts clear!'

'Darn it,' spat Whrod. 'Last. Got the nut? Lower South bolts clear!'

His declaration was echoed by the teams working on the ceiling and by shouts that came from higher up. Arthur looked and saw that there were other gangs on the higher floors and, amid them, several dull bronze automatons that looked like ambulatory jellyfish, round three-foot diameter globes that stood five feet tall and walked on four or five semi-rigid tentacles while they wielded tools in their other numerous appendages.

'Check chain!' shouted Alyse.

Whrod used the edge of his spanner to peel back what Arthur had thought was a solid part of the vertical frame but was in fact a red-painted cover or lid that fitted snugly on the beam. Under it, there was a smaller version of the Big Chain, big fat links four or five times the size of a bicycle chain. The chain ran on the inside of the U-shaped vertical beam, though it was not moving now.

'Chain present—looks all right!'

Diagonally opposite, another grease monkey confirmed that the chain was present there.

Alyse looked up, cupped her hands around her mouth, and shouted, 'Ready to rise! Shift them aside!'

Arthur looked up too, completely in the moment, all his troubles and responsibilities forgotten, replaced by curiosity as he wondered what exactly was going to shift aside.

CHAPTER FIFTEEN

The offices above Arthur creaked and rattled, then a whole line of them started to slowly move to the right, like carriages on a train being shunted off from a station. The next level up again, other offices were moving away in a different direction, and on the next level above that, and above that, presumably all the way up to level 61012, seventeen floors above.

As the vertical gap appeared that would allow the promoted Denizen's office to ascend, the barrage of cups, saucers and inkwells slowed and then stopped, as did the stream of abuse. But a lot more water started coming down, more than could be explained by the constant rain, and Arthur saw brief, hallucinatory images of giant buckets woven out of purple light that were upending themselves into the new, temporary shaft.

'Stand clear!' ordered Alyse. 'Not you, Ray. You stay with me. The rest of you, take the Big Chain to 61012.'

'Hey, I want to go up in this—' Suzy started to say, before Arthur made a gesture with his hand against his throat. She scowled, looked at Alyse, who met her eyes with an unflinching gaze, and then reluctantly followed the others back to the Big Chain.

Arthur moved to the middle of the office, ducked sideways to avoid a huge splash of water from above and stood next to the desk, which still had the Denizen under it. She looked at Arthur and sniffed.

'Take it up!' shouted Alyse. An automaton waved a tentacle in reply and a few seconds later, the office shook as the chains in the framework clanked into motion. Slowly, with a juddering screech, the office began to rise up towards its destination.

As it rose, a huge sheet of water came crashing down, so much that it couldn't run off fast enough, creating a temporary puddle as deep as Arthur's knees.

Arthur! I am spread throughout the—

It was the voice of Part Six of the Will.

'What was that?' asked a voice from under the desk. 'I smell sorcery!'

The Denizen poked her head out and sniffed the air, but quickly withdrew again when another great dump of water splashed across her face.

Arthur shook his head, sending a spray of droplets to join the rain.

Alyse looked at him suspiciously.

'Everything's fine,' said Arthur brightly. He lifted his spanner. 'All ready to get back to work.'

'Be sure you are,' Alyse replied.

Spread throughout . . . the what? thought Arthur. *The Will has spoken to me three times now, the last two times when I've just been soaked . . .*

'The rain,' Arthur whispered to himself. He tucked his spanner under his arm, put his hands together and held them out, watching the rain splash and fill his makeshift cup. Soon brimming over, he held his hands up under the green lamp on the desk, searching the clear water for an indication that he had guessed correctly.

Under the light, deep in the liquid, Arthur saw letters loop and twine, forming words that he knew well, breaking apart and forming again in a constant struggle against the fluid medium.

Part Six of the Will is in the rain. Broken across thousands—maybe millions—of raindrops. It's only able to come together a bit when water gathers. Like in that drain, or a big splash from above . . .

'What are you doing, Piper's child?' asked the Denizen, who had once again come out from under her desk. She bent under her umbrella and lifted the pince-nez spectacles that hung from a cord around her neck.

'I thought I saw something fall,' said Arthur. 'I caught it, but it must have been a piece of bread or something that fell apart.'

'Really?' asked the Denizen. She settled the pince-nez on her nose and blinked. 'I thought I smelled sorcery . . . and now I see there is something in your pouch. Give it to me.'

Arthur slowly shook his head and stepped closer, his spanner in his hand.

163

'Ray . . .' warned Alyse.

'Give it to me before I blast you to tiny shreds,' said the Denizen in a bored voice. 'I am a full sorcerer now, albeit only of the Fifth Grade for the moment. Hand it over!'

Her hand went to the umbrella, ready to fold and wield it.

Arthur struck as her fingers pressed the catch and the umbrella began to fold. His spanner bounced off the Denizen's head. She blinked once and said, 'No little Piper's child can hit hard enough to . . . to . . .'

She blinked again and slowly slid to the floor. Arthur, keeping them both covered and out of sight under the partly-folded umbrella, shoved her back under the desk.

'What have you done!' exclaimed Alyse in a furious whisper. 'You'll get us all executed!'

'I only knocked her out,' said Arthur. 'It had to be done. Tell me, is there somewhere all this rain goes? Like a big storm-water reservoir or something?'

'What?' asked Alyse. She peered under the desk and then looked back up. Her gang was already above, but so were a line of sad-eyed Sorcerous Supernumeraries.

'How did they get ahead of us?' asked Arthur.

'They caught a normal elevator like they always do!'

'They'll wonder what's happened to this sorcerer, won't they?'

'Of course they will!'

'Do the Denizens ever sleep at their desks?' Arthur asked. He was trying to think how to hide the sorcerer, but there wasn't anywhere completely

164

out of sight. They were surrounded by sorcerers at their desks, thousands of them . . .

'They always sleep at their desks,' said Alyse. 'But it's not night-time, is it? I knew I should have pushed you off the Big Chain!'

They were four floors away from their destination now. Arthur could see Suzy leaning over the edge, watching him. She waved again. Arthur responded by scratching his cap in an agitated way and throwing his hands up in the air, hoping that this might send a message that they were about to be in serious trouble. Not that there was anything Suzy could do.

All he could think of was to take out the Fifth Key, destroy as many of the Sorcerous Supernumeraries and the surrounding sorcerers in their offices as he could in a surprise attack, and then use the Key to escape. But that wouldn't free the Will and it would be very difficult to get back, even now that he'd seen the place and could use the Key, since there were all these sorcerers who would be watching for just such a thing.

'Have you ever had one keep hiding under a desk after they've risen up?' he asked Alyse.

'Of course not! Some of them have been waiting thousands of years to get promoted. They get out and dance on their desks half the time. Or start weaving spells to catch water and throw it down on their former fellows.'

Three floors away and there were more Sorcerous Supernumeraries staring mournfully down and shuffling on the edge of the temporary shaft.

'Right,' said Arthur. He quickly looked around to check that the office was above the eyeline of the Denizens around them. 'I'd better do something.'

'What?' asked Alyse.

'This,' said Arthur, and he shifted the umbrella so he and part of the desk were hidden from the sight of the Denizens above.

Alyse looked puzzled, an expression that changed to horror as Arthur suddenly reached out with his spanner and smashed the green desk lamp. It exploded with a vicious crack and a shower of sparks. A sheet of flame shot up and the rain falling on it created an instant pall of steam.

Moving through the cloud, Arthur sprang to the corner and stuck his spanner into the rising chain. Exerting all his unnatural strength, he tried to break one of the links open, but the spanner bent in half and snapped off in his hand. The chain kept rising with the broken head in it, and the office kept rising too . . . for about half a foot. Then there was a fearful screeching and the office suddenly lurched up on one side and down on the other. Arthur, Alyse, the desk and the unconscious Denizen began to slide off into an adjacent office.

'Shut down!' Alyse screamed up the shaft as she kicked the desk to push it against a corner. 'Chain break! Shut down! Chain break!'

Still obscured by steam, Arthur stopped the Denizen's slide, but the office was continuing to rise on the far side, tilting the floor even more.

'Shut it down!' Alyse continued to shout.

The chain suddenly stopped its mechanical shriek, the office juddered to a full stop at a thirty-degree angle, the flame from the green lamp sputtered out and the steam wafted away. Arthur quickly arranged the Denizen against the jammed-up desk, so she looked like she'd struck her head in the accident.

'Who would know where the water goes?' Arthur asked Alyse with some urgency.

'How dare you!' was Alyse's reply. 'We had such a good record!'

'Some things are more important,' said Arthur coldly. 'Like the fact that the whole House and the entire Universe is going to be destroyed unless I do something. So stop whining and tell me who might know where all the storm water goes!'

Alyse grimaced and looked up, rain tapping on her goggles. Then she looked back at Arthur.

'Dartbristle would know. Go and ask him and get away from us!'

'You all right down there?' called a grease monkey from above.

'Not exactly!' shouted Arthur. 'Just give us a minute!'

'Where would I find Dartbristle?' Arthur continued in a quiet tone. 'Also, I bet we need a pass or something to go back by ourselves, right?'

'There's a penny whistle by the drain you came up,' said Alyse. 'Play his tune on that and he'll come to the depot.'

'His tune? Oh yeah, the one he whistles—I remember that.'

Arthur had a very good musical ear, so good that people often assumed that he'd inherited it from his father, the lead singer of The Ratz, not knowing that Bob was actually his adoptive father.

'Do we need a pass to go back?'

'I'll write to say you're going to fetch a part we need.' Alyse got out her book and a blue pencil and quickly scribbled something on a page. Then

167

she tore out the page and handed it to Arthur, saying, 'That's it. Just go!'

'Everything's going to change,' Arthur told her. 'Whether you want it to or not. The only question is whether the change is for the better or the worse.'

'We just want to do our job,' said Alyse, repeating the words like a mantra.

The umbrella above them suddenly moved, a black-clad Sorcerous Supernumerary sweeping it aside. Another Supernumerary landed with a splash next to him and then a third jumped down. They ignored Arthur and Alyse, going to look at the unconscious sorcerer on the floor. Each of them, Arthur noticed, had the slightest of smiles that would not be visible to anyone further away than him and Alyse. They were pleased to see an unconscious sorcerer and a halted promotion.

'Boss? What do we do?' a grease monkey called from above.

Alyse looked up.

'Get yourself down here! You and Bigby and Whrod. I'm sending Ray and Suze back down to get a Number Three temporary chain bracket. The rest of you, I want every inch of horizontal chain from here to ten offices out in all directions checked for corrosion.'

'Corrosion accident causal effect?' asked a tinny, booming voice.

The speaker was one of the octopoidal automatons. It spoke through a valve under its central sphere, which rather horribly opened and shut as it talked.

'How would I know?' shouted Alyse. 'Most likely though. We'll have to look.'

'Higher authority approaches,' reported the automaton. 'Await instruction.'

'Big nob!' hissed one of the grease monkeys above.

The three Sorcerous Supernumeraries straightened like string puppets yanked to attention and rapidly climbed back up.

'Quick, you drop over the side to the next level, run through to the north side and use your wings,' Alyse told Arthur. 'A Sorcerer-Overseer will see who you are straightaway, up close.'

'Suze!' Arthur shouted. 'Get down here!'

He slid down the uneven floor and began to lower himself over the side, first making sure that he wasn't going to drop on the head of the Denizen below.

'Thanks,' Arthur said to Alyse. 'Suze! Come on!'

'I'm here!' Suzy called, landing with a *thump* near Arthur and almost rolling off before she got a good handhold. 'In a hurry, are we?'

'Yes,' said Arthur. He let go and dropped down to the next floor. He'd thought of aiming for the desk so he didn't have so far to fall, but decided against it. There was no point in attracting the attention of the sorcerer there, particularly since he'd just noticed that these Denizens with the purple umbrellas weren't writing. They still looked into the shaving-mirror viewers or whatever they were, but they weren't writing anything.

'Where we going?' asked Suzy.

'To the side and down,' Arthur said quietly as he led the way through an office and dodged around the occupant, who had pushed his chair back much further than normal. 'Flying. We have to find Dartbristle again and get him to lead us to

169

wherever the storm water goes.'

'Why not just ask Alyse? She's got that guide to the whole place and all.'

Arthur stopped suddenly and Suzy ran into his back.

'What guide?' he asked.

'That book—it's got maps and instructions and everything, for wherever the gang might have to go,' said Suzy. 'Least that's what Bigby was telling me. Kind of like your Atlas, only not as good.'

Arthur looked back. They'd only gone half a dozen offices.

'She just wanted to get rid of us,' he said.

'Fair enough,' said Suzy. 'Can't blame her for that.'

'Yes, I can.' Arthur was about to say more when a huge torrent of water crashed down between him and Suzy, knocking the Piper's child off her feet.

'This 'ere rain is a bit much,' Suzy said as she struggled to her feet. 'Wouldn't mind a bit of sunshine meself.'

'Wouldn't we all,' said the Denizen at the nearby desk. He didn't look away from his mirror-screen.

'Thought you lot weren't supposed to talk to us,' Suzy chided.

'We're not,' sighed the sorcerer. 'But it gets so boring just watching the mirror, waiting for something worth watching. What was that you were saying about someone wanting to get rid of you? I couldn't hear properly over the rain.'

'It was nothing,' said Arthur.

'Just the usual?' The Denizen sighed again. 'I thought you grease monkeys weren't so afflicted, not being eligible for promotion and so forth.'

'Afflicted?' asked Suzy.

'Resentful and envious,' said the Denizen. 'Take my last promotion, for example. The fellows I'd drunk tea with for the last thousand years, shared many a biscuit . . . they threw our department silver teapot at me as I rose above their heads.'

'Come on, Suze,' said Arthur. 'We need to go back up.'

'We do? What about that Overseer?'

'An Overseer?' squeaked the Denizen. 'Get away from me! I must attend to my studies!'

He immediately opened a book and began to read it quietly aloud while also watching his mirror, one eye focused left and one focused right, which was quite disturbing to see.

Arthur stood still for a minute, thinking, then started back towards the stalled office.

'What about that Overseer?' Suzy asked again in a whisper as she caught up with him.

'If we keep our distance, we should be fine,' Arthur assured her. He was so mad at Alyse that he didn't even consider the potential danger of being discovered. 'I'll get the information we need from Alyse and we'll go again.'

Four grease monkeys were working on the broken office, but Alyse herself was not there and neither were the unconscious sorcerer, the Sorcerous Supernumeraries or any other Denizens. Arthur watched for a few seconds to make sure the coast was clear, then climbed up the corner framework and back into the office.

Whrod looked over from where he was undoing a chain link.

'I thought Alyse sent you to get a chain bracket!'

'She did,' said Arthur. 'But I have to check something with her first. Where is she? With the

171

Sorcerer-Overseer?'

'What Overseer?' asked Whrod. 'There was an Automaton-Scheduler, but that's like five . . . four ranks below . . .'

'Where's Alyse then?'

'Dunno.' Whrod shrugged. 'Everyone's checking chain up on the next floor, except for us.'

'Right!' said Arthur. Flexing his knees, he jumped to the top of the desk, which had been tipped up to get it out of the way. From there, he jumped again to the next floor, a leap of at least eight feet.

'Show off,' grumbled Suzy, and climbed up the corner.

CHAPTER SIXTEEN

Alyse was one office away on the next level, rolling up a piece of paper to put in the message capsule that was on the sorcerer's desk. All the other grease monkeys were busy inspecting chains, spread out through all the offices around. There was no sign of the automatons or the Automaton-Scheduler.

Arthur bounded over to Alyse and grabbed her elbow, turning her round so their backs were towards the sorcerer.

'You tried to trick me,' whispered Arthur fiercely. 'Your handbook has the information I need.'

'Let go of me!' Alyse protested, but she was whispering too.

'Don't make a fuss,' warned Arthur, tightening

his grip on her arm. 'If they find out who I am, then the whole gang will be punished . . . maybe even executed.'

'All right,' said Alyse. 'What do you want?'

'I want to find a large reservoir or water store. But first I want to see that message.'

He reached over and took the paper before Alyse could snatch it away, and flicked it open one-handed.

To Senior Shift-Sorcerer 61580

Report two suspicious Piper's children
flying down to Grease Monkey Depot of
27th Chain and Motivation Maintenance
Brigade. Calling themselves Ray and Suze.

'You traitor!' spat Arthur.

'Is that message ready or not?' asked the sorcerer. He was unperturbed by the obvious animosity between Arthur and Alyse. 'I haven't got all day.'

'There's been a mistake,' said Arthur. 'No message, thanks.'

He forced Alyse towards the temporary shaft and handed the message to Suzy, whose face clouded as she read it.

'Us Piper's children always stick together,' whispered Suzy. 'Always!'

'The job comes first,' said Alyse.

'You hold her, Suzy, while I look up her book,' Arthur instructed. 'Act casual. Alyse—remember that if you try anything, the whole gang will cop it, one way or another.'

'What do you mean act casual?' asked Suzy as

she took Alyse's other arm.

'Act like you're friends looking at something on the floor together,' said Arthur. He opened Alyse's pocket and took out her handbook.

'It won't work for you,' said Alyse. 'Gang bosses only.'

'It had better work for me,' Arthur said as he opened it up. Alyse gasped.

'But you can't open it!'

Arthur ignored her and read the title page: *Chain and Motivation Maintenance Guide Registered No. 457589.*

Arthur flipped to the back. There was an index that just listed the capital letters A–Z. Arthur touched the W and the pages flipped to show a list of topics that began with that letter. He read through them quickly, until he saw *Water*, which had a long list of subtopics, including *Storage facilities, permanent* and *Storage facilities, transient*.

Under *Water, Storage facilities, permanent*, there were several listings, including *Central Rain Reservoir* and *Mid-tower Rain Booster Tank*. Arthur didn't even need to touch the latter topic; he just looked at it longer than any other line and the pages immediately flipped to show a cutaway drawing, a map and a list of technical details.

'There's a water store up higher; it's about a hundred offices square and sits between 61350 and 61399,' Arthur said. 'That'll probably do—it must be big enough.'

'Big enough for what?' asked Suzy, who was crouched down with Alyse, both of them apparently intent on the latticed floor.

'I'll tell you on the way.' Arthur checked the handbook again, closed it, and was about to put it in his pocket when it shook in his hand and made a rattling noise.

'What's that mean?'

'Change of orders,' said Alyse. 'Please, can I check it?'

Arthur hesitated. At that moment, he heard a sudden hiss and rattle erupt from everywhere around, followed a second later by the *pop* of capsules ejecting from the pneumatic message tubes and clattering on to every Denizen's desk within sight.

Arthur opened the handbook, which went straight to a page that said in large red type:

GENERAL MOBILISATION!
The tower has reached the target point underside of the Incomparable Gardens. All engineering gangs are to report immediately to Ground Floor Exterior Platform Lift One under the command of Saturday's Noon to secure and lift the assault ram.

Arthur looked around. Every single Denizen was standing up, and they were all removing and furling their umbrellas. Those who already had their umbrellas in hand were stepping out to form up in long lines, facing deeper into the tower, ready to march.

'Are the normal elevators that way?' Arthur asked Alyse.

'Yes,' she said. 'What are the orders? We must obey!'

Arthur gave her the handbook. As Alyse read, he looked around. The leader of the Sorcerous

Supernumeraries was reading a similar book to Alyse's. The Supernumerary looked up and her sad gaze met Arthur's. He quickly looked down, just in case she was powerful enough to recognise who—or what—he was.

'We have to get going!' repeated Alyse. 'This is it, the big one. We'll get to ride the cage all the way to the top!'

'What's this assault ram?' asked Arthur.

Alyse shrugged. 'Something big enough that it needs to go up on the outside cargo elevator. It's amazing—three hundred feet a side and no chain. It's self-propelling, driven by ten score senior sorcerers—'

'Can we ride up on that too?' asked Suzy, fired by Alyse's enthusiasm.

'No,' Arthur said decisively. 'Alyse, I'll let you and the gang go, but you have to promise that you won't tell and won't betray us.'

'Sure! Fine!' said Alyse, a little too quickly.

Arthur looked around. The closer sorcerers were marching away. Only the Sorcerous Supernumeraries were still close and they were watching the grease monkeys, who were mostly only pretending to inspect chains while they looked at Alyse and waited for her to tell them what was going on.

'Give me your hand,' he said quickly and quietly. 'And promise me, Lord Arthur, Rightful Heir of the Architect, that you will not betray us.'

Alyse took Arthur's hand.

'I promise you, Lord Arthur, that I won't betray you.'

A faint glow left Arthur's fingers and moved into Alyse's hand. She cried out, but Arthur didn't let her go until the faint light had disappeared.

'What occurs?' asked a slow, deep voice.

Arthur looked around. One of the Sorcerous Supernumeraries had sidled closer and was sniffing the air.

'Something shiny fell down from above and went across the floor somewhere,' Arthur said hastily. 'But I guess there's no time to look for it, what with this general mobilisation and all, right, boss?'

'Yes,' said Alyse slowly. She shook her head vigorously, sending a spray of water across Arthur and Suzy's faces. 'No time to waste . . .'

'Something from above? Something *shiny?*' asked the Supernumerary. He immediately knelt down and started sniffing the floor. Arthur and the others moved away.

'No time to waste!' shouted Alyse. 'Form up, gang! We're going down to the floor to work on Outside Elevator Number One!'

'Number One?' came a shouted question from the tilted office below. 'Outside Elevator Number One?'

'Yes!' yelled Alyse. 'Come on! Back to the Big Chain!'

The Supernumerary started to sniff towards Arthur's feet. More of the funereal Denizens were coming over, intent on what their sniffing companion was doing.

'We'll take the up chain when the first two take the down chain,' said Arthur as he and Suzy hurried after Alyse. All the offices were empty now, the Denizens and their umbrellas gone. 'Get to this water store, get Part Six of the Will and get out of here.'

'What about this 'ere ram thing and old Saturday

gettin' into the Gardens and everything?' asked Suzy.

'First things first,' said Arthur. The Big Chain was only a dozen offices ahead. He looked back. All the Supernumeraries were on the floor of the office where he'd been—a big, ugly pile of black-clad Denizens all trying to sniff at the floor. They reminded him of the writhing piles of sawfly larvae that fell from the trees in the garden at home.

I hope I can get back in time to make sure I have a home, he thought. *Though people are more important than places, and the house is probably far enough away to survive that nuke attack. But Leaf and everyone—they're too close, and I don't even know what I've done or how long it will last. I can't think about it now. I have to concentrate on what's in front of me . . .*

'What colour umbrellas do they have in the 61300s?' asked Arthur. 'If they haven't gone . . .'

'Checks of blue and yellow,' said Alyse.

'We'll have to count from here,' said Arthur as he looked up through the structure. He could see lines of moving Denizens, but they had their umbrellas furled and there were none still at their desks. 'You start heading down, Alyse. We'll go around to the up chain.'

'No hard feelings,' said Alyse.

'Speak for yourself,' Arthur replied.

I will return and punish her dreadfully, he thought, then suppressed the brief moment of rage. *There are more important things to do. Forget about it.*

'Wotcher, Alyse,' said Suzy. 'Don't get yer spanner in a twist!'

She waved cheerily as Alyse and another grease

179

monkey stepped out and into a moving link of the downward chain. Arthur hurried around to stand on the edge next to the rising chain.

'Easy does it,' said Suzy. Arthur took her hand and they both stood there for a few moments, watching the chain speed upwards, gauging when they should step on.

'Now!' said Suzy, and they stepped forward. Either Suzy wasn't as good at judging the speed as Alyse, or Arthur was worse with his eyes open than his eyes shut, because they mistimed it a little and were flung about. One of Arthur's feet trailed over the side before he got his balance and hastily pulled it in.

'Oopsie-daisy,' said Suzy. 'This is a bit of fun, this chain. We could do with one of these back in the old Lower House, I reckon.'

'There is no more Lower House,' said Arthur. He was trying to count the floors as they whizzed past.

'That's right,' said Suzy. 'I forgot. Oh well.'

Arthur stared at her. How could she have forgotten that so easily? Sometimes he thought the Piper's children were no more human than the Denizens, no matter that they'd started out as mortal kids.

Thinking about that made him forget to count.

'Drat! I suppose it won't matter if we're a few floors out. The Rain Booster Tank is huge, according to that guidebook. Which I should have kept.'

'Why do we want to go to a Rain Booster Tank?'

'Catch some of this rain and take a very close look.' Arthur cupped his hand to demonstrate, and Suzy followed suit, being careful not to stick her hand out too far beyond the chain, where it might get lopped off by a protrusion from an upper floor.

'What am I looking for?' she asked when her hand was brimful of clear water.

'Letters and words,' said Arthur.

'Yes! I see 'em!' exclaimed Suzy. 'O-r-l-g-w-x-s-t-r-e . . . orlgwxstre . . . hmmm . . . that sounds familiar but I can't quite put me finger on—'

'It's not an actual word!' said Arthur. 'It's just a random, jumbled up bit of the Will. It's split up among all these raindrops. That's why I need to find a place where lots of water comes together, because more, or even most, of the Sixth Part of the Will should be there.'

'Right!' Suzy nodded. 'So you get it and we get out?'

'Probably. I guess that's still the most sensible thing to do, though I wish I knew why Saturday wants to get into the Incomparable Gardens, and why she can't just go up in an elevator. Oh no!'

'What!?' Suzy looked around wildly.

'I've lost count again. Maybe we'll be able to see it, if the offices are empty.'

All the offices they had been passing were empty, but a flash of movement caught Arthur's eye a few floors up.

'That one was full—but they were standing at their desks, not sitting.'

'So's this one. What are they doing?'

The floors went by too quickly for Arthur to be sure, but as far as he could see, the offices they'd just passed were full of Denizens doing something that looked like t'ai chi—a formalised, slow dance, in their case performed at the side of their desks. Their umbrellas were furled too, so they were

181

dancing in the rain, kicking up arcs of spray as they slowly turned and jumped.

'I have no idea what they're doing,' said Arthur. He frowned and added, 'I'd hoped all the Denizens would have gone off to the elevators, to head wherever they're going. Keep an eye out for anything that might look like a water reservoir. We must be getting close.'

They went up past several more floors of sorcerers dancing at their desks, then there were more vacated floors, some with distant views of marching sorcerers heading off further into the interior of the tower.

'You look that way, I'll look the other,' Arthur said. 'I've got confused about which way is north. I really should have kept that guidebook. I don't know what I was thinking.'

'That Alyse needed it?' asked Suzy. 'Zounds! Is that it?'

Arthur spun around, which was not a good thing to do when travelling quite fast inside the link of a vast, moving chain. He nearly lost his balance and fell against Suzy, who staggered into the side of the link and almost lost her grip on the ring.

Recovering his stance, Arthur saw a glass wall some distance inside the tower, a glass wall that shimmered blue from the water inside it. The wall and the water continued up as they rose through the next floor, and the next.

'Do we keep going?' asked Suzy.

'To the top of it,' answered Arthur, who was counting very intently now. 'Get ready, it's forty-nine floors high.'

They stepped off at the forty-ninth floor, expecting to see either empty offices or offices with working sorcerers. But the office units here were not furnished with desks. Each ten-by-ten-foot office had a small lounge in it, and a standard lamp. The lounges were covered in different fabrics, ranging from black leather to bright floral patterns, and the standard lamps had matching shades.

'Artful Lounger territory,' whispered Suzy.

'Yep,' said Arthur. He looked around keenly. 'But there aren't any here.'

He started off towards the water tank. Though the rain obscured his view, he could see the clear glass wall of the tank through several floors and the open top of it up ahead, with its rain-dappled surface of clean blue water. It looked like an enormous aquarium and Arthur wondered if there were fish in it. Or other things . . .

'So do yer just stick your hand in, or what?' asked Suzy as they reached the edge of the huge tank and looked across the expanse of water.

We're ten thousand feet up a tower and this water 'tank' is about five hundred feet deep, thought Arthur, *with a surface area that's about equal to sixteen Olympic pools. That's some water storage!*

He bent down and dipped his hand in the water. Immediately he felt Part Six of the Will speak directly into his mind.

Arthur! I need your help to gather myself. Come into the water! There is no time to lose!

CHAPTER SEVENTEEN

'It wants me to go into the water,' Arthur told Suzy. He looked at the rain splashes and then back at the empty lounges behind them.

'So it's here?' Suzy asked. She kept looking back too.

'Yes,' said Arthur. 'I suppose I'd better go in. You keep watch.'

Suzy nodded and drew her spanner, slapping the heavy adjustable head against her open hand.

Five hundred feet deep, thought Arthur. *That's waaaay too deep . . . but I have to get the Will.*

Steeling himself, Arthur slid off the latticed iron floor and into the water. It was cold, but not as cold as he'd expected. It was definitely not as cold as it should have been that high up, but then neither was the air. Saturday might like the rain, but she clearly didn't want the cold of an earthly high altitude.

Good! the Will chimed in. *Swim to the middle and call me!*

Arthur trod water for a few minutes. He'd done lifesaving classes and had swum in his clothes before, but not with his boots on. He was about to kick them off, but decided not to. He wasn't having any trouble staying afloat. Possibly because he wasn't having any trouble breathing, and his strength and endurance were far greater than they'd ever been.

He struck out for the middle, using breaststroke rather than freestyle so he could see where he was going. It was slower, but safer. Halfway there, he rolled over on his back and did some backstroke so he could see Suzy. She waved and he waved back.

Good work, Arthur! Now call me with your mind.

Arthur trod water and watched the rain, visualising the tiny fragments of the Will that lay inside each raindrop.

Part Six of the Will of the Architect, attend upon me, Arthur the Rightful Heir, he thought, his brow furrowed in concentration. *Join together and come to me!*

Long threads of type began to glow and flow through the water, twining together like the tendrils of luminous sea plants. The rain shone with an inner light and began to drive towards Arthur rather than falling straight down through the latticework floors. Up above him, drips and drops that had been caught on the floors sprang into motion, rolling and spreading to the nearest gap to fall again.

Sixty floors below Arthur, a sorcerer stared at

her mirror in amazement. She hesitated for moment, then opened a small, secret drawer in the middle of her desk and depressed a dusty bronze button.

Around her, mirrors flashed. Denizens who had been paying scant attention leaned forward, snapping books shut and dropping pens. Above their heads, the pneumatic message tubes suddenly puffed and coughed, and red capsules began to fall upon the desks.

On the floors where the sorcerers danced, they all stopped in mid-beat. Umbrellas were snapped open, chairs dragged back as they sat down and thousands of small mirrors were turned for better viewing.

Higher up the tower, as high as you could get for now, until the assault ram was raised, a telephone rang and was picked up by a milk-white, silky hand.

Arthur watched the threads of type weave themselves through the water and he kept calling the Will inside his head. Slowly the lines of type began to take on a shape—the shape of a large bird. It turned a dark colour, a shining black, and its beak, head and ruffled neck rose up out of the water.

'Good, Lord Arthur,' croaked the raven. One text-wrought wing fluttered above the surface, while the other was still unformed threads of type. 'I am almost complete. A little more rain must fall and be gathered in.'

'Arthur!'

Arthur looked back to Suzy. She was pointing with her spanner.

'Artful Loungers! Lots of them!'

'A few more minutes,' said the raven. 'Keep

calling me, Lord Arthur!'

Arthur tried to jump up so he could see what Suzy saw, but even with his hardest kicking he could only just raise up seven inches or so. But that was enough. All around the offices beyond the reservoir, Artful Loungers were crawling out from *under* the lounges. They had been there all along, hidden and quiescent.

Now they were advancing on Suzy, with their curved blue-steel swords and Nothing-poison stilettos of crystal.

Suzy flicked her rain-cape behind her back and raised her spanner.

'Concentrate, Arthur! Call me!' said Part Six.

Arthur dived forward and broke into his fastest freestyle stroke.

'Arthur! I can't escape without you!'

Arthur ignored the raven and swam faster, piercing the water like a dolphin. But even though he was swimming faster than he ever had, after a dozen strokes he was no closer to the side, and after a dozen more he felt himself being pulled very strongly back. Rolling over, he was pushed sideways as well. As he swirled about, he felt a powerful tug at his ankles.

He was in a whirlpool. The water was running out of the tank and he was going with it.

'Suzy!' yelled Arthur. The water had sunk so quickly and he was being twirled round so fast that he could only see Suzy's head. 'Use your wings. Fly aw—'

Water filled his mouth. Flailing wildly, Arthur barely managed to get himself above the surface again. The suction was incredible, the action of tons and tons of water drawn into a ten-thousand-foot-high drain. Desperately he looked back, but he couldn't see Suzy, only the glitter of Artful Lounger swords, and through water-filled ears he heard the crash of metal and shouts and a single, cut-off scream.

Then he could only think of himself. He was drowning, his lungs filling with water as he was inexorably dragged below the surface. All his fears of a long, slow, underwater death were coming true.

He scrabbled at his belt pouch, thrusting his fingers in to touch the Fifth Key through the bag, not trying to get it out for if he did, he knew he would lose it for sure. He felt its power, weak though it was through the shielding metalcloth, and focused his mind to use its sorcery, only to be flung around so violently that his arms were twisted behind him and he was upended, driving head-first down the drain.

Water completely filled his lungs and the last, pathetic bubble of air left his mouth.

I refuse to die, thought Arthur. *I am no longer human. I am the Rightful Heir of the Architect. I am going to breathe the water.*

He opened his mouth and took a deep, refreshing intake of water. All his choking sensations vanished and his mouth, twisted moments ago in a panicked, silent scream, smoothed into something that was not quite a smile. He took another breath of water and pirouetted so he was upright, rushing feet-first rather than head-first down what must be an enormous pipe.

Suzy was probably only taken prisoner, he told himself. *I'll survive this and rescue her. It will be all right...*

The water rushing him down suddenly changed direction. Arthur hit something very, very hard. He screamed, but no sound came out, just a blast of water from his mouth. Then he was picked up again and slammed even harder, bumping and scraping as the water surged and corkscrewed, carrying him with it.

Still screaming, Arthur curled up into a ball to protect himself—and, like a ball, was swept on and on, down and along the huge storm-water pipe that switchbacked its way through and down ten thousand feet.

It took half an hour for the water to reach the bottom. In that time, Arthur was smashed a hundred times against the sides of the pipe. He hurt terribly all over, but the awful passage that would have killed any mortal at its beginning did not kill him.

At the bottom, the huge pipe spat out a waterfall that cascaded into a vast, underfloor lake, carved out of the bulwark rock under the Upper House. Arthur fell through the waterfall, sank to the bottom and just lay there until the pains that wracked him diminished from the level of blinding stabs to a steady, debilitating ache.

It still hurt to move, but Arthur forced himself to swim up to the surface. Breaking out of the water, he was afraid he might not be able to breathe air, but he could and it felt no different from when he was breathing the water.

Arthur wearily trod water and looked around. He could see the huge pipe and the waterfall that still cascaded from it, but little else. There was fog, or steam, obscuring everything. As the water drained from his ears, he became aware of sound, the dull, repetitive thud of mighty engines.

Back under the floor, he thought. *In the middle of a lot of water. Must be the central rain reservoir . . .*

'Part Six?' Arthur croaked. 'Will. Are you here too?'

A raven-head emerged from the water, but it was not glossy and black, and there were blank lines where parts of it were missing. It opened its beak and croaked, 'Most of me is here, Lord Arthur, but some fragments are yet to arrive. In fact, I believe the few paragraphs that make up my tail are still falling as rain and will not arrive here for an hour or more.'

'I doubt we've got an hour,' said Arthur. 'I was overconfident. Scamandros warned me that they could track any sorcery I did. I just didn't think calling you would count.'

'Saturday must have devoted a very large number of her Denizens to watch for any signs of sorcery,' said the Will. 'It is surprising, since she is also massing her forces to assault the Incomparable Gardens. If we are fortunate, that battle will have commenced and will serve as a distraction. In any case, we are a long way under the floor here and her servants do not like to venture into this region.'

'The Rat-catcher automatons do though,' said Arthur. 'Can you pull yourself together from anywhere in this pool?'

'Why, yes,' said the Will. 'Why?'

'You can do it from near solid ground then. I have to get out of the water. I feel like I've been run over by a mammoth. Which way is the closest shore?'

'Follow me,' said the raven-head, and it began to move away. It looked quite horrible, just the head of a bird and part of its neck, gliding across the water without obvious means of propulsion.

Arthur swam slowly and wearily behind it, thinking about Suzy and Leaf. He felt as if he'd abandoned both of them, but he hadn't meant to. It was just how things had worked out.

Not that that's an excuse, he thought gloomily. *Maybe Suzy's OK—they probably just took her prisoner. And maybe time has stayed stopped for Leaf. It seems so cowardly to wait for the Will and then take it back to the Citadel . . . but what else can I do?*

The steam clouds ahead parted to show a long stone quay or platform that was only a few inches above the water level. Arthur dragged himself up on to it and collapsed. The Will watched from the water and began to flex the beginnings of its left wing.

Arthur hadn't lain there very long when he heard something other than the steady hum and clank of the steam engines. A more surreptitious noise—like someone sweeping the floor, accompanied by a faint patter of feet and the suggestion of a whistle . . .

He sat up and looked along the quay. The whistle was very quiet, but he thought he knew what it was and his guess was confirmed as Dartbristle emerged out of the steaming mists. The Rat was holding a small crossbow in one hand and dragging a net full of something behind.

'Dartbristle!' Arthur called out.

The Raised Rat jumped, dropped the net and lifted his crossbow with both hands.

'Lord Arthur! What are you doing here?'

'I got washed down a drain. But I'm glad to see you. I need some directions. What are you doing?'

Dartbristle was aiming the crossbow at him, while also shaking his head. Arthur saw with horrid fascination that the crossbow bolt had a head made of Immaterial glass, like a sealed bottle, and a tiny piece of Nothing writhed inside.

'I'm sorry, Lord Arthur. I wish you weren't here! I have the strictest orders—'

'No!' shouted Arthur.

Dartbristle pulled the trigger and the Nothing-poisoned bolt sped straight for Arthur's chest.

CHAPTER EIGHTEEN

Arthur didn't have time to think or duck. He didn't need to. Without any active thought on his part, he leaned aside and caught the bolt as it passed, right in the middle of the shaft. The Nothing bottle on the end remained unbroken.

Arthur reversed the bolt to use it as a hand weapon and advanced upon Dartbristle, who was hastily cranking his crossbow to ready it for another bolt.

'The strictest orders,' panted the Rat. 'Shoot anyone who might interfere. I don't want to shoot you, but I must!'

Arthur stopped. Something—several somethings—were coming out of the steam clouds. Six Rat-catcher automatons, their long feelers testing the way ahead as they advanced down the quay.

Dartbristle saw the expression on Arthur's face and turned around, just as the closest Rat-catcher charged. The Rat threw his crossbow aside, picked up the net and hurled it into the water. He tried to draw his long knife, but throwing the net had taken all the time he had. The Rat-catcher's left claw caught him around the neck and snapped closed. Another automaton came up, wound its razor-edged feelers all around him and began to squeeze.

This was a mistake. Dartbristle was almost certainly already dead anyway, but the squeezing broke the Nothing bottles that were in their special wooden case on his back. Nothing exploded out and the Rat-catcher's feelers instantly dissolved. The automatons hummed and squealed in alarm as the Nothing ran like quicksilver over their claws and out along their bodies, dissolving everything it touched.

In a few seconds, no trace remained of either Dartbristle or the two Rat-catcher automatons. The Nothing coalesced back into a puddle of darkness and began to sink into the bulwark bedrock, cutting a deep shaft through the reinforced House material.

Arthur eyed the remaining four automatons and readied himself for their attack. But they didn't charge. They waved their feelers around and their red, central eye-things glowed, and then the four of them turned about and disappeared back into the warm fog.

'Recognised you weren't a Rat,' said the Will. It had two wings now and was hopping along the surface of the pool, albeit without having any claws or a tail. 'Which is lucky. I believe they have a bit of a problem with recognising their legitimate prey.'

'Poor Dartbristle,' said Arthur. 'He didn't want to shoot me, or at least not me in particular. What did he throw into the pool?'

'I shall take a look,' said the Will. It scuttled across the surface and grabbed the floating net in its beak to drag it back to Arthur, who sat back down on the edge of the pool and let his feet dangle in the water. His boots had come off after all, in his rapid descent, and his overalls were ripped to shreds below the knees and elbows. His belt was still on, fortunately, and Arthur tapped the pouch to confirm that the bag with the Key, the Mariner's medallion and Elephant was still there.

'These are things of sorcery,' said the Will as it dropped the net near Arthur. 'I do not know what they are for.'

Arthur picked up the net. There were three large, round glass floats inside. One red, one blue and one green. They looked like the same kind of glass that Simultaneous Bottles were made from.

'He threw these into the water, even though it meant he didn't have time to draw his weapon,' said Arthur. 'It was that important.'

'Then we should put them back in the water,' said the Will. 'To respect his dying wish.'

'What?' asked Arthur. This wasn't the kind of behaviour he was used to from any part of the Will.

'We should put them back in,' the Will repeated. 'As a matter of respect. Ah, the text for one of my tail feathers has just dropped in. Back in a moment.'

It left Arthur holding the net and scudded off towards the waterfall that issued from the downpipe.

Arthur lifted the red float and looked at it. It didn't seem particularly sorcerous. He held the floats for a minute, thinking about something his mother had once said to his sister Michaeli and she didn't even know he was listening: 'There is never any one absolutely right thing to do. All you can do is honour what you believe and accept the consequences of your own actions, and make the best of whatever happens.'

'I bet I'm going to regret this,' Arthur said aloud, and dropped the floats back into the water. They bobbed around his feet and then slowly began to drift out, so slowly that he couldn't be sure if they were actually propelling themselves or if there was some kind of current.

Arthur watched the floats bob away and tried to plan what he was going to do next. But he still hurt all over—apart from the physical pain, he felt a great load of guilt.

I should've got Suzy to swim out with me. I wasn't thinking. I was too confident. No—I've got to stop obsessing. It's done now. I just have to rescue her. I'll have to challenge Saturday for the Key anyway. But she has too many sorcerers. So I should go back and get the Army. And Dame Primus, or Dame Quarto and Thingo or whoever. At least the other Keys. But if I do that, it might take too long . . .

The Will came planing back on one claw a few minutes later, while Arthur wrestled with his conscience, his fears and his half-formed plans.

'Almost there!' cawed the Will. 'Only part of a

claw and a tail feather to go!'

'Good,' said Arthur. 'As soon as you're ready, I guess we'd better go back to the Citadel—'

He stopped talking and cocked his head.

'What is it?' asked the Will. It was preening its wing feathers with its beak.

'The steam engines,' said Arthur. 'They sound closer.' He stood up and turned around. 'Closer and coming from a different direction.'

The Will stopped preening and looked out across the water with its beady black eyes.

'Steamship,' said Arthur. 'Or steamships. That's what I can hear.'

'I can see them!' said the Will. 'Look! Eight of them.'

Arthur stared out across the lake. There was too much steam and smoke, but even if he couldn't see anything, he could hear the rhythmic beat of the engines and the sound of the ship's wake. Finally one sharp bow thrust its way through the fog and he saw the front of a Raised Rat steamship, with rank after rank of Newniths mustered on the foredeck.

'The Piper!' said Arthur. 'We've got to get out of here!'

'So much sorcery!' said the Will. 'Saturday is bound to respond at any moment!'

'I think she already has,' said Arthur. He pointed up at the clouds of smoke above them. A huge ring of fire was beginning to form above the ships, a ring the size of an athletics track, easily five hundred yards in diameter. Flames began to fall from it, small flames at first, like fiery rain, but they began to get bigger and, from the way they changed colour from yellow-red to blue and white, much hotter.

The ships responded by increasing their speed. They were heading straight for the quay where Arthur was standing, their funnels belching smoke as their engines were stoked for maximum power.

'They're going to run aground right here!' said Arthur. 'Are you complete?'

'Not quite,' said the Will calmly. 'Just one short paragraph to go, but an essential one, to make a flight feather . . .'

'Hurry up,' Arthur urged. As the ships came closer, the ring of fire was moving too and the storm of incendiary rain was increasing in ferocity.

But it wasn't setting the ships alight, Arthur saw, or even hitting the Newnith soldiers on the decks. The rain was sliding off an invisible barrier that stretched from the masts of the ships down to the side-rails, a sorcerous barrier that was, for the moment, proving impervious to Saturday's attack.

We don't have that barrier, Arthur realised. *That fire is getting way too close . . .*

He could feel the heat of the flaming rain now, fierce on his face. The drops were so hot he could see them keep going for several feet underwater, unquenched, their fire lasting for much longer than it should.

'Are you ready?' Arthur snapped again. 'We have to run!'

'Almost, almost, almost there,' crooned the raven.

Fiery rain drops were hissing into the water ten feet away. The ships, steaming at full speed, were three hundred yards away. A group of soldiers pointed at Arthur and suddenly there were arrows in the air, which flew true but didn't make it through the firestorm.

'Done,' said the raven. It flew up and perched on Arthur's shoulder. 'I am complete. I am Part Six of the Will of the—'

Arthur didn't wait to hear any more. He turned and ran along the quay as fast as he could go, flames spattering on the stone behind him. Steam klaxons sounded too, and the war cries of the Newniths, which he knew all too well from the battles in the Great Maze.

Through all that noise, through the hammering of engines, the scream of klaxons, the hiss and roar of the firestorm, and the shouts, there was still that other sound. A clear and separate sound, beautiful and terrible to hear.

The sound of the Piper, playing a tune upon his pipes.

'Ah,' said the raven. 'The Architect's troublesome third son.'

'Troublesome!' Arthur snorted. 'He's a lot worse than that.'

The quay ended at a solid rock face with no obvious exits. Arthur stared at it for a second, then started to hunt for protuberances or bits of stone that looked out of place. He quickly found one, pressed it—and rushed in as the rock-slab door groaned open.

The cavern beyond was an equipment room, the walls covered with racks of many different metalworking tools, which at a different time would have interested Arthur. With the Piper's Army landing behind him, he barely spared them a glance.

'How do I lock the door?' he asked the Will, after he made sure there was another exit.

'I have no idea,' the Will replied.

'You've been here for the last ten thousand years! Haven't you learned anything?'

'My viewpoint has been rather limited,' the raven explained. 'Not to mention extremely fragmented.'

Arthur grabbed several long iron bars and propped them up against the door, kicking them down so they were wedged in place.

'That might last a few minutes,' he said. 'Come on!'

'Where are we going?' asked the Will.

'Out of here, for a start.' Arthur opened the far door and looked up a circular stairway made of wrought red iron that was decorated with gilded rosettes in its railings and on the steps. 'The Piper will take a while to land all his troops, but they'll send out scouting parties for sure, and I guess Saturday will send forces down. We have to stay out of the way of both.'

'Saturday may well be occupied high above,' said the Will. 'Her tower has reached the underside of the Incomparable Gardens and the Drasil trees are no longer growing taller.'

Arthur started running up the steps, taking three at a time. The raven flew behind him, occasionally alighting on his head.

'Why does she want to get into the Incomparable Gardens?' Arthur asked as he climbed.

'Because the Incomparable Gardens are the first place the Architect made, and so shall be the last to fall,' cawed the raven. 'But also because Saturday believes that she should have always ruled there. She envies Sunday and would supplant him.'

'Even if it means destroying the House?' asked Arthur. The stairway was winding up between walkways like the one where he and Suzy had arrived out of the Simultaneous Nebuchadnezzar.

It would be really easy to enter the Improbable Stair right now, he thought. *Going up these steps makes it really easy to visualise . . .*

'She believes the Incomparable Gardens would survive even if the rest of the House crumbles into Nothing,' said the raven. 'She may even be correct. Making the lower parts of the House fall was the only way she could stop the Drasils from growing.'

'So she'll get in? Can't Lord Sunday stop her?'

'I know nothing of Sunday's current capabilities,' said the Will. 'Nor his intentions. We must find and free Part Seven to help us with that. But first, of course, you must claim the Sixth Key from Saturday, the self-proclaimed Superior Sorcerer.'

'I know,' said Arthur. 'But how am I supposed to do that?'

'Where there's a Will there's a—'

'Shut up!' protested Arthur. 'I'm sick of hearing that.'

'Oh?' asked the Will. 'Heard it before? I do apologise.'

'How about something a bit more concrete?' asked Arthur. 'Like a plan or some intelligent advice for a change?'

'Hmm,' said the raven. 'I take it my lesser parts have not endeared themselves to you?'

'Not exactly,' said Arthur. 'Some bits are better than others. How long is this stair going to go up?'

'I do have a plan actually,' said the Will, after another fifty steps.

'OK, what is it?' Arthur wasn't even slightly out

201

of breath, despite running up so many steps. He still found that incredible.

'Your friend, the Piper's child—you want to attempt a rescue?'

'Yes,' said Arthur. *If Suzy's still alive . . .*

He stopped and the raven almost crashed into his face before managing to land on his shoulder. 'Are you sure you're part of the Will?' Arthur had to ask. 'The rest of you doesn't usually care much about . . . anyone really.'

'It's all part of my plan,' the Will assured him. 'You see, when I was suspended in the rain, I did get to visit many nooks and crannies that were rarely visited by anyone else. Including the hanging cages where they put prisoners.'

'Hanging cages?' Arthur didn't like the sound of that.

'Yes,' said the raven eagerly. 'Now on the south and west sides of the tower, there's all the big lifting apparatus and so on. On the north side it's completely sheer and undisturbed. I don't know why. But on the east side there are lots of small extensions, platforms, balconies, crane-jigs and such-like. Towards the top, around 61620, the Internal Auditors have a buttress that sticks out about fifty feet, and from that buttress they hang cages for prisoners. That's probably where your friend is now. Unless the Artful Loungers killed her straight off. They are vicious creatures, and those Nothing-poison daggers of theirs—'

'Let's assume she's alive,' Arthur interrupted. Then he hesitated before adding, 'I want to rescue her—but how would we get to these cages and not attract the attention of the Internal Auditors? There's going to be battle going on—maybe two battles . . .'

'That will help us,' said the Will. 'But as to how we get there, it's rather simple. We disguise ourselves as a Bathroom Attendant.'

'Ourselves?' asked Arthur. 'As a Bathroom Attendant?'

'Yes,' croaked the raven happily. 'You're almost tall enough to be a short Bathroom Attendant and I can make myself into the mask.'

'But why would a Bathroom Attendant go up there in the first place?'

Arthur shuddered as a he remembered the gold-masked faces of the Bathroom Attendants who had washed him between the ears, temporarily removing his memory.

'Because they're Internal Auditors,' explained the Will. 'I mean, all Bathroom Attendants are Internal Auditors, though not all Internal Auditors are Bathroom Attendants.'

'You mean they work for Saturday? *She's* the one who wants all the Piper's children's memories erased?'

'Yes, yes,' said the Will. 'It's all got to do with trying to delay the appearance of the Rightful Heir. Or, if you get knocked off, another one, and so on.'

'So we disguise ourselves as a Bathroom Attendant, get to the Internal Auditors' offices and rescue Suzy from the hanging cage. But how does that fit in with getting the Key from Saturday? Or anything else, for that matter?'

'Well, there shouldn't be any Internal Auditors there,' said the Will. 'They're Saturday's best troops, so they'll be up top, ready to fight their way into the Incomparable Gardens. Like I said, it's the east side, so it'll be the quiet side. We rescue your friend, then we watch the Piper's troops fight Saturday's troops and, at the right moment, you open an elevator shaft to the Citadel and bring your troops through.'

'I don't know how to open an elevator shaft,' said Arthur.

'It's easy—or at least it will be then, because all of Saturday's sorcerers that are stopping the elevators will be distracted. Or if they're not, you use the Fifth Key to take us out, we regroup and then come back the same way. How does that sound?'

'Dodgy,' Arthur said. 'But the disguise part might work. If I can just rescue Suzy and all three of us can get out, that's enough for now. I have to go back to Earth too. There's something important I need to—'

'Forget Earth!' insisted the raven. 'Earth will be all right. It's the House we have to worry about.'

'Isn't that the same thing?' asked Arthur. 'I mean if the House goes, everything goes.'

'Nope,' said the raven. 'Who told you that?'

'But . . . everyone . . .' stuttered Arthur. 'The Architect made the House and the Secondary Realms . . .'

'That's Denizens for you,' said the raven. 'She made most of the House after she made the Universe. I bet Saturday made up that 'Secondary Realms' stuff, the sly minx. The Architect made the House to observe and record what was happening out in the Universe because it was so interesting. Not the other way around.'

'Most of the House,' said Arthur intently. 'You said 'most of the House'.'

'Yes, well, the Incomparable Gardens were first out of the Void.'

'So they are the epicentre of the Universe? What happens if the Incomparable Gardens are destroyed?'

'Everything goes, end of creation, the jig's up.'

'So basically what everyone has been saying is true,' said Arthur. 'It just means that until the last bit—the first bit—of the House is destroyed then the rest of the Universe will survive.'

'I suppose so,' said the raven. 'If you want to get technical. Is that a door?'

It flew ahead, up through the middle of the spiral stair.

Arthur followed more slowly, deep in thought.

CHAPTER NINETEEN

'Wait! Don't open it' Arthur said, but it was too late. The raven had jumped on the handle and ridden it down, and then pushed the door open with its beak. On hearing Arthur's call, it turned around and looked back at him, with the door left ajar.

'Yes?'

Arthur reached the doorway and carefully looked through, out on to a paved square at the foot of the tower. There were two Sorcerous Supernumeraries only three or four feet away, fortunately standing with their backs to the door. Beyond them, the square was packed with a crowd of Denizens. There had to be at least two thousand of them, including hundreds of Sorcerous Supernumeraries and many more full sorcerers of varying ranks, all with their umbrellas folded despite the rain.

The Denizens had their backs to Arthur. They were all looking at a huge iron platform at the base of the tower. As broad and long as a football field, it was about twelve feet high. Made from thousands of plates riveted together, it looked like the deck of a very old battleship, with its hull and upper works sliced off.

Located next to the tower, the massive platform had a dozen twelve-foot-high bronze wheels along two sides. On each corner there were raised, open-roofed turrets packed with sorcerers.

But it wasn't the platform all the Denizens in the square were looking at. They were staring up at the construction that stood *on* the platform, which looked like a giant bullet. It was a cylinder several hundred feet high, with its bottom half solid bronze and its top half an open framework of bronze rods like a baroque birdcage. This caged section was divided into eight levels, which had woven wicker floors like in a balloon basket. The floors were connected by spindly metal ladders that ran up the full length of the cylinder, from the solid 'cartridge' part to the top of the open section.

A dozen of the octopoidal construction automatons perched on the top of the rocket or whatever it was, flexing their tentacles. In the air around them flew fifty or sixty grease monkeys, their wings fluttering. Most of them held shiny pieces of metal.

Like the watching Denizens, all the grease monkeys were looking up. Arthur couldn't help but look up too, though he also eased the door shut a bit, to make it harder for him to be seen.

Blinking aside a raindrop that fell into his eye, Arthur saw a shape so dark it had to be composed of Nothing. It was slowly descending out of the rain towards the bronze-wire cylinder, so slowly that at first it appeared to be levitating of its own accord. It was only after Arthur's eyes adjusted to its darkness that he saw faint lines of light upon its surface, traces made by the Immaterial ropes that were being used by several hundred flying Denizens to bring the object over to the bronze rocket.

The ropes were bright, but it was the dark shape that hurt Arthur's eyes. He immediately knew what it was: a spike of sorcerously-fixed Nothing, like the one that the Piper had used to stop the movement of the Great Maze. This one was much, much taller, though it was also more slender. Arthur figured it to be a hundred feet long, with an incredibly thin, sharp point at the top.

The flying Denizens lined the spike up with the cylinder of bronze wire. When this was done, there was a shouted order from one of their number and together they released the ropes. The spike fell straight down the remaining few feet and was caught by the automatons, whose tentacles were cased in some kind of protective coating that sparked and glowed as they handled the Nothing. They moved the spike around, shifting it to the right position, and lowered it into place. Immediately the grease monkeys moved in, fitting a collar of a sparkling translucent material— probably Immaterial glass—to hold the spike in place atop the cylinder.

'Saturday's vehicle to pierce the underside of the Incomparable Gardens,' said the Will, not quietly enough for Arthur's liking. He eased the door shut and turned on the raven.

'You need to be quieter and more careful,' he whispered. 'There are thousands of Denizens out there.'

'I thought I was being quiet,' said the Will, lowering its voice only a little. 'I haven't been this corporeal for ages. It's hard getting used to having a throat . . . and a beak.'

'Well, try harder to be quiet,' Arthur admonished.

'Very well,' croaked the raven, its voice so quiet that Arthur could barely understand it. 'All I wanted to say was that if that's Saturday's vehicle for piercing the garden, then it's likely that all the Denizens down here will get in it. And when they get in it, we can get going.'

'It must be the assault ram mentioned in Alyse's orders. And that's the Exterior Lift One or whatever it was called.'

'It doesn't matter what it's called,' said the Will. 'As long as it goes. The sooner Saturday starts fighting with Sunday, the better for us to sneak up the other side of the tower.'

'OK.' Arthur looked down at his ragged overalls and bare feet. 'I have to get some clothes.'

'No problem!' said the Will. Before Arthur could stop it, it hopped to the door, prised it open and hopped out, transforming as it did so into a small, extremely dishevelled grease monkey.

He heard the Will say something to the closest Denizen, who answered loud enough for not only Arthur to hear, but every other Denizen within twenty yards.

'You sure? Asked for me, by name? Woxroth?'

'Yes,' said the Will. 'That was it. Woxroth. Just go in there.'

Arthur pressed his back to the wall and wished that he'd set some firmer ground rules with the Will. He didn't even have his spanner, and he was wondering whether he could actually strangle the Denizen or just hit him with his fist when the Sorcerous Supernumerary came in, closely followed by the Will, who shut the door behind them.

The Supernumerary looked at Arthur, who raised both his hands, then his fist. When the Denizen just kept staring at him with a sad expression, Arthur lowered them again and said, 'I just want your coat, hat and boots. Hand them over.'

'What?' asked the Denizen. 'Haven't you got a letter for me?'

'No,' said Arthur. He could feel the frustrated anger rising inside him again, the temper that appeared when his will was thwarted by insignificant creatures. 'I am Arthur! Give me—'

There was a loud *thock* and the Denizen suddenly crumpled to the ground. The raven jumped off the back of his head and dropped the cobble it had just used to great effect.

'What were you talking to him for?' it asked. 'Should have just bopped him one.'

'I was going to,' protested Arthur as he bent down to take off the unconscious Denizen's coat. 'He just looked so sad and pathetic.'

The coat and boots adjusted themselves as Arthur put them on, but they weren't a bad fit to start with. Arthur looked down at himself and wondered if he'd grown even taller, possibly just in the last few minutes, because he needed to look like a Denizen. If the Will thought that he could pass for a Bathroom Attendant, he must now be almost six foot tall. Almost as tall as his basketball-star older brother Eric, he realised, a stab of melancholy passing through him.

Eric might already be dead; he'll die when the hospital is bombed and the city goes with it. I shouldn't be this tall, not for years yet. I feel like my old self is slipping away . . . faster and faster . . . and I can never be normal again.

He'd just finished dressing, had transferred his precious bag to his coat pocket and was picking up the black umbrella, when the door suddenly flung open. The Will, quick as a flash, transformed into a blanket and threw itself over the unconscious Denizen on the floor.

A sorcerer with a yellow umbrella looked in.

'Hurry up, idiot!' she shouted at Arthur. 'We're boarding the assault ram! Come on!'

She stood there, watching as Arthur pulled the brim of his hat lower to hide his face and eyes, and tried to think. When he didn't move, she scowled and gestured with her umbrella.

'We haven't got all day! I'll put you on report in a minute. Woxroth, isn't it?'

'Sorry,' mumbled Arthur. He started over to her, thinking that he might drag the Denizen inside and shut the door, and the Will could conk her with its cobble. But there were more sorcerers looking in from behind her, their attention drawn by her shouting. So instead he just stumbled out of the door. As he shut it behind him, he caught a flash of movement and shuddered as he felt the Will run up his sleeve in the shape of something like a

211

cockroach.

The waiting Denizens were no longer an unruly crowd, staring up at the bronze rocket. They were lining up in a long queue that zigzagged back and forth through the square. The head of the line was at the assault ram, and the Denizens there were climbing the external ladders on the solid bronze part and forming up in ranks on the different floors.

Arthur joined the line, the last in the long queue. The Denizen in front of him, another Sorcerous Supernumerary, looked back at him for a moment, but only gave a mournful sigh and trudged on. Arthur copied her pose, dragging his feet and keeping his chin tucked almost to his chest so his hat shielded his face.

It took quite a while to get to the rocket. Arthur had time to estimate the number of sorcerers climbing into the assault ram. By the time they all got on, he reckoned, there would be five thousand sorcerers on board. Most of them were full sorcerers too, some of them with umbrellas of gold and silver, which meant they were from higher levels he hadn't even seen. And right at the top, where they might have been all along, there were dozens of Denizens wearing the shiny satin top hats of Internal Auditors, the same as the ones the Piper had killed in Friday's eyrie in the Middle House. A contingent of Artful Loungers, in one of the middle levels, sat at the side of the rocket and kicked their legs through the bars.

As they approached the base of the ram, Arthur saw that there was a rainbow umbrella sorcerer checking everyone off a list. But even worse than that, there was also a very haughty-looking, seven-foot tall Denizen dressed in an immaculate silver tailcoat, night-black breeches and super-reflective boots. He had a dove-grey greatcoat of seven capes draped over his shoulders, and any raindrops that got within a few feet of this sizzled themselves out of existence.

It's got to be Saturday's Dusk, thought Arthur. *He'll spot me for sure . . . and then there's five thousand sorcerers here to finish me off.*

Trying to act casual, Arthur raised his hand to his face and scratched his nose. With his mouth partially covered, he hissed, 'Will!'

An albino cockroach with *Will* written on its back in red letters crawled up Arthur's wrist and into the palm of his hand.

Think to me, said the Will silently. *You don't need to talk.*

Oh yeah, replied Arthur. *I forgot. That's Saturday's Dusk up ahead. I think I need you to distract him. Take the shape of a Raised Rat maybe, and run away. Then you'd better rescue Suzy, because I'm not going to get the chance—*

You don't know that, the Will replied. *Also I don't think Saturday's Dusk will know you. There's too much sorcery around for him to sniff you out. That bronze thing there is reeking with it, not to mention the platform it's on. They've got two hundred and fifty executive-level sorcerers preparing to lift that thing, you know. Just keep your head down.*

I still want you to go and rescue Suzy! Arthur insisted. *Go now, while there's still a chance.*

No, said the Will into Arthur's head. *My job is to find the Rightful Heir and now that I have, I'm sticking with you. We might even get a chance at the Key. Anything can happen now, with the Piper's*

213

Army below and Sunday's insects above.

I want you to go and rescue Suzy! I order you to do so!

'Name?' asked the gold-umbrella sorcerer.

Arthur dropped his hand, and the Will ran up his sleeve.

'Uh, Woxroth,' muttered Arthur.

'Last and least,' said the sorcerer. 'Get up the ladder and find your place.'

As Arthur scrambled up the ladder, the sorcerer turned to Saturday's Dusk, who had fastened a monocle in his right eye and was staring at the paved floor.

'Loading almost complete, sir.'

'Not a moment too soon,' replied Dusk. 'The Piper's forces have finished landing and are moving up. Well, they may have the floor. They will not get far up the tower and we will soon be in the Gardens.'

'Are they as beautiful and wondrous as they say?' asked the sorcerer as he started to climb, with Dusk coming up after him. He was about fifteen feet behind Arthur and the boy could hear every word.

'We will soon see,' said Dusk. 'Time we began, I think.'

He held on to the ladder with one hand and cupped the other around his mouth, calling out to another gold-umbrella sorcerer who stood watching in the nearest corner cupola on the platform.

'Take her up!' shouted Dusk. 'All the way to the top!'

CHAPTER TWENTY

The Sorcerous Supernumeraries were on the lowest level of the rocket, immediately above the solid brass case. In between the holes in the wicker floor, Arthur could see the metal. He didn't want to think about what might be packed inside the lower half of the rocket. Some kind of propellant, he assumed. It was clear that the assault ram was going to be fired at the underside of the Incomparable Gardens, and the most likely place for that to happen was from the top of the tower.

Arthur was lucky to be one of the last aboard, because that meant his position was right up against the bars. The Denizens were packed in shoulder to shoulder, but he could turn around and see outside.

There was no talk among the sorcerers around

Arthur. He looked out through the bars at the sorcerers in one of the corner cupolas on the platform below him. They were slotting their gold and silver umbrellas into holes in the ironwork. When the umbrellas were set, they turned the handles sideways to make them into something like music stands, and all together they placed open books upon the handles and without any visible or audible signal, began to write with peacock-feather pens.

Arthur felt power in whatever they were writing. It made him feel slightly ill and itchy all over. As they wrote, the platform silently rose off the floor and began to climb up the side of the tower.

As it climbed, the Sorcerous Supernumeraries began to whisper to each other.

'We're all going to die.'

'I bet I die first.'

'We'll all die together.'

'We might not. We might just be horribly injured and demoted again.'

'You always look on the bright side, Athelbert.'

'No, I don't. I do expect to get killed.'

'Surprised they put us down here. Thought we'd be first to the slaughter.'

'Nah, waste of time putting us up front. Those big beetle-things'd cut the likes of us up in a trice.'

'What beetle-things?'

'Quiet!' roared an authoritative voice from somewhere further inside the packed Denizen ranks.

Arthur shivered as he felt a new surge of sorcery from the writing Denizens in the cupolas, and the platform rose faster. He was on the far side of the rocket from the tower, so he couldn't see exactly

216

how far they'd already risen, but looking down he guessed they'd already gone up about two or three hundred levels.

'How come you've got a bit shorter, Woxroth?' asked a Denizen behind Arthur's back.

'Extra demotion,' grunted Arthur.

Awed silence greeted this answer, followed by a muttered, 'And I thought I had it bad. Demoted and then killed by a beetle, all in one day.'

Optimistic lot, aren't they? said the Will into Arthur's mind.

They might be realistic, thought Arthur. *Do you have any suggestions about what I can do?*

Bide your time and look for any opportunity. Then take it.

That's really helpful.

'Sorcerers with a clear view to the exterior, stand ready!' ordered a voice from inside, the command echoed on the floors above.

The Denizens on either side of Arthur shuffled and pushed to get their folded umbrellas pointing out through the bars. Arthur copied them, though he didn't know why they were doing it.

'We're approaching 61600, top-out's at 61850. Be prepared for a counter-attack. If it's green and iridescent, shoot it!'

'Woxroth,' whispered the Denizen to Arthur's left. 'For the radiant eradication of matter, do we start by visualising a glowing ember or the tip of the flame of a candle? I can't recall exactly . . .'

'Uh, dunno,' Arthur mumbled. He was trying to make his voice low and miserable, like the real Woxroth.

'An ember of course,' said the Sorcerous Supernumerary to Arthur's right. 'Did you fail

217

everything?'

'Almost everything,' replied the left-hand Supernumerary. 'Hoo! What's that? Glowing ember, glowing ember . . .'

'Hold on,' said the right-hand Denizen. 'They're our lot. On this side anyway.'

Arthur stared out through the bars. The platform was lifting the rocket up at a faster rate than he'd thought, at least as fast as the moving chain he'd ridden. So it was hard to see, with the air rushing through the bars, the slight rocking motion of the rocket and the constant mild jostling of all the Denizens.

Several hundred feet above them and closing rapidly, the sky was criss-crossed with smoky trails and sudden, sparking lights that blossomed like silent fireworks in brilliant colours, lasting only a few seconds. All Arthur could hear was the breathing of the Denizens around him and the low hum of the moving platform.

The sparks were being fired up and out by thousands of flying Denizens, who formed a circular perimeter several hundred yards out from the tower, surrounding it. At first Arthur couldn't make out what they were casting their silent, sparking spells at, there was so much smoke and light in the sky. Then he saw a green tendril that had to be at least four hundred feet long and ten feet thick suddenly lash out of the cloud and strike a flyer who had dared to climb too high. The tendril cracked like a whip, and Arthur and all the Denizens flinched at the sudden noise and the sight of the tendril smashing the Denizen's wings. The lash must have terribly injured the sorcerer as well, for he or she fell like a lump, straight down.

'Lashed to bits by a weed, that'd be right,' said one of Arthur's neighbours.

'Nah,' said someone else. 'That's a good fifteen hundred feet up. They're going to fire this thing from the top, a bit short of weed-range, and we'll slice through those tendrils like a hot knife through a butter cake. Course, after that, we'll be easy pickings for the beetles.'

'I've never even seen a butter cake.'

Arthur only half-listened to the complaints behind and around him. He watched the tendril strike again, still flinching at the whip-crack even though he knew it was coming. But the Denizen who'd said they wouldn't get close was right. The platform had slowed down a lot and was now manoeuvring sideways. Arthur could feel less sorcerous energy being expended by the Denizens in the driving cupolas.

The platform was also rotating, Arthur saw as his view changed. The corner of the tower came into sight and then the entire side. They were level with the top now, the ground out of sight at least seventeen thousand feet below.

Here at its peak, the tower was much, much narrower than the levels Arthur had visited. The last fifteen levels were the narrowest, composed of only five offices a side. At the very top, right in the middle, there was a single, much larger office that was the size of four of the usual cubes. Though its frame was iron, it had clear crystal walls and a roof made of the same material.

Someone was inside this crystal office, watching the platform and the rocket slowly slide across towards . . . towards *her*, Arthur saw.

Superior Saturday. It had to be her. She looked

eight feet tall at least and Arthur couldn't tell if she had shining blonde hair or was wearing a metallic helmet. She was certainly wearing some kind of armour, a breastplate of red-gold that shone like the setting sun, and leg and arm armour made from plates in different shades of evening sunlight.

The platform was turning so that the door in the lowest level of the rocket was lined up with her office. The door that Arthur was standing next to. The door that Superior Saturday clearly intended to use . . .

'Make way! Let's have a path through!' called the commanding voice. Denizens pushed at Arthur, driving him away from the door, packing him in even tighter against his comrades as a path was cleared from the doorway through to the interior ladder that led up to the next level of the rocket.

A Denizen pushed back right into Arthur's face, but he didn't complain. He shifted a little to his right and peered through the two-inch gap between two sorcerers' shoulders in front of him.

Superior Saturday touched the wall of her office and the crystal fell away, shattering into motes of light that spun around and wove themselves into a pair of shining wings that fell upon her shoulders and flapped twice as she launched herself across the empty air to the aperture between the bronze bars that served as a door for the rocket. She landed as if she were dancing in a ballet, and strode through the crowd without a sideways glance at the Denizens who bent their heads and tried to bow, despite the cramped space and many painful cranial collisions.

There, in her hand! called the Will. *The Key. You could call to it. No, on second thoughts, best not yet.*

Definitely not, thought Arthur. He stood on tiptoe and craned his neck to see what it was that Saturday held in her hand. It wasn't an umbrella or even anything as large as a knife, just something slim and short . . .

It's a pen, thought Arthur. *A quill pen.*

He lost sight of it and Saturday as well, as she climbed up the interior ladder. The platform rose up some twenty or thirty feet and drifted across to line up with the middle of the tower. Then, with a flourish of peacock quill pens, the entire platform settled on top of the tower with the groan and shriek of iron upon iron. A minute later, dozens of automatons climbed up, and grease monkeys flew up from below, and started to fix the platform to the tower.

Arthur looked across and up. It was hard to estimate, but he thought the clouds were only eight or nine hundred feet above them, and the tendrils that were still snapping down could reach about three hundred feet. So they had a six-hundred-foot safety margin. Presumably the assault ram had to be this close in order to have a chance of breaking through the underside of the Incomparable Gardens.

Someone shouted far below. Arthur looked back down. The grease monkeys and the automatons were disappearing back under the platform.

'Brace for launch!' called out the commanding voice inside the rocket.

The Denizens around Arthur grabbed the bars, and the Denizens further in grabbed each other. Arthur took a firm grip on the closest bar and bent

221

his knees.

'Light the blue touchpaper!' called out the voice.

Arthur couldn't see exactly what happened then, but somewhere over in the middle of the rocket, there was a sudden eruption, a vertical jet of white-hot sparks that reached the wicker floor above but somehow did not set it alight.

'Five . . . four . . . three . . . two . . . one!' called the voice. 'Fire!'

There was a loud fizzling noise, and nothing happened.

'Fire?' repeated the voice, somewhat less commandingly.

'What is going on down there?' asked a clear, cold female voice that made Arthur shiver. 'Must I do everything myself?'

'No, milady,' called the first voice, which was now beseeching. 'There is a second touchpaper. I will light it myself.'

A minute later, there was another violent stream of sparks.

'Five . . . four . . . three . . . two . . . one . . . um . . .'

A violent force struck the rocket, sending every Denizen to his or her knees. Arthur was thrown from side to side, smacking into the sorcerers around him, their umbrella-handles smashing into his ribs and thighs.

Huge clouds of smoke billowed up and out, and the rocket stormed up from the platform, accelerating faster than anything Arthur had ever experienced before.

Four seconds later, he heard the terrible crack of a tendril from above, closely followed by several more.

Crack! Crack! Crack!

The rocket shook with each impact and the bronze cage rods rang like bells. The assault ram did not deviate from its course, straight up into the underbelly of the Incomparable Gardens.

'Brace! Brace for impact!'

The warning was too late for most of the Denizens. Very few were still on their feet, the floor around Arthur resembling a particularly crazy game of Twister.

When the assault ram struck, everyone hit the ceiling and bounced back down. Arthur was bashed by what he thought was every possible combination of elbows, knees, umbrella points and handles, and if he were still human, he knew he would have broken every bone in his body and probably had several stab wounds as well.

But he was not human, which was just as well, for a human mind would have had as hard a time as a human body. As the rocket sliced through the underside of the Incomparable Gardens, the interior became suddenly dark. Then, as some of the less addled Denizens began to make their umbrellas glow with coloured light, they saw rich dark earth spewing through the bars, earth that flowed in like water, threatening to drown and choke them.

'Ward the sides!' someone shouted. Umbrellas flicked open and Denizens began to speak spells, using words that lanced through Arthur's forehead, though it wasn't exactly pain that he felt.

The opened umbrellas and the spells stemmed the tide of earth. The rocket began to slow and the anxious Denizens below heard cheering and shouting above. Then the rocket stopped completely, with nothing but the rich earth to see around them.

'Top floor's through!' called out a Denizen from above. 'We've breached the bed!'

'Come on!' shouted someone else. 'To the ladders and victory!'

Arthur scrambled to his feet, umbrella in hand. He was barely upright before he was knocked down again by a Denizen who screamed as she fell, her hands desperately gripping a huge, toothy-mawed earthworm that had struck through the bars. The earthworm was at least part-Nithling, for its open mouth did not show a fleshy throat, but the darkness of Nothing.

Arthur stabbed the worm with the point of his umbrella.

Die! he thought furiously and at the same time. *Glowing ember . . . candle flame . . . whatever, just die!*

CHAPTER TWENTY-ONE

A six-foot-long flame of blazing, white-hot intensity struck the worm and ran along its length without touching the Denizen it was trying to eat. She continued to hold its ashy remains for a millisecond, then, as they blew apart in her hands, she clapped and said, 'Cor!'

'So *you* didn't fail advanced blasting,' said someone else. 'Still, something let you down, made you just like us . . . ow! Another one!'

Flames, shooting sparks and bolts of frost shot out of numerous umbrellas as more of the huge, toothy earthworms thrust through the bars. Denizens shouted and screamed and fought, many falling to Nothing-infested earthworm bites and strangulation, as well as each other's sorcery.

'Up! Up!' someone roared. 'We have to get clear! This is not the battle!'

'Could have fooled me,' grunted someone close by Arthur's ear as he blasted another striking worm back into the earth it came from.

'Up!'

Arthur obeyed the command, backing towards the interior ladder. The Denizens behind him and the Sorcerous Supernumeraries at his side had the luxury of turning around, but the worms kept coming in. A shrinking ring of Denizens and constant sorcerous attacks were all that kept them back.

Finally, there was only Arthur and four other Denizens around the base of the ladder, desperately flaming the boiling sea of worms that was writhing and arching towards them.

'We can't climb up—as soon as one goes, they'll get the rest of us!' said a Denizen. 'I knew it would end like this—'

'Shut up!' yelled Arthur. There were too many worms and his lances of flame could only kill a few at once.

There's so much sorcery happening here, he thought. *No one could possibly notice me add some more.*

Arthur reached into his coat pocket with his left hand while he batted at a worm with his umbrella, temporarily just a lump of metal and fabric. One-handed, he fumbled open the bag that held the Fifth Key, pushing two fingers in until he touched the cold, smooth glass of the mirror.

'By the power of the Fifth Key,' he whispered, so low that he could not even hear himself above the hideous frying sounds of burning worms, 'destroy all the worms about me. Make them as if they had never been!'

There was an intense flash of light, accompanied by a single pure note of the most beautiful music, and the worms were gone. Even the ash and the burned bits of worm-meat were gone as well, as if they had never existed.

'Right,' said Arthur. He could hear shouting, explosions, and the hissing sound of fire and destruction spells going on up above. 'Up!'

The other Denizens looked at him, then turned and climbed at a speed that would have won them approval from Alyse.

'They are more afraid of you than they are of the worms,' chuckled the Will. It flew out of Arthur's sleeve as a three-inch-long raven and grew to full size as it landed on his shoulder. 'I should wait a moment before going up. She knows you are here now.'

'What?' asked Arthur. 'But I thought, there is so much sorcery . . .'

'Not of the kind made possible by the Keys,' said the Will. 'But it is a good time. She is beset by Sunday's defenders. We will assail her when they have done their work. Best to wait here till then.'

'Here?' asked Arthur. As if in answer to his question, the whole rocket shuddered and the floor suddenly dropped several feet and lurched to one side.

'Maybe not,' conceded the raven. 'Quick! Up!'

Arthur went up the ladder and the next and the one after that so fast he almost felt like he was himself a rocket. But he had to slow down as he caught up with the line of Denizens. They were climbing quickly too, for the rocket was shaking

227

and shifting. Looking back down, where the floors were still illuminated by the fading light from the umbrellas of dead Denizens, Arthur saw that parts of the assault ram had fallen away . . . or had been torn off.

'Hurry up!' shouted the Denizen ahead of Arthur. 'The ram's falling apart!'

She looked down and hastily amended, 'I mean it's falling back down!'

Arthur looked. The lower floors of the rocket were no longer there. Instead there was a gaping, roughly rocket-sized hole and at the end of it there were wisps of cloud. A long way below that, he could see a fuzzy green lump that was the top of the tower.

'Hurry up!' screamed the Denizen again, and everyone did hurry up as more and more bits of the rocket fell away below them and went down through the hole to either strike the tower or perhaps make the even longer journey—all twenty-odd thousand feet to the floor of the Upper House.

Arthur burst out on the top floor of the ram like a bubble from the bottom of the bath. The Nothing spike was gone, consumed by its purpose in cutting a way through the bed of the Incomparable Gardens.

Except it hadn't quite cut all the way through, or rather the rocket hadn't. Arthur looked around quickly, blinking at the soft, mellow sunlight. The top of the ram was about twenty feet below the rim of the hole made by the spike. Some of the interior ladders from the rocket had been ripped off and propped against the earth. From the shouting and general tumult, Arthur figured that's where everyone had gone.

The floor fell under Arthur's feet, slipping down several yards. He ran for a ladder and jumped halfway up it. As the floor fell, Arthur sprinted up the rungs, taking four at a time. Three rungs from the top, he hurled himself up with all the energy and concentration of an Olympic high-jumper. The Will helped too, gripping his head and flapping with all its might.

Arthur just made it, landing on the rim of the hole with his legs dangling, his fingers clawing into soft green turf that threatened to give way. Then he was scrabbling forward to safety as the top floor of the assault ram and a dozen luckless Denizens fell away behind him.

Before Arthur could get his bearings, he was almost cut in two by a pair of giant elongated jaws. Desperately he rolled aside, thrusting his umbrella up at the twelve-foot-long iridescent green beetle that loomed over him.

The beetle grabbed the umbrella and crushed it to bits, which would have been a good tactic against a normal sorcerer. With Arthur, it just gave him time to get the Fifth Key out of the bag. He held it up, focused his mind upon it and the beetle inverted to become a mirror-image of itself. Then it dwindled like a receding star into a mere pinprick of light.

There were many more beetles, but none were close enough to do harm. Arthur took a few seconds to take stock.

He was standing on a wonderful green lawn of perfect, real turf. It was in the shape of an oval, at least a mile wide, and was surrounded by a low ridge of heather and wildflowers, surmounted by a fringe of majestic red and gold autumnal trees that blocked further sight.

Only a hundred yards away, there was a ring of large silver croquet hoops, and it was here that Saturday and her remaining forces were defending themselves against a tide of long-jawed beetles. A long line of mainly headless Denizen bodies led from the hole behind Arthur to the ring of hoops. There was quite a pile of bodies near Arthur, so he ran over and crouched down behind this makeshift wall. None of the beetles came after him.

'You're all right,' said a voice by Arthur's knee. He recoiled in horror as a Denizen head without a body scowled up at him. 'Typical. Everyone else always has the luck, with promotions and everything. We'd better win, is all I can say. Are we winning?'

'I don't know,' said Arthur. It was difficult to tell what was happening. There were still at least a thousand sorcerers, plus Saturday herself. They'd made a kind of shield-ring of open umbrellas, and from behind that they were shooting spells of fire and destruction, explosion and implosion, unravelling and transformation. But there were at least as many of the beetles, and they were ripping sorcerers out of the shield wall and pulling them apart with their long pincer jaws.

'She's winning this round,' said the Will. 'She's using the Key on them as well as ordinary sorcery. Look.'

Saturday loomed tall in the middle of her troops, with two almost-as-tall Denizens at her side. She held the Sixth Key almost casually, like an orchestra conductor might hold her baton. As Arthur watched, she carefully wrote something in the air. A line of cursive, glowing letters twined out of the pen to make a flowing ribbon in the air.

When Saturday finished writing and flicked the pen, the ribbon of words flew over the heads of her sorcerers and bored straight through first one beetle, then another and another and another, as if it were a thread flowing behind the needle of a quick-handed seamstress. Wherever it passed, whether through head or limb or carapace, the beetle fell to the ground and did not move again.

'I think now is the opportunity,' said the Will. 'Claim the Key. It will come to you when you call.'

'But she's still got a ton of sorcerers and those beetles are dropping like . . . like flies,' said Arthur.

'I know, but what else is there to do?' asked the Will. 'I told you I'm not so good with plans. Besides, she's going to notice us in a second.'

'Think. I have to think,' muttered Arthur. He looked around. Where could he go if he got the Key? The trees were too far away and probably housed more horrible insects. He had no idea what lay beyond them. He had no idea if Lord Sunday would intervene, and if he did, on whose side.

Saturday's use of the Sixth Key had already been decisive, in only a matter of seconds. At least half of Sunday's beetles lay dead or immobile around the ring of defensive umbrellas. More were falling, to the cheers of Saturday's sorcerers.

'She's noticed us,' said the Will. 'Sorry about that. I think I moved my wings too much.'

Saturday was staring straight at Arthur, and so were her two cohorts, her Noon and Dusk.

Arthur looked behind him and made a decision. Transferring the Fifth Key to his left hand in one swift motion, he held up his right hand and called out as loudly as he could.

'I, Arthur, anointed Heir to the Kingdom, claim the Sixth Key—'

Lightning flashed from Saturday's hand. It forked to her Noon and Dusk, and then forked again to the sorcerers around them, splitting again at the next lot of sorcerers. Within a second, it had a hundred branches, and then in another second, a thousand, the force of Saturday's spell multiplying exponentially. As all the branches left the last line of outer sorcerers, they combined back to form a lightning strike greater than any ever produced by a natural storm.

The bolt came straight at Arthur. He raised the mirror, thinking to divert or reflect it, but it was too strong. He was blasted off his feet and thrown back twenty . . . thirty feet . . . the Will cawing and shrieking at his side.

Arthur hit the dirt on the very edge of the hole. For a second he teetered there, on the brink. His hat fell off the back of his head and the Will grabbed his arm so hard that golden blood welled up under the bird's claws as its wings thrashed the air.

'And with it the Mastery of the Upper House,' shrieked Arthur as he finally lost his balance. 'I claim it by blood and bone and contest . . .'

He fell, but even as he fell, he called out, his words echoing up to Saturday and her sorcerers.

'Out of truth, in testament and against all trouble!'

CHAPTER TWENTY-TWO

Leaf had only managed to move twenty people when Martine came back. The older woman did not offer any explanation, or even talk. She just appeared as Leaf was grimly trying to lift one of the sleepers on to a bed, and took over. Leaf gratefully assumed the role of lifting legs as Martine heaved the sleepers up under the arms.

In an hour, they moved fifty people to the operating-theatre complex and Leaf began to hope that there was a chance they would move them all. It was a small hope, but it was better than the drear fatalism that earlier had sat like a cold weight in her chest.

They were moving the fifty-first, fifty-second and fifty-third sleeper when the clock started to turn over again.

'Oh no!' Leaf cried as she saw the display slowly—very slowly—transform from 11:58 to 11:59.

'It's still slower,' said Leaf. 'Time. It's moving slower. We have more than a minute. Maybe it'll be really slow; we can go back up—'

Martine pushed the bed with sudden energy, pushing harder than she had before, too fast for safety, sending it rocketing out into the corridor so that it collided none too gently with the far wall. She pushed Leaf too, as the girl hesitated, thinking that maybe, just maybe she could get back up and get a few more sleepers, save just a few . . .

The clock turned to 12:00.

Leaf and Martine ran for the bed.

'Arthur, you have to come back and stop this now!' Leaf shouted at the ceiling. 'You can't let this happen!'

Martine grabbed the bed and turned it towards the operating theatre. Leaf sobbed and bit back a cry and started to push.

They were halfway along the corridor when the ground shook and all the lights went out. The shaking continued for at least a minute, and there was a terrible rattle and bang of things falling, some of them foam ceiling insulation tiles that fell on Leaf.

Then the ground was still again. Leaf crouched in the darkness, by the bed, holding Martine's hand. She could not think of what she should do, her mind paralysed by what had happened.

'I can't believe they did it,' she said. 'And Arthur didn't come back. And we only saved . . . we only saved so few . . . I mean, to be saved from Friday, only to get killed without even waking up . . .'

'We don't know what's happened,' said Martine, her voice scratchy and unfamiliar. 'We'll have to find out.'

Leaf laughed, a hysterical giggle of fear and anxiety that she only just managed to get under control. As she stifled it, the green emergency lights slowly flickered on, illuminating Martine's face as she bent down to look at Leaf.

'I'm sorry I ran away,' said Martine. 'You're braver than I am, you know.'

'Am I?' asked Leaf. She choked back a sob that was threatening to come out. 'You came back.'

'Yes,' said Martine. 'I think Arthur will come back too.'

'He'd better!' snapped Leaf. She stood up and checked the three sleepers. They were fine, apart from having a fine coating of dust and a few fragments of broken insulation.

'You hear that, Arthur!' Leaf said, looking up at the exposed wiring above her head. 'You need to come back and fix everything up! You . . . need to come back!'

CATALOGUE OF SEALS

IN THE

NATIONAL MUSEUM OF WALES

CATALOGUE OF SEALS
IN THE
NATIONAL MUSEUM OF WALES

Vol. I.

Seal Dies, Welsh Seals, Papal *Bullae*

David H. Williams

AMGUEDDFA GENEDLAETHOL CYMRU
NATIONAL MUSEUM OF WALES

CARDIFF 1993

First published in 1993
© National Museum of Wales

Published by the National Museum of Wales
Cathays Park, Cardiff, CF1 3NP

ISBN 0 7200 0381 4

Production: Hywel G. Rees
Typesetting: Cloud Nine, Cardiff
Type: Baskerville
Printing: South Western Printers, Caerphilly

CONTENTS

ACKNOWLEDGEMENTS

The compiler wishes to record his gratitude to Dr Michael P Siddons for his assistance in giving of his expert knowledge of Welsh heraldry, as also to the several scholars who have corresponded with him. The work stems from a invitation in 1979 from Mr George C Boon (then Keeper of the Department of Archaeology and Numismatics) and Mr John M Lewis (formerly Assistant Keeper of Medieval and Later Antiquities) to list the seals held by the National Museum of Wales. My thanks are due to both, and to Dr Mark Redknap (present Medievalist) who has assisted in building up the collection and in the production of this book. The many photographs have been prepared by the Department of Photography under the leadership of Mr Kevin Thomas, while Mr Edward M Besly has kindly provided polaroid prints for study purposes. The maps and diagrams are the work of Mr Tony P Daly and Ms Jacqui Chadwick of the Department of Archaeology and Numismatics. The conservation laboratory of the Department, and especially Mrs Louise Mumford, have prepared impressions and casts from numerous recent seal-finds, which have been very helpfully brought into the Museum by their finders for examination and often generously donated by their owners. Mrs Monica Cox assisted in the early stages of typing the manuscript. Finally, I am grateful to the present Keeper of the Department of Archaeology and Numismatics, Dr Stephen H R Aldhouse-Green for his continued support, and to Mr Hywel G Rees, Head of Publications at the Museum, for seeing this work through the press.

David H. Williams

ABBREVIATIONS EMPLOYED

Acc. No. : Accession Number (giving date of accession to the Museum's collections). If the seal is not held in the Department of Archaeology and Numismatics, the location is given after the accession number in brackets.

Acc. File. : Accession File, Dept. of Archaeology and Numismatics.

- - -

R.O. : Record Office.

- - -

BL : British Library.

BM : British Museum.

Glam. Archives : Glamorgan Archives.

HCA : Hereford Cathedral Archives.

NLW : National Library of Wales.

NMW : National Museum of Wales.

PRO : Public Record Office (Chancery Lane).

SA : Society of Antiquaries of London.

UCNW : University College of North Wales (Bangor, Gwynedd).

WFM : Welsh Folk Museum (St. Fagan's).

- - -

HMSO : Her Majesty's Stationery Office.

RCAHM : Royal Commission on Ancient and Historical Monuments in Wales.

VCH : *Victoria County History of England.*

- - -

Anglesey Antiq. Soc. : Anglesey Antiquarian Society.

Antiq. : The Antiquary.

Antiq. Jnl. : The Antiquaries Journal.

Arch. : Archaeologia.

Arch. Ael. : Archaeologia Aeliana.

Arch. Camb. : Archaeologia Cambrensis.

Arch. Cant. : Archaeologia Cantiana.

Arch. Jnl. : Archaeological Journal.

B.B.C.S. : Bulletin of the Board of Celtic Studies.

BM : British Museum Seal No. (as given in Birch 1887-1900).

Chester Arch. Soc. : Chester Architectural and Archaeological Society.

Cymm. Rec. Soc.: Cymmrodorion Record Society.

D.N.B. : Dictionary of National Biography.

Gentl. Mag. : The Gentleman's Magazine.

J.B.A.A. : Journal of the British Archaeological Association.

Jnl. N.L.W. : Journal of the National Library of Wales.

Lincs. Rec. Soc. : Lincolnshire Record Society.

Monm. Antiq. : The Monmouthshire Antiquary.

Mont. Collns. : Montgomeryshire Collections.

Norf. Arch. : Norfolk Archaeology.

PRO (M) : Seal Number accorded in Ellis (1986).

PRO (P) : Seal Number accorded in Ellis (I, 1978; II, 1981).).

Proc. Arch. Inst. Norwich : Proceedings of the Archaeological Institute of Norwich.

Proc. Soc. Antiq. : Proceedings of the Society of Antiquaries of London.

Trans. Shrops. Arch. Soc. : Transactions of the Shropshire Archaeological and Natural History Society.

Trans. Carms. Antiq. Soc. : Transactions of the Carmarthenshire Antiquarian Society.

Trans. Hon. Soc. Cymm. : Transactions of the Honourable Society of the Cymmrodorion.

Trans. Neath Antiq. Soc. : Transactions of the Neath Antiquarian Society.

Trans. Radn. Soc. : Transactions of the Radnorshire Society.

Y Cymm. : Y Cymmrodor.

- - -

Shape:

circ. : circular.

o. : oval.

p.o. : pointed oval.

References:

D: : Description or Notes, in other works.

E: : Other Examples of Original Impressions.

The Legend:

Bl. : Black Letter (Gothic) Script.

Caps. : Modern Capitals.

Lom. : Lombardic Capitals.

Pseudo-. : Imitation characters.

Ren. : Renaissance Capitals.

Rom. : Roman Capitals.

BIBLIOGRAPHY

Atkins and Margery (1985) : Atkins, M. and Margery, S., *Life on a Medieval Street* (Norwich Survey, 1985).

Banks and Dineley (1888) : Banks, R.W. and Dineley, T., *Official Progress of the Duke of Beaufort through Wales, 1684* (London, 1888).

Barber and Lewis (1901) : Barber, H. and Lewis, H., *History of Friars School, Bangor* (Bangor, 1901).

Barnard (1930) : Barnard, F.P., 'The Rawlinson Collection of Seal Matrices', *Bodleian Quarterly Record*, (1930, 2nd Qtr) VI.

Bedford (1897) : Bedford, W.K.R., *Blazon of Episcopacy* (Oxford, 1897 edn.).,

Bennett and Lawson (1906) : Bennett, J.H.E., and Lawson, P.H., 'An Index to the Wills Proved at the Peculiar Court of Hawarden', *Flintshire Hist. Soc. Publns.* 4 (1906).

Bertrand (1851): Bertrand, F., 'Sceau de l'Abbé et du Couvent du Mont Saint-Eloy', *Receuil de la Société de Sphragistique de Paris* I (1851).

Beverley Smith (1970) : Beverley Smith, J., 'The Middle March in the Thirteenth Century', *B.B.C.S.* XXIV: 1 (Nov. 1970).

Biddle (1990) : Biddle, M., *Object and Economy in Medieval Winchester* (Oxford, 1990).

Birch (1870) : Birch, W. de Gray., 'On the Great Seal of James I', *J.B.A.A.* XXVI (1870).

Birch (1872) : - - - ., 'On the Great Seals of King William II', *J.B.A.A.* XXVIII (1872).

Birch (1873) : - - - ., 'On the Great Seals of Henry I', *J.B.A.A.* XXIX (1873).

Birch (1876) : - - - ., 'Notes on the Seal of Simon de Montfort', *J.B.A.A.* XXXII (1876).

Birch (1887-1900) : - - - ., *Catalogue of Seals in the British Museum* (London, 6 vols. 1887-1900). *(This work does not include British non-armorial seals, for which reference should be made to the manuscript catalogues - as those of Doubleday and Laing; the Keeper of the Dept. of MSS (British Library) holds information as to seals acquired since Birch compiled his catalogue).*

Birch (1889) : - - - ., 'On Some MSS and Seals relating to Wales', *Arch. Camb.* 5th Ser. VI (No. XXIV, 1889).

Birch (1893-1905) : - - - ., *Descriptive Catalogue of the Penrice and Margam Manuscripts* (London, 4 vols. 1893-1905).

Birch (1897) : - - - ., *Margam Abbey* (London, 1897).

Birch (1902) : - - - ., *Neath Abbey* (Neath, 1902).

Birch (1912) : - - - ., *Memorials of Llandaff* (Neath, 1912).

Bishop and Chaplais (1957) : Bishop, T.A.M. and Chaplais, P., *English Royal Writs* (Oxford, 1957).

Blomefield (1741) : Blomefield, E.H., *History of City and County of Norwich* (1741).

Bloom (1906) : Bloom, J.H., *English Seals* (London, 1906).

Boon (1966) : Boon, G.C., 'Seal Matrix of Abergwili College, Carmarthenshire', *Antiq. Jnl.* 46 (1966).

Boon (1966a) : - - ., 'Leaden Sealing' in Lewis, J.M., 'Post-Roman Finds', *Monm. Antiq.* II: 2 (1966).

Boon (1983) : - - - ., 'Medals of the Anglesey Druidical Society', *Arch. Camb.* CXXXII (1983).

Boutell (1905) : Boutell, C., *English Heraldry* (London, 1905).

Boutell (1958) : - - - ., *Heraldry* (London, 1958 edn., revised by C.W. Scott-Giles).

Boys (1792) : Boys, C.W., *History of Sandwich* II (Canterbury, 1792).

Bradney (1904-33) : Bradney, J., *History of Monmouthshire* (London, 4 vols., 1904-33).

Brindley (1938) : Brindley, H.H., *Catalogue of Seals in the National Maritime Museum* (Greenwich, 1938).

Bullard (1934) : Bullard, J.V., *Constitutions and Canons Ecclesiastical, 1604* (London, 1934).

Burke (1847) : Burke, J., *General Armoury* (London, 1847, 3rd edn.).

Burtt (1872) : Burtt, J., 'The Muniments of the Abbey of Westminster', *Arch. Jnl.* XXIX (1872).

Canivez (1933-41) : Canivez, J.-M., *Statuta Capitulorum Generalium Ordinis Cisterciensis* (Louvain, 1933-41).

Cardwell (1892): Cardwell, E., *Synodalia* I (Oxford, 1892).

Carlisle (1818) : Carlisle, N., *Endowed Grammar Schools* II (London, 1818).

Carr (1982) : Carr, A.D., *Medieval Anglesey* (Llangefni, 1982).

Charles (1967) : Charles, B.G., *Calendar of the Records of the Borough of Haverfordwest (1539-1660)*, (Cardiff, 1967).

Cherry (1990) : Cherry, J., 'The seal matrix of Henry, Prince of Wales', *Antiq. Jnl.* LXX : II (1990).

Cherry (1992) : Cherry, J., 'The Breaking of Seals', *Medieval Europe* (1992) (pre-printed papers) Vol. 7.

Cherry and Redknap (1991) : - - . and Redknap, M., 'Medieval and Tudor Finger Rings', *Arch. Camb.* CXL (1991).

Clark (1910) : Clark, G.T., *Cartae de Glamorgan* (Cardiff, 6 vols. 1910).

Clarke-Maxwell (1929) : Clarke-Maxwell, Preb., 'Some Further Letters of Fraternity', *Arch.* LXXIX (1929).

Clarke and Williams (1992) : Clarke, S.J. and Williams, David H., 'A Personal Seal from Monmouth', *Monm. Antiq.* VIII (1992).

Clay (1928) : Clay, C.T. 'Seals of the Religious Houses of Yorkshire', *Arch.* LXXVIII (1928).

Corbett (1906) : Corbett, J.S., *Seal and Arms of Cardiff* (Cardiff Centr. Libr. MS 4.969 of 1906).

Coxe (1801) : Coxe, W., *Historical Tour through Monmouthshire* (London, 1801).

Cranmer (1641) : Cranmer, T., *Reformatio Legum* (London, 1641 edn. of this 1571 work).

Cronne and Davis (1968) : Cronne, H.A. and Davis, H.W.C., *Regesta Regum Anglo-Normannorum* (Oxford, 1968 edn.).

Davies (1979) : Davies, M.H., 'A Deed of Penmon Priory', *Jnl. N.L.W.*, XXI: 1 (Summer, 1979).

Delisle (1851) : Delisle, L., *Etudes sur la Classe Agricole en Normandie* (Evreux, 1851).

Demay (1880) : Demay, G., *Le Costume au Moyen Age d'apres Les Sceaux* (Paris, 1880).

Dillwyn (1840) : Dillwyn, L.W., *Contributions towards a History of Swansea* (Swansea, 1840).

Dineley (1888) : Dineley, T., *Progress of the Duke of Beaufort through Wales in 1684* (London,1888 edn.).

Donovan (1805) : Donovan, E., *Descriptive Excursions through South Wales* I (London, 1805).

Douce (1817) : Douce, F., 'Some Remarks on the Original Seal belonging to the Abbey of Wilton', *Arch.* XVIII (1817).

Douët D'Arcq (1868) : Douët D'Arcq, M., *Collection Des Sceaux De L'Empire* III (Paris, 1868).

Drake (1736) : Drake, F., *Eboracum* (London, 1736).

Druce (1911) : Druce, G.C., 'Notes on the Heraldic Jall or Yale', *Arch. Jnl.* LXVIII (1911).

Du Fresne (1736) : Du Fresne, C., *Glossarium* VI (Paris, 1736).

Dugdale (1846) : Dugdale, W., *Monasticon Anglicanum* (London, 1846 edn.).

Durrant Cooper (1860) : Durrant Cooper, W., 'Notes on the Great Seals between 1648 and 1660', *Arch.* XXXVIII: 1 (1860).

Ebblewhite (1895) : Ebblewhite, E.A., 'Flintshire Genealogical Notes', *Arch. Camb.* L (1895).

Edwards (1868) : Edwards, E., *The Life of Sir Walter Ralegh together with his Letters* II (London, 1868).

Edwards (1935) : Edwards, J.G., *Calendar of Ancient Correspondence Concerning Wales* (Cardiff, 1935).

Edwards (1940) : - - - ., *Littere Wallie* (Cardiff, 1940).

Egan (1985) : Egan, G., *Leaden Cloth Seals* (Finds Research Group Datasheet 3: Coventry, 1985).

Egan (1991) : - - ., 'Alnage Seals and the National Coinage', *British Numismatic Jnl.* 61 (1991).

Ellis (1817) : Ellis, H., 'Observations on the History and Use of Seals in England', *Arch.* XVIII (1817).

Ellis (1978) : Ellis, R.H., *Catalogue of Seals in the Public Record Office: Personal Seals* I (H.M.S.O. 1978).

Ellis (1981) : - - - ., *Personal Seals* II (H.M.S.O. 1981).

Ellis (1986) : - - - ., *Monastic Seals* I (H.M.S.O. 1986).

Emanuel (1947) : Emanuel, H., 'A Document relating to the Monastery of Caerleon', *Jnl. N.L.W.* V (1947-8).

Endrei and Egan (1982) : Endrei, W. and Egan, G., 'The Sealing of Cloth in Europe', *Textile History* 13: 1 (1982).

Evans (1927) : Evans, D.L., 'Some Notes on the History of the Principality of Wales', *Trans. Hon. Soc. Cymm.* (for Year, 1925-6; publ. 1927).

Evans (1928) : Evans, A.O., 'Nicholas Robinson', *Y Cymm.* XXXIX (1928).

Ewe (1972) : Ewe, H., *Schiffe auf Siegeln* (Berlin, 1972).

Eyre Evans (1902) : Eyre Evans, G., *Aberystwyth and its Court Leet* (Aberystwyth, 1902).

Eyre Evans (1919) : - - ., 'Geoffrey De Hennelawe', *Trans. Carms. Antiq. Soc.* XIV (1919-21).

Eyre Evans (1936) : - - ., 'Seal of Sir Rhys ap Thomas (1494)', *Trans. Carms. Antiq. Soc.* 26 (1936).

Forrer (1902-30) : Forrer, L., *Biographical Dictionary of Medallists* (London) I (1902), II (1904), III (1907), IV (1909), V (1912), VI (1916).

Foster (1904) : Foster, J., *Some Feudal Lords and their Seals* (De Walden Library, 1904).

Fox-Davies (1915) : Fox-Davies, A.C., *Book of Public Arms* (London, 1915).

Fowler (1925) : Fowler, R.C., 'Seals in the Public Record Office', *Arch.* 74 (1925).

Francis (1867) : Francis, G.G., *Charters granted to Swansea* (London, 1867).

Fryde (1974) : Fryde, N., *List of Welsh Entries in the Memoranda Rolls, 1282-1343* (Cardiff, 1974).

Gardner (1754) : Gardner, *Historical Account of Dunwich* (London, 1754).

Gatfield (1892) : Gatfield, G., *Guide to Heraldry and Genealogy* I (London, 1892).

Gough (1780) : Gough, R., *British Topography* I (London, 1780).

Gresham (1971) : Gresham, C.A., 'A Lease from the Last Prior of Bethkylhert', *Jnl. N.L.W.* XVII (1971-2).

Griffiths (1972) : Griffiths, R.A., *The Principality of Wales* (Cardiff, 1972).

Griffiths (1978) : - - -., *Boroughs of Medieval Wales* (Cardiff, 1978).

Hamper (1821) : Hamper, W., 'On the Seal of Evesham Abbey', *Arch.* XIX (1821).

Harmer (1952) : Harmer, F.E., *Anglo-Saxon Writs* (Manchester, 1952).

Hemp (1922) : Hemp, W.J., 'The Town Seal of Haverfordwest', *Arch. Camb.* LXXVII (1922).

Hemp (1939) : - - -., 'Five Welsh Seals', *Arch. Camb.* XCIV (1939).

Heslop (1986) : Heslop, T.A., 'Cistercian Seals in England and Wales', Norton, C. and Park, D. (edit.) *Cistercian Art and Architecture in the British Isles* (Cambridge, 1986).

Hope (1885) : Hope, W.H. St. John., 'Seals of the Colleges and University of Cambridge', *Proc. Soc. Antiq.* 2nd Ser. X (1885).

Hope (1893) : - - - ., 'The Seals of Archdeacons', *Proc. Soc. Antiq.* 2nd Ser. XV (1893).

Hope (1895) : - - - ., 'On the Municipal Seals of England and Wales', *Proc. Soc. Antiq.* 2nd Ser. XV (1895).

Hope (1895a) : - - - ., 'English Municipal Heraldry', *Arch. Jnl.* LII (1895).

Hopkin-James (1922) : Hopkin-James, L., *History of Old Cowbridge* (Cowbridge, 1922).

Howlett (1821-7) : Howlett, B., *Drawings of Welsh Ecclesiastical Seals* (Cardiff Centr. Libr. MS 4.335).

Hughes (1860) : Hughes, W., 'Welsh Gentlemen Serving in France', *Arch. Camb.* XV (1860).

Hunter Blair (1920) : Hunter Blair, C.H., 'A Note upon Medieval Seals', *Arch. Ael.* 3rd Ser. XVII (1920).

Hunter Blair (1927) : - - - ., 'Post-Reformation Ecclesiastical Seals of Durham', *Arch.* LXXVII (1927).

Hunter Blair (1943) : - - - ., 'Armorials on English Seals', *Arch.* LXXXIX (1943).

Hutchins (1861): Hutchins, J., *History of Dorsetshire* (London, 4 vols. 1861-70).

Isaacson (1917) : Isaacson, R.F., *Episcopal Registers of St. David's* (3 vols. Cymm. Rec. Soc. 1917-20).

Jacob (1774) : Jacob, E., *History of Faversham* (London, 1774).

Jeffreys Jones (1955) : Jeffreys Jones, T.I., *Exchequer Proceedings Concerning Wales* (Cardiff, 1955).

Jenkinson (1935) : Jenkinson, H., 'The Great Seal of England: Deputed or Departmental Seals', *Arch.* LXXXV (1935).

Jewitt and Hope (1905) : Jewitt, Ll. and Hope, W. H. St. John., *Corporation Plate* I (London, 1905).

Johnson (1720) : Johnson, J., *Collection of Ecclesiastical Laws* (London, 1720).

Jones (1871) : Jones, M.C., 'Abbey of Ystrad Marchell', *Mont. Collns.* IV (1871).

Jones (1883) : - - -., 'Seal of the Commissary of the Deanery of Arustley', *Mont. Collns.* XVI (1883), *Arch. Camb.* (1884).

Jones and Lloyd (1890a) : Jones, M.C. and Lloyd, W.V., 'The Seal of Montgomeryshire County Council', *Mont. Collns.* XXIV (1890).

Jones and Lloyd (1890b) : - - - - - .., 'County Council Seals of Wales', *Mont. Collns.* XXIV (1890).

Jones (1934) : Jones, E.A., 'The Nevin Borough Silver Seal', *Arch. Camb.* LXXXIX (1934).

Jones (1947) : Jones, E.D., 'Five Strata Marcella Charters', *Jnl. NLW.*, V : 1 (Summer, 1947).

Jones (1949) : Jones, F., 'Welsh Bonds for Keeping the Peace', *B.B.C.S.* XIII: 3 (Nov. 1949).

Kelly (1990) : Kelly, D.B., 'Archaeological Notes from Maidstone Museum', *Arch. Cant.* CVIII (1990).

King (1777) : King, E., 'The Great Seal of Ranulph, Earl of Chester', *Arch.* IV (1777).

Kingsford (1929) : Kingsford, H.S., 'Epigraphy of English Medieval Seals', *Arch.* LXXIX (1929).

Kingsford (1941) : - - - -., 'Some English Medieval Seal-Engravers', *Arch. Jnl.* XCVII (1941).

Laing (1850) : Laing, H., *Descriptive Catalogue of Impressions from Ancient Scottish Seals* (Edinburgh, 1850).

Laing (1866) : - - .., Supplemental *Descriptive Catalogue of Ancient Scottish Seals* (Edinburgh, 1866).

Lane Poole (1934) : Lane Poole, R.L., *Studies in Chronology and History* (edit. Lane Poole, A.L., Oxford, 1934).

Laws (1888) : Laws E., *Little England beyond Wales* (London, 1888).

Lee (1862) : Lee, J.E., *Isca Silurum* (London, 1862).

Lewis (1740) : Lewis, J., *A Dissertation on the Antiquity and Use of Seals in England* (London, 1740).

Lewis (1831) : Lewis, S., *Topographical Dictionary of England* (London, 1831).

Lewis (1833) : - - .., *Topographical Dictionary of Wales* (London, 1833).

Lewis (1968) : Lewis, J.M., 'Two Stone Seal-Dies from the Knighton Area', *Trans. Radn. Soc.* XXXVIII (1968).l

Lewis and Davies (1954) : Lewis, E.A. and Davies, J.C., *Records of the Court of Augmentations Relating to Wales* (Cardiff, 1954).

Llewellyn Williams (1916) : Llewellyn Williams, W., 'The King's Court of Great Sessions in Wales', *Y Cymm.* XXVI (1916).

Lloyd (1887) : Lloyd, J.Y.W., *Powys Fadog* V (London, 1887).

Lloyd (1935) : Lloyd, J.E., *History of Carmarthenshire* I (Cardiff, 1935).

Lloyd Parry (1909) : Lloyd Parry, H., *The Exeter Civic Seals* (Exeter, 1909).

Longueville Jones (1848) : Longueville Jones, H., 'Penmon Priory', *Arch. Camb.* III (1848).

Luard (1874) : Luard, H.R., *Matthew Paris: Chronica Maiora* (London, 1872-84).

Madden (1866) : Madden, T.F., *Matthaei Parisiensis: Historia Anglorum* (London, 1866-69).

Makower (1895): Makower, F., *Constitutional History of the Church of England* (London, 1895).

Marchegay (1879) : Marchegay, P., *Les Prieures Anglais De Saint-Florent Près Saumur* (Les Roches-Baritaud, Vendée, 1879).

Maskell (1872) : Maskell, W., *Description of the Ivories Ancient and Medieval in the South Kensington Museum* (London, 1872).

Massie (1857) : Massie, W.H., 'Remarks on the History of Seals', *Chester Archit. Soc.* I (1857).

Matthews (1898-1911) : Matthews, J.H., *Records of the County Borough of Cardiff* (Cardiff; 6 vols. 1898-1911).

Matthews (1910): Matthews, T., *Welsh Records in Paris* (Carmarthen, 1910).

Maxwell-Lyte (1926) : Maxwell-Lyte, H.C., *The Great Seal* (H.M.S.O., 1926).

Mein (1992) : Mein, A.G., 'A medieval Seal Mould', *Monm. Antiq.* VIII (1992).

Meyrick (1907) : Meyrick, S.R., *History of Cardiganshire* (Brecon, 1907 edn.).

Morgan (1885) : Morgan, O., 'On the Early Charters of the Borough of Newport', *Arch.* 48: 2 (1885).

Morgan (1966) : Morgan, F.C. and P.E., *A Concise List of Seals of Hereford Cathedral* (Publn. Woolhope Naturalists Field Club, Hereford; 1966).

Nelson (1936) : Nelson, P., 'Some British Medieval Seal-Matrices', *Arch. Jnl.* XCIII (1936).

Nicholas (1827): Nicholas, N.H., 'Seals attached to the Letter from the Barons of England to Pope Boniface the Eighth', *Arch.* XXI (1827).

Nichols (1846) : Nichols, J.G., *Topogr. and Geneal.* I (1846).

Ollard and Crosse (1919) : Ollard, S.L. and Crosse, G., *Dictionary of Church History* (London, 1919 edn.).

Oliver (1908) : Oliver, A., 'Municipal Seals exhibited at the Weymouth Congress', *J.B.A.A.* LXIV (1908).

Owen (1892) : Owen, George., *Description of Pembrokeshire* I (Publns. Cymm. Rec. Soc. I; London, 1892).

Owen (1906) : - - - ., *ibid.* III (1906).

Owen (1949) : Owen, H.J., 'Merionethshire Coat of Arms', *Jnl. Merioneth Hist. and Rec. Soc.* I (1949-51).

Owen and Blakeway (1825) : Owen, H. and Blakeway, J.B., *History of Shrewsbury* (London, 1825).

Owen Edwards (1929) : Owen Edwards, I. ab., *Catalogue of Star Chamber Proceedings Relating to Wales* (Cardiff, 1929).

Papworth (1874): Papworth, J.W., *Ordinary of British Arms* (London, 1874).

Pearson (1979) : Pearson, F., *Goscombe John* (National Museum, Cardiff; 1979).

Pedrick (1902) : Pedrick, Gale, *Monastic Seals of the Gothic Period* (London, 1902).

Pedrick (1904) : - - - ., *Borough Seals of the Gothic Period* (London, 1904).

Perceval (1877) : Perceval, C.S., 'On the seals under the Statute Merchant', *Proc. Soc. Antiq.* 2nd Ser. VII (1877).

Perceval (1881) : - - - ., 'Admiralty Seal of Richard, Duke of Gloucester, *Arch.* XLVI (1881).

Pettigrew (1856): Pettigrew, T.J., 'Notes on the Seals of the Endowed Grammar Schools': I, *J.B.A.A.*, XII (1856).

Pettigrew (1858): - - - ., Ibid. II, *J.B.A.A.* XIV (1858).

Pettigrew (1861): - - - ., 'On the Seals of Richard, Duke of Gloucester, and other Admirals of England', *Collectanea Archaeol.* I (London, 1861).

Phillip (1982-3) : Phillip, P., 'Seal of Neath Abbey', *Trans. Neath Antiq. Soc.* (1982-3).

Powell (1964) : Powell, A.D., 'Brilley Remembrance, 1590', *Trans. Radn. Soc.* XXXIV (1964).

Price (1900) : Price, P., 'The Arms of Cardiff', *Arch. Camb.* LV (1900).

Price (1952) : Price, G.V., *Valle Crucis Abbey* (Liverpool, 1952).

Price (1977) : Price, D.T.W., *History of St. David's University College, Lampeter* I (Cardiff, 1977).

Pritchard (1907): Pritchard, E.M., *History of St. Dogmael's Abbey* (London, 1907).

Randolph (1905) : Randolph, J.A., *Welsh Abbeys* (Carmarthen, 1905).

Rawlinson (1720) : Rawlinson, R., *English Topographer* (London, 1720).

Ready (1860) : Ready, R., 'Catalogue of Seals connected with Wales', *Arch. Camb.* (1860).

Rees (1975) : Rees, W., *Calendar of Ancient Petitions Relating to Wales* (Cardiff, 1975).

Riley (1868) : Riley, H.T., *Memorials of London Life* (London, 1868).

Rogers (1943) : Rogers, W.C., *The Swansea and Glamorgan Calendar*, Pt. I, Vol.2 (Swansea; typescript; 1943).

Round (1894) : Round, J.H., 'Introduction of Armorial Bearings into England', *Arch. Jnl.* LI (1894).

Round (1899) : - - - ., *Cal. of Documents in France* I (H.M.S.O., 1899).

Round (1964) : - - ., *Feudal England* (London, 1964 edn.).

Sayers (1957) : Sayers, R.S., *Lloyds Bank* (Oxford, 1957).

Scott-Giles (1933) : Scott-Giles, C., *Civic Heraldry* (London , 1933).

Scott-Giles (1953) : - - - ., *ibid*. (London, 2nd edn. 1953).

Sella (1937) : Sella, P., *I Sigilli dell' Archivio Vaticano* (Vatican City, 1937-46).

Siddons (1981) : Siddons, M., 'Welsh Seals in Paris', *B.B.C.S.* XXIX: 2 (Nov. 1981).

Siddons (1984) : - - ., 'Welsh Equestrian Seals', *Jnl. NLW* 23 (1983-84).

Siddons (1985) : - - ., 'Welsh Seals in Paris: Additions and Corrections', *B.B.C.S.* XXXII (1985).

Siddons (1989) : - - ., 'Welsh Seals in Paris: Further Additions', *B.B.C.S.* XXXVI (1989).

Siddons (1989a) : - - ., 'Welshmen in the Service of France', *ibid*.

Siddons (1991) : - - ., 'Heraldic Seals in the Gwent Record Office', *Monm. Antiq.* VII (1991).

Siddons (1991a) : - - ., *The Development of Welsh Heraldry* I (National Library, Aberystwyth, 1991).

Stanford London (1959) : Stanford London, H., 'The Greyhound as a Royal Beast', *Arch.* 97 (1959).

Storey (1969) : Storey, A., *Trinity House of Kingston-upon-Hull* II (Hull, 1969).

Surtees (1816) : Surtees, R., *County Palatine of Durham* (London, 1816-40).

Syer Cuming (1870) : Syer Cuming, H., 'On Dated Seals', *J.B.A.A.* XXVI (1870).

Syer Cuming (1871) : - - - ., 'Antiquities in the Possession of the Corporation of Dover', *J.B.A.A.* XXVII (1871).

Syer Cuming (1872) : - - - ., 'On Seals of the Corporation of Canterbury', *J.B.A.A.* XXVIII (1872).

Taylor (1890) : Taylor, H., 'The Arms of Flintshire', *Arch. Camb.* XLV (1890).

Taylor (1925) : - - ., 'The Arms of Flintshire', *Flintshire Hist. Soc. Publns.* 11 (1925).

Taylor (1935) : Taylor, G.A., 'Neath Borough Seals', *Neath Corporation* (Neath, 1935).

Taylor (1977) : Taylor, A.J., 'A Fragment of a *Dona* Account, 1284', *B.B.C.S.* XXVII: 2 (1977) 253.

Thomas (1908) : Thomas, D.R., *History of the Diocese of St. Asaph* I (Oswestry, 1908 edn.).

Thomas (1930) : Thomas, L., *Reformation in the Old Diocese of Llandaff* (Cardiff, 1930).

Thompson (1974) : Thompson, K.M., *Ruthin School* (Denbigh, 1974).

Tickell (1796) : Tickell, J., *History of Kingston-upon-Hull* (Hull, 1796).

Tonnochy (1945) : Tonnochy, A.B., 'English Armorial Signets', *J.B.A.A.* 3rd Ser. X (1945-47).

Tonnochy (1952) : Tonnochy, A.B., *Catalogue of Seal Dies in the British Museum* (London, 1952).

Tout (1911) : Tout, T.F., 'Flintshire: Its History and Records', *Flintshire Hist. Soc. Publns.* I (1911).

Traherne (1852) : Traherne, J.M., 'Notices of Caerleon and Llantarnam', *Arch. Camb.* VII (1852).

Tucker (1962) : Tucker, N.R.F., *The Councell Booke of Ruthin, 1642-1695* (Colwyn Bay, 1962).

Turner (1903) : Turner, Horsfall., 'Cardigan Seals and Badges', in his *Wanderings in Cardiganshire* (Bingley, Yorks., 1903).

Vaughan (1917) : Vaughan, H.M., 'Benedictine Abbey at St. Dogmael's', *Y Cymm.* XXVII (1917).

Venables (1891) : Venables, E. (edit.), *Chronicle of Louth Park Abbey* (Lincs. Rec. Soc. I, 1891).

Wagner (1959) : Wagner, A.R., 'The Swan Badge and the Swan Knight', *Arch.* XCVII (1959).

Wakeman (1849) : Wakeman, T., 'Seal of the Corporation of Caerleon', *Arch. Camb.* IV (1849).

Wakeman (1858) : - - ., 'On the Chancery Seal of Monmouth', (relates also to the Chancery Seal of Abergavenny), *J.B.A.A.* XIV (1858).

Walcott (1865) : Walcott, M.E.C., *Cathedralia* (London, 1865).

Walford and Way (1857) : Walford, W.S. and Way, A., 'Official Seal of King Edward IV for his Chancery of Monmouth', *Arch. Jnl.* XIV (1857).

Way (1851) : Way, A., 'Examples of Medieval Seals', *Arch. Jnl.* VIII (1851).

Way (1858) : - - ., 'Signet-Ring of Mary, Queen of Scots', *Arch. Jnl.* XV (1858).

Wheatley (1991) : Wheatley, K., 'Seals: The Stour Valley Collection', *The Searcher* (Sept. 1991).

Wilkins (1908) : Wilkins, C., *History of Merthyr Tydfil* (Merthyr Tydfil, 1908).

Williams (1859) : Williams, J., *History of Radnorshire* (Brecon, 1859).

Williams (1889) : Williams, S.W., *History of Strata Florida Abbey* (London, 1889).

Williams (1905) : Williams, Jonathan., *History of Radnorshire* (Brecon, 1905 edn.).

Williams (1962) : Williams, Glanmor., *Welsh Church from Conquest to Reformation* (Cardiff, 1962).

Williams (1964) : Williams, David H., 'Grace Dieu Abbey', *Monm. Antiq.* I:4 (1964).

Williams (1970) : - - - ., 'Goldcliff Priory', *Monm. Antiq.* III: 1 (1970-1).

Williams (1980) : - - - ., 'The Seal of Grace Dieu Abbey', *Monm. Antiq.* IV: 1-2 (1980).

Williams (1982) : - - - ., *Welsh History through Seals* (National Museum, Cardiff, 1982); and a Welsh translation (with amendments): *Hanes Cymru trwy Seliau* (1984).

Williams (1982a) : - - - ., 'A Churchstoke Seal', *Arch. Camb.* CXXXI (1982).

Williams (1984) : - - - ., 'Catalogue of Welsh Ecclesiastical Seals, I: Episcopal Seals', *Arch. Camb.* CXXXIII (1984).

Williams (1984a) : - - - ., *The Welsh Cistercians* (Caldey Island; 2 vols. 1984-5).

Williams (1984b) : - - - ., 'The Seal in Cistercian Usage with Especial Reference to Wales', Chauvin, B. (edit.), *Mélanges Anselme Dimier* II: 3 (Pupillin, France; 1984).

Williams (1985) : - - - ., 'Catalogue of Welsh Ecclesiastical Seals, II: Seals of Ecclesiastical Jurisdiction', *Arch. Camb.* CXXXIV (1985).

Williams (1986) : - - - ., Ibid. III: 'Capitular Seals', *Arch. Camb.* CXXXV (1986).

Williams (1987) : - - - ., Ibid. IV: 'Seals of Cistercian Monasteries', *Arch. Camb.* CXXXVI (1987).

Williams (1988) : - - - ., Ibid. V: 'Other Monastic Seals', *Arch. Camb.* CXXXVII (1988).

Williams (1989) : - - - ., Ibid. VI: 'Personal Seals with Religious Devices', (together with Addenda and Corrigenda to the Catalogue), *Arch. Camb.* CXXXVIII (1989).

Williams and Hudson (1990) : Williams, David H. and Hudson, Rodney., 'Gwent Seals: I', *Monm. Antiq.* VI (1990).

Williams and Hudson (1993) : - - - ., 'Gwent Seals V, *Monm. Antiq.* IX (1993).

Willis (1846) : Willis, R., 'On the History of the Great Seals of England', *Arch. Jnl.* II (1846).

Wise (1985) : Wise, P.J., *Hulton Abbey,* Staffs. Arch. Studies (Museum Arch. Soc. Report, N.S. 2: Stoke-on-Trent, 1985).

Wyon (1887) : Wyon, A.B. and A., *Great Seals of England* (London, 1887).

Wyon (1893) : Wyon, A., 'Royal Judicial Seals in Wales', *J.B.A.A.* XLIX (1893).

Wyon (1894) : - - ., 'Notes on Some New Seals of the King's Great Sessions of Wales', *J.B.A.A.* L (1894).

Yardley (1927) : Yardley, E., *Menevia Sacra* (Suppl. to *Arch. Camb.* 1927).

Other Significant References to Welsh Seals include:

Arch. Jnl. VI (1849), 73, 296, 403; XVII (1860) 62; XX (1863) 203; XXXVI (1879) 104.

Proc. Soc. Antiq. 1st Ser. I, 17, 18; 2nd Ser. IV, 44, 382-3; V, 180, 202-3; VI, 108; XIV, 10; XVIII, 69-70; XXVI, 120; and *Catal. to Bristol Mtng.* lxxxv.

and see the several individual entries in this Catalogue.

Other Manuscript References to Welsh Seals include:

Cardiff Central Library: MS 3.758 (Welsh description of Owain Glyn Dŵr's seals).

Carmarthen Record Office: Museum Colln. 283 (Autographs and Seals, Bishops of St. David's, 1718-37).

Gwent Record Office: D.361.F.P.8.116 (Official Seal of John Morgan, Esq., of Tredegar Park, Lord Lieutenant, 1715-19).

National Library of Wales:

MS 11724D (Issues and Profits of the Original Seal of Cos. Caernarfon, Anglesey, and Merioneth, 1704-5).

MS 11725E (*Ibid.* 1718).

MS 1396E (Papers, incl. the account of Thomas East, engraver, for various Welsh Judicial Seals, 1687).

MS 3854B (The Method of Proceeding in the Court of Great Sessions for Glamorgan, Brecon and Radnor, 1817).

Duchy of Cornwall Welsh Records, D 37 (Lease by Prince George of Wales of the issues and profits of the Original Seal in Cos. Denbigh and Montgomery, for an annual rent of £11-12-0; 1722).

Glansevern MS 14547 (Great Session: Rules of Court for the Counties of Montgomery and Denbigh, Early 19th C.).

Penrice and Margam Charter 1083 (Bond of Maurice Canon of Haverfordwest to Lord Mandeville in £500, for his proper execution and enjoyment of the office of Custodian of the Original Seal with its appurtenances in the Counties of Carmarthen, Pembroke and Cardigan (1638).

Trefor Owen MS 255 (The Legal Courts in Wales, and their Jurisdictions; *Ca.* 1780).

INTRODUCTION

The Significance of the Seal in Wales

From the earliest days of man's ability to communicate his thoughts in the written word and to set down his personal, business and legal transactions in formal documents, there has been a need for a mechanism which could both keep such writings and deeds secret and be able to assure the recipient and interested parties of their authenticity. This was especially important in an age of slow communications, when there could be no quick and ready contact between individuals, and when the handwriting might very often be that of a scribe, not of the sender. So it was that the use of seals evolved as far back as about 4,000 B.C., and massive and learned tomes have been written concerning the cylinder seals of Babylon and the scarab seals of Egypt dating from that time. The use of seals is well attested, too, in the Scriptures: *"Jezebel wrote letters in Ahab's name, and sealed them with his seal"* (1 Kings 21/8; *ca.*850 B.C.).

The significance of the seal was of no less importance in medieval Wales[1]. All persons of consequence had their own proper seal of recognisable design and legend, and bodies corporate, similarly, their 'common' seal. The earliest Welsh seals known date from the late twelfth century, from the age of the native princes, and attested deeds issued by princes like Llywelyn ab Iorwerth (*ca.* 1190-1240) and Gwenwynwyn of Powys (1195-1216). Their charters to Strata Marcella Abbey near Welshpool, underline the importance attached to the use of a seal in their day. Gwenwynwyn confirmed one of his grants, so that it could not later be questioned, 'with the protection of my seal'[2]. One of the objects of the design of a seal was that it should be distinctive from those of other people, so Llywelyn ratified his donation 'with the peculiar (*i.e: especial*) impression of my seal'[3]. Important transactions might bear the seals of several adjudicators and witnesses, their seals sometimes being appended (from left to right) in order of the precedence of their owners. An agreement between the Cistercian abbeys of Margam and Llantarnam (1256) bore not only their abbots' seals, but also those of the abbots of Tintern, Neath, Whitland, Strata Florida and Flaxley[4] (*Fig. 1*). A deed of release (1272) by Prince Rhodri in favour of his brother, Prince Llywelyn ap Gruffydd, was sealed 'for greater security' with the seals of the bishops and archdeacons of Bangor and St Asaph, as well as those of the abbots of Aberconwy, Basingwerk, and Bardsey[5]. When Bogo de Clare, Chancellor of Llandaff (1287) refused to append the chapter seal to the document certifying the election of Philip of Stanton as bishop, the personal seals of the canons had to attest it instead[6].

The importance attached to seals was also shown in the unease felt with a bull of Honorius IV approving the transference of Cistercian monks in North Wales from Aberconwy to Maenan (1284). Honorius issued his decree in the interval between his election and consecration in 1285; the attached seal impression raised doubts as to the document's authenticity and, at Edward I's request, his successor, Nicholas IV, confirmed his predecessor's deed. He found it necessary to state in so doing that 'papal bulls issued before their consecration bear no name on the lead seal, which has given rise to a popular error that such bulls are defective'[7]. In similar

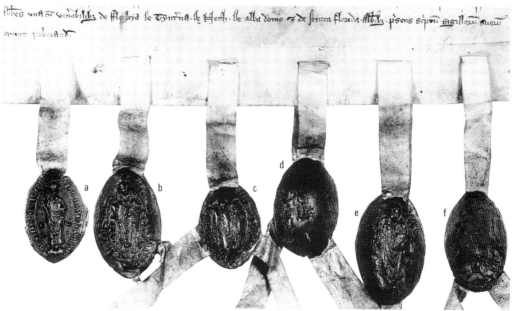

Fig.1: **Agreement between Margam and Llantarnam Abbeys (1256).**

(Seals of abbots of (**a**) Margam, (**b**) Tintern, (**c**) Neath, (**d**) Whitland, (**e/f**) Strata Florida and Flaxley.

BL, Harl. Ch. 75 A.37.

1

vein, the abbot of Neath (1336) requesting Edward III to confirm the charter granted to his monastery by King John (1207), noted that the charter has been 'so much ruined and worn by the wars in South Wales', that 'the seal is in part broken, but is recognisable enough'[8]. This underlies again the need felt for a seal to be distinctive, 'peculiar' or especial; proper to that person or body alone.

So far as corporate bodies were concerned, the importance of their common seals was emphasised when Edward II commanded the monks of Tintern (1314) to grant a corrody, 'making letters patent under their seal'[9], and when Lord Ferrers became Steward of St. Dogmael's Abbey towards the Suppression it was 'by letters patent, under the common seal'[10]. Officials taking up their positions needed immediate recourse to a seal, and so when during a vacancy in the see of St. David's (1407) a new vicar-general was appointed, the archbishop of Canterbury ordered the outgoing official principal to hand over with 'all possible speed, the seal of the officiality'[11]. Very rarely, in the later medieval period, is there to be found in Wales an alternative to the use of a seal. It comes when the archbishop of Canterbury set up a commission (1400) to enquire into the state of episcopal property in the diocese of St David's, following the death earlier of Bishop John Gilbert (1397). He requested the commissioners to return their findings 'sealed with an authentic seal, or strengthened by the sign and subscription of a notary public'[12] *(vide infra)*. The importance attached to the seal continued into modern times. Subsequent to the Acts of Union (1536 and 1542) the four judicial circuits established had their own proper seals. Another group of seals developed with the Elizabethan and Jacobean emergence of the grammar school: the statutes of Friars School, Bangor (1568) directed the trustees to obtain a common seal[13], as did the letters patent of Elizabeth I (1576) in respect of the Warden and Governors of the 'Free Grammar School of Carmarthen'[14]. The contemporaneous expansion of maritime trade saw not only the collectors of customs in Cardiff, Swansea, and Neath, having 'seals of office', but also the ordinance that 'seals be made in metal by the graver (in the Tower of London) for the chief creeks such as Newport and Chepstowe, and wooden seals for the petty creeks' (1615). An officer held the post of 'keeper of the cocket seal for the counties of Glamorgan and Monmouth' (1617)[15].

The accession of William of Orange (1688) saw many Welsh civic seals appended to expressions of loyalty[16]. The opening of the annual fair at Usk was accompanied by the proclamation that 'no leather, woollen or linen cloth be sold without first being sealed with the seal of the Borough'[17]. When St David's College, Lampeter, had been founded (1828), several ecclesiastical livings were placed in its gift, but the College found that it could not legally take possession of these without a common seal

which was, therefore, prepared[18]. In early modern times common seals, often with informative and sometimes topographical imagery, came to serve many bodies corporate: not only the grammar schools and the boroughs, but also tram- road, canal, and railway companies; friendly societies, poor law commissioners, banks, prisons, the newly-fledged county councils, and national institutions - such as the Eisteddfod and this Museum. Taken all in all, the seals of Welsh provenance known to us constitute a veritable 'mirror of history'[19].

The Collections of the National Museum

The National Museum holds a considerable number of seal dies (matrices) and casts or impressions. Mostly these are located in the Department of Archaeology and Numismatics, though some (chiefly dies) are located at the Welsh Folk Museum, St. Fagan's, and a very few are kept in the Departments of Art and of Industry. All told, at the time of preparation of this *Catalogue,* the total collection of the National Museum numbers 129 dies and 1896 casts and impressions (including numerous duplicates). In addition, most of the royal seals represented (and a few others) are paralleled by nearly two hundred plaster moulds. The collection can be summarised thus:

Seal Dies: .... 129.

Casts and Impressions: 1,896.

		(*English*:	Royal:	254.
Welsh:	498.		Ecclesiastical:	502.
English:	1,308.		Monastic:	257.
Scottish:	34.		Civic and	
Foreign:	55.		Corporate:	164
			Personal:	127).

Seal Moulds (imitation dies prepared from impressions): 195.

The great bulk of the seal casts and impressions derive from the Howell Collection presented to the former Cardiff Museum in 1883 *(Acc. Nos: Z.93)*, and the Mansel-Franklen Collection donated in 1925 *(Acc. Nos: 25.384)*. The seals preserved in the Cardiff Museum in turn included at least a few inherited from Caerleon Museum to which they had been presented by a man of antiquarian interests, F.J. Mitchell (1878), and included at least one notable matrix[20]. The curator of Cardiff Museum from 1876 to 1914 was the Revd. W.E. Winks, and 'as a reminder of the part he played', his son, L.F. Winks, F.I.C.S., of Powell Duffryn, Ltd., donated a leaden papal *bulla* to the National Museum (1954)[21]. The Mansel-Franklen Collection presented by Sir T. Mansel Franklen of St. Hilary, Cowbridge, came in a cabinet some time prior to 11th May 1925, before the National Museum had been officially opened. The cabinet was to be eventually returned to Sir Thomas, who said that his seals could be incorporated in the Museum's collection if so desired. The collection amounted to over 250 seals, and was accompanied by a manuscript catalogue drawn up by the Revd. Thomas Rackett, F.R.S., F.S.A., F.L.S., Rector of Spetisbury, Dorset, in 1835, and bearing the book-mark of the Revd. John M. Traherne, F.R.S., F.S.A., (1788-1860) of Coedriglan near Cardiff. Both he and Rackett were collectors of antiquities, including seals, and the nucleus of the collection was probably his[22]. There is other evidence (later) of their co-operation in the study of seals.

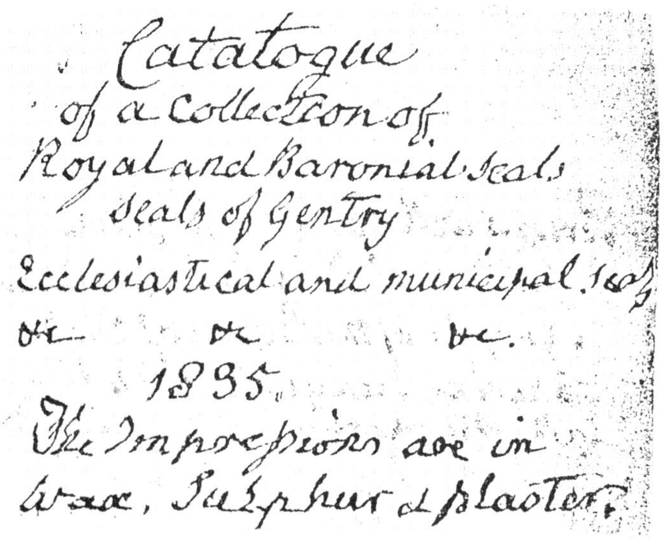

Fig. 2: Title-Page of Rackett's, *Catalogue of Seals, 1835.*

The initial collection inherited or donated to the National Museum has been built up further by purchase or donation over the intervening years. Donors of several seals have included H.J. Good *(Acc. Nos: 76/27H)*, W.J. Hemp *(Acc. Nos: 19/297, 20/420, 22/496)*, Major H. Lloyd Johnes *(Acc. Nos: 30.311)* and the Carmarthenshire Antiquarian Society *(Acc. Nos: 23/89)*. Mrs W.T. Wynne gave in 1921 the small collection made by her noted antiquarian father-in-law, W.W.E. Wynne of Peniarth (Merioneth; 1801-80) *(Acc.No: 21.24)*. Wynne had early written on the seal of Lewis Byford, bishop of Bangor, in the first volume of *Archaeologia Cambrensis*[22A]. Quite recently (1991) a number of replica casts of Welshmen serving in France in the fourteenth to fifteenth centuries have been purchased from the Archives Nationales in Paris[23]. Whilst Dr Cyril Fox was Director of the Museum (1926-48) a conscious effort was made to increase the representation of the judicial seals of the post-medieval Courts in Wales of the Great Sessions, and of the episcopal seals of post-disestablishment Church in Wales bishops. On Dr Fox's directive (17 October 1934) endeavours were made to obtain replicas of impressions of the judicial seals. Casts of three were supplied by the British Museum free of charge, and an estimate was given for a wider representation[24].

Later (28 March 1942) the Museum was to receive from A.J. Sylvester, C.B.E., the matrices of the judicial seal for the reign of George IV for Caernarfon, Merioneth, and Anglesey. It was one perhaps rarely used. It was war-time, and the Council of the Museum noted that 'we shall of course be storing the objects in a place of safety'. Sylvester had been given the matrix for the Museum by Sir Henry Fildes, J.P., M.P., who wished to remain anonymous in the matter[25]. A greater gift was that made (on permanent deposit) in 1940 by Lord Sankey of the silver matrices of the great seal of King George V in its original case. Sankey had received the seal as a perquisite of his office as Lord Chancellor. Staying with Sankey in 1938 was Canon Maurice Jones, the Principal of St David's College, Lampeter. He confided to his guest that 'he did not quite know what to do with the Great Seal, but felt it should be presented to a Museum'. Canon Jones suggested the National Museum. Matters lapsed until Dr Fox met Lord Sankey in London, received the Great Seal, brought it back to Cardiff and presented it to the Council on 26 January 1940[26].

On a train journey near Wrexham (October 1st, 1928) Dr Fox met Bishop Green of Monmouth who had one week previously been elected bishop of Bangor. The upshot of their conversation was that Dr Green presented to the Museum the matrix of his seal as bishop of Monmouth, trusting, he wrote, that 'you will start a case of episcopal seals'[27]. The Director was instructed by the Council of the Museum to endeavour to secure other such episcopal seals in order to achieve as large a series as possible. Dr Fox therefore wrote to Archbishop Edwards of St Asaph (November 28th) asking for his good offices in this matter, as he understood that 'the matrices of seals of Diocesan Bishops remain the property of their heirs-at-law'. The archbishop (who was a member of the Council of the Museum) agreed to look into the matter and gave Dr Fox's letter to the new bishop of Monmouth, Gilbert Joyce, to read. Bishop Joyce replied (December 1st) suggesting that 'ought not Mr Fox to write to the Registrars of the various dioceses'. This idea was taken up with varying results[28]. The diocesan registrar for Bangor placed three matrices on deposit, and the seal of recently retired Bishop Pritchard Hughes of Llandaff was presented at Dr Fox's request (June 2nd, 1931)[29]. Enquiries revealed that the seal of Bishop Owen of St David's (1897-1926) had passed to his widow, that of Bishop Vowler Short (1846-70) to one of his nephews, and that of Bishop Joshua Hughes, both of St Asaph (1870-89) to his son[30]. The seals of his two successors are preserved in the treasury of St Asaph Cathedral. When Dr Green in 1928 conveyed his seal as bishop of Monmouth to the Museum, he noted that his new seal as bishop of Bangor was 'even finer as a work of engraving'; latterly (1983) the Friends of the Museum have been able to purchase and donate this matrix[31].

The Matrices (Seal-Dies)

Matrices were commonly manufactured in copper alloys - brass, bronze or latten. Silver might be employed by people of higher rank and wealthier institutions, lead by poorer people. Some matrices were non-metallic, formed from stone or slate. Silver dies in the collection include those of a fifteenth-century abbot of Strata Florida, the judicial seals of the Courts of Great Sessions (*temp.* George II and IV), and the customs seal for Swansea (*ca.* 1605). Bronze and the like can get very worn with the passage of time, and if subject to corrosive agents - as in the soil, the edges may be especially affected, and as a consequence the legend is frequently indecipherable. Lead matrices, on the other hand, are usually found in a far better state of preservation, and give fine impressions even to-day. Lead was frequently used in making smaller personal seals in early thirteenth-century Wales. Another group of thirteenth to fourteenth-century seals mostly of Border provenance are those engraved in stone. One has been found in the vicinity of Churchstoke[32], another at Llangynllo, another in the Knighton area[33] - all three are circular in shape, and all three emanate from the same area of Powys. The shape of medieval matrices was almost invariably round or oval. Circular seals were used by civic bodies and by laymen of all ranks, oval seals by ecclesiastics and ladies; but there were numerous exceptions to these two generalisations. Pointed oval seals became common from the thirteenth century onwards. A stone block found in excavations at Trostrey, Gwent, would appear to have functioned as a mould for manufacturing (though not engraving) both round and oval matrices[34]. Carved out of oolitic limestone, it makes provision for the perforated hinges or loops on the reverse commonly added for purposes of handling and of securing lesser seals. Greater seals - as the medieval

chancery seal of Monmouth and the later judicial seals for the Great Sessions, had perforated lobes on one part of the double-matrix to take metallic projections borne by the other; this allowed of accurate centring during sealing. Early modern seals often came to have metallic or wooden handles.

Dating a Seal Matrix

When a seal impression is still attached to a document, the date the seal was used (though not of course the date it was engraved) can be pinpointed accurately. Where, however, a seal has become detached from its deed, or a matrix is newly discovered - perhaps embedded in soil, determining the date of its engraving is more difficult. Occasionally, the legend on the perimeter of the die may give the name of the person to whom it once belonged. A bronze matrix discovered in South Glamorgan in 1991 bore the ascription to Walter Wynter, archdeacon of Carmarthen; he is known to have been in office about 1328 to 1331, and so no problem arises in dating his seal. More often it will be necessary to gauge the rough date of a matrix by reference to the evolving styles of lettering employed in its legend.

The earliest seals of Welsh usage bear lettering commonly referred to as Roman Capitals, these held sway until 1180 to 1200. More florid Lombardic Capitals followed thereafter until about 1350, when Gothic characters (Black Letter script) ensued. This type can be

Fig. 3: **Mould for Seal Dies, Trostrey, Gwent.**

By courtesy of Mr A.G. Mein.   *Plate:* National Museum of Wales.

Roman Capitals
Seal of Milo of Gloucester
(1140-43).

Lombardic Script
Seal of Henry, Bishop of
Llandaff (1193-1218).

Black Letter
Seal of Thomas, Bishop of
Llandaff (1398-1407).

Renaissance Capitals
Seal of Arwystli Deanery
(c.1549-).

Fig. 4

divided into majuscules until about 1425, miniscules thereon. A sudden break then occurs with the re-emergence of capital letters, but smaller and sharper, and referred to as Renaissance Capitals. The differing styles can be exemplified by observing the form taken by the word *sigillum* (seal), or its contractions, *sigill'* and *sigillū*, on Fig. 4.

In medieval times the legend was given almost invariably in Latin, and this remained the practice until well into modern times. Only infrequently is the Welsh language used. The seal displaying the arms of the Games (later James) family of Breconshire is one example (1663):

Fig. 5.
(NLW, Badminton Deeds II, 10,744).

Reproduced by permission of His Grace the Duke of Beaufort.

('AB · DDYW · DYGYD' · COTH · GAMES ·)

6a: **First Chapter Seal of Llandaff.**

NLW, Penrice and Margam Charter 11. (Ca. 1175).

Courtesy of C. Methuen-Campbell, Esq. (Plate: National Library of Wales).

Seal Engravers

Next to nothing is known as to the engravers of seals used in medieval Wales. Comparison of certain seals does however suggest in some instances a common source. There is, for example, considerable similarity of style between the great seals of Prince Llywelyn ab Iorwerth (as used in 1208) and that of Gwenwynwyn of Powys (as employed in 1205)[35]. The early seals of the cathedral chapters of Llandaff and Hereford display a close likeness[36]:

Similarities of style and imagery also arise because lesser folk often bought their personal seal 'off the peg', so to speak. In some cases a personal ascription was added in the legend, in other cases the legend - perhaps a motto, cloaked the matrix in anonymity. The first type is well illustrated by the seal matrices of John Aduvar (possibly John ab Ifor) - found in the grounds of Cardiff Castle (1958) and that of Nicholas Chot - discovered in a field at Bonvilston (1986). The identical imagery - a symbolic floral design and the same diameter (26 mm) suggest a common, perhaps South Walian, engraver. Only the material of the matrix differs: lead (weighing 16.0 gms.) in the former case, latten (11.9 gms.) in the latter instance. Both were probably engraved in the early fourteenth century.

Fig. 6b: **First Chapter Seal of Hereford.**

Hereford Cathedral Archive 233. (Ca. 1190).

Courtesy of the Dean and Chapter. (Plate: Hereford Cathedral Library).

Fig. 7: **Seal of John Aduvar.**   Fig. 8: **Seal of Nicholas Chot.**

Impersonal seals of the second type known in Wales include that depicting a stag's head cabossed, with between the horns a cross paty, and bearing as legend the Latin motto: *Timete Deum.* One seal of this group has been found at Mathern, Gwent (1988) - perhaps lost by a visitor to the bishop of Llandaff's palace there; a second occurs attached to a deed (of 1295) issued at Eglwys-fach, Gwynedd. A third has been discovered at Thornicombe, Dorset (1991)[37A], whilst another was formerly in the Durden Collection[37B]. Yet another example, but oval in shape and with a star between the antlers, was found in excavations at Wolvesey Palace, Winchester (1960's)[37C].

Fig. 9a: **W430**
(Mathern, Gwent).
(Diameter: 18 mm.)

Fig. 9b:
(Thornicombe, Dorset).
(Diameter: 18 mm.)

Distinct similarities are also exhibited between the seals of certain of the later bishops of Bangor, but these are perhaps a reflection of matrices renewed and amended, rather than engraved afresh completely[37].

The costly official seals of royal government for Wales were engraved in London. Instructions were given (1326) for the 'manufacture of a seal for the liberty of Haverford, with the king's arms on one side, and two dragons on the other'[38]. Nicholas de Twyford, a London goldsmith was paid £5-10-0 in 1377 (during the minority of Thomas le Despenser, lord of Glamorgan), for engraving and making a seal ordered by Edward III for the lordships of Glamorgan and Morgannwg[39]. Shortly after the accession of Henry V (1413) John Bernes, another London goldsmith, received £10 for engraving two pairs of double seals for the principalities of North and South Wales[40]. Several notable engravers have served the Crown in modern times. Those who are known to have made seals for Welsh usage include Thomas Rawlins (chief engraver in 1647-8 and 1662-70), Thomas East (in 1687), and his nephew, John Roos (*d.* 1720). The latter

was but one of several instances where the engraving of coins, medals and seals, was a family craft. Amongst Rawlins' matrices were five judicial seals for the Welsh Courts of Great Sessions. They were necessitated by the restoration of the monarchy, and Rawlins worked on them from July 30th to September 24th, 1660, receiving a payment of £274-2-6. It has been said of Rawlins that he was 'although a talented artist, an uneven worker, and some of his productions betray no doubt the great haste with which he had to execute the king's commands'[41].

Fig. 10: **Account of Thomas East (1687).**

NLW, MS 1396 E.
(Plate: National Library of Wales).

Thomas East, who served James II, presented an account (1687) for making several seals necessitated by the accession of that monarch. They included two chancery and two judicial seals for Welsh circuits. His bill for the judicial seal for Denbigh, Montgomery and Flint, amounted to over £69[42]. East may have engraved the great seal of James II, which was lost in the Thames during the king's flight in December 1688. John Roos, chief engraver under Queen Anne and George I made (1716) amongst several important seals of state, a judicial seal also for the Denbigh, Montgomery and Flint circuit; he received for this alone £68-15-11. Of his craftsmanship, the officers of the mint reported that 'the work is good and he deserves the prices set down'[43]. A long line of state engravers knew the tribulations of political and religious changes, of mental stress, or of pecuniary embarassment. Rawlins, for example, had fled to the Continent after the downfall of Charles I, and then, back in London, was imprisoned for debt (1657) [44]. Throughout the nineteenth century, the work of engraving seals of state was synonymous with the name of members of the Wyon family. Thomas Wyon, the elder (*d.* 1830), cut the judicial seal (held in the Museum) of George IV for the counties of Caernarfon, Merioneth and Anglesey (*D. 47-8*). The influence of the Wyons extended into the twentieth century, and it was Allan Wyon, jnr., who engraved the seal of Dr Green as bishop of Bangor (1928) [45]. Their work reflected the words of Scripture: *'those who cut the signets of seals, each is diligent in making a great variety'* (Ecclus. 38/27).

Other occasional references to the manufacture of Welsh seal matrices occur in civic records. The Mayor of Haverfordwest's accounts (for 1581 and 1592) refer to the 'making of two seals' (for 1/-) and 'one seal of iron' (at 8d.). These must have been matrices for the office of mayor or lesser officials; clearly not the well-known common seal [46]. The borough of Ruthin had a series of seals. The medieval seal was replaced in 1711, only to give way to another engraved in 1809 to celebrate the golden jubilee of George III, to yield place in its turn (1835) to yet another consequent upon the Municipal Corporation Act which gave it a mayor [47]. The Court of Aldermen of Cardiff paid one John Thackwell, £10-14-0 (1819) for their new coporation seal [48]. Designers of modern Welsh seals have included C.R. Cockerell, the architect of St David's College, Lampeter, who also, in consultation with the College of Heralds, designed its seal (about 1830) [49]. Goscombe John, R.A., designed the corporate seals of Merthyr Tydfil (1907), the National Museum of Wales (1912), the National Library (about the same time), and of the Representative Body of the Church in Wales (1920), as well as being responsible for the projected Great Seal of Edward VIII [50].

Care and Custody of Seals

The importance of the seal meant that steps were often taken to protect it against casual damage. The monks of Ewenny Priory safe-guarded, for example, the seal of Gilbert de Turberville who had given them land by placing it in a green silk bag [51]. More often, precautions were necessary against possible mis-use of a seal. A corporate seal, such as that of a monastic community, might be kept in such a way that no one individual had access to it; this helped to guard against improper use. The common seal of Goldcliff Priory, Gwent, was 'closed with four locks' (*ca.* 1320) [52]. The common seal of Cwmhir Abbey, Radnorshire, was 'wont to be kept in a chest with two locks, the key of the one lock remaining with the abbot, and the other with one of the monks especially appointed for that purpose' (*ca.* 1520) [53]. The common seal of the newly founded Friars School at Bangor, Gwynedd, was ordered to be kept in a chest with two locks in the Cathedral Chapter House; the key to the one

lock remaining with the bishop, the other with the dean and chapter (1568) [54]. Such precautions meant, in general, a long life for the common seals of monasteries and collegiate establishments. The same matrices could be in use for two or three centuries. This may account for the indistinct nature of the known seal impressions of

Fig. 11: **Seal of Gilbert de Turberville** (Early 13th cent.)

Hereford Cathedral Archive 2295.
(By courtesy of the Dean and Chapter).

Cymer Abbey (1538-34) resulting perhaps from the use of a worn seal-matrix [55]. The same considerations may apply to the need felt by Strata Marcella Abbey (1531) to have 'a new seal' [56]. The matrices of both monasteries had lasted for at least two hundred years. Under the statutes of the newly-established Christ's Hospital in Ruthin, Clwyd (1590), the common seal was to be kept in a chest with double locks and two keys, then the chest in a strong hutch. Nothing was to pass under the seal without the assent of the President and the Warden [57]. That same (silver) seal happily survives in pristine condition to this day, although now kept in a bank vault. In more modern times, to guard against potential mis-use, the Court of Aldermen at Cardiff (1819) ordered that the corporation seal was not to be affixed to any deed or document 'unless at a Court of Common Council' [58].

Despite such precautions taken, there were several instances of the theft and subsequent mis-use of seals in both medieval and Tudor days. In an armed raid on Goldcliff Priory (*ca.* 1320) the locks of the seal-chest were torn off by William Walsh of Llanwern, Gwent, who then used its common seal to make grants of monastic property to himself [59]. Abbot John ap Rhys of Strata Florida, who had resigned from the abbacy of Cymer (about 1442), returned to the Gwynedd monastery with a band of cronies, evicted his successor and took the common seal using it to make grants and leases 'bearing date a long time before his resignation'[60]. Archdeacon John Smith of Llandaff admitted (in 1558) that 'he once broke the coffer, and took out thereof the chapter seal contrary to the bishop's will'[61]. Bishop Gervase, amongst the statutes he made for St. David's Cathedral (1224), ordered 'that a Chapter should be held every year on Easter Monday, (and) that ye Chapter Seal should at no other time be affixed to any confirmation, or alienation'[62]. This instruction, or at any rate its observance, perhaps soon fell into desuetude. There came to be 'three keys of the seal and treasure house' at St. David's. One was supposed to be held by the treasurer, another by the chancellor, and the third by the precentor. It was alleged (1572) that the precentor, Thomas Huett (living then at Aberduhonw, Builth) held them all and 'thereby hath given many and divers seals without any others assent or consent'[63]. This state of affairs was facilitated by the cathedral treasurer, Hugh ap Rhys (who lived in Rochester, Kent), being 'aged and impotent, and unable to travel'.

To protect against fraudulent use, when a seal expired it might well be broken up or defaced. The Earl of Norfolk writing, from Sheriff Hutton, to Cromwell (June 28th, 1537), told him that he had 'caused to be battered' the seals of three suppressed Yorkshire religious houses[64]; doubtless much the same happened in Wales. Seal matrices whose usefulness had passed might be melted down and the metal put to other purposes. With his conquest of Wales almost complete (1284), Edward I had the privy seal of Prince Llewelyn the Last - of whose great seal we have no knowledge, together with those of his wife, Eleanor, and his brother, Prince David, dealt with in this way. All three had lately died, and the silver metal of their privy seals was combined and turned into a

Fig. 12: **Defaced Seal of an Abbot of Strata Florida.** (15th cent.).

(Courtesy of the British Museum).

chalice[65]. A less drastic measure was once adopted at Strata Florida Abbey; perhaps in order to economise, and so that a new abbot could use the seal of his predecessor,

the latter's name was simply erased[66]. Public awareness of a new legitimate Crown seal was often facilitated by such matrices being handed over with great ceremony. When, in 1343, the Commissioners of the Black Prince delivered a new seal of office to the Chamberlain of the Exchequer at Caernarfon, it was done in the presence of a great company headed by the bishop of Bangor. The significance of the seal was reflected in the proclamation made that the old seal was of no further avail, and, to guard against fraudulent use, it was deposited in the king's chancery[67]. The matrices associated with the later spread of royal authority in Wales, via the Courts of Great Sessions, had official *keepers* appointed – to ensure the proper custody of those seals[68].

Fraudulent use of genuine seals was not the only hazard that needed to be guarded against; there was also the problem of forgeries. The need for care was exhibited when Bishop Guy of St. David's (1401) noted that a papal leaden *bulla* received was 'not injured, not abrased, but free from fault and sinister suspicion'. A successor, Bishop Hugh (1489) described the red wax seal impression on a missive from the papal penitentiary, as being 'sound, entire, not spoiled, not cancelled, not suspect in any part of itself, but entirely without flaw and suspicion.'[69] The forging of seals was not unknown. After the suppression of his abbey (1539), the last abbot of Strata Florida was alleged to have demised a grange (no longer his to do so) - 'by writing, under a counterfeit seal, like the convent seal of the monastery'[70]. At much the same time, Thomas Salisbury was accused of having appended two counterfeit seals to his supposed deed of collation to the parish of Denbigh[71]. Bishop William of Llandaff in the latter part of the sixteenth century, had occasion to complain to the Court of Star Chamber of forgeries made of the seals of his cathedral chapter and of the bailiff of Llandaff[72]. Forgeries were current in early Victorian days, when collecting seals was quite a hobby, both in Britain and on the Continent[73].

Discovery of Welsh Seal Matrices, and Seals found in Wales
As a detached object, seal matrices have often been lost by their owners - perhaps when on a journey, even sometimes stolen from them. Others in quite modern times have disappeared by mischance. The matrix for St. David's Hospital, Swansea (once in the Royal Institution of South Wales) is no more. The former seal of Aberystwyth Corporation having become obsolete (1875) was placed in the museum of the University College of Wales there, only to perish in the disastrous fire of 1885[74]. After comprehensive reorganisation of secondary education took place in Bangor the silver matrix of Friars School was found to be missing. One of the original seals of Cardiganshire County Council, left by the Clerk to the Council in his desk when the abolition of that Authority meant his transfer to another position, can no longer be

found despite a search. Lost seal matrices are, however, being discovered in increasing numbers, some by excavation, others by chance (as with a metal detector).

Some have been seal dies found in unexpected places: one (variously attributed to an abbot of Revesby or Tintern) in the moat of Ewenny Priory[75]; one of Bishop John of St. Asaph (1395-1410) at Glastonbury[76]; that of the Guild of the Holy Trinity, Cardiff, in a heap manure in a turnip field[77]; that of the Chancery of Monmouth in the bed of the River Wye - and later used as the bob of a clock pendulum[78]; that of a distant abbey (Sonnebeca in Belgium) in a field outside Bangor[78A]; that of the Peculiar Jurisdiction of Stratford-upon-Avon in a house near Denbigh[78B]. The eagle eyes of the young have been particulary successful. Miss Margaret Rowley was only eight years old in 1963 when, in a waste tip of spoil from the construction of the M1 motorway near Leicester, she found the late-fourteenth century die of the collegiate church of Abergwili[79]. Griffith Hughes of Castle Terrace, Dolwyddelan, Gwynedd, was but a young boy playing on

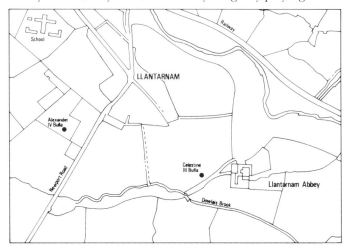

Fig. 13: **Find-spots of Papal _bullae_ near Llantarnam Abbey, Gwent.**

the wooded slope of Uchel-graig by the castle in 1875 when he fell from a tree branch on to a lot of small stones, and he later said: 'before I moved, with my hands all bruised, here was the seal before my eyes in the stones'. The seal in question was a lead _bulla_ of Pope Honorius III (1216-27)[80]. Lead wears well, and remains intact when the papal missive to which it was attached has long since perished. Similar lead _bullae_, one of Celestine III (1191-98) and one of Alexander IV (1254-61) were found in 1985 by Mr. K.L. Morgan, not un-naturally in the vicinity of Llantarnam Abbey, Gwent[81].

Another youngster to find a seal was five-year old Master B. Jones, of Cyncoed, Cardiff; taken on an outing to Barry Island in 1948 he spotted a leaden seal of Bishop Giraud of Vaison, France (1271-95) on the beach. The silver matrix of this seal is known, and some have thought it a forgery[82]. Such beach finds are not uncommon. At least two matrices have turned up from the same general

area of the foreshore of Swansea Bay; perhaps the consequence of shipwreck. The first to be found (in 1978) was the seal matrix of one William Malherbe (the surname may suggest a French provenance)[83]; the second, ten years on, was a substantial silver signet-ring, perhaps of the fifteenth century, and engraved with uncertain initials[84]. An interesting find at sea came when, about 1827, a James Murray fishing in the Clyde caught a very large cod (weighting 17¼ lbs.) in the gut of which he found a gold watch (with chain and seals attached) inscribed as belonging to one "Hugh Davies, of Wrexham"[85].

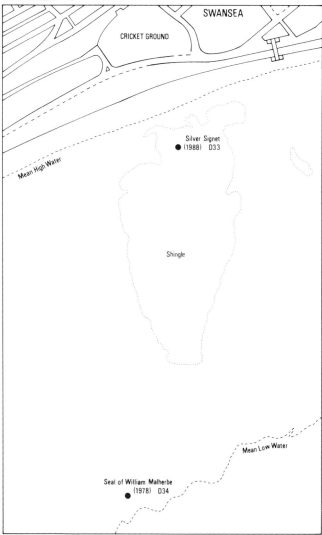

Fig. 14: **Seal finds in Swansea Bay.**

In the last few years, a number of small personal seal matrices have been found in Wales, notably in the excavations by Terrence James (on behalf of the Dyfed Archaeological Trust) at the Grey Friars, Carmarthen, and in the work of Steven Sell (on behalf of the Glamorgan-Gwent Archaeological Trust) at the assumed site of Ewenny Fair. Mostly they are of bronze and sometimes badly corroded, so that legends are not always decipherable with ease. The Carmarthen finds include a seal depicting the frequent device of a crow or hawk capturing a smaller bird or rodent with the legend, in French, 'Alas, I am taken'. A matrix with a similar device and with the same legend was discovered at the Wenallt, Cardiff (1983), but whereas the Carmarthen die was of latten and weighed under 7 gms., the Cardiff matrix is of lead, much denser of course, and weighing some 16 gms. Other seals brought recently into local museums for identification and comment include one of a Robert FitzMaurice found perhaps in the Penally area and examined at Tenby Museum; a seal of Philip ab Ieuan - possibly to be equated with the personage of that name active in a riot at Goldcliff Priory about 1321, discovered below water level in the Llandegfedd Reservoir and now on loan to Torfaen Museum; and the leaden early-thirteenth century seal of David Llywelyn found near St. David's, and now preserved at Scolton Manor Museum. Other investigators whose finds are represented in this *Catalogue* include Mr Charles Cater of Wrexham (and other members of the Mold Historical Research Society), and Mr K. Evans of Mathern, Gwent - who found the *Timete Deum* seal referred to above.

Fig. 15: **Seal of David Llywelyn.**
(found by Mr A. Duncan, 1987)
(Courtesy of Scolton Manor Museum).

Fig. 16: **Seal of ? Peter Sensis.**
(recorded by Mr S. Sell, 1986)
(Courtesy of the Glamorgan-Gwent Archaeological Trust).

More substantial seal matrices which have come to light in recent years include a fine die for the Chancery of Prince Henry (later King Henry V) as Lord of Carmarthen; it was acquired by the British Museum at a Bloomsbury Book Auction in 1987[86]. Mr. David Lewis, working with a metal-detector in the Portfield at Haverfordwest (about 1987) unearthed the obverse part of the early modern Seal for the Taking of Recognizances within the Town and County of Haverfordwest; hitherto it had only been known from its engraving in Lewis', *Topographical Dictionary*[87]. The matrix is now in the care of Scolton Manor Museum. A trial at Knightsbridge Crown Court (in late 1975) saw three brothers, demolition contractors, each fined £100 for being in possession of stolen property. The item concerned (or one of the items) was the silver matrix of the Judicial Seal of the Court of Great Sessions for Caernarfon, Merioneth and Anglesey, in the reign of George III. The brothers had found it when demolishing a house in Croydon, but such matrices were often legitimately conveyed to Crown officers once their time had expired[88]. During the trial a brother of the defendants sitting in court next to an expert witness called for the prosecution, confided in him that this seal with other property had been stolen by a footman in 1776[89]. The matrix is now in the custody of the British Museum, as is the fifteenth-century seal of the former Cornish borough of Grampound, discovered by a builder, Mr Hodson (1988), whilst replacing a sewer under No. 3, St. Mary's St., Carmarthen, at a depth of 12' below existing street level. This find-spot is not far from the Old Quay, raising the possibility that, for whatever reason the matrix reached West Wales, it may have done so by sea[90]. Other matrices which have found their way to Wales include a seal of Kelso Abbey in Scotland found in a garden at Conwil Elvet, Dyfed, some years ago[91]. Of great interest is the seal matrix of Archdeacon Walter Wynter of Carmarthen (*ca.* 1328-31) noted above, and found by Mr. D.G. Jones in 1991 in the vicinity of Castell Coch, Aberthin, South Glamorgan. The find was made not very far north of the medieval Portway (now followed in large measure by the A. 48 road), and this suggests that the archdeacon was on a journey well away from home when he lost his seal[92]. More recently, Mr. R. Jones has discovered the late-thirteenth century seal of William of Combe, close to the Raglan-Abergavenny Road[92A]. There are several localities named Combe in the south of England, and finds such as these are valuable as helping plot routes taken by medieval travellers. The Trostrey mould found by A.G. Mein (*supra*) must, however, be the pièce-de-resistance of recent seal finds in Wales.

Impressing a Seal

Few medieval eye-witness accounts survive as to the employment of seal dies, but at the Cistercian abbey of Louth Park (Lincs.), it is on record that in 1342 as a dying benefactor granted charters to the monastery, *'a monk heated the wax at the fire*, with which the deeds were sealed, his wife ministering the belt *(zonam)* with the seal'[93]. In Tudor Wales, Thomas Kynnyllyn of Monmouth (1538) asserted that when the now dissolved abbey of

Grace Dieu had made a grant of corrody, 'he wrote the grant, and was at the monastery when it was sealed and delivered'[94]. The later Courts of Great Sessions had *cursitors* appointed, whose task it was to impress the judicial seal to official documents, such as exemplifications of recovery[95]. Where seals were intentionally double-sided with separate matrices for the obverse and reverse impressions, the process of sealing was assisted either by perforated lobes extending from the matrices which carried metal pins (as in the Chancery Seal of Monmouth; *supra*), or by setting the opposing dies in blocks of wood (as the Town Seal of Haverfordwest)[96]. In cases where a seal had two faces sometimes the legend on the reverse is a continuation of that on the obverse.

It was important to affix a seal to a document in such a way that it could not be easily removed, for if it were the deed would be rendered worthless. Most seals were affixed either (1) by making incisions in the fold of the manuscript and passing a strip of parchment or a length of woven cord, often of coloured silk, through them, the seal being impressed over the ends *(Fig. 17a)*, or (2) by cutting a strip of parchment from the lower edge of the manuscript, and impressing the seal upon it *(Fig. 17b)*. As

Fig. 17b: **Ieuan ab Hywel of Margam** (as used in 1527).
NLW, Penrice and Margam Charter 283.
(Courtesy of C. Methuen-Campbell, Esq).

Fig. 17a: **Gilbert de Clare, lord of Glamorgan** (*Ca.* 1220)
NLW, Penrice and Margam Charter 2046.
(Courtesy of C. Methuen-Campbell, Esq).

an easy substitute for making a seal *pendant,* there developed in early modern times the practice of impressing a seal directly upon a document, *en placard*; worse still, in more recent times, by *embossing* without any wax being employed. A sad trait, as with some judicial seals from the eighteenth century on *(infra)*, was to protect the impressions by covering them with paper (seemingly before the wax had set completely solid), with the unfortunate result that the image of the seal was lost for ever[97].

To ensure the authenticity of a (great) seal, its owner might apply to the reverse of the wax impression his 'counter-seal', termed from its Latin form, *'contra-sigillum'*: 'placed *against the seal*'. This 'lesser seal' was alternatively called a 'secret' or 'privy' seal - a seal which might be used in its own right to close letters and to confirm lesser deeds. Prince Llywelyn ab Iorwerth sometimes used only his counter-seal (as in 1230) explaining that he was 'sealing the letters with his secret seal, because he has not his great seal with him'[98]. The primary purpose of a counter-seal was, however, that of guaranteeing and giving added force to the impression of a (great) seal attached to a deed. Prince Llywelyn, for example, also used his 'secret seal' on the reverse of the impression of his great seal on the occasion of his daughter, Princess Helen, marrying John the Scot, a nephew of the earl of Chester (1222)[99]. When Prince Llywelyn ap Gruffydd fell in battle (1282) his privy or

Fig. 18a: **Great Seal of
Llywelyn the Great.**
(*for original see* BL, Cott. Ch. XXLV, 17).

Fig. 18b: **Privy Seal of
Llywelyn the Great.**
(*for original see* BL, Cott. Ch. XXLV, 17).

'small seal' was found in his breeches[99A]. A counter-seal which testified directly its purpose was that of the bishop of Winchester (1174), with its legend: *'SVM CVSTOS ET TESTIS SIGILLI'*, (*'I am the keeper and witness of the Seal'*)[100]. This was a reminder, too, that the great seal of a notability was often kept in a chest or bag sealed with his privy seal. Occasionally, the legends of counter-seals contain other phraseology indicative of their purpose, as *'clavis sigilli'* ('the key of the Seal'), and *'fides sigilli'* ('the confidence of the Seal')[101]. In Norman times, and perhaps later, another way of adding to the authenticity of a seal impression was for a lock of the grantor's hair to be placed in the molten wax[102]. This perhaps gave greater physical strength to the seal, but it was meant to convey added force and good faith to the strength of the charter it attested.

Alas, many seal impressions have perished with the passage of time. Many more whose significance was not appreciated must have been cut off their charters when these were bound into volumes of deeds - at the British Library, the Public Record Office, and elsewhere. The result is that (as the letters of the Welsh princes have

been so bound) there is no extant example of the great seal of Prince Llywelyn the Last (*ob.* 1282). Certain charters of Welsh interest in Gloucester Cathedral archives have been bound but without losing their pendant seals. No doubt, too, Victorian seal-collectors are responsible for a certain amount of plunder, but natural wear and tear has also played its part. A box of deeds may well contain at its base seals which have become detached in the course of time.

In the early Middle Ages seals were impressed in pure beeswax and remained in its natural colour. Soon green coloured wax was adopted, especially on seals of state and of princes (like Llywelyn ab Iorwerth and Gwenwynwyn of Powys), of bishops (like Cadogan of Bangor), and of lesser lords (as Maredudd ab Hywel)[103]. It has been suggested that green wax was used by the noble classes to indicate the permanence of the charters they were granting; green implies life, evergreen meant permanent life, enduring validity[104]. Green was the dominant colour on Welsh episcopal seals down to the mid-14th century, thereafter red was increasingly employed[105]. By this time, turpentine was used in making sealing wax. It gave the impression greater hardness and a longer life, it also allowed a greater variety of colours to be adopted: red, brown, even white[106]. Various pigments were used to achieve such colouration: orpiment (to yield yellow wax), vermilion (to give red), verdigris (for green), or organic matter (for brown)[107]. So far as royal seals were concerned, it may be that green wax was used for important charters, brown for less significant documents, and red for privy seals and signets. Green re-asserted its importance, being often employed for impressing the seals of the Courts of Great Sessions; there is indeed a reference (in Carmarthenshire) to the *'Judicial Seal, otherwise called ye Greenwax Seale'* (1650)[108]. The clumsy use of coloured wax for a seal of Cwmhir Abbey (allegedly in 1502) led much later to its authenticity being doubted (1590); the Brilley Remembrance noting that 'this lease seemeth to be forged for the seal is of white wax set on the label with the head downwards, and fastened to the label with green wax on the backside'[109]. The use of opposing colours, whilst rare, did not of necessity suggest a forgery; seal impressions of Count Amedée of Savoy (1354) and Duke Charles of Lorraine (1424) both employed green wax for the obverse face but red wax for the counter-seal[110].

Welsh Sigillography

An interest in seals is not new. An English lawyer, Francis Tate, included (about 1591) a discourse entitled: 'Of the Antiquity of Seals', in a book he wrote[111], and later (in 1740) a cleric, John Lewis, Vicar of Minster in Kent, published a 'Dissertation on the Antiquity and Use of Seals in England'[112]. But by and large Britain lagged behind the Continent in this respect; so it was that (in 1780) Richard Gough wrote: 'other nations are before us in the useful design of collecting and engraving ancient seals', and he referred to works published in Bruges (1639), Leipzig (1719), and Florence (1739)[113]. He could have gone back further still, for in Germany Karl Pawlas published in the early 1960's the first three parts of his *Handbuch der Spragistik*[114]; the fourth part never appeared because Pawlas abandoned the project. This was a pity, for it was to have been a Bibliography of Sigillography stretching back to the fourteenth century.

In Britain a greater interest in sigillography developed towards the close of the eighteenth century and expanded in Victorian times[115]. George Vertue (1753) published accounts of the work of royal seal engravers, notably Thomas Symons[116]. Thomas Astle wrote a fairly comprehensive account of Scottish seals (1792)[117]. From this period perhaps date several British Library manuscript collections of engravings and drawings of British seals[118]. From this time on, too, came numerous references to seals in the annual volumes of *Notes and Queries* and the *Gentleman's Magazine*; studies which expanded in the periodicals published by the several nineteenth-century archaeological societies. By this time some British antiquarians collected seals, just as one might collect postage stamps today. A collector on a large scale was Bishop Richard Rawlinson (1690-1775) who amassed some 850 seals or replicas of seals. They were mostly of foreign origin, but included the hitherto unknown (and possibly suspect) matrices for Chepstow and Trellech in Gwent[119]. His collection, formerly in the Bodleian Library, passed to the Ashmolean Museum in 1927[120]. To aid seal collectors several engravers and modellers were active. Perhaps most notable was John Doubleday who, by 1849, had produced replicas of over 2,000 seal impressions found in the national collections of England and France. Alas, he also forged ancient and

Fig. 20: **Seal of St. Asaph Consistory Court** (*temp.* 1573-*ca.*1589) *BL, Harl. MS 1968, f.35r.*

modern coins for sale, and it could be that he forged some seals as well[121]. Henry Laing (*ob.* 1883) fulfilled much the same role for Scotland; at the age of fourteen he had been apprenticed to the modeller, William Tassie, whose work he continued[122]. As noted above, a long line of engravers suffered from incessant brainwork and financial anxiety[123]. One prolific Brooklyn engraver and modeller, G.H. Lovett (1824-94), died of nervous prostration, and his obituary aptly recorded: *'Death had set his seal upon him!'*[124].

So far as Wales was concerned two keen Victorian sigillarists were of note, whilst from its inception the Cambrian Archaeological Association displayed recent seal finds from the Principality in the Temporary Museums set up at its Annual Meetings (1847-)[125]. An early member who exhibited 'rare seals' was A.W. Franks, at the Caernarfon Meeting in 1848[125a]. The study of Welsh seals still owes much to men like Franks, and also to George Grant Francis, F.S.A., the Cambrians' Local Secretary for Glamorgan, who wrote (in 1858) that he proposed to bring together 'impressions of all the known Welsh seals, fix them on proper mounts, and place them for public sight' in the Royal Institution of South Wales at Swansea[126]. By 1875 he had assembled 872 casts of seals relating to Wales, and exhibited them at the Cambrians Annual Meeting that year[127]. Many casts, presumably from his day, still remain in Swansea Museum - a minority of them only 'in public sight'.

At much the same time, Welsh sigillography benefited greatly from the work of Robert Ready. Born in Norwich (1811), he found himself in the 1840's relying for his income 'entirely upon work in connection with medieval seals and kindred objects of glyptic art'[128]. By the mid-1850's he was selling casts of seals, executed in sulphur or gutta-percha, from addresses in Cambridge and

Fig. 19: **Seal of Bishop Nicholas Robinson of Bangor** (1566-85) *BL, Harl. MS 2176, f.28d.*

elsewhere in East Anglia[129], and he made copies of the seals appended to the muniments of Pembroke College, Cambridge[129A]. In 1858 he was described as 'a perambulating dealer, who is generally on a tour after fresh seals'[130]. The next year his collection of seals 'connected with Wales', and cast in gutta-percha, comprised 271 specimens and copies of the collection were held at Carmarthen, Ludlow (still bearing the original enumeration), and Swansea Museums, and

Fig. 21:
George Grant Francis
(1814-82)
Courtesy of Swansea Museum: Swansea City Council Leisure Services

Fig. 22:
Robert Ready
(1811-1901)
from *L. Forrer, Biographical Dictionary of Medallists (1912).*

Fig. 23:
Walter de Gray Birch
(1842-1924)
from *The Illustrated London News; courtesy of National Portrait Gallery.*

Ready published in *Archaeologia Cambrensis* a catalogue of them[131]. A complete set could be purchased for six guineas[132]. Ready was now employed as a 'modeller' at the British Museum (1859-97), combining his work there with his private practice[133]. He died in Camden Town in 1901, and his son, Augustus P. Ready - who had worked at the Museum with his father, took on his mantle and succeeded him. So perfect were the replicas of Greek coins they produced that - save for the difference in weight - they could hardly be distinguished from the real thing. So perfect, too, were their electrotype copies of seal matrices - a process they pioneered, that as a means of precaution (against being mistaken for the originals), they were stamped on the rim with: **R** (Ready), **RR** (Robert Ready), or **MB** (Museo Britannica)[134]. Augustus' work included replicas (in 1915) of the seals of Ithel ap Bleddyn and the Carmarthen Staple, and he was a donor of seals to Carmarthen Museum[135].

Another member of staff at the British Museum was the prolific scholar, Walter de Gray Birch (*ob.* 1924), son of the Keeper of Oriental Antiquities there. Apart from his monastic researches, a textbook on seals, and his monumental and pain-staking six-volume catalogue of seals in the British Museum (most non-armorial personal seals being excluded), he also found time to publish a short treatise in *Archaeologia Cambrensis* (1889): *'On Some MSS and Seals Relating to Wales in the British Museum'*[136]. In that article he expressed the hope that a member of the Cambrian Archaeological Association 'might some day write a descriptive account of Welsh seals, destined for liberal illustration in *Archaeologia Cambrensis*'[137]. That wish has, in part, been fulfilled a century later[138]. When Birch died he left a box containing plaster casts of seals of the bishops and cathedral chapter of Llandaff. Through the good offices of a neighbour (H.L. Mann, a member of the Ecclesiological Society) they were presented to the National Museum by his daughter, Miss U. Birch of Chiswick.[139]. Two other sigillographers are worthy of mention. First, Bartholomew Howlett (1767-1827), who had made drawings of over one thousand seals for Caley's edition (1817-30) of Dugdale's *Monasticon Anglicanum*. His last years were clouded by financial difficulties, but he executed (between 1821 and 1827) a small volume of drawings of Welsh ecclesiastical seals - displaying two which can no longer be traced. His work is now in Cardiff Free Library[140]. He compiled a similar collection for Herefordshire[141]. Second, Michael Siddons - a noted heraldist, who in recent years used the opportunity of residence on the Continent (as a medical adviser to the European Commission), to bring to notice a number of Welsh seals attached to deeds in the Archives Nationales of France[142].

The National Museum is not the only repository of seals in Wales. Collections of modern casts and replicas of Welsh seals are to be found not only there and in Swansea Museum, but also amongst the collections of the

Society of Antiquaries of London, at Ludlow Museum, and to a lesser extent in the Ashmolean Museum, Oxford, and the local museums of Abergavenny, Abergwili (Carmarthen), Newport (Gwent) and Tenby. Welshpool's Powysland Museum has some eighty seal impressions - mostly English, but including two or three of Welsh interest. Of especial note are the casts (together with the dies) of Welsh railway seals held in the National Railway Museums at Swindon and York. Original impressions occur attached to Welsh deeds not only at the British Library (Dept. of MSS), the Public Record Office, and the Archives Nationales of Paris, but also at all the County Record Offices of Wales. Welsh original seals are also to be found in the cathedral archives at Durham, Gloucester, and Hereford. Other locations are noted later in this *Catalogue*. The most fruitful sources of original impressions are the archives of the University College of North Wales, Bangor, and undoubtedly, and above all, those of the Department of Manuscripts and Records at the National Library of Wales, Aberystwyth - (where also in a tin box, the Wyndham Clark collection of seals). A small collection is also held in the Department of Maps and Prints, and derives at least in part from a gift by the executors of Lady Mansel Franklen in 1938. Some of its contents were formerly the property of the Revd. J.M. Traherne referred to before, and the seals are accompanied by manuscript notes in the hand of the Revd. Thomas Rackett also alluded to above.

Welsh Seals at the National Museum

Certain classes of Welsh seals held are worthy of fuller comment:

1. The *Judicial Seals*. The Act of Union of 1536, uniting England and Wales, supplemented by a further act in 1542, established county boundaries in the Principality which endured until 1974. To counter the prevalent state of lawlessness in parts of Wales, the country (Monmouthshire excepted) was divided into four judicial circuits of three counties each, for the purposes of the Great Sessions[143]. The circuits were: Anglesey, Caernarfon, and Merioneth; Denbigh, Flint, and Montgomery; Cardigan, Carmarthen, and Pembroke; Brecon, Glamorgan, and Radnor. George Owen (1603) told how *'thear is in every sheere a great sessions or assisses houlden every yeare twyce, and a justice of assise for every three sheeres'* [144]. Each circuit had its own Judicial Seal which (on the obverse) displayed the monarch on horseback, and (on the reverse) a shield of the royal arms, with the Prince of Wales' feathers at the base. On the obverse, below the feet of the horse, a few of the seals displayed a local landscape: as Cardiff with the Herbert mansion (W.34), Caernarfon Castle with sailing ships on the Menai Straits (W.36), and Denbigh Castle with its circumventing wall (W.42). Mostly the judicial seal was impressed on deeds such as exemplifications of fines and of recovery. The issuing of writs in the first instance before the Great Sessions was by means of the 'original

seal' of the local chancery. The 'Method of Proceeding in the Court of Great Sessions for Glamorgan, Brecon and Radnor' (1817) noted an Original Seal for issuing writs and a Judicial Seal for witnessing judicial process[145]. The custodian of the judicial seal, or his lessee, was entitled to the perquisites deriving from it. This was made clear in a grant of James I (in 1608) to David Staverton of the City of London, gentleman, of *'all those issues which are profits of his highness' Judicial Seal, together with all fines or the king's Silver and Exemplifications as well at the great Sesssions of the Counties of Brecon, Radnor and Glamorgan, from time to time held or to be holden, as in time of vacation every year happening and every other time whatsoever'* [146]. The Courts of Great Sessions were abolished in 1830, and had perhaps become somewhat superfluous before this date.

2. The *Episcopal Seals*[147]. A bishop might possess no less than three or four seals to be used as occasion demanded. Most significant was his 'great seal' - used for all major charters and deeds; his seal *'ad causas'* - used for lesser business or when the 'great seal' was not at hand; his 'privy' seal - also used for lesser business and very often on the reverse of the 'great seal' to attest it; his 'signet seal' - used for private letters and the like, and often on a finger ring. A study of Welsh episcopal seals shows that the great seals down to the mid-fourteenth century portrayed the bishop standing (generally on a corbel), accompanied perhaps (from the early fourteenth century) by heraldic devices. From the mid-fourteenth century images other than those of the bishop frequently occur. These were often of the Saints, occasionally of the Holy Trinity, and in such cases the bishop is usually portrayed in a niche at the base of the seal engaged in prayer. After the Reformation the seals show a considerable change of emphasis, depicting, as they sometimes do, the Risen and Glorified Christ, or scenes from the Scriptures (examples including the Fall

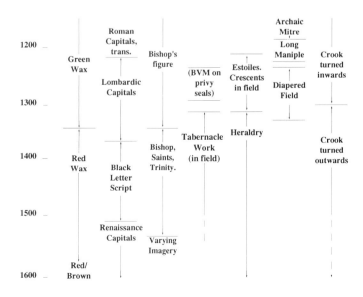

Fig. 24: **Dating an Episcopal Seal.** (*Arch. Camb.* CXXXIII (1984) 108, reproduced by permission of the Editor).

of Man, the Sacrifice of Isaac, and the Parable of the Sower). The seals are valuable for their portrayal of the varying emphases and developments in the vestments worn by the bishops of the time. Worthy of especial note are: (1) the archaic mitre, with lateral horns, worn until around 1170; (2) the breast-plate or *rationale* incised with a cross, frequently observed from about 1205 to 1280, and a precursor of the later pectoral cross; (3) the long pronounced maniple which features from about 1190 to 1230; (4) the decorated dalmatic which is especially prominent from the early fourteenth century onwards; (5) the changes wrought by the Reformation - a cope, or even a preaching gown or rochet and chimere, replacing the chasuble. The changes to be observed on Welsh episcopal seals over the centuries can be expressed diagrammatically; were such a seal to have lost its legend and ascription to a particular bishop, its period of engraving could easily thus be determined.

3. Seals of *Ecclesiastical Jurisdiction*[148]. The need for these was stressed in the *Constitutions* of Otto, Legate in England of Pope Gregory X (1237). He ordained that 'because notaries public are not used in England, and therefore there is more frequent occasion for authentic seals, not only bishops but their officials, also archdeacons and their officials, and rural deans' were to have their proper seals with their dignity or office 'graven in plain letters or characters'. If the office was for life or an indefinite term, a 'perpetual' one, then the personal name of the dignitary or official was also to be engraved upon his seal. If it was an office 'which is but for a time', as that of rural deans and their officals, then the name of the holder was not to appear upon it[149]. The *Constitutions* by emphasising the need of rural deans to have seals of office, reflect the greater importance of that office in the thirteenth century when it waned whilst the influence of the archdeacon increased[150]. The *Constitutions* further provided that upon the expiration of their office, rural deans and other holders of non-'perpetual' appointments were 'to resign their seals without trouble to him from whom they received it'. Finally, the *Constitutions* also enjoined both care in the custody of a seal of office, and caution 'in setting the seal'.

4. Seals of *Cathedral Chapters*[151]. The *Constitutions* of Otto further provided that deans and and also 'the chapters of cathedral churches, and other collegiate bodies' should have their especial seals. As cathedral and collegiate chapters were continuing corporate bodies, their seals usually enjoyed a long life. The second or third 'great seal' of Bangor was in use, for example, by 1383 down to at least 1544; the second seal of Llandaff, in existence perhaps by as early as about 1200, was still employed as late as 1545. Only one 'great seal' is known for St. David's; in use by 1367 and probably well before then, it so continued until at least 1543[152]. The seal impressions for Bangor show a predominance of green wax until 1426, but red or brown thereafter[153].

5. *Cistercian Seals*[154]. It is evident that by the close of the twelfth century, a variety of practice concerning seal design and usage had developed within the Cistercian Order. This led the General Chapter meeting at Cîteaux in 1200 to attempt to regularise matters. It ruled that each member abbey was to employ only its abbot's seal, and this was not to bear the abbot's personal name[155]. It was further laid down that the seal might take one of two forms for its device. There might be either an effigy of an abbot holding a pastoral staff, or else simply his hand clutching the staff. In the former case the abbot is generally seen standing on a corbel, vested in chasuble or cowl, his right hand holding the staff, his left hand clasping against his chest a book (presumably the *Rule of St. Benedict*). In the second type an abbot's cowled forearm is usually depicted, and the hand occasionally appears to be gloved with tassels hanging from the wrists. Some monasteries appear to have ignored these instructions, for in 1218 the General Chapter ordered any abbey which possessed a common seal to destroy it[156]. Cwmhir, therefore, when attaching its abbot's seal to a document (about 1235) felt constrained to explain that 'it is not a custom of our Order to have a common seal except the seal of the abbot'[157]. The General Chapter of that year also insisted that each abbot should possess only one seal[158]; a precaution against fraud and mis-use.

Change was to come. It was heralded in England and Wales by the Statute of Carlisle (1307) which provided that 'there be a common seal for religious houses in the custody not of the abbot, but of the prior and four worthy monks, and be placed in safe keeping under the private seal of the abbot'. The statute also implied that no deed was valid unless the common seal was attached[159]. Not long afterwards, in 1335, Pope Benedict XII in his Constitution for the Reform of the Cistercian Order (*Fulgens sicut stella*) laid down that each Cistercian house was to have its 'proper and especial seal', to be kept under lock and key[160]. The General Chapter amplified this instruction by ordering that such common seals were to be 'made rounded, of copper, and engraved with the image of the Blessed Virgin, in whose honour are founded all the monasteries of our Order'[161]. Pope Benedict's Constitution also provided that henceforth the seals of abbots were to have the personal names of the owners engraved in the legend. This was to avoid fraud, for in important business the abbatial seal was to be used in conjunction with the common seal, and being so inscribed made it easier to verify 'by whom and in whose time' a particular transaction took place[162]. These seals also often came to bear an image of the Blessed Virgin Mary, and to be far more elaborate in design than the abbatial seals of the thirteenth century. The common seals, as well as displaying the Blessed Virgin (and sometimes an abbot kneeling in supplication before her), also frequently came to portray relevant armorial bearings[163]. In Tudor times, and before, several abbeys applied a small abbatial signet to the reverse of impressions of the common seal[164].

6. *Other Monastic Seals*[165]. The statutes regarding seals which emanated from the Parliament at Carlisle (1306-7) applied to all religious houses, and not simply Cistercian ones. They were reinforced by Archbishop Cranmer who ruled that the seals of 'chapters, hospitals, and other societies' were not to be applied to any document whatsoever, save with the agreement of the 'greater part' of their members[166]. The imagery employed was diverse, although the Blessed Virgin Mary continues to be frequently displayed. There were also scriptural scenes (as the Resurrection on the seals of Goldcliff Priory and Christ's Hospital, Ruthin); biblical imagery (as the eagle on the seals of Brecon and Carmarthen Priories); and national and local saints (as in the cases of St. David's Hospital, Swansea, and St. Seiriol's Priory, Penmon). Worthy of especial note is the close resemblance in design between the common seals of Usk Priory (Benedictine nuns) and of St. Dogmael's Abbey (Tironian monks), once again suggesting a common designer or engraver.

Fig. 25: **St. Dogmael's Abbey** (1534).
(PRO, E 25/40).

Fig. 26: **Usk Priory** (1534)
(PRO, E 25/111, pt.2).

7. *Civic Seals*[167]. One lasting consequence of Edward I's Conquest of Wales lay in his building a series of castles at strategic points. In many cases a borough was established near the castle, a number of which lay by the sea. The granting of a charter and corporate status to such settlements meant the emergence of civic common seals which frequently incorporated the two elements of the castle and the sea in their design. The first corporate seals of Chepstow, Criccieth, Denbigh, and Harlech, all displayed a castle; that of Conwy showed a castle by the waves of the sea; that of Beaumaris exhibited a castle and a ship; those of Haverfordwest and Tenby had engraved a ship on the obverse face, a fortification on the reverse. Early seals of Monmouth (on the River Wye) and Newborough, and the second seal of Beaumaris, displayed a sailing vessel only. The medieval and modern seals of Cowbridge were allusive, showing a *cow* walking across a *bridge*. There was a variety of other imagery employed on Welsh civic seals. The engraving of such corporate seals in the early Middle Ages can be ascribed to within a few years at most of the granting of the charter concerned; that of Denbigh suggests a hurried and unfinished design. Later charters frequently authorise the possession of a corporate seal, as the royal charter to Brecon in 1556: *'and that the aforesaid bailiff, aldermen and burgesses, may have a common seal to serve their businesses, and to break, change, and make anew that seal at their pleasure'*[168]. The granting of this new charter meant the design of a seal displaying a cape or mantle of state ermine lined, replacing the seal hitherto used of Edward Stafford, Duke of Buckingham and Lord of Brecon[169], and bearing the arms of Braose and Bohun, two of the town's earlier lords[170]. Occasionally, a seal is precisely dated. The second seal of Beaumaris concludes its legend with the year, '1562', and inscribed on the hull is the further date, '8 Feb'. Its new charter was granted by Elizabeth I on June 22nd, 1562; perhaps '8 Feb' refers to the date of engraving the following year[171] - then calculated as 1562 until Lady Day (March 25th).

8. *Personal Seals.* People of substance often employed a seal which was either *equestrian* - showing them on horseback, or *armorial* - displaying on a shield (very often) their family heraldry. Persons of yet greater consequence might have a two-faced seal: equestrian on the obverse side, heraldic on the reverse[172]. Even small land-owners and the peasantry[173] needed sometimes to use a personal seal; as was foreshadowed in Scripture: *'Fields shall be bought for money, and deeds shall be signed and sealed and witnessed'* (Jeremiah 32/44). It was noted (1283) that the Welsh jurors involved in an extent of Tempsiter (Salop) had no seals with which the extent could be sealed[174], but all the substantial freeholders of Rhos and Rhufoniog (Gwynedd) had their personal seals (1283-95)[175]. There was in fact in the medieval period a wide variety of often quite small personal seals for lesser folk. Sometimes these were distinctive to themselves, having their own name inscribed in the legend;

sometimes they were bought (already bearing a device) 'off the peg', so to speak, from a dealer, and their personal name was added[176]; others were impersonal, the matrix revealing no clue to its owner if found detached. Something of this has been noted above. Some seals were allusive: a member of the Butler (pincerna) family shown holding a cup[177]; a seal of the Luvel family displaying a wolf (Fr. 'louve')[178]; the porter of Cardiff grasping a key[179], and so on. Others might depict a common emblem of the times, as the fleur-de-lys, or as (frequently in NE Wales) ears of wheat, reflecting the agrarian society of the day[180]. Taken together, an interesting group of seals (mostly thirteenth century and from the Margam region) display the pastime of hunting: a hunter with his horn, a bow and arrow, a stag at speed, and a wolf[181]. The seal of a lady of noble or knightly birth frequently showed her holding two shields: in her right hand that bearing the arms of her husband, in the left hand that displaying the heraldry of her father[182]. Lesser individuals frequently made use of the seal of another person when transacting business, either because he or she had no seal or their seal was not well enough known. The seal they might well then employ would very often be that of their superior lord. Gwenwynwyn of Powys (about 1200) sealed with his own seal the deed of sale of Perbethgefn by Meurig Sais to Strata Marcella because Meurig had no seal, and very probably Gwenwynwyn wanted to secure the gift for his foundation[183]. The seal of Maurice Grammus was similarly used (about 1250) upon the occasion of a grant to Margam Abbey by Alice vergh Alexander[184]. Much later (1554), John Hughes, surrogate for the Keeper of Spiritualities in the diocese of Bangor, somewhat surprisingly employed the seal of a former archdeacon of Carmarthen (Henry ab Hywel: 1494-1509). He had to affix a seal to a probate document, and seems to have used the one nearest to hand[185].

Notes:

1. Williams (1982) 4-5.

2. Jones (1947) 51.

3. Ibid. 52.

4. BL, Harl. Ch. 75 A.37; cf. *Arch. Ael.* 3rd Ser. XVII (1920) 262.

5. Edwards (1940) 85.

6. Williams (1962) 68.

7. Cal. Papal Registers (Letters) I, 500-01; cf. Edwards (1940) 183.

8. Rees (1975) 404.

9. Cal. Close Rolls, *1314*, 192.

10. Vaughan (1917) 25.

11. Isaacson (1917) II, 407.

12. Ibid. I, 169.

13. Barber and Lewis (1901) 156.

14. Carlisle (1818) II.

15. Jeffreys Jones (1955) 215-6.

16. PRO, C 219/72.

17. *Usk Town Trail*, (handbook to the *Inner Route*) 7; for a lead cloth seal found in excavations at Abergavenny (1972-73), see: *Monm. Antiq.* X (1994).

18. Cardiff Central Library, Tonn MS 3. 104, vol.2, p.185.

19. Williams (1982) 5.

20. Acc. File 31. 78/1-9; the matrix was that of Edward IV for his Chancery of Monmouth (D. 27).

21. Acc. File 54.484.

22. Acc. File 25.384; for something of Rackett, see: *Gentl. Mag.* 100:I (1830) 449, and N.S. IV (1835) 220; for an obituary of Traherne, see: *Gentl. Mag.* 1860 : I, 517.

22a. *Arch. Camb.* I (1846) 148-9.

23. Siddons (1981) 531-44, (1985) 233-240, (1989) 185-6.

24. Acc. File 34.665.

25. Acc. File 42.133.

26. Acc. File 40.47.

27. Acc. File 28.582.

28. Acc. File 29.327.

29. Acc. File 31.234.

30. Acc. File 29.327.

31. Friends of the National Museum of Wales, *Annual Report* (Cardiff, 1983) cover, and pp. 4, 9.

32. Williams (1982a) 139, Pl. XVII.

33. Lewis (1968) 66-7, Pl. Ib.

34. Mein (1992) 25-8.

35. Williams (1982) 18-9.

36. Williams (1983) 102.

37. Ibid. 102.

37a. *The Searcher* (Sept. 1991) 27 (No. 9).

37b. Tonnochy (1952) 201 (No. 931).

37c. Biddle (1990) 754.

38. Fryde (1974) 64 (No.5040).

39. Clark (1910) IV, 1344.

40. *Arch. Jnl.* XCVII (1940) 174.

41. Forrer V (1912) 38-9, 51-2; *D.N.B.* 47 (1896) 326..

42. Forrer II (1904) 4-5; NLW, MS 1396E; *Brit. Numis. Jnl.* 1st Ser. VI, 263-4.

43. Forrer V (1912) 210.

44. Ibid. 38-9.

45. Forrer VI (1916) 579-657.

46. Charles (1967) 186, 215.

47. Tucker (1962) 57.

48. Matthews II (1900) 346.

49. Cardiff Central Library, Tonn MS 3.104, vol. 2, p. 185.

50. Pearson (1979) 44, 47-8, 50, 75, 81-5; Wilkins (1908) 569-70.

51. Hereford Cathedral Archive 2295; Williams (1982) 17.

52. Rees (1975) 118.

53. PRO, C 24/29 (pt.2).

54. Barber and Lewis (1901) 156.

55. NLW, Dolrhyd Deed 1, Peniarth (Hengwrt) Deed 208; UCNW, Nannau MS 863.

56. Glam. Archives, CL/Deeds II/ Monts./Box 3 (R.2): kind information of Mr. Graham Thomas.

57. Ruthin Hospital Charities, *Christ's Hospital, Ruthin, Clwyd: A Brief History* (1990) 2.

58. Matthews IV (1903) 379.

59. Rees (1975) 118; *Monm. Antiq.* III : 1 (1971) 44.

60. Williams (1984a) 76.

61. Thomas (1930) 87.

62. Yardley (1927) 44-5.

63. PRO, C 3/6/57; Huett, precentor from 1562 to 1588, was a noted biblical scholar and translator; he lived at the former Cistercian grange of Aberduhonw south of Builth: Owen (1892) 241-2.

64. *Cal. Letters and Papers (Domestic), temp. Henry VIII* (Rolls Ser.) XII: pt.2, 53 (No. 159).

65. Taylor (1977) 253; a seal suggested as being that of an earlier Prince David (1240-46) is more probably that of Henry III : Owen and Blakeway I (1825) 118.

66. Williams (1982) 6 (No.3).

67. Williams (1982) 17.

68. NLW, MS 3854B (of 1817) 4, 17.

69. Issacson I (1917) 201, 207; III (1920) 68.

70. PRO, E 321/10/45.

71. PRO, C 1/951/82/.

72. Owen Edwards (1925) 102.

73. *Arch. Jnl.* XVIII (1861) 48; cf. *Jnl. Brit. Arch. Assoc.* XIII, 348-50, 353-5.

74. NLW, MS 13,482C (Evans, G., *Cardiganshire Notes, II*) 119.

75. *Arch. Camb.* 1856/370.

76. *Arch. Camb.* 1879/142-3; *Arch. Jnl.* VIII, 76; *Proc. Soc. Antiq.* 2nd. Ser. 108 (where ascription to Revesby doubted); NLW, Map Room Seal Collection, for manuscript attribution to Tintern.

77. *Arch. Camb.* 1856/370.

78. *Arch. Camb.* 1857/426, 1886/26-7; cf. *Jnl. Brit. Arch. Assoc.* XIV, 56-8.

78A. *Arch. Camb.* 1893/187.

78B. *Arch. Camb.* II (1847) 19-20.

79. *Antiq. Jnl.* XLVI (1966) 104-6.

80. Acc. File 38.422.

81. *Monm. Antiq.* VI (1990) 56-7.

82. Acc. File 55.202.

83. Acc. File 83.13H (found at approx. NGR SS 641919).

84. A replica (D 33) is in the Museum's collections.

85. NLW, Penralley MS (Suppl.) 28.

86. *Antiques Trade Gazette*, 28th Febr. 1987; Bloomsbury Book Auctions, *Sale Catalogue* - 12th March 1987 (No.135).

87. *Arch. Camb.* 1851/335-6; for some other seal finds in Wales, see: *Proc. Soc. Antiq.* 2nd Ser. VI, 108; XIV, 10.

88. PRO (Chancery Lane) files, Case 25/1 (1975-6).

89. Letter to compiler from Mr. Roger Ellis, F.S.A (formerly of the P.R.O): 20th Jan. 1992.

90. Information of Mr. Hodson, the builder; find date: 12th April 1988.

91. Now in the Carmarthen Museum, Abergwili, Dyfed.

92. D 12.

92a. *Monm. Antiq.* IX (1993) in press.

93. Venables (1891) 59.

94. Williams (1984a) I, 169.

95. NLW, MS 3854B (of 1817) 4, 17.

96. Williams (1982) 8-9 (No.8).

97. E.g: NLW, Bronwydd (Group II) Deeds 2077, 3095; Edwinsford Deeds 2446, 2464.

98. Edwards (1935) 51, cf. 24.

99. BL, Cott. Ch. XXLV, 17.

99a. Siddons (1991a) 281.

100. Demay (1880) 43.

101. Ibid. 45; other terms Demay cites includes, but rarely used: 'anti-sigillum' and 'sub-sigillum'; for the last mentioned, see also: Canivez III, 540 (of 1363).

102. *Notes and Queries*, 1st Ser. V (3 April 1852) 317; Du Fresne VI (1736) 487.

103. Williams (1982) 18-9 (Nos. 36-7), 22 (No.42), 27 (No.57).

104. Lewis (1740) 18-9, Du Fresne VI, 489.

105. Williams (1984) 106.

106. Bloom (1906) 7-9.

107. Williams (1982) 11; BL, Sloane MS 73, f. 128b-129 (regarding the manufacture of vermilion and verdigris); *Encycl. Brit.* (11th edn.,) XXIV (1911) 538.

108. *Trans. Carms. Antiq. Soc.* IX (1913), 94.

109. Powell (1964) 24, 27.

110. Demay (1880) 43-4.

111. Gough (1780) xliii, Lewis (1740) 9.

112. London, 1740.

113. Gough (1780) xliii.

114. Schloss Burgpreppach, 1964.

115. See, for example, Gatfield I (1892) 66-9.

116. *Medals, Coins, Great Seals of Thomas Simon* (1st edn., London, 1753); *Catalogue of Engravers* (1888) in Walpole, H., *Anecdotes of Painting in England*, Pt.3 (1888).

117. *An Account of the Seals of the Kings, Royal Boroughs, and Magnates of Scotland* (London, 1792).

118. As, for example, BL, Cott. MS Jul. C. vii (of 1611); Add. MSS 8157; 21,056; 24,480; 26,759; Stowe MSS 289-90, 504; Harleian MS 6107.

119. Gough (1780) xxxix; *Notes and Queries* 159 (1930) 343; *Monm. Antiq.* VI (1990) 55-8; *Arch. Jnl.* XIX, 369.

120. Barnard (1930) 132-8; *Notes and Queries* 159 (1930) 343; *D.N.B.* 47 (1896) 332.

121. Forrer I (1904) 612, *Numis. Chr.* (1849), and see his MS Catalogue of Seals (British Library, Dept. of MSS).

122. Forrer III (1907) 271; and see Laing (1850) and (1866).

123. Forrer IV (1909) 169-72.

124. Forrer III (1907) 480-3.

125. Commencing with the Temporary Museum set up at the Cardiff Meeting (1849) which exhibited seals loaned by the Revd. J.M. Traherne: *Arch. Camb.* IV (1849) 320.

125A. *Arch. Camb.* III (1848) 352.

126. *Arch. Camb.* 1858/316.

127. *Arch. Camb.* 1875/419.

128. Forrer V (1912) 53-4.

129. *Notes and Queries* 2nd Ser. II (1855) 509, *Arch. Jnl.* XVII, 62.

129A. *Arch. Jnl.* XII (1855) 108.

130. *Notes and Queries* 2nd Ser. V (1858) 367.

131. *Arch. Camb.* 1860/281-4; see also: *Arch. Camb.* 1858/466, 1859/350.

132. *Arch. Camb.* 1859/310.

133. Forrer V (1912) 53-4; *Notes and Queries* 3rd Ser. V (1864) 185, 5th. Ser. VI (1876) 475, XI (1879) 176.

134. Forrer V (1912) 54.

135. Noted at the Carmarthen Museum, Abergwili; *Trans. Carms. Antiq. Soc.* XII (1917-8) ix.

136. *Arch. Camb.* 5th Ser. VI (1889) 273-92.

137. *Arch. Camb.* 5th Ser. VI (1889) 273.

138. In the compiler's six-part *Catalogue of Welsh Ecclesiastical Seals* (*Arch. Camb.* 1984-9).

139. Acc. File 44/171.

140. Cardiff Central Library MS 4.335; *D.N.B.* 28 (1891) 127.

141. BL, Add. MS 24,101.

142. Siddons (1981) 531-44, (1985) 233-40, (1989) 185-6, (1991a) 8-10, 18.

143. Jenkinson (1935) 325-6; Llewellyn Williams (1916) 13, Williams (1982) 32-3, Wyon (1893) 1-14; NLW, MSS 3854B (pp. 4, 17), 11724D, 11725E.

144. Owen III (1906) 40. .

145. NLW, MS 3854B.

146. NLW, Misc. Deeds, Box 1 (Wales).

147. For further details, see: Williams (1984) 105-9.

148. For further details, see: Williams (1985) 162-4.

149. Johnson (1720) Pt.2 : MCCXXXVII/28; cf. Bloom (1906) 154-5.

150. Williams (1985) 163, Ollard and Crosse (1919) 527-8.

151. For further details, see: Williams (1986) 154.

152. Williams (1986) 154.

153. Williams (1989) 76.

154. For further details, see: Williams (1984b) 249-547, (1987) 138-40.

155. Clay (1928) 7, *Proc. Soc. Antiq.* 2nd Ser. IX, 197-9.

156. Canivez I, 251-2 (1200/15), 487 (1218/17), cf. 493 (1218/45).

157. Beverley Smith (1970) 91.

158. Canivez I, 487 (1218/13).

159. Clay (1928) 7.

160. Canivez III, 411 *(bulla* 2).

161. Canivez III, 437 (1335/2).

162. Canivez III, 415 (Constit. 1335/9).

163. Williams (1987) 139-40.

164. Williams (1987) 140.

165. For further details, see: Williams (1988) 119.

166. Cranmer (1641) 228-9.

167. For further details, see: Williams (1982) 24-6, 38-41.

168. NLW, *Royal Charter of the Borough of Brecon, 1556*, p. 5; cf. *Trans. Carms. Antiq. Soc.* XIX (1925) 86, where Richard II (1379) granting a charter to Llandovery provided that there was to be *'a common seal used in the affairs of the borough'*.

169. Banks and Dineley (1888) 216, 220; Scott-Giles (1933) 56-7.

170. Griffiths (1972) 54.

171. Williams (1982) 38 (No.87).

172. Hunter Blair (1920) 273-80.

173. Delisle (1851) 182.

174.   *Cal. Inq. Misc.* (Rolls Ser.)., I, 371 (No.1272).

175.   Jones (1949) 142-4.

176.   Atkins and Margery (1985) 18.

177.   Williams (1982) 15 (No.32).

178.   Ibid. 14 (No.29); Siddons (1991a) 260.

179.   Ibid. 25 (No.54).

180.   Ibid. 15 (Nos. 30-1, 33).

181.   Ibid. 14 (Nos. 26-9).

182.   Ibid. 13 (No.21).

183.   Jones (1871) 304.

184.   Birch (1897) 196, cf. 199.

185.   Clwyd (Ruthin) R.O., DD/WY/842.

GROUP D : SEAL DIES

WALES

ECCLESIASTICAL

D 1.   ABERGWILI, Dyfed : Collegiate Church of St Maurice.
Common Seal.
Post-1334 (when the position of precentor was established). Brass, 38.6 g., on reverse a soldered emplacement for a hinged handle; p.o., 60 x 37 mm.
Within a canopied niche, St Maurice, in full plate armour of Lancastrian period style; in base: the precentor in prayer to left.
* **S' precentoris / et / capitili / ecclesie / collegiate / de / abergwilly** (Bl.)
The matrix was found in 1963, by eight-year old Margaret Rowley in spoil from construction of the M1 motorway near Leicester, in a waste tip near the south-west of the town. The spoil may have come from the vicinity of Abbey Farm.
Acc. No: 65.80.
D: Boon (1966) 104-6; Isaacson (1917) I, 160; II, 437; Williams (1982) 28 (No.62), (1986) 161 (No.214a).

D 2.   ARWYSTLI, Powys : Deanery of.
Royal Seal for Ecclesiastical Causes.
1549-53 (temp. Edw. VI). Brass, 99.5 g., with folding scrolled handle; p.o., 78 x 54 mm.
The royal arms, France (Modern) and England quarterly, ensigned with the imperial crown; supporters: *dexter*, a lion guardant crowned; *sinister*, a dragon; ensigned with a crown; in base: the ascription: **PRO : COMISSARIO : ARWYSTLEY.**
+ SIGILLVM : REGIAE : MAIESTATIS : AD : CAVSAS : ECCLESIASTICAS (Ren.)
The matrix was found, about 1875, in Cooper's Fields, Cardiff - near the site of the Black Friars, and was presented (in 1880) to Cardiff Museum by G.E. Robinson, Esq.
Acc. No: 03.229.
D: Arch. III, 414-6; *Arch. Camb.* 1884/228-32, *Mont. Collns.* XVI, 259-62; *Proc. Soc. Antiq.* 2nd Ser. IX, 39-40; Williams (1985) 166 (No.105; (where also notes on this class of seals in general); *Eighteenth Annual Report of the Cardiff Free Library and Museum, 1879-80* (Cardiff, 1880) 15.

D 3.   BANGOR, Gwynedd; Bishop of: J.C. Campbell, D.D.
1859-90. Brass, p.o., 97 x 65 mm.
A shield ensigned with a mitre; *dext.* a bend gutty (de poix) between two pierced mullets, BANGOR; *sin.* gyronny of eight quartering a lymphad, CAMPBELL.
THE SEAL OF JAMES COLQUHOUN CAMPBELL D D BISHOP OF BANGOR 1859 (Caps.)
Acc. No: 29.327/1 (WFM).
Seals D 3 - 5, and 9, presented by A. Ivor Pryce, Diocesan Registrar of Bangor.
D: Bedford (1897) 21.

D 4.   BANGOR, Gwynedd; Bishop of: D.L. Lloyd, S.T.R.
1890-99. Brass, p.o., 83 x 61 mm.
A shield ensigned with a mitre; *dext.* BANGOR (as No. 3); *sin.* a spear's head embrued between three scaling ladders, on a chief a castle, LLOYD, (the coat attributed to Cydifor ap Dinawal).
+ SIGIL : DANIEL LEWIS LLOYD : S : T : R : EPI : BANGORIENSIS A : S : MDCCCXC (Pseudo-Lom.)

Acc. No: 29.327/2 (WFM).
D: Bedford (1897) 20.

D 5.   BANGOR, Gwynedd; Bishop of: D. Davies, D.D.
1925-28. Bronze, p.o., 74 x 58 mm.
A shield ensigned with a mitre, BANGOR (as No. 3).
+ SEAL + OF + DANIEL + DAVIES + D.D. + BISHOP + OF + BANGOR + 1925 (Caps.)
Acc. No: 29.327/3 (WFM).
D: Y Cymm. XXXIX (1928) opp. p. 149.

D 6.   BANGOR, Gwynedd; Bishop of: C.A.H. Green, D.D.
1928-44. Gilt brass, p.o., 104 x 71 mm.
A shield ensigned with a mitre, heavily worked and with prominent *infulae; dext.* BANGOR (as No. 3), *sin.* three stags trippant, GREEN.
Sig : Caroli : Alfredi : Hoell : Green S:T:P : Bangoriensis : Epi : mdmxxviii (Pseudo-Early Bl.)
On the reverse is stamped the name and address of the well-known seal engraver, Allan Wyon, 80 Boundary Road, London, N.W. (WFM). Presented by the Friends of the Museum in 1983.

D 7.   *Fob Seal.*
1928-44. Amethyst in gold bezel, 19 x 16 mm.
A shield: BANGOR (as No. 3).
Acc. No: 44.298/5 (WFM)

D 8.   BRECON, Powys; Christ's College.
1541- . Brass replica, p.o., 61 x 45 mm.
Our Lord on the Cross; to either side a shield: *dext.* on a cross five cinquefoils, ST DAVID'S; *sin.* quarterly FRANCE (Modern) and ENGLAND (for Henry VIII, founder); the college chapel (formerly part of the Dominican Friary in the background.
(A.D) SIG. COLLEG · CHRIST · DE · BRECKNOCK (1541) FVND · A · SER · DOM · REG · HENRIC? OCTAV? (Ren.)
The matrix was a duplicate seal engraved for Bishop D.L. Lloyd of Bangor, whilst he was Headmaster of Christ's College.
Acc. No: 29.327/4 (WFM).
D: Williams (1982) 412 (No.98), (1986) 161 (No. 215a).

D 9.   CARDIFF, S.Glam; Fraternity of the Holy Trinity.
15th cent. Brass, with remnants of hinge emplacement on reverse; circ., 30 mm.
The Blessed Trinity: God the Father seated, supporting His Crucified Son, above the Father's right shoulder is the Holy Spirit descending as a dove; cusped border.
S · frīs · trinitatis · de · kerdif · in · galis (Bl.)
The matrix was found in a heap of manure (brought from Cardiff) in a turnip field at Llantwit Major, and presented by J. Stradling Carne.
Acc. No: 83.4.
D: Antiq. VII (1883) 275, *Arch. Camb.* 1856/370, CXXXVII (1988) 133 (No. 299a); *Antiq.* VII (1883) 275; *Arch. Jnl.* VIII (1851) 76; *J.B.A.A.* II (1847) 346: *Proc. Soc. Antiq.* 1st. Ser. 168; Matthews (1898) I, 261; VI, cxi; *21st Annual Report of the Cardiff Free Library and Museum, 1882-3* (Cardiff, 1883) 19.

D 10. CARDIFF, S. Glam; Church Congress.
1889. Bronze, p.o., 49 x 34 mm., with wooden handle.
The Holy Spirit descending as a dove above an angel in glory bearing two shields: uppermost (and surmounted by a cross botonny), (Sable) two croziers in saltire, on a chief (Azure) three mitres, LLANDAFF; and beneath, (Or) three chevronels (Gules) CLARE (for *Cardiff*); in base, an eagle, and a scroll inscribed: '*Ye Gifte of Counseil*'.
CHURCH CONGRESS CARDIFF A.D. 1889   (Pseudo-Lom.)
Presented by Canon Thompson, D.D., to Cardiff Museum.
Acc. No: 01.347.
D: Annual Report Cardiff Public Museum and Art Gallery, 1901-02 48.

D 11.   *Metal stamp* (as No. 10).
Acc. No: 01.410.

D 12. CARMARTHEN, Dyfed; Archdeacon of: Walter Wynter.
Ca. 1328-31. Bronze, 16.94 g., p.o., 42 x 25 mm.
Under a trefoiled canopy, decorated by quatrefoils and supported by side-shafts with tabernacle work, St Stephen vested in alb and dalmatic (the robes of a deacon), holding two of his traditional symbols - three stones upraised in his right hand, (indicative of the manner of his martyrdom); a Book of the Gospels in his left. In base, under a carved gothic arch, the archdeacon two-thirds length gowned (or surpliced) and capped, in prayer to the left.
S' WALTR' WYNT' A R C HID̄ DE KERM̄DYN   (Lom.)
The matrix was found by Mr. D.G. Jones (Whitefield Farm, Cowbridge) in 1991 in the vicinity of Castell Coch, Aberthin, S. Glam., at approx. NGR ST 07/SW 027748. The find was made not very far north of the medieval Portway (now followed in large measure by the A. 48 road), and this suggests that the archdeacon was on a journey well away from when he lost his seal.
Acc. No: 92.69H.

D 13. GRACE DIEU, Gwent; Cistercian Abbey of the BVM.
Common Seal.
13th-early 14th cent. Gilded brass, p.o., 49 x 28 mm., small handle on reverse.
A tonsured abbot standing in eucharistic vestments upon a corbel, a book held in his left hand, his pastoral staff held by his right hand (crook turned outwards); in field, *sin.* an estoile above a mullet; *dext.* the words **ET CONVENT'** appear to have been added to the legend following either the Statute of Carlisle (1307) or the Constitution of Pope Benedict XII (1335), both of which decreed the use of common seals in the Cistercian Order; possibly this abbey (only a small one) did not want to bear the cost of engraving of a new seal, and so in this way converted its abbot's seal into its common seal.
Mr M Corfield first noticed that this is a gilded matrix, and Susan LaNiece and M.S. Tite of the Research Laboratory of the British Museum make this further report: 'The lettering and detail are sharply engraved but show evidence of wear consistent with frequent use. The uppermost star engraved beside the figure appears less worn and it is suggested that this is a later addition. The gilding is visible to the naked eye in many of the recesses but no traces are present on the flat face of the seal matrix'.
+ SIGILLVM : ABBATIS : DE GRACIA · DEI (ET CONVENT')   (Lom.)
Sometime after the suppression of the abbey, the matrix passed into the possession of the Lorymers of Perthir, Monmouth; it was presented to St Gregory's College, Downside, in 1830, who in turn gave it to the Society of Antiquaries in 1935. It is currently on long loan to the National Museum.
Acc. No: 79.99H.
E: NLW, Milborne MS 4876 (of 1473 A.D.) - see No. W 167 in this
       Catalogue. A different design apparently occurs on the seal of Grace
       Dieu attached to Hereford Cathedral Archive 1775.
D: *Downside Review* VII 115-6; Coxe (1801) 289, 427; Williams (1964) 94,
       (1980), 54, (1987) 148 (No.242a), (1989) 77.

D 14. LLANDAFF, S. Glam; Bishop of: J.P. Hughes, D.D.
1905-31. Brass, p.o., 81 x 54 mm.
A shield: *dext.* (Sable) two croziers in saltire, on a chief (Azure) three

mitres with their *infulae*, LLANDAFF; *sin.* a lion a lion rampant, on a chief arched (Gules) two crosslets, HUGHES.
+ THE : SEAL : OF : JOSHUA : PRITCHARD : HUGHES /
BISHOP : OF : LLANDAFF   (Caps.)
Presented by the bishop on 2 June, 1931, at the request of Dr Cyril Fox, Director.
Acc. No: 31.234 (WFM).

D 15. LLANDAFF, S. Glam; Bishop of: J. Morgan, D.D.
1939-57. Bronze, p.o., 89 x 59 mm.
A shield: LLANDAFF (as D. 14 *dexter*) ensigned with a mitre.
+ The · Seal · of · John · Morgan · D : D : Bishop
· of · Llandaff · Mcmxxxix   (Pseudo-Bl.)
Acc. No: 58.1.

D 16.   *Duplicate.*
Acc. No: 58.1.
D 15 and D 16 were deposited in the Museum consequent upon a wish the archbishop expressed during his life. The one matrix was of an inferior type of metal and became unsuitable for use, so a second was engraved. This differed very slightly in design.

D 17. LLANDAFF, S. Glam; Chancellor of: G. Harris, LL.D.
1756-96. Steel, p.o., 81 x 56 mm.
A shield: *dext.* LLANDAFF (as D. 14 *dexter*), *sin.* a lion rampant in an orle of cinquefoils, HARRIS perhaps the coat attributed to Gwynfardd; in base: a bust.
· THE · SEAL · OF · GEO · HARRIS · LL · D · CHANCELLOR ·
OF · LLANDAFF · 1756   (Caps.)
Presented by Viscount Sankey.
Acc. No: 48.115 (WFM).

D 18. LLANDAFF, S. Glam; Chancellor of: Viscount Sankey, K.C.
1909-14. Brass, p.o., 70 x 50 mm.
A shield: LLANDAFF (as D. 14 *dexter*).
+ THE SEAL OF JOHN SANKEY M.A B.C.L K.C
CHANCELLOR OF LLANDAFF 1909   (Caps.)
Acc. No: 40.48 (WFM)

D 19. LLANDAFF, S. Glam; Parish Burial Board
19th cent. Steel, p.o., 62 x 44 mm.
The west front of the cathedral; the field surrounded by foliage.
+ LLANDAFF PARISH + BURIAL BOARD   (Pseudo-Lom.)
Acc. No: 27.456.

D 20. LLŶN, Gwynedd; Rural Dean of: Eynon.
Early 13th cent. Slate, 42.5 g., p.o., 48 x 27 mm.
A fish, perhaps a pike. (The initial **S** of the legend is reversed).
+ SIGILL ENNII DECANI DE LEIN   (Lom.)
This matrix was found about 1890 at Mynydd Ednyfed, near Criccieth.
Presented by W.J. Hemp, HM Office of Works.
Acc. No: 20.119.
D: Proc. Soc. Antiq. 2nd Ser. XXX, 183-4; Hemp (1939) 200; Williams
       (1985) 188 (No. 189a).

D 21. MEIRIONYDD, Archdeacon of: Richard Langford.
1717-32. Silver, oval, 47 x 37 mm; with wooden handle.
A cartouche bearing arms: a shoveller, wings close, LANGFORD; above is the date: **1717**.
SIGILLVM · RICH · LANGFORD · A · M · ARCHDIAC · MERIONETH · (Caps.)
Presented by an anonymous donor.
Acc. No: 86.15H.
D: Hemp (1939) 202-3.

D 22. MONMOUTH, Gwent; Bishop of: C.A.H. Green, D.D.
1921-28. Brass, p.o., 93 x 75mm.
A shield, ensigned with a mitre: *dext.* two croziers in saltire between in chief a roundel charged with a lion passant guardant, in fess two fleurs-de-lis, and in base a fleur-de-lis, SEE OF MONMOUTH, impaling *sin.* three stags trippant, GREEN.

THE : SEAL : OF : CHARLES : ALFRED : HOWELL : GREEN : D : D : BISHOP :
OF MONMOUTH : 1921   (Pseudo-Lom.)
Presented by the bishop subsequent to a conversation in a train near
Wrexham with Dr Cyril Fox, Director.
Acc. No: 28.582 (WFM).
D: Williams (1982) 45 (No. 107).

D 23.   *Signet*
1921-28. Amethyst in seal ring, 19 x 16 mm face.
The arms of Dr Green as Bishop of Monmouth (as No. 22), but the seal
defaced - probably after his translation to Bangor.
Presented by the Hon Mrs C.A.H. Green.
Acc. No: 44.298/4 (WFM).

D 24.   STRATA FLORIDA, Dyfed; Cistercian Abbey of the B.V.M.
Abbatial Seal
15th cent. Silver (with loop handle on reverse; p.o., 44 x 28 mm.
Under a gothic-type canopy with side pinnacles, the Blessed Virgin
seated and crowned, her left hand grasps a sceptre fleury, her right arm
supports the Child; in base: within a rounded niche flanked by
masonry, the abbot, cowled and tonsured, clasping his pastoral staff,
kneels in prayer facing half-right; to either side a shield: *dext.* a crosier
in bend, *sin.* an eagle. In the legend the abbot's name has been
obliterated, probably after his death or cession to allow use of the seal
by his successor, and thus obviate the cost of engraving a new one.
sigill'. / / / / / / abb'is de strata florida   (Bl.)
The matrix was found locally about 1807; it is currently on loan from
the British Museum (Dept. of Medieval and Later Antiquities). It is of
exceptionally fine craftsmanship.
Acc. No: 80.27H.
D: Arch. Camb. 1848/191, Meyrick (1907) 246; Tonnochy (1952) 184
    (No. 858), Williams (1889) 87, 107; Williams (1987) 145 (No. 234a);
    Trans. Carms. Antiq. Soc. XI (1916-7) 62, notes a letter of 7th June,
    1901, from W. de Gray Birch to G. Eyre Evans, stating that 'a silver
    electrotype of this original matrix was made a few years ago', and was
    then in Cardiganshire.

**D 25.   TALLEY, Dyfed; Premonstratensian Abbey of the B.V.M. and St
John the Baptist.**
Common Seal.
15th cent. Brass replica, 68.3 g., circ., 48 mm.
A mitred abbot, his pastoral staff with crook turned outwards grasped
obliquely by his left arm, seated in an acute-arched niche with
decorated lateral pillars; the niche is surmounted by the inscription: **ave
maria** (for the primary patron); above is the Agnus Dei with cross and
banner unfurled (for the secondary patron); in field, to either side, a
flowering plant in a vase; cusped edge to field, and beaded border.
(There is no evidence that the abbots of Talley were ever mitred, so the
effigy displayed is somewhat problematical. It might relate to a fond
remembrance of Abbot Iorwerth who, in 1215, became bishop of St
David's.)
*   S'abbtis t convent' monstri · b'e · marie · de · talley   (Bl.)
The original matrix was found in Wymondham, Norfolk.
Acc. No: 35.303.
D: Arch. XXXII, 404; *Arch.Camb.* 879/166, 187-8; Lloyd (1935) 342;
    Norfolk Arch. VII (1872) 350; *Norwich Museum Catalogue* 98 (No. 914);
    Proc. Arch. Inst. Norwich (1847) xlvii; *Proc. Soc. Antiq.* I, (1849) 155;
    Williams (1988) 130 (No. 292a).

D 26.   Miscellaneous Religious Device.
14th/15th cent. Bronze signet ring, 6.3 g; face: 11 x 6 mm.
Inscribed: **i h c**
Acc. No: 92.70H
Found at Cardiff Castle in 1884.

MEDIEVAL ADMINISTRATION

D 27.   MONMOUTH, Gwent; Chancery of.
Obverse only.
Temp. Edward IV. (In use by 1473 until at least 1622).
Brass, circ., 66 mm.
Equestrian: the king on horseback to right; his shield and horse
caparisons bear: three lions passant guardant, a label of three points
each charged with three fleurs-de-lis, DUCHY OF LANCASTER (of
which Monmouth then formed part); no crest on helmet, wreath and
mantling only; field diapered lozengy with a sun or a rose alternately in
each compartment. (The compiler is grateful to Sir Robert Somerville,
F.S.A., for pointing out that the arms borne on the shield were those of
the Duchy of Lancaster (letter, 23-7-1983); and to Mr. A.L. Jones (6-3-
1992) and Dr. M. Siddons (13-3-1992) for their correspondence
regarding this seal). The ascription to the reign of Edward IV stems
from that monarch being not only king but also Duke of Lancaster.
Once engraved as the chancery seal it remained unchanged, and was
used (still bearing the name of Edward) both as the Chancery and
Exchequer Seal for Monmouth as late as 1622.
S : Edwardi : dei : gra : reg : Angl : t : Francie : cancellerie :
sue : de : Monemouth̄   (Bl.)
This matrix was discovered in the river Wye about 1850 by a poor man,
and for some time was used as the weight of a clock pendulum. It bears
one of the (originally four) perforated lobes by which it would be fixed
to the now lost counter-seal in the process of sealing; the other three
projections have been sawn off. Presented by F.J. Mitchell to Caerleon
Museum.
Acc. No: 31.78/4
E: NLW, Badminton Deeds I, 802 (fragment of 1602), 1695 (1567),
    1775 (1621), 1776 (chipped, 1622), 1777 (fragment, 1622);
    Badminton Deeds II, 10,637 (large fragment, 1567); 10,638 (1571,

broken); Badminton Manorial 2458 (1574), 2461 (small fragment,
1618), Milborne Deeds 79 (1552), 154 (1473), 936 (1605); PRO, E
40/5538 (small fragment, 1598).
D: Arch. Camb. 1857/426, 1886/26-7; *J.B.A.A.* XIV (1858) 56-8;
    Williams (1982) 9 (No. 9).
For an earlier seal of the Exchequer of Monmouth, see: NLW, Badminton
Deed I, 1565 (of 1452); Milborne Deed 103 (fragment, 1447).

For other Chancery seals, see:
Abergavenny: Gwent R.O. D 8/1/0156 (1490), D 2/34 (1492; both of
    Jasper Tudor); NLW, Badminton Deed I, 1684 (small fragment,
    1419); Abergavenny Museum Collections., *J.B.A.A.* XIV, 57.
Carmarthen: Carmarthen Museum Collections.
Cardiff: Gwent R.O. D 8/1/1794 (1493), D 8/1/1814 (1487; both of
    Jasper Tudor); NLW, Penrice and Margam Charters 229 (1358), 266
    (1471).
Cydweli: PRO, DL 7/1, No. 64 (1442).
Pembroke: BL, Sloane Chs. XXXII, 5 (1448), 9 (1424), 19 (1387), 20
    (1459); Add. Ch. 6,000 (1426), *and see W. 414 infra;* NLW, Bronwydd
    Deed 1415 (1510); PRO, E 212/114 (? 1485 or 1509).
Usk: NLW, Badminton Manorial 2291 (1441).

For other Exchequer Seals, see:
BL, Add. Ch. 8640 (for Holt Castle, 1450); 8647 (First Seal for
    Caerleon, 1520); 8649 (Second Seal for Caerleon, 1546).
NLW, Bachymbyd Deed 94 (for North Wales, 1428); Dolfrïog Deed 512
    (for North Wales, 1495); E. Francis Davies Deed 86 (for Chirk,
    1545); Penrice and Margam Charter 244 (for South Wales, 1422).
PRO, E 211/236 (of *temp.* Edward VI, for Caernarfon; still in use in
    1580).

MEDIEVAL PERSONAL SEALS

D 28. ADUVAR, John; possibly John ab Ivor.
Early 14th cent. Lead, 16.0 g., with small projection on reverse for handling; circ., 26 mm.
A conventional floral design. (The legend, unusually for lead seals, is too far worn to decipher the surname accurately).
• S' IOHANES ADUVAR   (Lom.)
This matrix was found by Edward Stowell whilst gardening in the grounds of Cardiff Castle, and presented by Master David Stowell of Canton in 1958. The advice of Prof Wiliam Rees was sought regarding John ab Ivor, but he knew 'of no historical personage of that name'.
Acc. No: 58.153.

D 29. CHOT, Nicholas.
Early 14th cent. Latten, 11.9 g., with pierced attachment loop on reverse; circ., 26 mm.
A conventional floral design.
• S' NICOLAI   CHOT   (Lom.)
This seal is almost identical (save for the legend) in size and design to No. 28. The matrix was found in a field at Bonvilston adjacent to the Llancarfan road in December 1986. A common, perhaps South Walian engraver, is to be assumed. Presented by H.R. Axford of Fairwater, Cardiff.
Acc. No: 87.27H

D 30. Uncertain.
Late 13th to mid-14th cent. Copper alloy (very worn), circ., 18 mm.
Perhaps a wheat-sheaf with fallen grain. (No legend).
Found in the summer of 1992 by Mr. E.R. Mitchell to the east of Marcross, S. Glam. (NGR: 928693).
Acc. No: 92.231H.

D 31. DIGBY (?) Sir John.
(?)-1533. Brass replica, rectangular face, 13 x 11 mm.
Crest of Digby: ostrich with horseshoe in beak.
God pleysed
The gold signet ring was found at Cedweli Castle, Carms. and presented by the Earl of Cawdor to the British Museum, from whom this electrotype replica was supplied for three guineas on 24 May 1935.
Acc. No: 35.268.

D 32. HAWYS, Lady of Cyfeiliog.
Late 13th cent. Bronze replica, damaged; p.o., 49 x 28 mm.
The lady Hawys standing full-length on a corbel, wearing a long cloak over a girdled dress, a necklet with pendant jewel, wimple and flat cap with hair in a network; in each hand a shield: *dext.* a lion rampant (POWYS WENWYNWYN; for her husband), *sin.* two lions passant (arms of LE STRANGE, her paternal descent).
• S' HAWISIE D̄N̄E DE KEVEOLOC   (Lom.)
The original matrix, found in the ground at Oswestry, is preserved in Shrewsbury Museum, and bears a metal loop on reverse for attachment and handling. (The lady Hawys was the wife of Gruffydd ap Gwenwynwyn, lord of Southern Powys and Cyfeiliog).
Acc. No: 79.100H   BM 6670.
D: Arch. Camb. 1853/200-1, 1895/11; *Arch. Jnl.* X, 143-4; *Chester Arch.*

Soc. I, 173, 175 (and illus. opp. 161, 162); *J.B.A.A.* VII, 433-4; *Mont. Collns.* I, 49-50; *Trans. Shrops. Soc.,* V (1882) 419, 430; Siddons (1991a) 291-2 (Fig. 95).

D 33. ? I.R.
15th cent. Replica cream plaster-cast, oval face, 12 x 11 mm.
An uncertain monogram.
From a substantial signet ring found on the foreshore of Swansea Bay by Mr. H.C. Challacombe in 1988.
Acc. No: 92.71H.

D 34. MALHERBE, William.
Ca. 1270-1300. Lead, 8.3 g., remnant of attachment loop on reverse; circ., 23 mm.
A cinquefoil.
S' WILLI · MALHERBE   (Lom.)
Acc. No: 83.13H.
This matrix was found in 1978 on the foreshore of Swansea Bay, at NGR SS 641919.

D 35. WILLIAM, Hywel ap.
Early 14th cent. Stone, 43.5 g., circ., 40 mm.
No device.
+ S' ⁞ HOWELI ⁞ AP ⁞ WILLH̄   (Lom.; *for* WILLMI)
The matrix - which is perforated, probably for the emplacement of handle or for purposes of suspension, was found in a field at Vron-ladies Farm, Llangynllo, Powys, in 1966, by Mr. Elwyn Breeze who presented it to the Museum.
Acc. No: 67.155.
D: B.B.C.S. XXII: 4 (May, 1968) 416-7; Lewis (1968) 66-7.

D 36. W..........
15th-16th cent. Pewter signet ring; circ., face, 14 mm.
'W' ensigned by a coronet.
Found at Denbigh Castle, Clwyd.
Acc. No: 81.111H.
E: (For original examples of similar seals, see: NLW, Peniarth Deed 92 (of 1475), and Peniarth (Flintshire) Deed (NLW 1516/D) No. 271 (of 1494).

D 37. W..........
Late medieval/Early modern. Brass signet ring; 16.6 g., circ. face, 14 mm.
'W' ensigned by a coronet.
Probably found in Gwent, as transferred from Caerleon Museum.
Acc. No: 31.78/9.

D 38. ...ILEL, Jordan; (? Wilel.... Jordan).
? Mid.-late 13th cent. Lead, 9.48 g., circ., 28 mm.
A fleur-de-lis.
+ S' JORDANI ...ILE'L   (Lom.)
The matrix was found in the Cowbridge area by Mr Peter Williams, and brought into the Museum by Mr P.G. Jones of Welsh St Donat's.
Acc. No: 92.72H.

MEDIEVAL MISCELLANEA

D 39.   13th cent. Bronze, 20.5 g., with perforated lobe for attachment; o., 41 x 30 mm.
A symbolic tree in leaf, bearing berries: possibly a love-seal.
+ SECRETVM MEVM TIBI   (Lom.)
Acc. No: 86.40
D: Cf. *Arch. Ael.* 3rd Ser. XV, 138, for this same legend, but not device, on a seal of A.D. 1174.

D 40.   *Ca.* 1270-1300. Bronze, 4.3 g., with small handle for suspension on reverse; circ., 18 mm.
A stag's head cabossed, between the attires a crude shield: a cross paty, above and below the cross five stops or roundles. 'The device and legend were based on the vision, attributed to both St. Eustace and St. Hubert, of the cross between the antlers of a stag' (Cherry, J. in Biddle (1990) 754). Beaded borders. The legend commences with a cross patonce or paty:

+ TIMETE DEVM (Lom.)
Found by the donor, Mr. K. Evans of Mathern, Gwent, in November, 1988, at approx. NGR ST 59 SW-511926. The seal may have been lost by a visitor to the bishop of Llandaff's palace at Mathern.
Acc. No: 92.73H.

E: For a like seal, see: P. 119 *(infra)* found at Thornicombe, Dorset, and PRO, DL L 2064 (of 1295, on a deed sealed at Eglwys-fach, Gwynedd: *B.B.C.S.* XIII: 3 (Nov. 1949) 143-4.

D 41. (?) Early 14th cent. Bronze, 5.9 g., with perforated handling projection on reverse; circ., face, 16mm.
A hawk preying on a sedentary bird.
ALAS IE SV PRIS (Lom.)
('Alas! I am caught')
Found at Wenallt, Cardiff, at approx. NGR: ST 151831, and presented on indefinite loan by C.W. Shepherd of Pontypridd.
Acc. No: 83.126H.

D 42. 13th-early 14th cent. Brass, with handle; 5.7 g., circ., 16mm.

A red squirrel, to the right, holding a nut in its paws; beaded borders.
* **I CRAKE NOTIS** (Lom.)
Found in Gwent, and transferred from Caerleon Museum; for a similar seal found in Gwent, see W 438.
Acc. No: 31.78.7.

D 43. (?) 14th cent. Glass intaglio, o., 15 x 13 mm.
An open crown, surmounted by an orb, between two sceptres.
Found on the site of University College, Cardiff.
Acc. No: 24.520.

D 44. (?) 14th/15th cent. Silver signet ring; hexagonal face, 17 x 15 mm.
The letters **b.o.f.** surmounted by a crown.
Found at Cydweli Castle, prior to 1846, and presented by the Earl of Cawdor, F.S.A.
Acc. No: 32.177.
D: Arch. Camb. 1846/81-2; *Arch. Jnl.* IV, 358; RCAHM V, *County of Carmarthen* (1917) 56 (No. 160A).

JUDICIAL SEALS

Counties of Glamorgan, Brecknock and Radnor
Temp. **George II (1727-60).**

D 45. *Obverse (engraved in 1729).* Silver, circ., 105 mm.
The king on horseback, to right; in armour, a sword in his right hand; the Prince of Wales' feathers and motto, **ICH DIEN**, in field; in base, beneath the horse's feet, a representation of Cardiff, the Herbert mansion (Grey Friars) being prominent.
GEORGIVS · II · DEI · GRATIÆ · MAGNÆ · BRITANNIÆ · FRANCIÆ · ET · HIBERNIÆ · REX · FIDEI · DEFEN · ETꟼ (Ren.)
The seal was purchased for £26-5-0, subsequent to a sale at Sotheby's.
Acc. No: 55.76.

D 46. *Reverse.* Silver, circ., 105 mm.
A shield: the royal arms (of 1714-1801) ensigned by the royal crown; supporters: *dext.* a greyhound collared, *sin.* a hind ducally gorged with a coronet and chained; in base: the Prince of Wales' (three ostrich) feathers enfiled by a coronet, and a scroll with motto: **ICH DIEN**; Dr. M. Siddons points out (20-8-92) that the ostrich feathers are strictly speaking not the badge of the Prince of Wales as such, but of the heir to the throne, who is of course usually created Prince of Wales.
SIGILL · IUDI · PRO · COMITA · GLAMORGAN · BRECKNOK · ET · RADNOR (Ren.)
Acc. No: 55.76.

Counties of Caernarfon, Merioneth and Anglesey
Temp. **George IV (1820-30)**

D 47. *Obverse.* Silver, circ., 100 mm.
The king on horseback, galloping to left; design as his great seal *(No. R 89)*, but the feathers and motto of the Prince of Wales in the exergue instead of the date.
GEORGIUS QUARTUS DEI GRATIA BRITTANIARUM REX FIDEI DEFENSOR (Ren.)
The matrix bears projections designed to fit apertures attached to the reverse. It is inscribed on exterior: *T. WYON FECIT.* As the Courts of Great Session were abolished in 1830 this seal was one of the last of its class to be engraved. It was presented to the Museum by A.J. Sylvester, C.B.E., on behalf of Sir Henry Fildes, J.P., M.P., who did not want his name publicly mentioned.
Acc. No: 42.133.
D: J.B.A.A. XLIX (1893) 11-2, Pl. 7.

D 48. *Reverse.* Silver, circ., 100 mm.
A shield: the royal arms (of 1816-37), ensigned with the royal crown; supporters, *dext.* a greyhound, *sin.* a stag. In base: three ostrich feathers enfiled by a coronet, and with a scroll inscribed: **ICH DIEN**.
SIGILLUM JUDICALE PRO COMITATIBUS CARNARVON MERIONETH ET ANGLESEA (Ren.)
Acc. No: 42.133.
(For other matrices of Judicial Seals, see: Tonnochy (1952) 18, Nos. 53 (George III, for Caernarfon, Merioneth and Anglesey), 54 (George III, for Denbigh, Montgomery and Flint), 55 (George IV, for Denbigh, Montgomery and Flint). The British Museum also holds a further matrix for the first-mentioned reign and circuit, *see the Introduction to this Catalogue).*

MODERN ADMINISTRATIVE AND CORPORATE BODIES

D 49. **ANGLESEY, Druidical Society.**
1772-1884. Silver, with ivory handle; o., 35 x 30 mm.
The head of a druid between two oak boughs.
NIS CWYR NAMYN DIWYD DDERWYDDON (Caps.)
INST : OCT : 1772
('Only diligent druids know')
Presented on 14 June 1934 by J. Gilbert of Nantwich, through the good offices of Sir Charles Bird. The next day, the Assistant Keeper-in-Charge wrote to Mrs Prichard of Llanerchymedd, Anglesey, whose family held the Society's goblets and medals, wondering whether she could furnish

any information about the seal.
Acc. No: 34.372 (WFM).
D: Anglesey Antiq. Soc. 1925/64; Boon (1983) 117, 120 (for notes on the legend), Pl. XVI:2; Williams (1982) 40 (No.92).

D 50. *Private Seal.*
As D 49. Quartz set in gold surround, for attachment to watch chain; o., 27 x 22 mm.
A seal perhaps used by members of the Society.
Acc. No: 90.29H.

CARDIFF, S.Glam.

D 51.   Common Seal of the Bailiffs and Burgesses.
1819-35. Steel, 147.1 g., broken ivory handle; o., 50 x 41 mm.
A coat of arms: quarterly: 1. and 4. a Tudor rose, 2. and 3. (Gules) three chevronels (Or), CLARE; crest: a lion rampant arising from a coronet; supporters: *dext.* a horse, *sin.* a lion rampant; motto on scroll: **OPIBUS FLORENS ET NOMINE PRISCO** (*'Flourishing in wealth and in its ancient name'*).
+ SIGILL : COMM : BAILLIV : ET : BURGENS : CAERDIFF :   (Caps.)
The engraving of this seal (by John Thackwell) was ordered by the court of Aldermen in 1818. It cost £10-14-0. It was superseded upon the reform of local government (and abolition of the bailiffs) in 1835. The matrix was presented to Cardiff Museum by the Corporation.
Acc. No: 30.398.
D: Arch. Camb. 1900/161; *Cardiff. Rec.* I, 261; II, 346; IV, 374, 379; Williams (1982) 39 (No. 89); *Ann. Rep. Cardiff Public Museum and Art Gallery 1894-5*, 17.

D 52.   Guardians of the Poor Law Union.
19th cent. (*ca.* 1834-1930). Steel, o., 50 x 47 mm.
A crown.

THE GUARDIANS
OF THE
CARDIFF UNION
IN THE
COUNTIES OF
GLAMORGAN AND MONMOUTH   (Caps.)

This series of seals were donated in August 1930 by the City of Cardiff Public Assistance Committee, the Board of Guardians being defunct by virtue of the provisions of the Local Government Act of that year.
Acc. No: 30.398.
E: Glam. Rec. Off., CL U/C 74-5 (1887-1900), 79 (1898-1903), 82 (1853-63), 90 (1894-99), (all red wax).

D 53.   *Duplicate.*
(Acc. No: 30.398). Steel, 77.1 g., circ., 32mm.

D 54.   *Duplicate.*
(Acc. No: 30.398). Brass, with wooden handle; o., 30 x 25 mm.

D 55.   *A Variant Seal.*
1836-1930. Steel, circ., 50 mm.
A crown.

THE COMMON SEAL OF THE
GUARDIANS
OF THE POOR OF THE
CARDIFF UNION
IN THE COUNTY BOROUGH
OF
CARDIFF
AND THE
COUNTY OF GLAMORGAN   (Caps.)

Acc. No: 30.398.
E: Glam. Rec. Off., CL U/C 76 (1901-07), 80-1 (1903-15), (all red wax).

D 56.   *Duplicate.* Brass, 132.3 g., with attachment for handle; o., 47 x 41 mm.
Acc. No: 30.398.

D 57.   Fortitude Lodge.
Early to mid-19th cent. Copper, 84.9 g., with handle; circ., 45 mm.
Masonic symbolism, including a coffin with **M.M.** (for Master Mason status), a sword (for keeping intruders away), a cock, a death's head (also associated with the third degree), candles, the sun, an hour-glass; also a Cross and Paschal Lamb.
✳ **FORTITUDE LODGE N.. 207 N:1 JERSEY**   (Pseudo-Ren.)
Fortitude is one of the cardinal masonic virtues.
Presented to Cardiff Museum by Mr J. Woodman.
Acc. No: 91.443.

D: Twentieth Ann. Rep. of Cardiff Free Library and Museum, 1881-2 (Cardiff, 1883) 28.

D 58.   National Museum of Wales.
1912- . Letter Press die; circ., 51 mm.
A seated female figure holding a tablet showing the Welsh dragon.
SÊL AMGVEDDFA GENEDLAETHOL CYMRY
SEAL · OF · THE · NATIONAL · MVSEVM · OF · WALES   (Pseudo-Rom.)
Designed by Goscombe John, R.A.
D: Williams (1982) 44 (No. 105).

D 59.   CHEPSTOW, Gwent; 'Creek of', in the Port of Cardiff.
Seal of the Customer of Poundage and Tonnage.
Ca. 1605- . Copper, 20.7 g; circ., 35 mm.
A cinquefoil rose ensigned with a crown.
S'CVST! POND' ET · TON · PRO · CHEP' IN · PORT! CARD!   (Ren.)
On reverse , an emplacement for a folding handle.
Acc. No: 09.16.
D: Proc. Soc. Antiq. 2nd Ser. IX, 44-5; Matthews VI (1911) cxi, cxvi; Jeffreys Jones (1955) 215-6; *Western Mail*, Sept. 28, 1908; *Report of the Welsh Museum, 1908-09*, 30.

D 59a.   HAVERFORDWEST, Dyfed; Seal for the Taking of Recognisances.
Resin cast. (See W 245 for details).

D 60.   LLANFABON, Mid-Glam; Independent Order of Oddfellows (Manchester Unity): Lord Nelson Lodge.
1865- . Copper, with wooden handle; circ., 25 mm.

1685   (sic)
(A Hand)
M.U.
M.U. 1685 LORD NELSON LODGE LAVABON

Acc. No: 36.605 (WFM).

D 61.   NEWTOWN AND MACHYNLLETH, Powys; Railway Company.
1857- . Steel, in wooden stand; circ., 47 mm.
Two shields (of ancient Welsh arms) *accolés: dext.* (Vert) three eagles displayed in fess (OWAIN GWYNEDD), *sin.* (Or) a lion rampant (for POWYS; probably deriving from the arms of BLEDDYN AP CYNFYN); above: a harp, below: rose, leek, thistle and shamrock, for the United Kingdom.
1857 THE NEWTOWN AND MACHYNLLETH
RAILWAY COMPANY   (Caps.)
This railway, largely the work of David Davies of Llandinam, opened in 1863.
Acc. No: 33.167 (Dept. of Industry).

D 62.   SIRHWYI, Gwent: Independent Order of Oddfellows (Manchester Unity): Sir William Penn Lodge.
1867- . Brass, circ., 25 mm.

M U
(A Hand)
1967   (sic)
M.U. 1867 SIR WILLIAM PENN LODGE SIROWY WORKS   (Caps.)

Acc. No: 50.374/1 (WFM).

D 63.   SWANSEA, West Glam; 'Creek' of, in the Port of Cardiff.
Customs Seal.
By 1605- . Silver, 15.7 g., circ., 32 mm.
A unicorn supporting a harp, on the harp a slipped rose.
+ S: CONT : DE · SWANSEY · IN · PORT · CARDIFFE   (Ren.)
Presented to Cardiff Museum by Mr Matthew Jones of Cardiff, a descendant of a former portreeve (mayor) of Swansea.
Acc. No: 94.142.
D: Arch. Camb. 1894/157; ; Francis (1867) 143-7; Matthews I (1898) vi, cxi, 261; Jeffreys Jones (1955) 215-6; *2nd Ann. Report, Cardiff Museum and Art Gallery, 1893-94*, 21.

**D 64.   TREORCI, Mid-Glam; Philanthropic Order of True Ivorites:
'Tab Dewi' Lodge.**
(?) 19th cent. Brass, circ., 25 mm.
Inscribed: **UNDEB IFORAIDD 820**
                                        TAB DEWI TREORCI
Acc. No: 62.53/3 (WFM).

D 65.   *Another Seal.* Brass, circ., 25 mm.
Inscribed: 844
                CANGEN FFRWYTHLAWN CYFRINFA IFORAIDD TREORCI (Caps.)
Acc. No: 62.53/4 (WFM).

MODERN PERSONAL SEALS

D 66.   AMBROSE, William; used by.
19th cent. Quartz, with brass handle; oblong face, 16 x 14 mm.
Motto: **FIDE ET FORTITUDINE**, encircling the letters: **JJC**, and ensigned
with a boar's head couped.
Acc. No: 66.459 (WFM).

D 67.   *Another Seal* (on 2nd face of D 66).
19th cent. Semi-precious purple stone, with brass handle; oblong,
17 x 14 mm;
A coat of arms: a rose between three boars' heads couped; crest: a
boar's head couped; Motto: **FIDE ET FORTITUDINE.**
Acc. No: 66.459 (WFM).

D 68.   *Another Seal* (on 3rd face of D 66).
19th cent. Quartz, 17 x 14 mm.
Small shield with indistinct device; motto: as D 67.
Acc. No: 66.459 (WFM).

D 69.   *Another Seal.*
Amethyst, rounded oblong, 17 x 13 mm.
A boar's head, surmounting the letters:

JJ
G
I

Acc. No: 66.459 (WFM).

D 70.   O.H.B
? 19th cent. Brass, o., 15 x 21 mm.
Inscribed: **O.H.B.**
Acc. No: 58.318 (WFM).

D 71.   (?) CHOLMELEY (from Glansevern, Berriew, Powys).
? 19th cent. Bezel, o., 18 x 16 mm.
Crest of Cholmeley: out of a coronet, a lion rampant reguardant.
Acc. No: 63.70/26 (WFM).

D 72.   COUPLAND (of Welshpool, and Preston; from Glansevern,
Berriew, Powys).
Late 18th cent. Precious stone, o., 28 x 22 mm.
On a cross (Sable) between four trefoils, five mullets, COUPLAND; a
crescent (indicating the second son); crest: a clenched hand grasping a
trefoil.
Acc. No: 63.70/10 (WFM).

D 73.   *Another Seal.*
Late 18th cent. White metal, o., 21 x 19 mm.
Arms and crest of COUPLAND (as D 72).
Acc. No: 63.70/22 (WFM).

D 74.   D.D. (of Batsley Farm).
(?) 19th cent. Brass, with wooden handle; circ.
Inscribed: **D. D**
                        BATSLEY ✳ FARM ✳   **(Caps.)**
Acc. No: 12.211/18 (WFM).

D 75.   DAVIES, JONES and HUMPHREYS (from Glansevern,
Berriew, Powys).
Late 19th cent. Black semi-precious stone, o., 16 x 14 mm.
Crest: a nag's head.
Acc. No: 63.70/13 (WFM).

D 76.   EVANS (from Glansevern).
19th cent. Amethyst, o., 24 x 21 mm.
A shield: quarterly, 1. and 4. a lion rampant within a bordure, EVANS;
2. and 3. a chevron between three Cornish choughs or cormorants,
WARBURTON; crest: a stag trippant; motto: **FLECTI NON FRANGI.**
Acc. No: 63.70/24 (WFM).

D 77.   *Another Seal.*
19th cent. Semi-precious stone, o., 26 x 21 mm.
Arms and crest of EVANS (as D 76).
Acc. No: 63.70/11 (WFM).

D 78.   *An uncertain Glansevern Seal.*
19th cent. Rock crystal., o., 21 x 19 mm.
A shield, surmounted by a decorative escallop: quarterly, 1. and 4.
quarterly, i. and iv. (Gules) a fret; ii. and iii. unclear; 2. and 3. a chevron
(Azure) between three birds (perhaps meant for cormorants) facing
sinister, WARBURTON; impaling: the same, but with a baton *?*gobony,
probably for a difference, over all. (Dr M. Siddons in commenting upon
this coat suggests that it indicates a marriage between two persons of
the same family; letter, 15-11-92).
Acc. No: 63.70/25 (WFM).

D 79.   EVANS, E., of Tymawr, Tywyn, Gwynedd.
(?) 19th cent. Steel, with steel handle; o., 19 x 15 mm.
Inscribed: **E.EVANS**
                                        TYMAWR
                                        TOWYN   **(Caps.)**
Acc. No: 30.429/1 (WFM).

D 80.   GLANSEVERN, Berriew, Powys.
(?) 19th cent. Red semi-precious stone, with brass handle; oblong face,
14 x 12 mm.
Glan Severn
Acc. No: 63.70/14 (WFM)

D 81.   From GLANSEVERN, Berriew, Powys.
(?) 19th cent. Semi-precious stone, o., 20 x 18 mm.
A female bust, Regency hairstyle.
Acc. No: 63.70/9 (WFM).
D: Personal communication of Dr. M. Redknap.

D 82.   *Another Seal.*
(?) 19th cent. Quartz, octagonal, 10 x 8 mm.
Male bust, facing left.
Acc. No: 63.70/16 (WFM).

D 83.   *Another Seal.*
(?) 19th cent. Semi-precious black stone, with brass handle, linked to D
82; o., 21 x 19 mm.
Male bust, facing right.
Acc. No: 63.70/17 (WFM).

D 84.   *Another Seal.*
(?) 19th cent. Semi-precious stone with brass handle; o., 18 x 15 mm.
Bearded man's bust.
Acc. No: 63.70/20 (WFM).
E: Cf. NLW, Glansevern MS 10,484 (red wax, 1844).

D 85. *Another Seal.*
(?) 19th cent. Semi-precious stone with brasswork handles, linked to D 84; o., 17 x 11 mm.
Crossed branches, enclosing a heart.
Acc. No: 63.70/21 (WFM).

D 86. GOODMAN, Gabriel, D.D., Dean of Westminster, and of Ruthin, Clwyd.
Ca. 1600-10. Crystal bezel, set in a gold signet ring; o., 22 x 19 mm.
A coat of arms: per pale Ermine, a two-headed eagle displayed, charged with a crescent for difference; on a canton a martlet of the third, GOODMAN (coat granted in 1572). Inside the hoop of the ring is a grasshopper worked in green translucent enamel.
W .J. Hemp (Royal Commission on Ancient Monuments in Wales) asserted that this matrix had been 'quite improperly' bequeathed by the Hon Mrs L. Brodrick of Coed Coch, Abergele. It was loaned to the 'Reign of Queen Elizabeth' Exhibition at 22 Grosvenor Place, London, SW1, from January to March in 1933.
Acc. No. and File: 30.236/2 (WFM).
D: J.B.A.A. 3rd Ser. X, 44, Pl. XVIc; Thompson (1974) 194 (No.38).,

D 87. HUMPHREYS from Glansevern, Berriew, Powys.
Ca. 1876. Steel, circ., 20 mm.
A nag's head.
Motto: **PREMIUM VIRTUTIS HONOR** (Caps.)
Acc. No: 63.70/27 (WFM).

D 88. HUMPHREYS-OWEN, A.C., of Glansevern, Berriew, Powys.
1876- . Red semi-precious stone, oblong face: 22 x 18 mm.
Coat of arms: quarterly, 1. a tilting spear erect, the head imbrued between three scaling ladders, on a chief a fort triple-towered, OWEN (arms granted posthumously in 1838); 2. a lion rampant within a bordure of mullets, for heiress of CEFN HAFOD; 3. a lion rampant guardant, EVANS; 4. three nags' heads, DAVIES; crest: a wolf salient supporting a scaling ladder; motto: **TORAV CYN PLYGAF.** (In 1876, A.C. Humphreys was allowed to use the surname, and bear the arms, of Owen).
Acc. No: 63.70/12 (WFM).
D: Mont. Collns. III, 233; X, 415-6, 420-2; NLW, Glansevern MS 10675.

D 89. I.H.T.
(?) 19th cent. Dark-green semi-precious stone with silver handle; shield shaped, 12 x 10 mm.
Hand clutching an arrow.
Inscribed above: **I.H.T.**
Acc. No: 68.234/57 (WFM).

D 90. K, from Bryn Rhedyn, Gwynedd.
- - Brass, with ebony handle; circ., 11 mm.
Inscribed: **K**
Acc. No: 51.438/40 (WFM).

D 91. P.L. from Fairwater, Cardiff, S.Glam.
Early 20th cent. Silver plate, and like handle fashioned as an eagle; circ., 19 mm.
Inscribed: **P.L.**
Acc. No: F 76-90/19 (WFM).

D 92. OWEN, Sir Arthur Davies, of Glansevern, Berriew, Powys.
1752-1816. Silver gilt, o., 23 x 21 mm.
Inscribed: **A.D.O.** in an elaborate double monogram.
Acc. No: 63.70/30 (WFM).
E: For a seal attributed to Sir Arthur, see: NLW, Glansevern Deed 13669 (where arms are as for Evans and Warburton, D 76 *supra*).

D 93. OWEN, William, K.C. (Second husband of Anne Warburton Owen, of Glansevern, Berriew, Powys).
Ca. 1818-37. Silver gilt, o., 25 x 16 mm.
Inscribed: **W**
Acc. No: 63.70/29 (WFM).

D 94. A.W.P., from Llangollen, Clwyd.
- - - Brass, with handle; circ. face, 19mm.
Inscribed: **A.W.P.**
Acc. No: 63.282/2 (WFM).

D 95. D.P. and **C.P.**
- - Slate rod with engraving at each end; oblong faces, 12 x 10 mm.
Inscribed: **DP + CP**
Acc. No: 43.264/1 (WFM).

D 96. PRICE, Dr William (of Llantrisant, Mid-Glam.).
1800-93. Ivory matrix, with brass handle; o., 14 x 12 mm.
A coiled snake.
Acc. No: 50.5/7 (WFM).

D 97. J.L.R. (from Bryn Rhedyn, Anglesey)
- - Brass, circ., 10 mm.
Inscribed: **J.L.R**
Acc. No: 51.438/39 (WFM).

D 98. SLAUGHTER, Elizabeth (a relative of Anne Warburton Owen, of Glansevern, Berriew, Powys).
Late 18th cent. White metal, black, o., 21 x 18 mm.
An elaborate monogram: **E.S**
Acc. No: 63.70/18 (WFM).

D 99. SLAUGHTER, Capt. Thomas (father of Anne Warburton Owen, of Glansevern, Berriew, Powys).
Ca. 1800. White metal, o., 24 x 22 mm.
A bust, beneath which an elaborate monogram: **T.S**
Acc. No: 63.70/23 (WFM).

D 100. H.R.W. (from Newport, Gwent).
- - Brass, circ., 17 mm.
Inscribed: **H R W**
Acc. No: 71.316/16 (WFM).

D 101. WALDRON, James.
Mid-19th cent. Fob seal, o., 25 x 19 mm.
Bust facing left.
Acc. No: 32.572/5 (WFM).

D 102. WARBURTON, of Glansevern, Berriew, Powys.
19th cent. White metal, o., 22 x 19 mm.
A coat of arms: a chevron between three cormorants or Cornish choughs, WARBURTON; crest: a Saracen's head.
Acc. No: 63.70/19 (WFM).

D 103. WARBURTON, Anne (mother of Anne Warburton Owen, of Glansevern, Berriew, Powys).
Ca. 1780. Silver gilt, o., 17 x 14 mm.
Inscribed: *Anne Warburton*
Acc. No: 63.70/28 (WFM).

D 104. *Another Seal.*
Semi-precious red stone, with brass handle; sub-rectangular face, 14 x 11 mm.
Inscribed: **Anne Warburton**
Acc. No: 63.70/15 (WFM).

D 105. Uncertain, from Newport, Gwent.
1582. Brass signet ring, o., 20 x 18 mm.
Inscription resembling: **RL** (or **FL**) and **S.C.O** (in style of a monogram) above: **38,** below: **1582**
Acc. No: 44.16 (WFM).

D 106. (?) **Merchant's Mark** (from Gwent)
17th cent. Iron signet ring, o., 11 x 10 mm.
Formerly in Caerleon Museum.
Acc. No: 31.78/9 (WFM).

MISCELLANEOUS

D 107.   - - Quartz, with brass handle; oblong, 15 x 13 mm.
A snake in the grass; inscribed above: **BEWARE**
Acc. No: 51.323/1 (WFM).

D 108.   - - Bezel, o., 17 x 14 mm.
A jug and a tree; inscribed below: **KEEP A REGRET**
Acc. No: 51.323/2 (WFM).

D 109.   - - Steel, with decorative horn and silver handle; oblong, 17 x 14 mm.
Inscribed: **COFIA FI** (*'Remember me'*).
Acc. No: 62.411/16 (WFM).

D 110.   - - Amethyst, oblong, 14 x 12 mm.
Inscribed: **FORGET THEE! NO!**
Acc. No: 50.5/16a (WFM).

D 111.   19th cent. Amethyst set in brass fob seal, oblong, 15 x 12 mm.
A 'busy bee'.
Inscribed: **INDUSTRY**
Found by Mr S.J. Gowen of Hirwaun at a Victorian picnic site above Maerby, Aberdâr, in 1979.
Acc. No: 79.95H.

D 112.   19th cent. Crystal, oblong, 14 x 11 mm.
A bird, guarding her offspring in their nest.
LIVE AND DIE FOR THOSE WE LOVE   (Caps.)
Acc. No: 50.5/15 (WFM).

D 113.   19th cent. Crystal, polygon, 12 x 11 mm.
A plant.
MAY YOU POSSESS IT   (Caps.)
Acc. No: 50.5/16 (WFM).

D 114.   *From Swansea, West Glam.*
19th cent. Brass multiple-matrix, each face circular, 12 mm.

1. A steam locomotive, inscribed:	**QUICK.**	
2. A peacock (?)	"	**PEACE.**
3. An oak trunk (?)	"	**OLD YET FIRM.**
4. An hour glass	"	**TIME IS SHORT.**
5. A hand	"	**LOVE TRUTH.**
6. A red deer lodged		- -
7. A prosperous woman	"	**BY HONESTY.**

Acc. No: 60.83/15 (WFM).

D 115.   *From Bryn Rhedyn, Gwynedd.*
- - Brass, with decorative ivory handle, circ., 16 mm.
Cross-hatch pattern.
Acc. No: 51.438/38 (WFM).

D 116.   *From Bryn Rhedyn, Gwynedd.*
- - Silver gilt, circ., 10 mm.
A flower.
Acc. No: 51.438/41 (WFM).

D 117.   *From Maesteg, Mid-Glam.*
- - Ivory, circ., 9 mm.
Curved cross-hatching.
Acc. No: 60.11/32 (WFM).

D 118.   - - Topaz matrix for watch-chain; three-sided, octagonal, 18 x 12 mm.
No device.
Acc. No: 60.425/8 (WFM).

ENGLAND

ROYAL

GEORGE V (1910-36)
First Great Seal (1911-30)

D 119.   *Obverse.* Silver, circ., 160 mm.
The sovereign enthroned in state, his right hand holding his sceptre, his left hand the orb topped by a short cross paty, all under a gothic-type canopy; in niches above, and both spearing the serpent, are the figures of, *dext.* St. George, and *sin.* St. Michael ; in both inner, canopied side-niches, is a shield: quarterly, 1. and 4. three lions passant guardant in pale, ENGLAND; 2. a lion rampant within a double tressure flory counterflory, SCOTLAND; 3. a harp, IRELAND; the arms of the UNITED KINGDOM; in outer carved and canopied niches, the figures of, *dext.* Justice, and *sin.* Fortitude. To either side of the footboard a lion sejant rampant; beneath the footboard, between two lions sejant rampant, a shield: St. George on his horse to right, slaying the dragon. The general design recalls that of the gold sovereign introduced by Henry VII in 1489.
: GEORGIVS V D:G: BRITT : ET TERRARUM TRANSMAR :
QVAE IN DIT : SUNT BRIT : REX F : D : IND : IMP :   (Pseudo-Lom.)

Both obverse and reverse have the pierced lugs for fixing during the process of sealing. Both parts are kept in a green leather box inscribed: LORD CHANCELLOR, and were presented by Viscount Sankey who formerly held that office. The gift came as a result of a conversation Lord Sankey had in 1938 with Canon Maurice Jones, Principal of Lampeter. The Great Seal was placed on special exhibition in the Museum in March 1940.
Acc. No: 40/47.
D: Antiq. Jnl. XVI, 10-11.

D 120.   *Reverse.* Silver, circ., 160mm.
The King, in the uniform of an Admiral of the Fleet, standing on the deck of a Dreadnought, the three lanterns emblematic of his rank under his feet, and a trident in waves above them, and the motto: **DIEU ET MON DROIT**. To either side of the king's legs, a lion assis upon a pedestal carved with three scallops, beneath which a coat of arms: UNITED KINGDOM. No legend. Border of oak leaves. (This seal marks a break with tradition, in that it no longer depicts the sovereign seated on a charger).

OFFICIAL

D 121. Subsidy on Cloth, *? for Berkshire or Buckinghamshire.*
(?) Late 13th cent. Bronze, 28.2 g., circ., 27 mm.
A demon's head, over a fleur-de-lis.

S : S·VBSIDII : PANNORV̄ : IN : COM : B   **(Lom.)**

The matrix, found near Manton, Wilts., has been attributed as a subsidy seal of Edward I made for sealing a tax on the counties of Wiltshire and Berkshire for the expedition into Wales. Presented by Capt. Henry Lewis of Tongwynlais. (For further notes on this class of seal, see *Vol. 2*).
Acc. No: 27.377.
D: Gentl. Mag. LXV, 1077.

D 122. GOVERNOR OF VIRGINIA : Sir Walter Raleigh.
1584. Silver replica, 63.3 g., circ., 55 mm.
A coat of arms: five fusils in a bend with a martlet for difference, RALEIGH; helm with mantling and crest: a stag statant. Supporters: two wolves. In the field, the date: **1584**; below, on a scroll, the motto:

AMORE ET VIRTVTE.

 ✱ **PROPRIA + TNSIHNIA** *(for insignia)* **+ WALTERI + RALEGH + MILITIS + DOMINI +& GVBERNATORIS + VIRGINIAE +&t**   **(Ren.)**

Seals D 122-124 were presented by R. Rickards of the Priory, Usk.
Acc. No: 16.28/1.
D: Gentl. Mag. LVII (1787;1) 459, Pl. II/3; *J.B.A.A.* XXVI, 217; 3rd Ser. X, 46, Pl. XVIII; Tonnochy (1952) 73 (No. 347).

D 123. WARDEN OF THE STANNARIES, CAPTAIN OF THE QUEEN'S GUARD, GOVERNOR OF JERSEY : Sir Walter Raleigh.
1585. Silver replica, 47.9 g., circ., 47 mm.
A fully armed and plumed knight riding on horseback to the left, his right hand holding a sword upraised, his left grasping a shield: five fusils on a bend, RALEIGH; these arms also borne on the horse-trappings; inner pearled border. Legend occupies two lines:

+ · SIGILL · DN̄I . WALTERI : RALEGH : MILITIS : GARDIAN : STANNAR : CORNVB : ET : DEVON : /
+ CAPITAN : GARD : REG : ET : GVBERNATOR : INSVLAE : DE : IERSEY.   **(Ren.)**

Acc. No: 16.28/2.
D: Gentl. Mag. LVII (1787:1) 459, Pl. II/1; *J.B.A.A.* 3rd Ser. X, 45-6, Pl. XVIII; Tonnochy (1952) 73 (No. 346).

PERSONAL

D 124. RALEIGH, Sir Walter.
Late 16th cent. Silver replica, 28.8 g., circ., 40mm.
A shield of arms, with sixteen quarterings (tracing his pedigree): 1. Raleigh, 2. Stockhay, 3. Peverell, 4. Lamborne, 5. Beaupel, 6. ? D'Amory, 7. un-identified, 8. Clare, 9. Fitzhamon, 10. Marshall, 11. Clare (co. Pembroke), 12. Peverell, 13. Colleton, 14. Mewton, 15. Dawnay, 16. Ferrers; supporters: two wolves, three helms with crests: 1. a

fleur-de-lis, 2. a stag's head caboshed with a fleur-de-lis between the attires, 3. a stag statant; at the foot, on a scroll, the motto:

AMORE ET VIRTVTE   **(Ren.)**

Acc. No: 16.28/3
D: Gentl. Mag. LVII (1787:1) 459; *J.B.A.A.* 3rd Ser. X, 46; Pl. XVIII; *Reports and Trans. of the Devonshire Assoc.* XXXII, 309 *et seq.*, Edwards II (1868) 496; Tonnochy (1952) 74 (No. 348).

MISCELLANEOUS

D 125. Unidentified.
(?) Early 14th cent. Brass (worn), 6.9 g., circ., 18 mm.
A coat of arms, ensigned with a cross: 1. and 3. *poss.* a mitre, a hare, or a head erased; 2. and 4. an annulet; perhaps false heraldry. The legend is very indistinct but commences with the usual: **S'**, and is in Lombardic Capitals.
The matrix is of uncertain origin, but perhaps emanates from East Hatley, Cambridgeshire.
Seals D 125-127 were presented by Major H. Lloyd Johnes of Monmouth.
Acc. No: 30.311/110.

D 126. A Porter's Seal (unidentified, but perhaps emanating from Ely, Cambs.).
Mid-13th to early 14th Cent. Brass, 12.0 g., p.o., 35 x 21 mm.
A key, wards uppermost.

S' NETLAVE ELLISIS   (possibly for: .. **DE CLAVE** ...; **Lom.**).
The matrix, which has a loop on the reverse for suspension and handling, was dug up about 1900 by a labourer at East Hatley, Cambridgeshire. (It is remotely possible that this was the seal of the porter of Ely).
Acc. No: 30.311/112.
D: Proc. Soc. Antiq. 2nd Ser. XX, 240.

D 127. H........
(?) Early Modern. Brass, with handle; oblong face, 17 x 15 mm.
Small shield, bearing the letter **H** on a diapered surface.
Found in East Hatley, Cambs.
Acc. No: 30.311/111.

FOREIGN

D 128. MONT ST-ELOI ABBEY, near Arras, France.

Common Seal.

13th cent. Brass replica, 37.2 g., p.o., 55 x 32 mm.

A mitred abbot standing upon a corbel, his left hand holding his pastoral staff (crook turned away from him), his right hand upraised in blessing.

+ S· AB̄B̄IS : t OVĒTVS : DE MŌTE : SC̄I : ELIGII : AD : CA⁻   **(Lom.)**

(*'Seal of the Abbot and Convent of Mont St-Eloi* ad causas*'*)

Seals D 128-129 were presented by A.W.S. Jones of Bournemouth, and Sqdr. Ldr. E.M. Jones of Ottawa.

Acc. No: 50.433.

D: Bertrand (1851) 72-5.

D 129.   MAINZ, West Germany : St Ignatius Church.

Seal of the Fabric.

(?) Early 14th cent. Brass replica, 40.8 g., p.o., 53 x 33 mm.

St. Ignatius standing beneath a carved canopy and wearing Eucharistic vestments, his right hand holds his pastoral staff (crook turned outwards); his left hand clasps a book; in field, to either side, a sprig.

+ S . FABRICE · S · IGNACII MAGVT   **(Lom.)**

(*'Seal of the Fabric of St Ignatius of Mainz'*)

Acc. No: 50.433.

GROUP W : SEAL IMPRESSIONS

WALES

Unless otherwise stated, the impressions have been made in modern times: the date given is that of the engraving of the original matrix.

ROYAL

Princes of Wales

W 1.   LLYWELYN AB IORWERTH.   (*Ca.* 1194-1240).
Great Seal.
1222. Red-brown plaster cast, circ., 64 mm (when complete).
Equestrian: the prince in armour galloping on horse to the right, wearing hauberk, surcoat, round helmet; a broad sword held in his right hand, scabbard at his waist; shield slung by a strap over his right shoulder.
+ SIG.....................E   (Lom.)
From the bequest of T.H. Thomas, R.C.A.
Acc. No: 16/68/108.   BM 5547 Ø.
E: NLW, Wynnstay MC 28(8) (of 1208); Paris, Arch. de l'Empire J 655, No. 14 (variant, 1212); BL, Cott. Ch. XXIV, 17 (of *ca.* 1222).
D: Williams (1982) 18 (No. 36); Siddons (1981) 539-40 (No. XII); (1984) 304-5 (Nos. XIII, 1-2).

W 2.   *Another Impression.*
Buff plaster cast, imperfect, circ., 71 mm.
Acc. No: 12.175.

W 3.   *Privy Seal.*
1222. Red-brown plaster cast, o., 32 x 25 mm.
A boar passant to the right under a tree.
+ SIGILLVM SECRETVM LEWLINI   (Lom.)
Acc. No: 69.97/1.   BM 5547 R.
E: BL, Cotton Ch. XXIV, 17 (of *ca.* 1222).
D: Williams (1982) 19 (No. 38); Siddons (1981) 540 (No. XII).

W 4.   EDWARD 'of Caernarfon', (later King Edward III).
Obverse.
1301-07. Green plaster cast, circ., 82 mm.
The prince in armour, on horse galloping to the right, and bearing a shield: three lions passant guardant, ENGLAND, a label of three points for difference.
EDWARDVS ILLVSTRIS REGIS ANGLIE FILIVS   (Lom.)
Acc. No: 69.97/2.   BM 5549 Ø.
D: Williams (1982) 21 (No. 41).

W 5.   *Reverse.* Green plaster cast, circ., 85 mm.
Armorial: within a carved rosette of eight semi-circular cusps and suspended from an oak tree, a shield of arms: ENGLAND, with a label of five points.
..WARDVS PRINCEPS + WALLIE COMES CESTRIE ET PONT..IVI..   (Lom.)
Acc. No: 69.97/2.   BM 5549 R.

W 6.   EDWARD, 'the Black Prince'.
Obverse.
1343-76. Green sulphur cast, circ., 94 mm.
The prince seated under a carved canopy with tabernacle work at the sides; in field, to either side, an ostrich feather labelled, over them the initials: **E.P.**
S' EDVARDI : PRIMOGENITI : REGIS : ANGL': P'NCIPIS : AQVITANNIE : ET : WALLIE : DVCIS : CORNVBIE : ET :COMITIS : CESTRIE   (Late Lom.)
Acc. No: 25.384.   BM 5551 Ø.
D: Arch. XXXI, 361-2; *Arch. Jnl.* XIV, 351-2.

W 7.   *Reverse.* Green sulphur cast, circ., 95 mm.
The prince on a horse galloping to left, bearing a shield: quarterly, 1. and 4. semée of fleurs-de-lis, FRANCE (Ancient); 2. and 3. three lions passant guardant, ENGLAND, with a label of three points; all indistinct on this impression. (Legend as on obverse).
Acc. No: 25.384.   BM 5551 R.

W 8.   OWAIN GLYN DŴR (self-styled Prince of Wales).
Great Seal.
Obverse.
As used in 1404-06. Yellow plaster cast, circ., 91 mm.
Owain seated under a gothic-type canopy, wearing a cloak over a girdled robe, and having a bifid beard (similar to that on the seal of Richard II); his head bears a diminutive coronet, and he holds a sceptre in his right hand; the arms of his throne terminate in dragons' heads, its feet are claws; Owain's feet rest on two lions passant guardant coward addorsed; behind him supported by two angels is a mantle, semée of lions rampant.
owynus .... princeps : wallie   (Bl.)
Acc. No: 92.74H/1.
E: Paris, Arch. de l'Empire, J 623, No. 96 (of 1405); J 516 (No. 29, of 1406).
D: Arch. XXV, 619-20, Pl. LXXI; *Arch. Camb.* 1851/121-2. 1853/193-5; Siddons (1981) 540-1 (No. XIII/2a), (1985) 235 (No. XIII); (1991a) 285 (Fig.91)., Cardiff Central Libr. MS 3.758 (in Welsh); Williams (1982) 23 (No. 46).

W 9.   *Another Impression.* (Acc. No: 92.75H/1). Green plaster cast.

W 10.   *Another Impression.* (Acc. No: 92.76H/1). Orange wax.

W 11.   *Another Impression.* (Acc. No: 25.384). Buff sulphur cast, cracked.

W 12.   *Another Impression.* Bronze cast.
Acc. No: 16.68/108 (from the bequest of T.H. Thomas, R.C.A).

W 13.   *Another Impression.* Dark-brown wax, cracked.
Acc. No: 16.68/108 (from the bequest of T.H. Thomas, R.C.A).

W 14.   *Reverse* (of W 8). Yellow plaster cast, circ., 91 mm.
Owain in armour, on horseback to the right; his right hand holds a
sword extended, his left hand grasps a shield: quarterly, a lion rampant
in each quarter; a *kerchief de plesaunce* pendant from his right wrist; his
helmet surmounted by crown and mantling, and crest of winged dragon
with two feet; horse's trapper bears quarterly, four lions rampant, and
its head a crest of a similar winged dragon; in field, flowering foliage.
(The four lions rampant, the ancient arms of Gwynedd, summed up
Owain's aspirations).
+ owynus · dei · graci. (princeps) : wallie   (Bl.)
Acc. No: 92.74H/2.
E: Paris, Arch. de l'Empire J 623, No. 96.
D: Siddons (1981) 541 (No. XIII, 2b), (1984) 304 (No. XII), (1985)
    235 (No. XIII), (1991a) 236, 285-6 (Fig.92).

W 15.   *Another Impression* (*reverse* of W 9). Green plaster cast.
Acc. No: 92.75H/2.

W 16.   *Another Impression* (*reverse* of W 11). Buff sulphur cast.
Acc. No: 25.384.

W 17.   *Another Impression* (*reverse* of W 12). Bronze cast.
Acc. No: 16.68/108   (from the bequest of T.H. Thomas, R.C.A).

W 18.   *Another Impression* (*reverse* of W 13). Dark-brown wax.
Acc, No: 16.68/108   (from the bequest of T.H. Thomas, R.C.A).

W 19.   *Another Impression.* (Acc. No: 92.76H/2). Brown plaster cast.

W 20.   *Privy Seal.*
As used in 1404. Yellow plaster cast, circ., 55 mm.
A shield, surmounted by a crown, decorated with fleurs-de-lis: quarterly,
each quarter charged with a lion rampant; 1. and 4. hatched;
supporters: *dext.* a winged dragon with two feet; *sin.* a lion guardant
crowned.
sig................. p(rincip)is : (wallie)   (Bl.)
Acc. No: 92.77H/1.
E: Paris, Arch. de l'Empire J 392, No. 27 (of 1404).
D: Arch. XXV, 619-20, Pl. LXXI; *Arch. Camb.* 1851/121-2; Siddons
    (1981) 540 (No. XIII/1); Williams (1982) 3 (No. 1).

W 21.   *Another Impression.* (Acc. No: 92.77H/2). Yellow plaster cast.

W 22.   *Another Impression.* (Acc. No: 25.384). Brown sulphur cast.

W 23.   *Another Impression.* Bronze cast.
Acc. No: 16.68/108 (from the bequest of T.H. Thomas, R.C.A).

W 24.   *Another Impression.* Brown wax.
Acc. No: 16.68/108 (from the bequest of T.H. Thomas, R.C.A).

Other original impressions of the seals of Princes of Wales include:
Princess Joan (1383): BL, Egerton Ch. 2130.
Prince Edward (1478): NLW, Misc. Deeds (County Boxes) Box 5; (for
    him, *Cf.* BL, Detached Seals XCVI, 80-81).
Prince Arthur (1500): NLW, Ashburnham II, 100/4 (signet).

For an etching of an original seal, see:
Prince Richard of Wales (1376): Dineley (1888) 262.

OFFICIAL

W 25.   OWEN, John : Vice-Admiral of North Wales.
1660-66. Red wax, circ., 34 mm.
A ship with three masts and two tiers of guns; to one mast is appended
sail-wise, a scutcheon of arms: quarterly, 1. and 4. a chevron between
three lions rampant (HWFA AP CYNDDELW), 2. and 3. three eagles
displayed (OWAIN GWYNEDD), in fess.
JOHN · OWEN · COLL · VICE · ADMIRALL · NORTH · WALLIENSIS   (Ren.)
The matrix was formerly at Porkington (now Brogynton) Salop.
Acc. No: 92.78H.
D: Arch. XLVI, 369-70; *Arch. Jnl.* VI, 403; *Chester Arch. Soc.* I, 166 (illus.);
    Trans. Shrops. Soc. V (1882) 419.

COURTS OF GREAT SESSIONS : JUDICIAL SEALS

Brecknock, Glamorgan and Radnor.
temp. Henry VIII.
As used in 1543-7. Buff plaster casts, circ., 74 mm.

W 26.   *Obverse.*
The king on horse-back to the right; the coronet borne on his helmet is
ensigned with a lion statant guardant crowned; in his right hand is
drawn a long sword, his left hand holds a shield: quarterly, 1. and 4.
three fleurs-de-lis, FRANCE (Modern); 2. and 3. three lions passant
guardant, ENGLAND; horse caparisoned and armoured, with a plume
of three ostrich feathers.
...II DEI..... ANGL' FRANC... HIBIE REX FIDEI DEFES' Ŧ
INT'RA. E...... EMV'. CAPV...   (Ren.)

These matrices were presented by Cardiff Corporation.
Acc. No: 12.163   *Cf.* BM 5581
D: Cf. *Arch. Jnl.* LXVIII, 175; *J.B.A.A.* XLIX (1893) 2-3; Pl. I; *Y Cymm.*
    XXVI (1916) 13.

W 27.   *Reverse.*
A shield: quarterly, FRANCE (Modern) and ENGLAND, ensigned with
the royal crown; supporters: *dext.* a greyhound (? ducally gorged), *sin.*
largely lost (probably a hind) but chained. In base, the Prince of
Wales's feathers and motto: **ICH DIEN.**
..GILL................COMITATIBVS · BREKNOK · RADNOVR · ET ·
GLAMOR............   (Ren.)
Acc. No: 12.164.

temp. Edward VI.
1547-53. Buff plaster casts, imperfect, circ., 68 mm.

W 28. *Obverse.*
The king on horse-back to the right, his sword held with his right hand; horse caparisoned with the royal arms: quarterly, FRANCE (Modern) and ENGLAND, reversed.
All that survives of the legend is:

....ANGL C...... (Ren.)

The word *ANGL* seems to have been mis-placed on restoration of the seal. The matrices were presented by Cardiff Corporation.
Acc. No: 12.176.
D: Matthews (1903) IV, 48; Cf. *J.B.A.A.* XLIX, 2-4.

W 29. *Reverse.*
A shield: quarterly, FRANCE (Modern) and ENGLAND, ensigned with the royal crown; supporters: *dext.* wanting, *sin.* partly lost (perhaps a hind) but chained. Only the first word of the legend survives:

..SIGILLVM........... (Ren.)

temp. Elizabeth I.
1558-1603. Cream plaster casts, circ., 62 mm.

W 30. *Obverse.*
The queen, on horseback, seated sideways on a pillion, her person facing the spectator; she holds the bridle with her right hand, and bears a sceptre in her left; in field, a portcullis crowned; at base, clumps of foliage.

+ ELIZABETH : DEI : GRAC.............LIE : FRANCIE :
...........GINA FIDEI DEFENSOR (Ren.)

Acc. No: 12.164.
D: Cf. *J.B.A.A.* XLIX, 5-6.

W 31. *Reverse.*
A shield: quarterly, 1. and 4. FRANCE (Modern), 2. and 3. ENGLAND; ensigned with a crown; supporters: *dext.* a greyhound collared, *sin.* a hind collared and chained; in base, the Prince of Wales's feathers and motto (obscured).

+ S' IVDICIALɆ DOMINE REGIN.......IBVS BREKNOK RADNOR
Ŧ GLAMORGAN (Ren.)

temp. James I.
1603-25. Buff plaster casts, circ., 100 mm.

W 32. *Obverse.*
The king on horseback to left, in armour with crown, holding aloft a sword with his right hand; horse bearing a plume of three ostrich feathers and passing over foliage. In field, over tail of horse, a portcullis with chains, surmounted by a royal crown; below the horse, a greensward with flowers, a rose and ? thistle.

⁑ IACOBVS ....LIÆ ⁙ SCOTIÆ ⁙ FRANCIÆ ⁙
ET HIBERNI............... DEFENSOR (Ren.)

Acc. No: 12.165.   BM 5571.
D: *Arch.* XCVII, 141; Pl. XLI(d); Cf. *J.B.A.A.* XLIX, 6-7; Matthews IV (1903) 209.

W 33. *Reverse.*
A shield: the royal arms, 1603-88; quarterly, 1. and 4. quarterly, FRANCE (Modern) and ENGLAND, 2. a lion rampant within a royal tressure, SCOTLAND, 3. a harp, IRELAND; ensigned with the royal crown. Supporters: *dext.* a greyhound (collar not seen), *sin.* a hind ducally collared and chained. In base, three ostrich feathers (for the Prince of Wales) with a scroll bearing the motto: **ICH DIEN.**

+ SIGILLVM IVDICALE PRO · COMITATIBVS BRECKNOK ⁙ RADNOR
ET · GLAMORGAN ⁙ (Ren.)

temp. George II.
1727-60. Mauve silicon rubber, circ., 102 mm.

W 34. *Obverse.* See D 45 above. Acc. No: 55.76.

W 35. *Reverse.* See D 46 above. Acc. No: 55.76.

Caernarfon, Merioneth and Anglesey.
temp. George III.
1760-1820. Buff plaster casts, circ., 90 mm.

W 36. *Obverse.*
The king on horseback to the right; in the field behind, the feathers and motto, **ICH DIEN**, of the Prince of Wales; under the body of the horse, a landscape depicting Caernarfon Castle with two three-masted ships on the Menai Straits adjacent.

· GEORGIUS TERTIUS DEI GRATIA BRITANNIARUM REX
FIDEI DEFENSOR (Ren.)

These impressions were presented by the Trustees of the British Museum.
Acc. No: 34,665/1.
D: *Arch.* XCVII, 141; Cf. *J.B.A.* XLIX, 10-11.

W 37. *Reverse.*
A shield: the royal arms, 1816-37, bearing the inescutcheon of HANOVER, ensigned with the royal crown; supporters: *dext.* a greyhound, *sin.* a stag. In base: three ostrich feathers enfiled by a coronet, and a scroll bearing the motto: **ICH DIEN.**

SIGILLUM JUDICALE PRO COMITATIIBUS CARNARVON
MERIONETH ET ANGLESEA (Ren.)

Acc. No: 34.665/2.

temp. George IV.
1820-30.

W 38. *Obverse.* White plaster cast.
See D 47. Acc. No: 42.159.

W 39. *Another Impression.* (Acc. No: 92.79H/1). Pale brown wax.

W 40. *Reverse.* White plaster cast.
See D 48. Acc. No: 42.159.

W 41. *Another Impression.* (Acc. No: 92.79H/2). Brick coloured wax.

Denbigh, Montgomery and Flint.
temp. George III (1760-1820).
Post-1811. Buff plaster casts, circ., 90 mm.

W 42. *Obverse.*
The king on horseback to the right; in the field behind are the feathers and the motto, **ICH DIEN**, of the Prince of Wales; under the body of the horse, a landscape surmounted by Denbigh Castle with its circumventing wall, below which three cattle byres.

⁙ GEORGIUS TERTIUS DEI GRATIA BRITANNIARUM
REX FIDEI DEFENSOR (Caps.)

Presented by the Trustees of the British Museum.
Acc. No: 34.665/3.
D: *J.B.A.A.* XLIX, 10-11.

W 43. *Reverse.*
A shield: the royal arms, 1816-37, ensigned with the royal crown; supporters: *dext.* a lion guardant crowned; *sin.* (? a buck) ducally gorged and crowned. In base, three ostrich feathers enfiled by a coronet, and a scroll bearing the motto: **ICH DIEN.**

SIGILLUM JUDICALE PRO COMITATIBUS DENBIGH
MONTGOMERI ET FLINT (Caps.)

Acc. No: 34.665/4.

temp. George IV.
1820-30. Buff plaster casts, circ., 93 mm.

W 44. *Obverse.*
The king on horseback galloping to the left; design as his Great Seal (*Seal No. R 90*), but the feathers and motto, **ICH DIEN**, of the Prince of

Wales in the exergue instead of the date.
∴ GEORGIUS QUARTUS DEI GRATIA BRITANNIARUM
REX FIDEI DEFENSOR   (Caps.)
Presented by the Trustees of the British Museum.
Acc. No: 34.665/5.
D: J.B.A.A. XLIX, 11-14; Griffiths (1972) 37-41.

W 45.   *Reverse.*
A shield, and legend, as W. 43.
Acc. No: 34.665/6.

-    -   -   -

Known original impressions of Judicial Seals of the Court of Great
Sessions, include *inter alia*:

for *Glamorgan, Brecknock and Radnor:*
A.D. 1543 : NLW, Penrice and Margam Ch. 1794 (fragment).
     1548 : NLW, Penrice and Margam Ch. 2816 (imperfect).
     1556 : NLW, Penrice and Margam Ch. 1572.
     1564 : NLW, Penrice and Margam Ch. 1798.
     1567 : NLW, Penrice and Margam Ch. 2123b (imperfect).
     1568 : NLW, Penrice and Margam Ch. 1582.
     1569 : NLW, Penrice and Margam Ch. 1583.
     1570 : NLW, Penrice and Margam Ch. 2125b (fragment).
     1571 : NLW, Penrice and Margam Ch. 2931.
     1573 : PRO, C 106/100 (box 1).
     1576 : PRO, C 106/100 (box 2; fragment).
     1576 : NLW, Penrice and Margam Ch. 2940.
     1576 : NLW, Quaritch Deed 599.
     1583 : Nottage Court (Glam.) MS 53.
     1600 : PRO (Chancery Lane) C 106/100 (Box 1).
     1606 : BL, Add. Ch. 26,508.
     1607 : NLW, Penrice and Margam Ch. 1831.
     1616 : NLW, Penrice and Margam Ch. 1255 (fragment).
     1616 : HCA 3173 (fragment).
     1665 : NLW, Penrice and Margam Ch. 1881 (indistinct).
     1667 : NLW, Penrice and Margam Ch. 1008.
     1677 : NLW, Penrice and Margam Ch. 3065.
     1682 : NLW, Penrice and Margam Ch. 3450 (imperfect).
     1702 : NLW, Misc. Box No. 3 (worn).
     1723 : NLW, Penrice and Margam Ch. 3614 (fragment).
     1741 : NLW, Penrice and Margam Ch. 6484.
     1746 : NLW, Penrice and Margam Ch. 1164.
     1772 : NLW, Penrice and Margam Ch. 1766.
     1794 : Glamorgan Archives D/D. Xdt. 3.

D: NLW, Misc. Docs. Box 1: *Grant of profits of the Judicial Seal* (1608);
   NLW MS 3854B: *Method of Proceeding in the Court of the Great Sessions*
   for Glamorgan, Brecon and Radnor (1817); *Arch.* XCVII, 141, Pl. XLId;
   Arch. Jnl. LXVIII, 175; Matthews IV (1903) 48, 209; *J.B.A.A.* XLIX
   (1893) 2-7; *Y Cymm.* XXVI 1916) 13.

for *Denbigh, Montgomery and Flint:*
A.D. 1543 : NLW, Wigfair Deed 83 (fine fragment).
     1545 : BL, Add. Ch. 8650.
     1551 : BL, Add. Ch. 8528.
     1559 : NLW, Wigfair Deed 441 (small fragment).
     1565 : NLW, Ruthin Lordship Deed 29 (fragment).
     1571 : NLW, Wigfair Deed 466 (fragment).
     1578 : BL, Add. Ch. 41,406.
     1579 : NLW, Ruthin Lordship Deed 1113.
     1583 : Shrewsbury Local Studies Libr., Deed 110 (chipped).
     1586 : NLW, Ruthin Lordship Deed 1110 (indistinct).
     1586 : NLW, Cernioge Deed I, 79.
     1592 : NLW, Wigfair Deed 1021 (large indistinct fragment).
     1593 : NLW, Celynog Deed 22.
     1595 : NLW, Ruthin Lordship Deeds 1078-9.
     1597 : BL, Add. Ch. 8534 (partly indistinct).
     1598 : NLW, Coed Coch Deed 233.

     1600 : BL, Add. Ch. 8656 (partly indistinct).
     1602 : NLW, Ruthin Lordship Deed 1063 (indistinct).
Temp. Eliz. I: See W 478.
     1604 : NLW, Ruthin Lordship Deed 1976 (fine fragment).
     1605 : NLW, Ruthin Lordship Deed 1112 (indistinct).
     1606 : NLW, Ruthin Lordship Deed 1111 (indistinct).
     1606 : NLW, BRA Deposit (1936) ? No. 94.
     1614 : NLW, Ruthin Lordship Deed 1116 (fragment).
     1616 : NLW, McEwen Coll. 6a.
     1617 : NLW, Ruthin Lordship Deed 1168.
     1618 : BL, Add. Ch. 8658.
     1619 : BL, Add. Ch. 8657.
     1619 : NLW, Nanhoron Deed 19 (fragment).
     1623 : NLW, Coed Coch Deed 303.
     1624 : NLW, Wigfair Deed 737 (fragment).
     1624 : NLW, Plas-yn-cefn Deeds 126 (fine, but damaged),
           422, 1199 (large fragment), 1217
     1631 : NLW, Ruthin Lordship Deed 1050 (fine).
     1639 : NLW, Coed Coch Deed 1538.
     1650 : NLW, Ruthin Lordship Deed 32 (fragment).
     1666 : BL, Egerton Ch. 1666.
     1669 : NLW, Wigfair Deed 1326 (fine impression).
     1679 : NLW, Wigfair Deed 1357 (large fine fragment).
     1682 : NLW, Wigfair Deed 1326 (flattened, but date of 1661
           visible in legend).
     1769 : NLW, Misc. Box No. 13 (image lost, fragile).
     1787 : BL, Add. Ch. 41,243.
     1814 : NLW, Wigfair Deed 1744 (paper masked).

D: Arch. Jnl. XVII, 62; *J.B.A.A.* XLIX, 10-14; *Mont. Collns.* XXVI, 162);
   Williams (1982) 32 (No. 74).

for *Anglesey, Caernarfon and Merioneth:*
A.D. 1545 : NLW, Sotheby Deed 161.
     1550 NLW, Sotheby Deed 171.
     1563 : NLW, Carreg-lwyd Deed 2055.
     1578 : UCNW, Baron Hill Deed 1741 (fragment).
     1591 : UCNW, Baron Hill Deed 1262 (fragment).
     1601 : UCNW, Baron Hill Deed 1264 (small fragment).
     1616 : NLW, Carreg-lwyd Deed 1752.
     1633 : UCNW, Baron Hill Deed 707 (good impression).
     1639 : UCNW, Baron Hill Deed 1245.
     1639 : NLW, Sotheby Deed 509.
     1640 : UCNW, Baron Hill Deeds 79, 1266.
     1641 : NLW, Sotheby Deed 514.
     1643 : NLW, Carreg-lwyd Deed 1606 (fragment).
     1648 : *See* BL, *Det. Seal* XXXVII, 75.
 *Ca.*1650 : NLW, Sotheby Deed 522 (detached).
     1659 : NLW, Sotheby Deed 539.
     1660 : NLW, Wigfair Deed 1233 (fractured and indistinct).
     1668 : NLW, Carreg-lwyd Deed 2412 (fragment).
     1671 : NLW, Sotheby Deed 571 (imperfect).
     1684 : NLW, Nanhoron Deed 303 (imperfect fragment).
     1685 : NLW, Sotheby Deed 596 ((imperfect).
     1689 : Gwynedd Record Office XD 2/27394.
     1692 : NLW, Sotheby Deed 603 (paper masked).
     1707 : NLW, Sotheby Deed 639 (paper masked).
     1709 : NLW, Sotheby Deed 640 (paper masked).
     1723 : NLW, Boderwyd Deeds 167 and 168 (paper masked).
     1732 : NLW, Sotheby Deed 648 (fragment).
     1749 : NLW, Nanhoron Deed 229 (needs cleaning).
     1764 : UCNW, Penrhyn Further Additions (Box Gaflogeon).
     1794 : NLW, Nanhoron Deed 310 (fine impression).
     1820-30 : *See D. 43-44.*

D: Arch. XCVII, 141; *J.B.A.A.* XLIX (1893) 10-12, Pl.7.

for *Pembroke, Carmarthen and Cardigan:*
A.D. 1551 : Dyfed Archives (Carmarthen), Lort 22/895.
     1557 : NLW, Edwinsford Deed 2672.

37

1560 : NLW, Bronwydd (Group II) Deed 1311 (fragment).
1573 : PRO, E 156/37/42 (fragment).
1576 : NLW, Cwmgwili Deed 47 (small fragm.).
1577 : NLW, Bronwydd (Group II) Deed 928.
1579 : NLW, Bronwydd (Group II) Deeds 1409, 1417 (fragment).
1582 : NLW, Bronwydd (Group II) Deeds 860-1 (fragments).
1583 : NLW, Bronwydd (Group II) Deeds 1184, 1203 (fine fragment).
1585 : NLW, Bronwydd (Group II) Deed 862 (fragment).
1586 : NLW, Bronwydd (Group II) 1183.
1588 : NLW, Edwinsford Deed 670.
1593 : NLW, Slebech Deed 673.
1594 : NLW, Cilymaenllwyd Deed 84.
1596 : NLW Deed 188 (fragment).
1605 : NLW, Dynevor Group A, Suppl. 6.
1606 : NLW, Misc. Docs. Box 14 (N. 13).
1607 : NLW, Bronwydd (Group II) Deed 921.
1611 : NLW, Edwinsford Deeds 2084 and 2085 (good impression).
1612 : NLW, Dynevor Group A, Deed 20.
1612 : Dyfed Archives (Carmarthen), Lort 19/733.
1613 : NLW Deed 191.
1613 : NLW, Edwinsford Deed 523 (fine, but cracked).
1613 : BL, Add. Ch. 979.
1614 : NLW, Bronwydd (Group II) Deed 1212 (fragment).
1630 : Dyfed Archives (Carmarthen), Lort 26/990.
1630 : NLW, Edwinsford Deed 2097.
1639 : Dyfed Archives (Carmarthen), Lort 24/942.
1640 : NLW, Edwinsford Deed 2557 (indistinct).
1648 : NLW, Edwinsford Deed 1184 (injured).
1650 : NLW, Edwinsford Deed 1189.
1651 : Dyfed Archives (Carmarthen), Lort 17/769.
1657 : NLW, Bronwydd (Group II) Deed 2234.
1658 : Dyfed Archives (Carmarthen), Lort 17/677.

1661 : NLW, Edwinsford Deed 1535 (fine large fragment).
1663 : Dyfed Archives (Carmarthen), Lort 24/943 (fractured).
1665 : NLW, Edwinsford Deed 703 (imperfect fragment).
1671 : Dyfed Archives (Carmarthen), Lort 26/988 (fractured).
1681 : Dyfed Archives (Carmarthen), Lort 26/996.
1685 : Dyfed Archives (Carmarthen), Lort 26/987 and 989.
1688 : Dyfed Archives (Carmarthen), Lort 24/958.
1688 : NLW, Dynevor Group A, Suppl. 10.
1689 : NLW, Bronwydd (Group II) 1607.
1692 : Dyfed Archives (Carmarthen), Lort 12/578 and 24/946.
1696 : NLW, Edwinsford Deed 2439 (small fragment).
1698 : NLW, Edwinsford Deed 2643 (fragment).
1702 : NLW, Edwinsford Deed 2454 (paper masked small fragment).
1740 : NLW, Bronwydd (Group II) 1562.
1760 : NLW, Edwinsford Deeds 2446 and 2464 (paper masked).
1777 : NLW, Bronwydd (Group II) 2931.
1779 : NLW, Bronwydd (Group II) 1759.
1783 : NLW, Cwrt Mawr Deed 740 (paper masked).
1793 : NLW, Bronwydd (Group II) Deed 3095 (paper masked).
1819 : NLW, Bronwydd (Group II) Deed 2077 (paper masked.

D: NLW, Penrice and Margam Ch. 1083: *Appointment of Custodian of the Seal* (1638); *Arch.* XXII (1829) 417, XXXI (1846) 461-2, 495-6; *J.B.A.A.* XLIX (1893) 1-14, L (1894) 66-70; *Trans. Carms. Antiq. Soc.* V (1909) 53.
(The assistance of Carmarthen Record Office is acknowledged here).

(Some modern casts of Welsh Judicial Seals, of various reigns, are also to be found amongst the Detached Seals of the British Library (Department of Manuscripts), and a few in the collections of the Society of Antiquaries of London).

ECCLESIASTICAL

Episcopal

W 46. BANGOR, Bishop of: D.L. Lloyd, S.T.R.
1890-99. Red wax, p.o., 79 x 53 mm.
See D 4 above. Acc. No: 79/107H.

W 47. BANGOR, Bishop of: C.A.H. Green, D.D. (2nd Archbishop of Wales)
1928-44. Green wax, p.o., 99 x 67 mm. (in leather bound case)
See D 6 above. Acc. No: 44.298/3 (WFM)

W 48. *Fob seal.* Red wax, oval, 19 x 16 mm.
See D 7 above. Acc. No: 44.298/5 (WFM).

W 49. LLANDAFF, Bishop of: William Saltmarsh.
Obverse.
1186-91. Pale brown plaster cast, p.o., 71 x 44 mm.
The bishop in pontifical eucharistic vestments and short mitre; his left hand holds his pastoral staff, his right hand raised in blessing.
SIG............................EPI   (Rom.)
Acc. No: 44.171.   BM 1861 Ø.
E: BL, Harl. Ch. 75 A. 16 (Und.), A. 17 (1190).
D: Williams (1984) 116 (No. 28); Birch (1912) 373-4.

W 50. *Another Impression.* Pale brown sulphur cast.
Acc. No: 25.384.

W 51. *Counter-seal.*
1186-91. Ochre sulphur cast, oval, 34 x 30 mm.
Impression of an ancient Christian gem; a long cross between two couped busts facing each other.
+ IN..........TAT OMNE VERBVM   (Rom.)
The seals bearing the Acc. No: 44.171 were formerly the property of Walter de Gray Birch, and presented to the Museum by his daughter, Miss U. Birch of Chiswick, through the good offices of her neighbour, H.L. Mann, a member of the Ecclesiological Society.
Acc. No: 44.171.   BM 1861 R
E: BL, Harl. Ch. A. 16 (Und.).
D: Williams (1984) 116 (No. 30); Birch (1912) 374.

W 52. *Another Impression.* (Acc. No: 92.80H). Pale brown plaster cast.

W 53. *Variant Counter-seal.* Off-white plaster cast, oval, 34 x 27 mm.
Impression of an ancient gem; an imperial bust, in profile to the right, couped at the neck.
Acc. No: 44.171.   BM 1863 R
E: BL, Harl. Ch. A. 17 (1190).
D: Williams (1984) 116 (No. 29); Birch (1912) 374.

W 54. LLANDAFF, Bishop of: Henry of Abergavenny.
First Seal.
1193- *ca.*1203. Brown sulphur cast, p.o., 62 x 41 mm.

The bishop standing, in pontificals with short archaic mitre, a long maniple attached to his left arm; right hand raised in blessing, left hand grasping his pastoral staff turned towards himself.
..SIGILL : HENRICI (: LANDA)VENSIS : EPISCOPI **(Early Lom.)**
Acc. No: 25.384 BM 1865Ø
E: BL, Harl. Ch 75 A. 18 (1199), A. 21 (Ca. 1199), A. 23 (Undated)., Canterbury Cath. *Cart. Antiq.* L. 130 (of 1200).
D: Williams (1984) 117 (No. 31). Birch (1912) 374-5.

W 55. *Another Impression.* Cream plaster cast. Acc. No: 44.171.

W 56. *Counter-seal.* Brown sulphur cast, p.o., 36 x 23 mm.
The Archangel Gabriel, sword in right hand.
+ SECRET / HENR · LANDAV · EPISCOP · **(Early Lom.)**
Acc. No: 25.384. BM 1865 R.
E: BL, Harl. Ch. 75 A. 18 (1199), A.21, 22 and 23 (all undated); NLW, Penrice and Margam Ch. 48, 102 (both undated).
D: Williams (1984) 117 (No. 33); Birch (1912) 374.

W 57. *Another Impression.* Cream plaster cast. Acc. No: 44.171.

W 58. *Second Seal.*
Ca. 1203-13. Yellow sulphur cast (cracked), p.o., 68 x 44 mm.
The bishop standing on a columnar pedestal, in pontificals but with the folds of his chasuble differing from those in W 54; again there is a pronounced maniple and also a *rationale* (a cross-bearing breast-plate); his left hand holds his pastoral staff turned towards himself, his right hand is raised in blessing.
+ SIGILL': HENRICI · DEI · GRACIA · LANDAVENSIS · EPISCOPI **(Lom.)**
Acc. No: 25:384. BM 1869 Ø.
E: BL, Harl. Ch. 75 A.20, A.22; NLW, Penrice and Margam Ch. 48, 102 (all undated)
D: Williams (1984) 117 (No. 32); Birch (1912) 375.

W 59. *Another Impression.* Dull yellow sulphur cast (cracked).
Acc. No: 25.384

W 60. *Another Impression.* Brown sulphur cast (base wanting).
Acc. No: 25.384.

W 61. *Another Impression.* Cream plaster cast (head wanting).
Acc. No: 25.384

W 62. *Another Counter-seal.*
Undate. Cream plaster cast, p.o., 38 x 24mm.
A cherbub on a platform.
....L' H'DI G·AA : LAND' E... **(Lom.)**
Acc. No: 44.171.
D: Williams (1984) 117 (No. 34); Birch (1912) 375.

W 63. LLANDAFF, Bishop of: William of Goldcliff.
1219-30. Brown sulphur cast, p.o., 66 x 42mm.
The bishop standing on a corbel; in eucharistic vestments with a short mitre and long maniple; in his left hand his pastoral staff turned towards himself, his right hand raised in blessing.
+ SIGILL' : WILL'I : DEI : GRA. . A : LANDAVENSIS : EPI **(Lom.)**
Birch (in BM 1879Ø, and *Memorials* 376), wrongly attributes this seal to Bishop William of Christchurch (1240-44).
Acc. No: 25.384.
E: BL, Harl. Ch. 75 D.16 (Undated).
D: Williams (1984) 118 (No. 35).

W 64. *Another Impression.* Cream plaster cast. Acc. No: 44.171.

Counter- or Privy Seal.
W 65. Undated. Brown sulphur cast, p.o., 44 x 25 mm.
St. Peter, standing on a bracket, book in left hand, keys in right.
+ SECRET' : W. LANDAVENSIS : EP : ł **(Lom.)**
Acc. No: 25.384. BM 1879 R.
E: BL, Harl. Ch. 75 D. 16
D: Williams (1984) 118 (No. 36); Birch (1912) 376.

W 66. *Another Impression.* Cream plaster cast. Acc. No: 44.171.

W 67. LLANDAFF, Bishop of: Elias of Radnor.
1230-40. Off-white plaster cast, p.o., 74 x 44 mm.
The bishop standing on a pedestal, in pontificals - with developed mitre, apparelled alb and embroidered dalmatic beneath his chasuble; his left hand holds his pastoral staff turned towards himself, his right raised in blessing; in field, *dext.* a crescent; *sin.* an estoile of six points.
+ ELIAS : DEI GRACIA : L . . . AVENSIS : EPISCOPVS **(Lom.)**
Acc. No: 44.171. BM 1872 Ø.
E: BL, Harl. Ch. 75 A.25 (*ante*-1234), A.26 (1239), B.6 (*Ca.* 1234), B.8 (1234), B.9 (1234), B. 40 (1234); HCA 886 (1230-31), 515 (un-dated fragment); NLW, Penrice and Margam Ch. 136 (1239), 137 and 139 (both undated).
D: *Arch. Camb.* 1867/23, 1868/185-6, Williams (1984) 118 (No. 37); Birch (1912) 375-6.

W 68. *Another Impression.* Brown sulphur cast. Acc. No: 25.384.

W 69. *Counter- or Privy Seal.*
1230-40. Off-white plaster cast, p.o., 36 x 26 mm.
A right hand of blessing, issuing from wavy clouds, or a vested arm.
+ SECRETV̄ : ELIE : LANDAVENSIS : EPISCOPI **(Lom.)**
Acc. No: 44.171. BM 1872 R.
E and *D:* as for W 67.

W 70. *Another Impression.* Brown sulphur cast. Acc. No: 25.384.

W 71. LLANDAFF, Bishop of: John of Egglescliffe, O.P.
1323-47. Cream plaster cast, p.o., 68 x 41 mm.
Under a gothic-type canopy, the bishop standing in pontificals on an elaborately decorated and layered corbel, wearing an embroidered and sharply pointed mitre; his left hand holds his pastoral staff turned away from him, his right hand raised in blessing; the field diapered lozengy, a rose in each space. In field, two shields of arms: *dext.* three lions passant guardant, ENGLAND; *sin.* a stork statant, EGGLESCLIFFE; over the canopy, *dext.* a small crescent; *sin.* ? an estoile.
........S · IOHA.............CIA EPIS.... .ANDAVENSIS **(Lom.)**
Acc. No: 44.171. BM 1882.
E: BL, Add. Ch. 20,610 (1333); NLW, Penrice and Margam Ch. 215 (1339), 216 (1339).
D: Williams (1984) 120 (Nos. 45a, 45b); Birch (1912) 377-8.

W 72. *Another Impression.* Yellow sulphur cast (upper portion wanting).
Acc. No: 25.384.

W 73. *Another Impression.* Yellow plaster cast (sides chipped).
Acc. No: 25.384.

W 74. LLANDAFF, Bishop of: Thomas Peverell, O.Carm.
1398-1407. Buff sulphur cast, p.o., 62 x 34 mm.
Under a gothic-type canopy, the Blessed Trinity: God the Father seated and supporting the Crucified Christ, by His left shoulder an eagle (? dove) representing the Holy Spirit descending; foliage by the Father's right shoulder and in the field; in base, the bishop kneels to the left in prayer, mitred and with his pastoral staff, with *sinister* a shield: a bend, in chief a book or billet (*poss.* a canton), for PEVERELL (though not the usual family arms). Some see the seven tall pinnacles adorning the canopy as alluding to the 'mystic seven of the candlesticks' - the churches of Asia Minor and the gifts of the Holy Spirit. Cabled border.
Sigillum : thome : peuerell : epis̄ *(?)* : landauen' : **(Bl.)**
Acc. No: 44.171. BM 1884.
E: Glamorgan Archive D/D F.1853 (fragment from 1403).
D: Williams (1984) 121 (Nos. 47a, 47b); Birch (1952) 379-80; Tonnochy (1952) No. 805.

W 75. *Another Impression.* (Acc. No: 92.81H). White silicon rubber.

W 76. LLANDAFF, Bishop of: John Hunden, O.P., D.Th.
1458-76. Red wax, p.o., 77 x 50 mm.
Beneath an elaborate gothic-type canopy, a key-bearing St. Peter; in side niches, *dext.* a sword-carrying St. Paul; *sin.* probably St. Teilo, a primatial cross in his left hand; in smaller niches above, two bishops, probably SS. Dyfrig and Euddogwy (all being co-patron saints of the Cathedral); beaded border; in base, under a pointed arch, the bishop in prayer to the front. mitred and vested, between two shields: *dext.* sword and key in saltire, LLANDAFF; *sin.* semée of crosslets fitchy, three talbots' heads erased, HUNDEN.
Sigillum : iohĩs : episcopi : landaui : ordin' · p'dicatoru⁻ (Bl.)
The matrix was found in soil near St. Asaph Cathedral about 1800; its present whereabouts are unknown. (The seal has occasionally been attributed to Bishop John Burghill : 1396-98).
Acc. No: 25.384.
D: Williams (1984) 121-2 (No. 49); Birch (1912) 380-1; *Proc. Soc. Antiq.* 2nd Ser. XI, 289.

W 77. LLANDAFF, Bishop of: Richard Lewis, D.D.
1883-1905. Red wax (paper masked), p.o., 71 x 48 mm.
A shield, ensigned with a mitre: *dext.* (Sable) two croziers in saltire, on a chief (Azure) three mitres labelled of the second, LLANDAFF; impaling *sin.* (Gules) three serpents nowed, LEWIS (probably a differenced version of the coat attributed to Ednywain ap Bradwen).
THE SEAL OF RICHARD LEWIS D.D. BISHOP OF LLANDAFF 1883 (Caps.)
Acc. No: 92.82H.
D: Bedford, *Blazon* 81; M.P. Siddons (letter, 19-8-92).

W 78. LLANDAFF, Bishop of : J.P. Hughes, D.D.
1905-31. Red wax, p.o., 81 x 54 mm.
See D 14. Acc. No: 31.234 (WFM).

W 79. *Another Impression.* (Acc. No: 92.83H). Pale mauve silicon rubber.

W 80. LLANDAFF, Bishop of: J. Morgan, D.D.
1939-57. Red wax, p.o., 79 x 52 mm.
See D 15. Acc. No: 92.84H/1.

W 81. *Another Impression.* (Acc. No: 92.84H/2). Grey silicon rubber.

W 82. See D 16. (Acc. No: 92.85H). Grey silicon rubber.

W 83. MONMOUTH, Bishop of: C.A.H. Green, D.D.
1921-28. Grey silicon rubber, p.o., 90 x 72 mm.
See D 22. Acc. No: 92.86H.

W 84. *Another Impression.* Red wax (WFM).

W 85. *Another Impression.* Steel cast (WFM).

W 86. ST. ASAPH, Bishop of: John Lowe.
Signet
1433-44. White silicon rubber, circ., 11 mm., (with a replica of the matrix).
An eagle displayed, facing half-left and standing on its left leg; above its head the word: **John**; two other indistinct words may be **Asaph** and **Lowe**. (Miss N. Aubertin-Potter, Sub-Librarian at All Souls, kindly supplied this information).
The matrix is preserved in the Ashmolean Museum, Oxford.
Acc. No: 92.87H.
E: Bodleian Libr. Oxford (All Souls, Llangennith MS 2 of 1441).
D: Williams (1984) 126 (No. 67), (1989) 74 (No. 67).

W 87. ST. ASAPH, Bishop of: A.G. Edwards.
1889-1934. Pale red silicon rubber, p.o., 76 x 53 mm.
A shield, ensigned with an ornamental mitre: *dext.* (Sable) two keys in saltire, wards uppermost (ST. ASAPH), impaling *sin.* (Argent) a chevron engrailed (Gules) between three fleurs-de-lis, EDWARDS. A border of small crosses surrounds the legend:
+ SIGILLUM ALFREDI GEORGII EDWARDS EPISCOPI ASAPHENSIS MDCCCLXXXIX (Caps.)
The brass matrix is preserved in St. Asaph Cathedral treasury.
Acc. No: 92.88H.
D: Williams (1982) 45 (No. 106).

W 88. ST. ASAPH, Bishop of: W.T. Havard.
1934-50. Pale red silicon rubber, p.o., 74 x 52 mm.
A shield, ensigned with a worked mitre: *dext.* (Gules) two keys in saltire, wards uppermost, ST. ASAPH, impaling *sin.* a bull's head cabossed, between three mullets (Gules), HAVARD. The legend is bordered by small crosses.
+ SIGILLUM WILHELMI THOMAE HAVARD EPISCOPI ASAPHENSIS MCMXXXIV (Caps.)
Acc. No: 92.89H. (The brass matrix is preserved in St. Asaph Cathedral treasury).
(N.B: Impressions en placard of the seals of bishops of St. Asaph from 1715 to 1846 (Bishop Wynne through to Bishop Vowler Short) are also kept in the treasury. Other St. Asaph episcopal impressions of the period occur in NLW, Misc. Deeds: Boxes 9 and 12).

W 89. ST. DAVID'S, Bishop of: Henry Chichele.
1407-14. White plaster cast, p.o., 76 x 49 mm.
In two lateral niches, the co-patrons of the Cathedral: *dext.* St. Andrew (head wanting); *sin.* St. David with his primatial cross; tabernacle work to the sides. In base, under a rounded arch, the bishop in prayer to front, flanked by two shields: *dext.* quarterly, FRANCE (Modern) and ENGLAND; *sin.* a chevron between three cinquefoils or roses, CHICHELEY.
.... : dei et aP̄lice sedis : gratī : menev....... (Bl.)
Acc. No: 92.90H.
E: Paris: Ministere D'Etat, Archives De L'Empire J 646, No. 74; Glam. Archives, CL/Deeds I/3682 (fragment., 1411).
D: Douët D'Arcq III (1868) 299 (No. 10234); Williams (1984) 131 (No. 91), (1989) 75 (No. 91).

W 90. ST. DAVID'S, Bishop of: R. Lowth, D.D.
1766. White plaster cast, p.o., 91 x 62 mm.
An oval, and ornamental, shield: *dext.* (Sable) on a cross (Or) five cinquefoils, ST. DAVID'S; impaling *sin.* (Gules or Sable ?) a wolf salient, LOWTH. Carved outer border. (A sharp ridge across the middle of the impression reflects a deep horizontal cut on the matrix, presumably made for the purpose of cancelling the seal's validity. Lowth held the see but for a few months).
THE · SEAL · OF · ROBERT · LOWTH · D.D · BISHOP · OF · ST · DAVIDS · 1766 (Caps.)
Presented by the Department of Medieval Antiquities at the British Museum.
Acc. No: 92.91H.
D: Tonnochy (1952) 167 (No. 812).
For a series of seals impressions of early modern bishops of St. David's, see: Carmarthen R.O., Museum Collection. No. 283: "Autographs and Seals, Bishops of St. David's".

W 91. SWANSEA AND BRECON, First Bishop of : E.L. Bevan, D.D.
1923-34. Copper cast, p.o., 74 x 45 mm.
A shield, ensigned with a mitre: per fess in chief, surmounting a demi-wheel (from the prophecy of Ezekiel) an eagle rising reguardant *(the arms of the medieval BRECON PRIORY)*; in base, a fleur-de-lis.
+ THE SEAL OF EDWARD LATHAM BEVAN . D.D.
+ BISHOP OF SWANSEA AND BRECON . 1923 (Caps.)
Acc. No: 34. 627 (WFM).

W 92. WESTERN DISTRICT (including Wales), Vicar Apostolic of: P.A. Baines, O.S.B; Bishop of Siga.
1829-40. Green sulphur cast, oval, 25 x 21 mm.
A shield, ensigned with an episcopal hat; a crescent, in chief *(?)* two

wolves' heads erased; crest: a lion passant, *dext.* of which, a mitre; *sin.* a pastoral staff; motto: *?* **STUDIT ET ERUDIT**. These arms are not those on his tomb in Downside Abbey, Bath. (The ascription to Bishop Baines comes from a 19th-century hand on the reverse: *'Bp. Baynes'*).
Acc. No: 25.384.

W 93. *Another Seal.* Red wax, rectangular, 20 x 18 mm.
A shield, surmounted by a cross botonny and ensigned with an episcopal tasselled hat: *dext.* the arms of the BENEDICTINE ORDER incorporating its motto, *Pax*, impaling *sin.* (Azure) a tower triple-

towered (for SIGA; his see 'in partibus infidelium'). This seal was traced through the researches of Mrs G Elwes of Wanborough, Guildford; the impressions were prepared by the Rev. M. Jones-Frank from the matrix, the property of the Bishop of Clifton, to one of whose predecessors it was sent on 22 August 1909 by the Prior of Downside.
Acc. No: 83.96H.
D: Thesaurus Ecclesiae Cliftoniensis.

W 94. *Another Impression.* (Acc. No: 92.92H). Red wax.

OFFICIAL

W 95.   ARWYSTLI, Powys: Deanery of.
Royal Seal for Ecclesiastical Causes. Red wax, p.o., 77 x 54 mm.
See D 2 above. Acc. No: 80.11.

W 96.   *Another Impression.* (Acc. No: 92.93H). Red wax.

W 97.   CARMARTHEN, Archdeacon of: Walter Wynter.
Ca. 1328-31. White plasticine, p.o., 42 x 25 mm.
See D 12. Acc. No: 92.94H/1.

W 98.   *Another Impression.* (Acc. No: 92.94H/2). Red silicon rubber.

W 99.   *Another Impression.* (Acc. No: 92.94H/3). Red silicon rubber.

W 100.   CEREDIGION, Archdeacon of: William.
1292. Red wax, p.o., 45 x 28 mm.
The Blessed Virgin seated and crowned, in a niche under a trefoiled arch, supporting the Child on her left knee; beaded border; in base, under a cusped pointed arch, the archdeacon, half-length, in prayer to right. A small bird terminates the legend.

S' : W : ARCHIDIACONI : DE : K'DYGAN   (Lom.)
Acc. No: 92.95H.   BM 2187
(where referring to BL. Det. Seal XLVII, 192, mistakenly entered as XLVIII, 192).
D: Williams (1985) 185 (No. 178).

W 101.   LLANDAFF, Chancellor of: G. Harris, LL.D.
1756-96. Grey silicon rubber, p.o., 79 x 55 mm.
See D 17. Acc. No: 92.96H.

W 102.   LLANDAFF, Secular Registry: Court of Probate.
Post-1857. Red wax (paper masked), circ., 77 mm.
Arms, crest and supporters of Queen Victoria, with the letters: **V.R.** to either side of crest; in base, a small shield of arms, LLANDAFF.
+ SEAL · OF · THE · COURT · OF · PROBATE   LLANDAFF
· REGISTRY   (Caps.)
Acc. No: 16.68/106.
From the bequest of T.H. Thomas, R.C.A.

W 103.   MEIRIONYDD, Gwynedd; Archdeacon of.
? 17th cent. Dark pink silicon rubber, p.o., 46 x 30 mm.
A demi-figure of God the Father, in a pillared throne, supporting the crucified Son, the Holy Spirit in the form of a dove proceeding from His mouth; beneath, is a death-head, with a garland, emblematical of the victory over death.
+ S + ARCHID + DE + MERION +   (Ren.)
Acc. No: 85.16H.
From the ivory matrix in the Ashmolean Museum, Oxford.
D: Arch. Camb. 1847/19, 1886/110-11, CXXXIV (1985) 183 (No. 170);
   Catal. Ashmolean Museum (1836) 142 (No. 410); Maskell (1872) 164.

W 104.   MEIRIONYDD, Archdeacon of: R. Langford.
1717-32. Red wax, oval, 44 x 34 mm.

See D 21 *supra.* Acc. No: 17.190.
Presented by W.J. Hemp, North Rd., Aberystwyth.
(For the seal of Archdeacon Hugh Wynne (1733-..), see: UCNW, Mostyn Deed 1157 (of 1733).

W 105.   *Another Impression.* (Acc. No: 92.97H). Red wax.

W 106.   MONMOUTH, Gwent; Archdeacon of: C.A.H. Green, D.D.
1914-21. Red wax, oval, 70 x 47 mm.
A coat of arms: three stags trippant, GREEN.
+ SEAL OF CHARLES ALFRED HOWELL GREEN. D.D.
ARCHDEACON OF MONOUTH 1914
Acc. No: 44.298/1 (WFM).

ST. ASAPH, Clwyd: Chancellors of.
(From the matrices preserved in the Cathedral Treasury)

W 107.   C.S. Luxmoore, M.A.
1826-54. Red silicon rubber, oval, 62 x 50 mm.
A coat of arms: *dext.* two keys in saltire, ST. ASAPH; impaling *sin.* quarterly, 1. and 4. a chevron (Azure) between three moorcocks, 2. and 3. on a bend (Azure) three escallops; and barry of six (Argent) and (Azure), in chief three roundels, with a label of three points, BARNARD (Luxmoore's mother's family). Carved outer border. The legend commences with a pierced mullet:
· THE SEAL OF C·S· LUXMOORE · A · M · CHANCELLOR OF
S^{T} ASAPH 1826   (Caps.)
Acc. No: 92.98H.

W 108.   C.B. Clough, M.A.
1854-59. Red silicon rubber, oval, 61 x 49 mm.
A coat of arms: *dext.* (Sable) two keys in saltire, ST. ASAPH, impaling *sin.* quarterly, 1. (Azure) a greyhound's head couped between three mascles, CLOUGH; 2. per fess (Azure) the Jerusalem Cross between four crosses crosslet and on either side a sword point up; and in base (Or) a lion passant *(the augmentation coat given to or adopted by Sir Richard Clough after his return from a pilgrimage to the Holy Land)*; 3. (Argent) a chevron (*?* Sable) between three boars' heads couped, POWELL; 4. (Azure) three covered cups, BUTLER. Carved outer border.
+ THE SEAL OF CHARLES BUTLER CLOUGH M.A.
CHANCELLOR OF S^{T} ASAPH   (Caps.)
Acc. No: 92.99H.

W 109.   R.B. Maurice Bonnor, M.A.
1859-86. Red silicon rubber, oval, 62 x 51 mm.
A coat of arms: *dext.* two keys in saltire, ST. ASAPH, impaling *sin.* quarterly, 1. and 4. on a bend three escallops, BONNOR; 2. and 3. a lion passant guardant within a border indented, MAURICE. (For these arms see: *Mont. Collns.* V (1872) 268, where the lion is said to be rampant). Carved outer border.
+ THE SEAL OF R.B.M. BONNOR. M.A.
CHANCELLOR OF S^{T} ASAPH. 1859   (Caps.)
Acc. No: 92.100H.

W 110.   F.J. Jeune, M.A., Q.C.
1885-91. Red silicon rubber, oval, 62 x 49 mm.
A coat of arms: *dext.* two keys in saltire, ST. ASAPH; impaling *sin.* a stag trippant between *?* four estoiles or six-pointed mullets, JEUNE. Carved outer border. The legend commences with a quatrefoil:
**THE SEAL OF F.H. JEUNE M.A. CHANCELLOR OF
Sᵀ ASAPH 1885**   (Caps.)
Acc. No: 92.101H.

W 111.   H.C. Raikes, M.A., LL.D., P.C.
1891. Red silicon rubber, oval, 63 x 52 mm.
A coat of arms, supported by foliage, and ensigned with the Agnus Dei; *dext.* two keys in saltire, ST. ASAPH; impaling *sin.* a chevron engrailed ermines between three eagles' heads couped, RAIKES. Outer border beaded.
**+ THE : SEAL : OF : HENRY : CECIL : RAIKES : LL.D :
CHANCELLOR : OF : Sᵀ : ASAPH : 1891**   (Pseudo-Lom.)
 Acc. No: 92.102H.

W 112.   W.T. Parkins, M.A.
1891-?1908. Red silicon rubber, oval, 63 x 52 mm.
A coat of arms, supported by foliage in the field, and surmounted by a plate inscribed: **A.D. 1891**; *dext.* two keys in saltire, ST. ASAPH, impaling *sin.* per bend sinister Ermine and (Erminois) a lion rampant, PARKINS. Outer border beaded.
**+ THE : SEAL : OF : WILLIAM : TREVOR : PARKINS M.A :
CHANCELLOR : OF : Sᵀ : ASAPH**   (Pseudo-Lom.)
Acc. No: 92.103H.

W 113.   F. Williams, Q.C.
1965-82. Red silicon rubber, oval, 62 x 50 mm.
A coat of arms: *dext.* two keys in saltire, ST. ASAPH, impaling *sin.* (*?*Sable) two foxes counter-salient in saltire (two leaping cross-foxes) the sinister surmounted of the dexter, WILLIAMS   (perhaps meant for

the coat of Cadrod Hardd). Cabled outer border. Legend commences at the base of the seal:
**+ THE SEAL OF FRANCIS WILLIAMS, Q.C.
CHANCELLOR OF Sᵀ ASAPH 1965**   (Caps.)
Acc. No: 92.104H.

W 114.   ST. DAVID'S, Dyfed; Official Principal of Bishop Henry Morgan.
1554-59. Red wax, p.o., 78 x 55 mm.
Under a Palladian-type canopy of late style, Saint David, full-length, in cope and mitre, pastoral staff in his left hand turned towards him; at base, a shield: on a chevron between three plates, each charged with a pyncheon, three pansies stalked, MORGAN.
**(+) SIGILLV + OFFICIALIS + PRINCIPALIS + MENEVENSIS
+ EPISCOPI**   (Ren.)
The matrix was found in soil at Caerleon, Gwent.
Acc. No: 25.384.   BM 2186.
D: Williams (1985) 175-6 (No. 147); Donovan (1805) 152.
E: Cf. NLW, Misc. Deeds: Box 7 (for seals of some 18th C. Vicars General); for a drawing of the seal of John Cruso, LL.D, Vicar-General from the 1660's until his death in 1682, see: Dineley (1888) 374.

W 115.   CHURCH IN WALES, Representative Body of.
1920- . Black wax, p.o., 81 x 45 mm.
St. David in eucharistic vestments, his pastoral staff held in his left hand, his right hand raised in blessing; in rear, a canopied altar (inscribed **DEWI SANT**); a dove above, a Welsh dragon beneath.
**THE · SEAL · OF · THE · REPRESENTATIVE BODY
OF · THE · CHURCH · IN · WALES**   (Caps.)
Designed by Goscombe John, R.A. (Art Dept.).

W 116.   *Another Impression.* Red wax (Art Dept.).

CAPITULAR

W 117.   LLANDAFF; First Seal of the Chapter.
Late 12th cent. Off-white plaster cast, p.o., 85 x 58 mm.
The cathedral (seen from the north side) as built by Bishop Urban (*Ca.* 1130) with a campanile and spires.
(+ S)IGILLVM L(ANDAVENSIS EC)CLESIE   (Rom.)
Acc. No: 44.171.   BM 1887.
E: BL, Harl. Ch. 75 A.18 (1199), 75 B.25 (late 12th C.); NLW, Penrice and Margam Ch. 10 (late 12th C.), 11 (*Ca.* 1170-80).
D: Cardiff Centr. Libr. MS 4.335; Williams (1982) 27 (No.59); (1986) 157 (No. 197).

W 118.   *Another Impression.* Buff sulphur cast.
Acc. No: 25.384.

W 119.   *Second Seal.*
In use *ca.* 1200-1545. Off-white plaster cast, p.o., 68 x 45 mm.
The cathedral (from the west) with details of Norman architecture, central tower and two pinnacles, porch, etc., probably reflecting continued re-building of the nave.
(+) SIGILL' CAPITVLI · LANDAVENSIS ECLESIE⁻   (Early Lom.)
Acc. No: 44.171   BM 1890 Ø.
E: BL, Harl. Ch. A.20 (*Ca.* 1200), B.6 (*Ca.* 1234), B.8 (1234), B. 9 (1234); Glamorgan Archives, D/D C(arne) 665 (1448), 668 (1522); D/D F(onmon) 2654 (1417); NLW, Badminton Deeds I, 109 (1541), 110 (1545),; Penrice and Margam Ch. 241 (1397); PRO, E 25/72 (1534).
D: Clark IV (1910) 1481; Williams (1986) 157 (No. 198).

W 120.   *Another Impression.* Buff sulphur cast.
Acc. No: 25.384.

Counter-, or Privy Seal.
W 121.   Early 13th cent. Off-white plaster cast, p.o., 42 x 29 mm.
The Agnus Dei with banner-bearing cross, all symbolic of Christ, the sacrificial Lamb.
SECRETVM LANDAVENSIS ECCLESIE   (Lom.)
Acc. No: 44.171.   BM 1890 R
E: BL, Harl. Ch. 75 B.6 (*ca.* 1234); NLW, Penrice and Margam Ch. 145 (1246).
D: Williams (1986) 158 (No. 201).

W 122.   *Another Impression.* Brown sulphur cast, (base wanting).
Acc. No: 25.384.

W 123.   *Another Seal.*
*?*Late 16th cent. Red wax *en placard*, p.o., 68 x 44 mm.
The cathedral, depicting the west front and south side, foliage in the field; below is a motto: **INTRATE** (*'Enter'*).
· SIGILLVM ∴ CAPITVLARE ∴ : LANDAVENSIS ∴ ECCLESIÆ   (Ren.)
Acc. No: 25.384.

W 124.   ST. ASAPH, Second Seal of the Chapter.
Mid-15th cent. Red silicon rubber, circ., 84 mm.
Within three lateral niches, under a triple gothic-style canopy of late design, *centre:* St. Asaph standing in eucharistic vestments with pastoral staff held in his left hand (its crook turned outwards), his right hand upraised in blessing; *dexter:* the diocesan bishop similarly attired, kneeling in veneration, his hands clasped in prayer (its crook turned towards him); *sinister:* a holy abbess standing, probably St. Winifride, holding her crook (turned outwards) with her left hand, in her right hand an uncertain object, perhaps a reliquary; *below:* in a round-arched

niche, the dean to front in prayer, to either side of him some seven canons facing inwards and also kneeling in devotion. (D.R. Thomas, *The History of the Diocese of St. Asaph*, Oswestry, 1908, I, 376-7, quotes another view that the central figure is that of St. Kentigern, the founder of the diocese, and that the kneeling bishop is St. Asaph; this is not proven as one would expect St. Asaph to be haloed - as are both the standing figures). Foliage in field. In the legend a sprig occurs between each word:

Sigillum / capitulare / ecclesie / cathedralis / assavensis   (Bl.)
Acc. No: 92.105H.
E: BL, Harl. MS 2099, f. 58d (illus.); Clwyd (Hawarden) R.O. Gwysaney MS B.427 (1544); NLW, Crosse of Shaw Hill Deed 8 (1492), Downing MS A.13 (2nd; 1514), Plymouth MS 1658 (4th seal; 1552).
D: Williams (1986) 159 (No. 206), (1989) 77 (No. 206).

RURIDECANAL

W 125.   LLŶN, Gwynedd: Eynon, dean of.
Early 13th cent. Red wax, p.o., 48 x 27 mm.
See D 20. Acc. No: 19.297.

W 126.   *Another Impression.* (Acc. No: 92.106H/1). Red wax.

W 127.   *Another Impression.* (Acc. No: 92.106H/2). Red wax.

PAROCHIAL

W 128.   LLANDAFF, S. Glam; Parish Burial Board.
See D 19. Grey silicon rubber, p.o., 60 x 41 mm.
Acc. No: 92.107H.

COLLEGES, FRATERNITIES, HOSPITALS, ETC.

W 129.   ABERGWILI, Dyfed : Collegiate Church of St Maurice.
See D 1. (Acc. No: 92.108H/1). Red wax, p.o., 60 x 37 mm.

W 130.   *Another Impression.* (Acc. No: 92.108H/2). Red wax.

W 131.   *Another Impression.* (Acc. No: 92.108H/3). Dark-orange plasticine.

W 132.   BRECON, Powys : Christ's College.
See D 8. Red wax, p.o., 63 x 43 mm.
Acc. No: 79.87 H.

W 133.   CARDIFF, South Glam. : Fraternity of the Holy Trinity.
See D 9. (Acc. No: 92.109H/1). Red wax, circ., 30 mm.

W 134.   *Another Impression.* (Acc. No: 92.109H/2). Buff plaster cast.

W 135.   *Another Impression.* (Acc. No: 92.109H/3). Brown wax (cracked).

W 136.   *Another Impression.* (Acc. No: 92.109H/4). Red wax.

W 137.   *Another Impression.* (Acc. No: 92.109H/5). Red wax.

W 138.   *Another Impression.* (Acc. No: 92.109H/6). Red wax.

W 139.   *Another Impression.* (Acc. No: 92.109H/7). Red wax (cracked).

W 140.   *Another Impression.* (Acc. No: 92.109H/8). Red plaster cast.

W 141.   CARDIFF, S. Glam. : Church Congress.
See D 10. Red wax, p.o., 46 x 31 mm.
Acc. No: 01.347.

W 142.   LLANBEDR-PONT-STEFFAN (Lampeter), Dyfed : St David's College.
Ca. 1830-. White silicon rubber, p.o., 99 x 56 mm.
St. David in full pontificals, a book held in his left hand, his pastoral staff (turned away from him) in his right hand, in a pillared niche beneath a dome-shaped canopy; the field filled with foliage and charged with four pierced cinquefoils. The words of the legend are separated by an ornate stop:
· sigil' · com · coll · s · david   (Pseudo-Bl.)
This seal was designed about 1830 by the college architect, C.R. Cockerell, in consultation with the College of Heralds. It is incorrectly ascribed in Birch, *Catal. of Seals in BM* II (No. 3954) to St Mary's College at St David's, Dyfed. The matrix is in the keeping of the Principal of St David's University College.
Acc. No: 92.110H.
D: Cardiff. Central Libr., Tonn MS 3.104, Vol. 2, p. 185; Williams (1982) 4, 43 (No. 102).

W 143.   RUTHIN, Clwyd : Christ's Hospital.
1590- . Red wax, circ., 60 mm.
The Risen Christ emerging from the tomb decorated by seven cinquefoils, his hand and side bearing the marks of nail and spear, a rayed nimbus around his head, his right hand upraised in blessing, his left grasping a long cross to which is attached a banner, in the shape of a dove, depicting a cross; to either side are bemused guards with spears and lances, and on scrolls in the field occurs the text: **EGO SVM**

RESVRRECTIO ET VITA (*'I am the Resurrection and the Life'*; *St. John 11/25*). Beaded borders.

· SIGILLVM HOSPITALIS CHRISTI IN RVTHIN 1590

ELIZABETH 32 (Ren.)

The silver matrix is in safe-keeping for the Warden of Ruthin.
Acc. No: 92.111H.
E: NLW, Ruthin Lordship Deed 889 (fragment of 1594).
D: Williams (1982) 42 (No. 101), (1988) 132 (No. 296).

W 144. SWANSEA, West Glam.: Hospital of St David.
Ca. 1332-1548. Buff sulphur cast (cracked and worn), p.o., 47 x 31 mm.
Saint David standing in a pillared and canopied niche, the primatial cross in his left hand, his right hand raised in blessing; a pectoral cross possibly hangs over his chasuble; in base, under an arch, a *?*quatrefoil, with two smaller quatrefoils, one to each side, in the interstices below the corbel or platform.

SIGILLVM CŌE' DOM : BEATI DAVID DE : SWEYNESE (Lom.)

Acc. No: 25.384.
E: NLW, Marquess of Bute Collection, Packet F, Box 63, No. R (1543).
D: *Arch. Camb.* 1876/17, 1888/8 (illus.); Cardiff Central Libr. MS 4.335; *Proc. Soc. Antiq.* 1st Ser. I, 111; Dillwyn (1840) 46; Williams (1982) 28 (No. 61), (1988) 132-3 (No. 297).

W 145. *Another Impression.* Buff sulphur cast (cracked and worn).
Acc. No: 25.384.

W 146. Counter-seal.
1334 (used by the Master, John de Accum). Yellow sulphur cast, oval, 28 x 24 mm.
A bust facing right.

+ SIG' : SECRET..... DAVID ... (Lom.)

This impression derives from the former Mansel Franklen Collection.
Acc. No: 1986.96H.
D: *Arch. Camb.* 1876/8-9, Williams (1988) 133 (No.298); Cardiff Central Library MS 4.335 (drawn after an impression attached to a missing Duchy of Lancaster deed).

W 147. UNKNOWN LOCATION; Fraternity of St Peter.
? 15th cent. Green gutta-percha, p.o., 58 x 37 mm.
Saint Peter standing upon a curved corbel in full pontificals but haloed and wearing a cap rather than mitre or tiara, a large-key held in his left hand, his right hand upraised in blessing; abundant foliage in the field, Cabled border. A leafy shoot occurs between each word of the legend.

+ Sigillum / Fraternitatis / Sc̄i / Petri (Bl.)

The bronze matrix, found at Radnor Castle, Powys, is numbered amongst the collections of Rowley's House Museum, Shrewsbury; as is also the possible counter-seal.
Acc.No: 25.384.
D: *Arch. Camb.* 1855 (opp. p. 47), Williams (1988) 134 (No. 300); *Trans. Shrops. Arch. Soc.* V (detailing Shrewsbury Museum *Catalogue*) 430, No. 581; Williams (1859) Pl. opp. p. 122.

MISCELLANEOUS RELIGIOUS DEVICES
(*where no owner known*)

W 148. I.H.C. Red wax, oval, 11 x 6 mm.
See D 26. Acc. No: 92.112H.

W 149. Agnus Dei.
Ca. 1300. Off-white plasticine, circ., 18 mm.
The Lamb of God, with cross and banner. The legend may be an abbreviation of 'prophet' or 'predicator' (forerunner, herald, preacher) of Jesus.

PRDIVE'S'V (Lom.)

From a matrix in the possession of Mr E.A. Roberts of Monkton, Dyfed.
Acc. No: 92.113H.
D: Williams (1989) 70 (No. 311). (For a seal with similar device and legend found in Cornwall see *Arch. Jnl.* XXIX, 188; and, for two of this type found in close proximity, in an unspecified Norfolk field, see: *The Searcher* 77 (Jan. 1992) 19-20; for seals with same device but differing legends, see Williams (1989) 70 (Nos. 312-3); for seals with the same legend but differing device, see *Arch. Jnl.* IV, 360; NLW, Penrice and Margam Ch. 314; Tonnochy (1952) Nos. 696-7; a seal with the same legend but with a lamb passant to the right and lacking the cross and banner, was found by metal detector in 1990 at Tarrant Rushton, Dorset; (information of Mr. K. Wheatley of Wareham).

W 150. The Blessed Virgin Mary.
? 14th cent. Yellow sulphur cast, circ., 20 mm.
The Blessed Virgin standing, and holding her Child; to the right, a person kneeling in supplication. Legend illegible.
Acc. No: 92.114H.

W 151. St Mary Magdalene.
Medieval. Cream plaster cast, circ., 17 mm.
Possibly a miniature of St Mary Magdalene kneeling *sinister* in the garden, before the banner-bearing Risen Lord standing *dexter*. No clear legend.
From a bronze matrix found in top soil near Ewenny Priory (Site PRN 1812M) by S. Sell.
Acc. No: 92.115H/1.

W 152. *Another Impression.* (Acc. No: 92.115H/2). Blue silicon rubber.

W 153. *Another Impression.* (Acc. No: 92.115H/3). Blue silicon rubber.

W 154. St John the Baptist.
? Early 14th cent. Red wax, oval, 21 x 18 mm.
St John the Baptist holding the Agnus Dei, a person kneeling to the right in supplication; cusped border ornamented by *?* roses.

* IOH'E · VOTV · PRECO · XPI · SVSCIPE · TOTVM (Lom.)

(*'John, herald of Christ, accept all our vow'*)
The silver matrix was found on the site of St John's Priory, Carmarthen, and presented to the Carmarthenshire Antiquarian Society Museum by 19 October 1935; its present location is unknown.
Acc. No: 38.145/1.
D: Williams (1982) 13 (No. 23), (1989) 71-2 (No. 319).

W 155. *Another Impression.* (Acc. No: 92.116H/1). Red wax.

W 156. *Another Impression.* (Acc. No: 92.116H/2). Red wax.

W 157. *Another Impression.* (Acc. No: 92.116H/3). Red Wax.

W 158. Westminster; Dean of : Gabriel Goodman, D.D. of Ruthin.
See D 86. Red wax, oval, 22 x 19 mm.
Acc. No: 30.236/2.

MONASTIC

W 159.   Dominican Friars; Seal of the Provincial Prior in England.
Early 16th cent. Buff sulphur cast, p.o., 68 x 44 mm.
Within a pillared niche of Palladian design, a bearded figure standing, probably for God the Father, an aureole of rays behind His head and shoulders, the Child supported on His right arm; all upon a corbel ornamented with flowering foliage; beaded border.
**SIGILLV! PRIOR' : PROVĪCIALIS : ANGLIE : ORDINIS :
FRATRV̄! PREDICATORVM**   **(Ren.)**
The latten matrix, found in Pembroke, Dyfed, is in the collections of Tenby Museum.
Acc. No: 25.384.
D: Arch. Camb. 1851/249, 336; *J.B.A.A.* VI (1851) 452; *Proc. Soc. Antiq.*
    1st Ser. II, 100; Laws (1888) 257; Williams (1988) 130 (No. 291).

W 160.   *Another Impression.* Red wax.
Acc. No: 25.384.

W 161.   CHEPSTOW (alias STRIGUIL), Gwent : Benedictine Priory of the Blessed Virgin Mary.
Second Common Seal.
Late 15th cent.-1534. Green plaster cast, p.o., 64 x 40 mm.
The Blessed Virgin, crowned and seated in a canopied niche of late gothic-type style, the Child supported by her right arm; in base, a shield: a gate or portcullis with pendant chains *(R.H. Ellis)*, a bascule - one of the badges of the Herberts, Earls of Pembroke of the first creation (Wm. Herbert, *ob.* 1469; *Siddons (1991a)* 244-5). In chief a saltire between defaced charges.
S'coe / sc̄e / marie ....guil   **(Bl.)**
Acc. No: 25.384.   BM 2898.
                                                                  PRO M.188.
E: NLW, Badminton Deeds I, 1038 (fragment of 1504); PRO, E 25/30
    (Pt.1; of 1534), E 326/B.8080 (fragment of 1482).
D: Williams (1988) 125 (No. 276).

W 162.   *Another Impression.* Buff sulphur cast.
Acc. No: 25.384.

W 163.   EWENNY (or OGMORE), S. Glam. : Benedictine Priory of St Michael.
Seal of the Prior.
Ca. 1175. Yellow sulphur cast (cracked), p.o., 68 x 43 mm.
A tonsured prior, turned to the left, holding a book in his left hand, a scroll in his right.
+ SIGILLVM ꞉ PRIORIS ꞉ S'CI (MIC)HAEL ꞉ DE ꞉ VGGOMOR ⁻   **(Early Lom.)**
Acc. No: 25.384.
E: NLW, Penrice and Margam Ch. 16 (undated), 17 and 19 (*Ca.* 1175).
D: J.B.A.A. LVIII, 74 (illus.); Birch (1897) 30, (1902) 199; Williams
    (1988) 125 (No. 278).

W 164.   *Another Impression.* Yellow sulphur cast (cracked).
Acc. No: 25.384.

W 165.   GOLDCLIFF, Gwent; Benedictine Priory of St Mary Magdalene.
First Seal of Prior William de St. Aulbyn (1319-27 and 1336-49)
In use *ca.* 1340. Buff sulphur cast, p.o., 40 x 25 mm.
The Blessed Virgin crowned and standing full-length, the Child borne in her left arm, a sceptre clasped by her right hand; field diapered lozengy, beaded borders; in base, under a pointed and decorative archway, the prior half-length in prayer to right.
SIGILLVM : FRATRIS WILL'I : DE : SC̄O : ALBINO (*possibly* **AUBINO**) **(Lom.)**
Acc. No: 25.384.   PRO M 353.
E: PRO, E 42/343R, 415R, 416R, 417R (all of 1340).
D: Williams (1988) 127 (No. 282).

W 166.   *Second Seal of Prior William de St Aulbyn.*
In use *ca.* 1340 as the *Common Seal.* Buff sulphur cast, p.o., 53 x 32 mm.
The garden of the Resurrection *(St. John 20/17)*; beneath a double-arched canopy, and above two corbels each ornamented by a trefoil, St. Mary Magdalene bearing her vase of spices and kneeling before the Risen Christ, who holds in his left hand a long cross with banner unfurled, a tree (representing the Garden) separating them; field diapered lozengy and bounded by beaded borders; in base, under a pointed arch decorated by crosslets, the prior tonsured and kneeling to right in prayer.
S'FRĪS WILL'I DE SC̄O (?AUBYN) PRIORIS DE GOLDCLIVIA   **(Lom.)**
                        (?ALBINO)
(Whilst catalogued, for the sake of convenience, as the prior's first and second seals, one of the matrices may well have dated from his first term as prior).
Acc. No: 25.384.   BM 3214.
                                                                 PRO M. 352.
E: PRO, E 42/343 , 415 . 416 , 417 (all of 1340).
D: Williams (1970) 44, (1988) 127 (No.283); Rees (1975) 118.

W 167.   GRACE DIEU, Nr. Monmouth, Gwent : Cistercian Abbey of the Blessed Virgin Mary.
Common Seal.
1473 (from NLW, Milborne Deed 4876). Red wax, p.o., 46 x *Ca.* 30 mm.
See D 13. *supra.*
Acc. No: 80.36H (original impression, on loan from the National Library of Wales).

W 168.   *Another Impression.* Green wax, p.o., 47 x 28 mm.
Acc. No: 79.83H (made from D 13 above).

W 169.   *Another Impression.* (Acc. No: 92.117H). White silicon rubber.

W 170.   LLANTARNAM (alias CAERLEON), Gwent : Cistercian Abbey of the Blessed Virgin Mary.
Seal of the Abbot.
Early 13th cent. Red wax, circ., 28 mm.
A cowled forearm issuing from the right, with tassels pendant at the wrist, and gloved hand clasping a pastoral staff (crook turned towards the holder); three estoiles in the field.
.........Abb'īs de CARLIO...   **(Mixed Lom.)**
Acc. No: 31.78/11.   BM 2825.
E: BL, Harl. Ch. 75 A.32 (1203).
D: Monm. Antiq. II: 3 (1967) 131-2; Williams (1987) 144 (No. 228).

W 171.   MARGAM, West Glam. : Cistercian Abbey of the Blessed Virgin Mary.
Second Common Seal.
Mid-14th cent.-1536. Buff sulphur cast, p.o., 55 x 36 mm.
The Blessed Virgin crowned, standing under an elegantly carved canopy, the Child supported with her left arm, a sceptre topped by a rose-flower held with her right hand; in field, to each side, a shield: *dext.* three clarions, two and one (badge of the CLARES, later lords of Glamorgan and 'patrons'); *sin.* three chevrons, CLARE; above each shield, a small quatrefoil slipped; below them, in opposing positions, a crescent enclosing a roundle, and an estoile; beaded border. In base, under a carved arch surmounted to either side by a quatrefoil, an abbot, pastoral staff in hand (crook turned inwards) kneeling in prayer to the right.
· SIGILLVM : ABBATIS : ET : CONVENTVS : DE : MARGAN   **(Lom.)**
Acc. No: 25.384   BM 3608
E: BL, Harl. Ch. 75 A.48 (1525); Glamorgan Archives CL/BRA 247/70
    (1485), CL/BRA 247/47 (1514); NLW, Penrice and Margam Ch.
    268 (1484), 273 (1509), 274 (1510), 276 (1514), 277 (1516), 279

(1518), 280 (1518), 281 (1521), 2068 (1509), 2071 (1519), 2072 (1520), 2073 (1529), 2074 (1530).

D: Cardiff Central Libr. MS 4.335; Birch (1897) 30, 357; (1902) 97; Williams (1982) 20 (No. 70), (1987) 149-50 (No. 246).

W 172. *Another Impression.* Off-yellow sulphur cast, p.o., 52 x 40 mm. Acc. No: 25.384.

W 173. *First Seal of the Abbot* (temp. **Conan** or **John**).
Ca. 1170-80. Yellow sulphur cast (worn), p.o., 43 x 28 mm.
An abbot, three-quarters length, in *?* eucharistic vestments, an ornamented book held in his left hand, his right hand clasps his staff (crook turned outwards); in field, above his left shoulder, five pellets arranged in *quincunx,* but not apparent on all impressions.
+ SIGILLVM : ABBATIS : DE : MARGAN   (Lom.)
Acc. No: 25.384.
E: NLW, Penrice and Margam Ch. 6 (*Ca.* 1170-80), 26 (*Ca.* 1170), 27 (1170), 151 (1249).
D: Birch (1897) opp. p. 30; Williams (1987) 142 (No. 220).

W 174.   NEATH, West Glam. : Cistercian Abbey of the Blessed Virgin Mary.
Third Common Seal.
15th cent.- 1539. Brown sulphur cast (flattened), p.o., 49 x 40 mm.
Under a pinnacled niche, on a platform the edge of which is decorated with nine estoiles, the Blessed Virgin crowned, in her right hand a sceptre surmounted by a fleur-de-lis, her left arm supporting the Child; in field, *dext.* a stem, possibly of palm; *sin.* a crozier, its crook turned to the outside; in base, a shield: three clarions, two and one (badge of the DE CLARES, later lords of Glamorgan); beaded border.
.. Sigillum : comune monasterii beate : marie : de : neth   (Bl.)
Acc. No: 25.384   PRO M 594.
E: PRO, C 106/100 (Box 1; 1535); SC 13/R.41; Nottage Court, Glam. MSS (1515 and 1536).
D: Cardiff Central Libr. MS 4.335; *J.B.A.A.* IV, 355; Birch (1897) 332, (1902) 97; Siddons (1991a) 263, Williams (1987) 150 (No. 248).

W 175.   STRATA FLORIDA, Dyfed : Cistercian Abbey of the Blessed Virgin Mary.
Seal of an Unknown Abbot.
15th cent. Red silicon rubber, p.o., 42 x 27 mm.
See D 24 above. Acc. No: 80.27H.

W 176. *Another Impression.* Red wax.
Acc. No: 38.145/1. Presented by R.D. Roberts.

W 177. *Another Impression.* Red wax (chipped).
Acc. No: 92.118H.

W 178.   TALLEY, Dyfed : Premonstratensian Abbey of the Blessed Virgin Mary and St. John the Baptist.
See D 25 above. Red wax, circ., 44 mm.
Acc. No; 35.303.

W 179. *Another Impression.* Red wax.
Acc. No: 35.303.

W 180. *Another Impression.* (Acc. No: 92.119H/1). Red wax (cracked).

W 181. *Another Impression.* Blue plasticine (poor impression).
Acc. No: 35.172

W 182. *Another Impression.* (Acc. No: 92.119H/2). Red wax.

W 183. *Another Impression.* (Acc. No: 92.119H/3). Red wax.

W 184.   TINTERN, Gwent : Cistercian Abbey of the Blessed Virgin Mary.
First Seal of the Abbot.
Early 13th cent. Red plaster cast, p.o., 42 x 27 mm.
A cowled lower arm issuing from the left, hand grasping a pastoral staff held upright (crook turned outwards); in field, a mullet above the crook, a crescent above the wrist, with foliage sinister.
+ SIGILLVM ABBATIS DE TINTERNA   (Lom.)
Acc. No: 31.78/2.   BM 4194.
E: BL, Harl. Ch. 75 D.11 (fragment; 1253); Canterbury Cathedral *Carta Antiqua* I, 234 (1245).
D: Williams (1982) 30 (No. 67), (1987) 144 (No. 230).

W 185.   Second Seal of the Abbot.
Mid-13th cent. Pale-brown sulphur cast, p.o., 42 x 26 mm.
An abbot standing in eucharistic vestments on a corbel, a book held in his left hand, his right hand clasping his pastoral staff (its crook turned outwards); foliage in field.
- + SIG........BATIS . DE . TIN......   (Lom.)
Acc. No: 25.384.   BM 4196.
E: BL, Harl. Ch. 75 A.37 (Seal No. 2; 1256).
D: Williams (1987) 143 (No. 226).

W 186. *Common Seal.*
14th cent.-1536. Pale brown sulphur cast (upper part wanting), p.o., 58 x 37 mm.
The Blessed Virgin crowned and seated in a pillared niche, the Child supported by her left arm, her right hand holding *?* an orb; in base, under a rounded decorative arch, an abbot half-length, in prayer to left, clasping his pastoral staff (its crook turned towards himself).
.....BBATIS ET CONVENTVS ..BEATE MARIE DE T.......   (Lom.)
Acc. No: 25.384.   BM 4193.
                                                       PRO M 856.
E: BL, Cott. Ch. XXI, 41 (1524); PRO, E. 326/9180 (fragment; 1514).
D: *Arch. Camb.* 1856/370, Dugdale (1846) V, 267; Williams (1987) 152 (No. 252).

W 187. *Another Impression.* Red plaster cast.
Acc. No: 31.78/3.

W 188.   USK, Gwent : Benedictine Priory (Nunnery) of the Blessed Virgin Mary.
Common Seal.
13th cent.-1536. Red plaster cast, p.o., *ca.* 60 x 40 mm.
Seated on a throne with lateral knobbed pillars, supported by a carved triple-tiered corbel, and culminating in a church-like canopy, the Blessed Virgin crowned, the Child on her left knee, above her shoulder an estoile of six points, above the right a crescent enclosing a ray; beaded border.
S : SC̄E : MARIE : ET CONVENTVS : DE VSKA   (Lom.)
Acc. No: 25.384   BM 4231.
                                                       PRO M 877.
E: PRO, E 25/111, Pt.2 (1534); E 326/B. 7987 (1496).
D: Cardiff Central Libr. 4.335; Dugdale (1846) IV, Pl. XXVI/5; Williams (1980) 2 , 45; (1988) 129 (no. 289).

*(**For other Welsh Ecclesiastical Seals:** see Williams (1984) 110-35, (1985) 166-89, (1986) 156-62, (1987) 142-55, (1988) 121-34, (1989) 68-77).*

CIVIC AND CORPORATE

W 189.   ABERAFAN, West Glam.
15th cent. Brown wax, circ., 22 mm.
An estoile. A leafy shoot separates the words of the legend:
+ ihc̄ / he / ll' / ine   (Bl.)
   (alt. be)
Acc. No: 25.384.
D: Lewis (1833) B I.

W 190.   ABERGAVENNY, Gwent; Corporation of.
Temp. Charles II (1660-85). Red wax, oval, 38 x 32 mm.
A fleur-de-lis.
· THE · COMMON · SEALE · OF · BERGEVENNY   (Caps.)
Acc. No: 92.120H.
D: Arch. Camb. 1876/349.

W 191.   ABERYSTWYTH, Dyfed; Corporation of.
1810-32. Brown wax, circ., 27 mm.
A lion rampant reguardant, PRYSE of GOGERDDAN (the arms
attributed to Gwaithfoed of Ceredigion).
ABERYSTWITH · CORPORATION ·   (Caps.)
The legend was changed about 1832, and the device in 1875. The seal
was defaced in 1885 and placed in the U.C.N.W. Museum where it
perished in the fire of 1885. It had originally been purchased by the
Corporation from Mr. Edward Evans, perhaps the engraver.
Acc. No: 76.27 H 11.
D: Eyre Evans (1902) 140-1, 195-7, and his *Cardiganshire Notes* II, 119
    (NLW, MS 13,482 C); Lewis (1833) I.

W 192.   ABERYSTWYTH, Dyfed; National Library of Wales.
1907- . Red wax, circ., 64 mm.
A triple horned dragon grasping a shield bearing the arms of the
UNITED KINGDOM.
THE · SEAL · OF · THE · NATIONAL · LIBRARY · OF · WALES   (Caps.)
(Art Dept.).

W 193.   *Another Impression.* Red wax (cracked).
(Art Dept.).

W 194.   ANGLESEY; Druidical Society.
1772-1844. Red wax, oval, 35 x 29 mm.
See D 49. Acc. No: 79.88H.

W 195.   *Fob Seal* of the Society. Red silicon rubber, oval, 27 x 22 mm.
See D 50. Acc. No: 92.121H.

W 196.   BEAUMARIS, Anglesey; Second Common Seal.
1562- . Red silicon rubber, circ., 66 mm.
A single-masted carvel-built warship (possibly reflecting the strategic
importance of Beaumaris) showing two decks of gun-ports; main mast
with main yard and square sail, and fighting top provided with spears or
pikes; square stern-castle and beak at bow. At either end are displayed
the two maces the borough was ordered (in 1562) to possess. The
charter and privileges granted to Beaumaris by Edward I (1296) were
confirmed and extended by Elizabeth I (22nd June 1562), and resulted
in this new common seal being engraved. The date of **8 FEB.** engraved
on the hull, and the year **1562.** inscribed in the legend, suggest that the
seal was made, or came into use, on 8th February 1563 (the calendar
year then extending until Lady Day, 25th March). It replaced an earlier
medieval seal which also depicted a single-masted ship, together with an
escutcheon and castle.
+ SIGILLVM · COMVNE · BVRGI + DE · BELLO MARISCO ·
AŌ 1562   (Ren. Caps.)
Acc. No: 92.122H.
E: PRO, Wards 2/53ᶜ/9, ¹/28, ᵏ/8, ᵏ/9 (all of 1568); UCNW, Baron Hill
    Deeds 592 (1563), 596 (1565), 607 (1568), 611 (1569).
    For the First Common Seal, see: UCNW, Baron Hill Deeds 462 (1443),

525 (1485), 588 (1469; fine), 591 (No. 2; 1537).
    For the Third Common Seal, see: PRO, C 219/90 (of 1700).
D: Williams (1982) 38 (No. 87); personal communication of Dr. M.
    Redknap.

W 197.   CARDIFF, S. Glam; Common Seal.
14th cent. and in use in 1690. Buff plaster cast, circ., 42 mm.
On a pyramidal mount, or cairn of stones, two lions rampant
combatant, supporting aloft a shield: three chevrons (deriving from the
arms of the DE CLARES, for long Lords of Glamorgan with their
chancery at Cardiff).
S'COMMVNE : DE KERDIF   (Lom.)
Presented by Cardiff Corporation.
Acc. No: 01.9.   BM 4791.
E: PRO, C 219/78 (poor, 1690), C 219/82 (1690).
D: Arch. Camb. 1900/161-2; Cardiff Central Library MS 4.969 (where
    Corbet, *Seal and Arms of Cardiff*); Matthews II (1900) II, 43, VI
    (1911) cix-cx; Dineley (1888) cclxxx, 357; Siddons (1991a) 296; *Cf.*
    BL, Add. MS 6,331, f. 15.

W 198.   *Another Impression.* (Acc. No: 01.9). Buff plaster cast.

W 199.   *Another Impression.* (Acc. No: 01.9). Buff plaster cast (worn).

W 200.   Seal of the Bailiffs.
Obverse.
As used in 1544, but of 13th cent. engraving. Dark-red wax, circ., 31 mm.
A shield: charges indistinct, but three chevronels, CLARE; supporters: *?*
two lions rampant. (Legend wanting).
Acc. No: 92.123H.
E: PRO, E 213/57.

W 201.   *Reverse.* Dark-red wax, circ., 31 mm.
A shield: *?* a Tudor rose; supporters: *dext. ?* a gryphon or wyvern, *sin.* a
lion rampant.
..... OFFICI : BAILIFF : DE...........   (Lom.)
Acc. No: 92.123H.
(For an early 13th-century seal of the **Porter of the Town Gate of Cardiff,**
see: BL, Harl. Ch. 75 C. 44).

W 202.   Borough Seal.
1608- . Red wax, circ., 28 mm.
A cinquefoil rose; cabled border.
+ CARDIF ·:· VILLA   (Caps.)
E: PRO, C 219/86 (1698, damaged), C 219/106 (1708).
D: Corbett (1906), Matthews II (1900) 43, Lewis (1833) I.
Acc. No: 92.124H/1.

W 203.   *Another Impression.* (Acc. No: 92.124H/2). Red wax.

W 204.   *Another Impression.* Buff plaster cast.
Acc. No: 01.10. Presented by Cardiff Corporation.

W 205.   *Another Impression.* (Acc. No: 92.124H/3). Red wax.

W 206.   *Another Impression.* (Acc. No: 92.124H/4). Red wax.

W 207.   *An Impression from a different matrix.* Red wax (paper masked),
circ., 28 mm.
Same device, but legend having variant stops:
*   · CARDIF · · · VILLA ·   (Caps.)
Acc. No: 92.125H.

W 208.   *Common Seal of the Bailiffs and Burgesses.*
1819-35. Red-brown silicon rubber, oval, 48 x 40 mm.
See D 51. Acc. No: 95.68.

W 209. *Another Impression.* (Acc. No: 92.126H). Red wax (cracked).

W 210. Seal of the Guardians of the Cardiff Poor Law Union.
19th cent. Bronze-coloured steel cast, oval, 43 x 38 mm.
See D 52. Acc. No: 30.398.

W 211. *A Later Seal.* Red-brown silicon rubber, oval, 45 x 38 mm.
See D 55 and 56. (Acc. No: 92.127H).

W 212. *Another Impression.* Bronze cast.
Acc. No: 30.398.

W 213. Seal of Fortitude Lodge (Cardiff).
See D 57. (Acc. No: 92.128H). Buff silicon rubber, circ., 45 mm.

W 214. Seal of the Gorsedd of Bards, National Eisteddfod (Cardiff).
1899. Blue wax, circ., 40 mm.
A dragon rampant, with nowed tail. The legend derives from the arms
of Cardiff:

Y DDRAIG GOCH A DDYRY GYCHWYN (Caps.)
(*'The Red Dragon sets the pace'*)
above which: **GORSEDD Y BEIRDD**
Acc. No: 92.129H.
D: Cardiff Eisteddfod Handbook (1899); Scott-Giles (1933) 140 (where
   a similarity noted to the seal of Prestatyn U.D.C.), 308; Williams
   (1982) 44 (No. 104).

W 215. *Another Impression.* Grey wax.
Acc. No: 99.394.

W 216. National Museum of Wales (Cardiff).
1912- . White plaster cast, circ., 70 mm.
See D 58. Acc. No: 92.130H.

W 217. *Another Impression.* Dark brown electrotype.
(Art Dept.).

W 218. *Another Impression.* Red wax.
(Art Dept.).

W 219. CARMARTHEN : Chancery of Prince Henry
(*later King Henry V*) **as Lord of Carmarthen.**
Probably 1408-13. Bright red wax, circ., 68 mm.
Against a field strewn with sprigs and over a greensward, the prince on
horseback galloping to the right; in armour with visor closed, and for
crest on a chapeau a lion statant guardant with a label of three points;
his right hand holds his sword aloft behind him; a shield slung over his
right shoulder and held by his left hand before him: quarterly, 1. and 4.
three fleurs-de-lis, two and one, FRANCE (Modern); 2. and 3. three
lions passant guardant, ENGLAND; the same arms occur on the horse
trappings, and a fan-shaped plume adorns the horse's head; borders
decorated with quatrefoils.
S' henr' principis Wall' duc' acquit' lancastr' t cornub'
comes cestr' de : dm'o de Kermerdyne (Bl.)
From the matrix purchased by the British Museum in 1987.
Acc. No: 92.131H.   BM 5573.
D: Arch. 85 (1933) 327; Arch. Jnl. XIII, 189-90; *Antiques Trade Gazette*,
   28th Febr. 1987; Bloomsbury Book Auctions, Sale Catalogue for
   March 12th, 1987 (No. 135); Cherry (1990) 461-2, Plate LXV.

W 220. *Seal of the 'New Custom' of the Port* (*Carmarthen*).
Temp. Edward I or II (*ca.* 1284-1326). Red-brown gutta percha
(cracked), circ., 30 mm.
A shield: three lions passant guardant in pale, ENGLAND; with scrolls
of sixfoils in the field; legend within pearled borders.
✠ S'NOVE · CVSTVME · REGIS IN PORTV · KERMERDYN (Lom.)
Acc. No: 25.384.
D: Tonnochy (1952) No. 45.

W 221. *Another Impression.* Brown wax.
Acc. No: 76.27H/2.

W 222. *Another Impression.* Cream plaster cast.
Acc. No: 23.89/2.
Presented by Carmarthenshire Antiquarian Society.

W 223. Seal of Delivery of Wool and Hides (Carmarthen).
Obverse.
Temp. Edward I or II (*ca.* 1284-1326). Green gutta percha (cracked),
circ., 45 mm.
A shield: the arms of ENGLAND (as W 220), suspended by a strap from
a hook between two wavy rose branches; legend within pearled borders,
a rosette between each word.
· SIGILL' · EDWARDI · REGIS · ANGL' · APVD · KERMERDYN (Lom.)
Acc. No: 25.384.   BM 5572 Ø.
D: Arch. Jnl. XIII, 190; *J.B.A.A.* I, 130; Tonnochy (1952) No. 37.

W 224. *Another Impression.* Cream plaster cast.
Acc. No: 23.89/3.
Presented by Carmarthenshire Antiquarian Society.

W 225. *Reverse.* Green gutta percha (cracked), circ., 43 mm.
Three lions passant guardant, ENGLAND.
· PRO · LANIS · ET · COREIS · LIBERANDIS (Lom.)
Acc. No: 25.384.   BM 5572 R.
D: As W 223.

W 226. *Another Impression.* Cream plaster cast.
Acc. No: 23.89/3.
Presented by Carmarthenshire Antiquarian Society.

W 227. CARMARTHEN, Mayor of.
Obverse. Dark-red wax, circ., 38 mm.
As used in 1453.
A triple-towered fortress with curtain wall breached by a central portal;
a bird standing on each lateral turret.In field, to either side: an ostrich
feather each with a scroll on the point, with the Prince of Wales' motto,
ICH DIEN inscribed. In base, a lion passant guardant sinister.
.................nove villa......... (Bl.)
Acc. No: 92.132H.
E: PRO, E 210/10863.
   For *Second Common Seal*, see: PRO, C 108/275 (1566).
   For *Third Common Seal*, see: NLW, Br. Rec. Ass. 1931 Deposit, No. 81
      (1786).
   For *Fourth Common Seal*, see: PRO, J 90/684 (1820).
   (*Carmarthen Museum, Abergwili, has casts of several Carmarthen seals*).

W 228. CARMARTHENSHIRE, Dyfed : Seal of the County Council.
1889-1974. Red wax (in wooden case), circ., 54 mm.
A shield: per pale, 1. a harp, 2. a leek; crest: a dragon; motto: **'RHYDDID
GWERIN FFYNIANT GWLAD'**, (*'A free people, a prosperous country'*).
**✶ THE COMMON SEAL OF THE CARMARTHENSHIRE
COUNTY COUNCIL** (Caps.)
Acc. No: 92.133H.
Presented by Ald. Gwilym Evans (Chairman, 1892-95).
D: Mont. Collns. XXIV (1890) 306-7; *Annual Report of Cardiff Public
   Museum and Art Gallery, 1894-95*, p.21.

W 229. CEDWELI (Kidwelly) Dyfed : Second Common Seal.
17th cent. (*possibly* 1619-). Brown wax, oval, 27 x 25 mm.
Between foliage in field, a shield: (Azure) a wolf salient (Argent) facing
right; probably taken from the arms of DWNN of CEDWELI; crest: a
helmet (to left) visor closed.
· COMMVN SIGILLVM · DE · KIDWELLY (Ren.)
Acc. No: 76. 27H/10.
E: For the *First Common Seal*, see: NLW, Muddlescombe Deed 31
   (fragment; 1575).
D: Lewis (1833) I.

W 230. **CHEPSTOW (alias STRIGUIL), Gwent : Common Seal.**
? Early 14th cent. White silicon rubber, circ., 48 mm.
An imposing keep, with double turreted curtain wall; beaded borders.
· : SIGILLVM : COMVNE : DE : STRVGVLLIA :   **(Lom.)**
From the brass matrix (No. 797) at the Ashmolean Museum, Oxford.
The seal has been previously ascribed, probably wrongly, to Strongoli in Calabria.
Acc. No: 92.134H.
D: Catal. Ashmolean Museum (1836) No. 797; *Monm. Antiq.* VI (1990) 55-6, 58 (No. 5).

W 231. **Customer of Poundage and Tunnage, (Chepstow, Gwent; Creek of, in the Port of Cardiff).**
See D 59. Red wax, circ., 33 mm.
Acc. No: 09.16.

W 232. *Another Impression.* White plaster cast.
Acc. No: 09.16.

W 233. *Another Impression.* Red wax (cracked).
Acc. No: 09.16.

W 234. **CONWY, Gwynedd : Seal of the Provost.**
14th cent.-1426 (when in use). Brown plaster cast, circ., 34 mm.
A triple-towered castle, fronting on waves of the sea.
· S' PROVESTRIE : DE : CONEWEY   **(Lom.)**
Acc. No: 76.27H/8.
E: NLW, Chirk Castle Deeds, F. 12,685 (fragment of 1384); UCNW, Baron Hill Deed 2149 (of 1426); Penrhyn Further Additions, Box *Villa de Conwey* (1574, broken).
    Gwynedd Archives (Caernarfon); examples of 1762, 1806, and 1850, occur in Caernarfon Corporation papers and unlisted material.
D: Lewis (1833) I; Williams (1982) 24 (No. 48).

W 235. **CRICCIETH, Gwynedd : Common Seal.**
? Late 13th cent. White plaster cast, circ., 42 mm.
A central battlemented tower with doorway, flanked by two smaller similar towers; upon the *dexter*, a dragon with floriated tail; upon the *sinister*, a man, his feet dangling over the edge and blowing a horn; all enclosed by a curtain wall with two smaller watch-towers; beaded border. The legend is rudely engraved; the initial **S** is reversed, and the second **C** should read **D**:
+ : S : COMVNE CE CRVKIN IN WAL': ·   **(Lom.)**
Criccieth became a borough in 1284 or 1285. This impression derives from the matrix found at Trawsfynydd, Meirionydd, about 1900, and presented by the British Museum.
Acc. No: 92.135H.
D: Antiq. Jnl. IV, 254-5; *Proc. Soc. Antiq.* 2nd Ser. XVIII, 69-70; Hemp (1939) 200-1, Tonnochy (1952) 27 (No. 172); Williams (1982) 7 (No. 5).

W 236. **DENBIGH, Common Seal of the Burgesses.**
Obverse.
As used in 1285. Green wax, circ., 55 mm.
A triple-turreted castle, for Denbigh Castle (rebuilt in 1282 and protecting an English settlement). The seal would appear to have been unfinished at this date, the upper half remaining blank.
S' CŌMVNE : BVRGENSIV̄ : DE : DINBEY   **(Lom.)**
Acc. No: 92.136H.
E: PRO, DL 27/33 (of 1285).
    For the Second Common Seal, perhaps subsequent to the charter of 1662, see: NLW, Chirk Castle Deeds, Gp. C. 15-16 (1727), F. 793 (1734). *Later came a smaller version, with no legend:* F. 4012 (1747), F. 4013 (1761), F. 4015 (1780), F. 4485 (1784); *also a seal used by individual burgesses:* F. 4015 (1780). *See also:* Clwyd (Ruthin) R.O.: BD/A/97 (*for a smaller version, without legend, used by the Sheriff's Court for the Recovery of Debts);* 604 (*for modern casts*).
D: Williams (1982) 24 (No. 49).

W 237. *Reverse.* Red wax, circ., 33 mm.
No device; apparently also an unfinished matrix.
+ SECRET' : C..... : DINB'   **(Lom.)**
E: PRO, DL 27/33 (of 1285).

W 238. **FESTINIOG AND BLAENAU RAILWAY CO., LTD; Gwynedd.**
1868-83. Brown plaster cast, circ., 42 mm.
A coat of arms: (Azure) a goat rampant, from *dexter* base a rising sun (possibly derived from the alleged ancient arms of MEIRIONYDD).
THE FESTINIOG & BLAENAU RAILWAY COMPANY LIMITED   **(Caps.)**
Acc. No: 79.89H.
The copyright of this impression rests with Thamesdown Borough Council (Swindon).
D: Cf. Arch. Camb. 1847/135; *Mont. Collns.* XXIV (1890) 313.

W 239. **GLAMORGAN, High Sheriff of : William Simons, Esq.**
1929-30. Red wax, oval, 46 x 38 mm.
A coat of arms: quarterly, 1. (Gules) three chevronels (Or), CLARE; 2. and 3. (Sable) a chevron between three spear-heads, BLEDDYN ap MAENYRCH; 4. (Azure) six roundels (Argent), three, two, one; On a chief (Or) a demi-lion issuant, Sir Gregory SEYS; crest: a demi-lion rampant, dexter paw grasping a spear-head; motto: **CRESCIT SUB PONDERE VIRTUS.**
WILLIAM SIMONS ESQUIRE HIGH SHERIFF OF GLAMORGAN
· 1929-30 ·   **(Caps.)**
Acc. No: 92.137H.
Seal designed by J. Kyrle Fletcher.

W 240. **GLAMORGANSHIRE BANKING COMPANY.**
1884-98. Buff plaster cast, circ., 50 mmm.
A shield: three chevrons, CLARE (for Glamorgan).
THE GLAMORGANSHIRE BANKING COMPANY · LIMITED ·
ESTABLISHED 1836   INCORPORATED 1884   **(Caps.)**
From the matrix at Lloyds Bank Head Office, London.
Acc. No: 79.74H.
D: Cf. Sayers (1957) 286; Williams (1982) 41 (No. 96).

W 241. **HARLECH, Gwynedd : Common Seal.**
1286 to at least 1594 (when in use). Brown wax (chipped), circ., 34 mm.
A triple-towered castle, masoned and embattled with round-headed doorway; field diapered lozengy.
*   SIGILLV̄ : COMMVNE : DE HARDLECH   **(Lom.)**
Acc. No: 76.27H/3.   BM 4973
E: BL, Add. Ch. 8486 (1529); Clwyd (Ruthin) R.O. DD/WY 2163 (1573); Gwynedd (Dolgellau) R.O. Z/DV 79 (1531), 85 (1538), 86 (1538; fragment), 92 (1549), 309 (1592; fragment); UCNW, Maesynuadd Deed 239 (1594), Mostyn MS 3531 (1577).
D: Arch. Camb. 1846/246, 1875/115; *Arch. Jnl.* VI, 403; *Gentl. Mag.* LXXIII (1803 : 2) 909-10; Williams (1982) 24 (No. 50). (1982) 24 (No. 50).

W 242. *Another Impression.* Red wax (flattened and indistinct).
Acc. No: 92.138H.

W 243. **HAVERFORDWEST, Dyfed : Common Seal.**
Ca. 1291- . Red plaster casts, circ., 64 mm.
Obverse.
A single-masted ship with fore-, and back-stays, shrouds and halliards, a clinker-built hull, a side-rudder, embattled fore-, after-, and top-castles; in the fore-castle, a mariner blowing a horn; in the after-castle, a fellow sounding a trumpet; a six-foil and two quatrefoils in field upper.
+ SIGILLUM : COMVNE : DE : HAWERFORDIA   **(Lom.)**
Impression made from the matrix in Haverfordwest Town Hall, and presented by W.J. Hemp, High Wycombe, Bucks.
Acc. No: 22.496/1.
E: Dyfed Archives (Haverfordwest) Haverfordwest Borough MS 1044 (fragment; 1537); NLW, Haverfordwest Rec. 988 (fragment; 1315); PRO, C 219/74 (1689, paper-masked).
D: Hemp (1922) 383-9; Williams (1982) 8 (No. 8).

For other seals of Haverfordwest, see: Charles (1967) 186, 215; Fryde (1974) 64; Lewis (1833) I; NLW, Haverfordwest Rec. 782 (of 1392); *Pembroke County Guardian*, 1st Febr. 1902 (contributed by Mrs M.I. Dawson, in *Pembrokeshire Antiquities*); PRO, HCA 32 (1775); Dineley (1888) 277.

W 244. *Reverse.*
A castle with a gate-house; on the castle tower, a man blowing a trumpet; in field - *dext.* a lion rampant; *sin.* a perched eagle, above which two quatrefoils; in base, a wyvern.
+ O LECTOR : SALVE : CELI : PATEANT : TIBI : UALVE (Lom.)
('*Hail! O Reader, may the gates of heaven open wide for you*')

W 245. Seal for the Taking of Recognisances within the County and Town of Haverfordwest.
Obverse only.
? Late 16th-17th cent. Blue silicon rubber, circ., 49 mm.
A triple-towered, embattled castle, with portcullis closed; from the central tower a man blows a horn to the right; in each side-tower flies a standard of conventional heraldry; supporters: *dext.* a lion rampant, *sin.* a bird (? eagle) resting and reguardant. Cabled borders.
SIGILLVM · AD · RECOGNICIONEM · INFRA · COMITATV ·:· (Ren.)
From the brass matrix discovered by metal-detector, by Mr. David Lewis (about 1987), in the Portfield, Haverfordwest.
Acc. No: 92.139H/1.
D: Lewis (1833) I, where both obverse and reverse illustrated, and the legend completed.

W 246. *Another Impression.* (Acc. No: 92.139H/2). Red-brown silicon rubber.

W 247. *Another Impression.* (Acc. No: 92.139H/3). Red-brown silicon rubber.

W 248. *Another Impression.* (Acc. No: 92.139H/4). Red-brown silicon rubber.

W 249. KENFIG, Mid-Glam; Common Seal.
As used *ca.* 1250-1325. Yellow sulphur cast (broken), circ., 33 mm.
A quatrefoil between four pellets.
S' : C͞OMVNE : DE KENEF' (Lom.)
Acc. No: 25.384.
E: NLW, Penrice and Margam Ch. 198 (2nd seal; before 1320), 199 (2nd seal; 1321), 200 (2nd seal; 1325), 2059 (2nd seal; undated).
D: Birch (1897) 210; Williams (1982) 25 (No. 51).

W 250. LLANFABON, Mid-Glam; Independent Order of Oddfellows (Manchester Unity), Lord Nelson Lodge.
1865- . Red wax, circ., 25 mm.
See D 60 *supra.* Acc. No: 36.605 (WFM).

W 251. MERTHYR TYDFIL, Mid-Glam; Seal of the Corporation.
1905- . Red wax, circ., 64 mm.
A coat of arms: the Virgin Tudfil, with distaff - denoting the industry of the borough, between two daggers - symbolising her martyrdom here early in the sixth century, encircled by the motto: NID · CADARN · OND · BRODYRDDE, and surrounded by an oak wreath ensigned with a crown, and bearing three discs displaying a blast furnace, Trevithick's engine (launched here), and the local Morlais Castle.
+ SEAL · OF · THE · MAYOR · ALDERMEN · AND · BVRGESSES OF ·
THE · BOROVGH · OF · MERTHYR TYDFIL (Pseudo-Lom.)
Designed by Goscombe John, R.A., on Merthyr receiving its new charter in 1905. This impression was formerly the property of Sir Isambard Owen.
Acc. No: 51.384/5.
D: Wilkins (1905) 569-70, Williams (1982) 39 (No. 89).

W 252. *Another Impression.* Silvery-grey electrotype (Art Dept).

W 253. *Another Impression.* Red wax (Art Dept).

W 254. MONMOUTH, Gwent : Chancery of.
Obverse. Black gutta percha, circ., 65 mm.
See D 27. Acc. No: 25.384.

W 255. *Another Impression.* Red gutta percha; bears marks of the lobes of the matrix.
Acc. No: 31.78/4.

W 256. *Another Impression.* (Acc. No: 25.384). Green gutta percha.

W 257. *Another Impression.* (Acc. No:31.78/4). Red plaster cast.

W 258. *Another Impression.* (Acc. No: 92.140H). Red-brown silicon rubber.

W 259. *Reverse.* Black gutta percha (cracked), circ., 65 mm.
A shield: three lions passant guardant, a label of three points each charged with three fleurs-de-lis, DUCHY OF LANCASTER; field diapered lozengy with suns and *?* moons.
· Sigill.m : edwardi (dei : gracia : reg') angl ꞁ francie :
cancell(arie : nre : de : monem)outh (Bl.)
Acc. No: 25.384
D and *E:* see D 27.

W 260. *Another Impression.* Red gutta percha (cracked); (bears marks of lobes of the matrix).
Acc. No: 31.78/4.

W 261. First Common Seal of the Borough (Monmouth).
? 13th cent. - 1675. Brown wax, circ., 37 mm.
An ancient single-masted ship, each end of the vessel having the figure head of an animal (thus resembling a Viking boat); at the masthead a flag with streamer.
+ COMMVNE SIGILL' MONEMVTE (Early Lom.)
A different seal was employed from 1675, subsequent probably to the charter granted by Charles II to the borough.
Acc. No: 76.27H/7. BM 5186.
E: Monmouth Museum (impression of 1616); NLW, Badminton Manorial 724 (1569), 790 (1391); PRO (Chancery Lane) E 42/277 (1397).
(*For impressions of the later seal, see:* PRO (Chancery Lane) C 219/72 (1688), C 219/80 (poor, 1695), C 219/104 (1708).
D: Brindley (1938) 15, Lewis (1831) III, 317; Scott-Giles (1933) 239; Williams (1982) 26 (No. 56); *For the later seal:* Dineley (1888) 388, Ewe (1972) 76, 160 (No. 118).

W 262. *Another Impression.* Green plaster cast.
Acc. No: 31.78.

W 263. William Jones' Charity (Monmouth).
1614- present day. Red wafer seal, oval, 52 x 37 mm.
A shield: a lion rampant; crest: on a helm, a Cornish chough.
WILLIAM JONES (Ren.)
Acc. No: 79.73H.
D: J.B.A.A. XII (1856) 225-6, Pl. 29/3; Williams (1982) 42 (No. 100).

W 264. NEATH, West Glam; 'Creek of', in the Port of Cardiff.
By 1605- . Red wax, circ., 34 mm.
A shield: a lion rampant.
✦ Costomer Neathe in Porte Cardiff (? Pseudo-Bl.)
Acc. No: 92.141H.
D: Jeffreys-Jones (1955) 215-6.

W 265. Second Common Seal of the Borough (Neath).
1706-*ca.*1925. Brown wax, circ., 46 mm.
A tower supporting two trumpets; in foreground, the waters of the River Neath; to either side (?) warehousing, and pennants resembling 'the booths and flags of a race course' (Grant Francis).
+ SIGILLUM COMMUNE · VILLÆ DE NEATH (Ren.)
The matrix, engraved by J. Sturt and presented by the Mine

Adventurers Company in 1706, replaced an earlier seal which had been in use at latest by 1397.
Acc. No: 76.27H/6.
E: Glamorgan Archives D/D. Gn. 545 (1707), 548-9 (1708).
D: Trans. Neath Antiq. Soc. 2nd Ser. I, 76-9; II, 55; III, 35-7; V, 40-2; Lewis (1833) I; Taylor (1935).

W 266. NEWBOROUGH, Anglesey; Common Seal.
As used in 1426. Red wax, circ., 40 mm.
A clinker-built single-masted ship with large crenellated stern-castle and smaller fore-castle, which supports a bowsprit. The mast supports a crows' nest and pennant flag. The stern-castle is reminiscent of the (late 14th cent.) Bremen *cog*, but the flat bed and straight stern and stern-posts of the cog are not visible, and the method of construction suggests another ship-type.

: sigillū : comunitatis : de : neuburgh   **(Bl.)**
This 19th-century impression derives from the antiquarian collections of Stephen W. Williams (County Surveyor of Radnorshire, 1864-99) and has been placed on loan by Rhayader Museum.
Acc. No: 91.82H.   BM 5188.
E: BL, Add. Ch. 8642 (of 1426).
D: Carr (1982) Pl. 10; Williams (1982) 25 (No. 52) incorrectly ascribes to Newborough the seal of Newport (Salop); personal communication from Dr. M. Redknap.

W 267. NEWTOWN AND MACHYNLLETH, Powys; Railway Company.
See D 61. (Acc. No: 92.142H). White silicon rubber, circ., 49 mm.

W 268. PORT TALBOT, West Glam; Common Seal.
1921- . Mauve wax, circ., 50 mm.
A triangular panel enclosing a shield *couchée:* four lions rampant; ensigned with a helmet; background diapered (?) lozengy, a quatrefoil in each compartment.
Inner Legend: **SEEL WILLAVME SIRE DE FRISE**   **(Lom.)**
Outer Legend: **+ Common : seal : of : the : borough : of : port : talbot : restored : mdccclxi**   **(Pseudo-Bl.)**
An unusual seal which incorporates the mid-14th century seal of the lord of Frisia : one of the titles of Count William III *(ob. 1337)* and IV *(ob. 1345)* of Holland. In 1861 a rim was added to make this the *'common seal of the borough of Aberavon'*. This, in turn, was altered to read *'port talbot'* when the borough of Aberafan was merged into the new borough of Port Talbot in 1921. (The connection with the lord of Frisia is uncertain, but Elizabeth, daughter of Edward I, was married to Earl John of Holland and Frisia, before she wed Humphrey de Bohun). For an earlier alleged seal of Aberafan, see W 189 *supra*.
Acc. No: 92.143H/1.
D: Arch. Jnl. X, 74; *Proc. Soc. Antiq.* 2nd Ser. II, 88-9; Lewis (1833) I (under Aberavon); Williams (1982) 39 (No. 90).

W 269. *Another Impression.* Red wax (cracked), circ., 38 mm.
This impression lacks the rim and outer legend.

W 270. RUTHIN, Clwyd : Third Seal of the Corporation.
1809-35. Dark brown wax, rounded oblong, 23 x 18 mm.
A shield: a three towered and embattled castle.
ALDERMEN AND CORPORATION OF RUTHIN   **(Caps.)**
This seal was adopted by a resolution (25th October 1809) of the Aldermen and Common Council of Ruthin in order to celebrate the Golden Jubilee of the accession of George III.
Acc. No: 76.27H/4.
D: Arch. Camb. 1856/293-6; Clwyd R.O. (Hawarden) Letter: R/21/DCC/MAE of 13-9-79; Lewis (1833) I, Tucker (1962) 57.
E: For an example of an earlier common seal, see: NLW, Ruthin Lordship Deeds 788-9 (of 1759; which displays a castle gateway flanked by two embattled towers, but with no legend).

W 271. Fourth Seal of the Corporation.
1835- . Red wax (cracked), rounded oblong, 39 x 35 mm.
A shield: a three towered and embattled castle.

MAYOR ALDERMEN AND BURGESSES OF RUTHIN   **(Caps.)**
This seal was consequent upon the Municipal Corporation Act of 1835, when mayors were created. This impression came from the bequest of T.H. Thomas, R.C.A.
Acc. No: 16.68H/105.
D: Arch. Camb. 1856/293-6; Jewitt and Hope I (1905) 114, Tucker (1962) 55.
(The existence of at least two earlier common seals for the borough of Ruthin, is attested in a letter sent on June 23rd 1711, by Ellis Meredith to the Rev. Thomas Lloyd at Chirk Castle *(NLW, Chirk Castle Deeds, F. 11552)*: 'Be pleased dear sir, to acquaint Sir Richard *(Sir Richard Myddleton of Chirk Castle)* that Mr. Roberts, upon whom I waited last Wednesday, told me he has consulted Baron Price , who was of opinion that Ruthin being an ancient corporation and having had a seal, might assume a seal, to be used as their common seal, without further ceremony, upon which, as soon as the Baron has pitched upon a device (several figures being to be laid before him by Hugh Meredith) the seal is ordered to be made accordingly of silver and is expected by Mr. Roberts to be brought down by Hugh Meredith'.)
(For a seal engraved for the king's officers at Ruthin, see: NLW, Coed Coch Deed 1041 (of 1567).

W 272. SIRHYWI, Mid-Glam; Independent Order of Oddfellows (Manchester Unity), Sir William Penn Lodge.
1867. Red wax, circ., 25 mm.
See D 62. Acc. No: 50.374/1 (WFM).

W 273. SWANSEA, West Glam; ? Second Common Seal.
? 15th cent.-1548 (when in use). Off-white plaster cast, circ., 38 mm.
An embattled gateway with portcullis raised; from each tower a flagstaff, thereon a banner, that on the *dexter* charged with a lion rampant (possibly for BRAOSE of Gower), that on the *sinister* bearing an eagle displayed; upon an inescutcheon in the centre chief point a bird reguardant with wings displayed and inverted, holding in the beak a fish by its tail-end.
Sigillū : comune : burgensiū : ville : de : sweӯse   **(Bl.)**
Acc. No: 92.144H.
D: Fox-Davies (1915) 764, Francis (1867) 143-7, Rogers (1943) Pt.I, vol. II, p.125 - which tells of this seal falling into abeyance (until 1843) in favour of one depicting the portcullis of the Beaufort family. An original impression of the latter is to be found in PRO (Chancery Lane) HCA 32 (Prize 318) of 1780. In 1843 there was a partial return to tradition which explains the two matrices of differing size once again exhibiting an embattled gateway and now preserved in the Royal Institution at Swansea; *for the latter seal, see:* PRO, WO 44/523 (of 1852); Dineley (1888) 298.
For the seal of the Portreeve of Swansea, see: NLW, Coleman Deed 854 (of 1737).

W 274. 'Creek of Swansea', in the Port of Cardiff : Customs Seal.
Ca. 1650. White plaster cast, circ., 31 mm.
See D 63. Acc. No: 94.142.

W 275. *Another Impression.* (Acc. No: 92.145H/1). Red wax.

W 276. *Another Impression.* (Acc. No: 92.145H/2). Red wax (cracked).

W 277. TENBY, Dyfed : Common Seal.
15th cent. White plaster casts, circ., 71 mm.
Obverse.
A single-masted ship of the period in full sail flying a flag displaying (incorrectly) the royal arms - perhaps for Jasper Tudor (who embarked here for France after the Lancastrian defeat of 1471); in the stern a mariner blows a horn (less likely, observes through a telescope); over the nearside lean two other figures; foliage in the field; cabled borders.
+ Sigillum : comune : burgensium : ville : tenebie   **(Bl.)**
Both impressions derive from electrotype matrices sent to the Museum by Tenby Town Council in 1968 for examination. The dies are now preserved in Tenby Museum.
Acc. No: 92.146H.

W 278. *Reverse.*

A portcullis-gate flanked by two towers on each of which a trumpeter; in centre chief an inescutcheon: in chief barry of three charged with as many martlets, two and one, and in base a like number of cinquefoils, two and one; these arms perhaps deriving from DE VALENCE (William de Valence, Earl of Pembroke, having given the borough its first charter). The legend is the same as on the obverse.

E: Dyfed Archives (Carmarthen) Lort 17/680 (of 1595; fractured); Essex R.O. D/DP T1/1493 (fragment of 1424); Tenby Museum Deeds SE 8/3/290 (1820; paper-masked); 8/3/310 (1841; paper-masked); 8/3/420 (1847; paper-masked); 8/3/460 (1867; en placard). The matrix, or its electrotype replica, appears to have been lost for a period some time after this; *see below*).

D: *Arch. Camb.* 1857/333; *Pax* 61 (May 1921) 65-6; *Proc. Soc. Antiq.* 2nd Ser. XV, 446; Ewe (1972) 91, 201 (No. 200); Laws (1888) 417, Williams (1982) 26 (No. 55).

W 279. Seal of the Mayor (Tenby).

? 17th cent.-1896 (when in use). Bronze coloured wax, oval, 38 x 35 mm.

An embattled two-towered gateway (portcullis raised) approached by a flight of steps; in chief centre point an inescutcheon *(as in W 278).*

+ SIGILLVM · MAIORIS · VILLA · TENBY (Ren.)

This seal may post-date the charter given by Charles II to the borough.
Acc. No: 76.274/9.

E: Tenby Museum SE 8/3/620 (1885), 8/3/630 (1889), 8/3/640 (1891), 8/3/650 (1896). *For a smaller version of the seal (26 x 21 mm.) see:* SE 8/3/600 (1885; when used as the 'corporate seal' of the borough'); 8/3/420 (1893), 8/3/690 (1902); *for an earlier seal,* described as 'the common seal of the mayoralty' (35 mm; circ.) see: BL, Harl. MS 2093, f. 248 (1632).

W 280. Seal of Office of the Common Clerk of the Borough (Tenby).

1760-1881. Red wax (chipped and cracked), oval, 30 x *Ca.* 24 mm.
A three-masted warship in full sail; in base, the ascription: **TENBY.**
Acc. No: 16.68/104 (from the bequest of T.H. Thomas, R.C.A.).

E: Tenby Museum Box 88 (1760-1), and SE 8/3/550, 560, 570, 580 (all of 1881, when used as the 'Corporate Seal'). (The steel die of a smaller version of this seal (21 x 19 mm.) is also preserved in Tenby Museum).

W 281. *Another Impression.* Brown wax.
Acc. No: 76.27H/5.

W 282. TRELLECH, Gwent; Common Seal.

? Late 13th cent. White silicon rubber, circ., 40 mm.
A shield (ensigned with foliage): three chevrons, DE CLARE (Lords of Usk; that lordship incorporating Trellech), between *dext.* a crescent; *sin.* a star of five rays; beaded borders.

+ S' : COMVNITATIS : BVRG. : DE TRILL' (Lom.)

This seal, from the bronze matrix in the Ashmolean Museum, Oxford (No. 317) has been incorrectly ascribed to both Triel (Seine and Oise, France) and to Trill (Devon). No known medieval impressions from it are extant.
Acc. No: 92.147H. BM 5467.

D: Rawlinson (1720) 40-1; *Catal. Ashmolean Mus.* (1836) No. 317; Williams (1982) 25 (No. 53), Williams and Hudson (1990) 55-6, 58 (No. 6); Bradney (1904) II, Pt. 2, p. 134, tells how in 1677 'the burgesses (of Trellech) were aggrieved, in regard they have not their charters renewed'.

W 283. TREORCI, Mid-Glam; Philanthropic Order of True Ivorites, 'Tab Dewi' Lodge.

? 19th cent. Dark red wax, circ., 25 mm.
See D 64. Acc. No: 62.53/3 (WFM).

W 284. *Another Seal.* Dark red wax, circ., 25 mm.
See D 65. Acc. No: 62.53/3 (WFM).

W 285. USK, Gwent : Borough of.

? 18th cent. Pale blue silicon rubber, oval, 30 x 22 mm.
Per fess wavy, in chief a tower between two battle-axes erect; in base, the ripples of the river Usk.

USK · BOROUGH (Caps.)

From the matrix preserved at Gwent Record Office (Cwmbran). In 1833, the seal (described as 'antient') was in the custody of the Recorder (the Clerk of the Portreeve when sitting as a magistrate).
Acc. No: 92.148H.

D: Bradney (1921) III, Pt. 1 (1921) 17; Evans (1953) 510; *Usk Town Trail (Inner Route)* 7; BL., Add. MS 24,480, f. 155 (*ca.* 1702-14).

Some Original Impressions of Welsh Civic Seals not contained in the Museum's collections and not listed above.
(This list is not exhaustive).

Brecon, Powys:
2nd Common Seal: PRO (Chancery Lane) C 219/54 (1678, 219/70 (subsequent to (1685), 210/74 (1689), 219/78 (1685), 219/90 the charter of 1556. (1700), 219/106 (two examples of same date: 1708).

Caernarfon, Gwynedd:
1st Common Seal: NLW, Peniarth Deed 2043 (1430); UCNW, Baron Hill Deed 3188 (fragment of 1643); PRO (Chancery Lane C 219/74 (1688), 219/86 (1698). *See also:* BL, Add. MS 24, 480, f.155r.
Later Common Seal: NLW, Llanfair and Brynodol MS D 495 (1801; three imperfect impressions). (See: *Arch. Camb.* 1857, pp. 173, 177-8).

Cardigan, Dyfed: NLW, Misc. Record 458 (1813; indistinct).

Cowbridge, S. Glam:
1st Common Seal: NLW, Penrice and Margam Charter 2810 (1521; injured, and image almost entirely lacking).
2nd Common Seal: Glamorgan Archives, B/Cow. 139 (1817). *See also:* BL, Add. MS 24, 480, f.155d.

Flint, Clwyd: BL. Harl. MSS 2040, ff. 32d, 186d; 2099, f.97d *(drawings of the common seal).*

Holt Castle, Clwyd: Clwyd R.O. (Hawarden) D/PT 251 (of 1454), 1091 (1521) *inter alia;* (Ruthin) DD/WY/70 (1473), 1628 (1459); BL, Harl. MSS 1968, f.32d; 1970, f.104d.

Laugharne, Dyfed: NLW, SD/Misc/153, 154 (1886; poor impression).

Llanidloes, Powys: PRO (Chancery Lane) H 045/2525 (plain seal of 1849; perhaps not the seal adopted in 1833).

Montgomery, Powys:
1st Common Seal: NLW, Powysland Club Deposit, 1982: in Box 27 (impressions of 1394 and 1549).
2nd Common Seal: PRO (Chancery Lane) C 219/78 (poor; *temp.* 1689-94); C 219/82 (fragment, 1695).

Newport, Dyfed: NLW, Misc. Deeds, Box 14 (Envelope No. 7) (1884). *See also:* NLW, Bronwydd (Gp. II) Deed 1426 (1606).

Newport, Gwent:
1st Common Seal: NLW, Tredegar Park Muniments Pt. 2; Box 56, No. 188 (of 1580; imperfect).
2nd Common Seal: NLW, Tredegar Park MSS 225 (*ca.* 1770), 228 (1794; paper masked).
also: NLW, Tredegar Park Muniments 62/29 (small seal, perhaps personal, of Wm. Kemeys, mayor (1444).

Pembroke, Dyfed: PRO, HCA 32 (1705; en placard, indistinct). *Seal of the Mayor:* PRO, C 219/90 (*Ca.* 1700), C 219/106 (1708).

Secondary impressions and casts of Welsh Civic Seals, are also to be found in the collections of the British Library (Dept. of MSS), Ludlow Museum, and the Royal Institution at Swansea, amongst other repositories. A considerable number are to be found in the seal collections of the Society of Antiquaries (Burlington House, London):

Drawer 1: Aberafan, Aberystwyth, Beaumaris.
Drawer 2: Caerleon.
Drawer 3: Cardiff, Cardigan, Carmarthen, Chepstow.
Drawer 4: Cowbridge, Criccieth.
Drawer 5: Flint.
Drawer 6: Harlech, Haverfordwest.
Drawer 7: Laugharne.

Drawer 9: Monmouth, Montgomery, Neath, Newport (Gwent), Newport (Dyfed).
Drawer 10: Pembroke, Pwllheli.
Drawer 11: New Radnor, Ruthin.
Drawer 13: Swansea, Tenby, Trelech, Usk.
Drawer 14: Welshpool.
Drawer 15: Wrexham.

Numerous references and drawings of civic seals occur in works on local history and other books listed in the Bibliography; note especially: Dineley (1888), Lewis (1833) I, and so far as the former Monmouthshire is concerned: Scott Giles (1933) is also very helpful.

For **Pwllheli** (Gwynedd), see: Lloyd Hughes, D.G., *Pwllheli: An Old Welsh town and its history* (Gomer Press, 1991) Appendix A, pp. 337-41.

Lords of Glamorgan : Chancery of Cardiff

(The impressions with Accession Nos. in the ranges of 01/11-19 and 12/166-175 were presented by Cardiff Corporation).

W 286.   MILES FITZWALTER of Gloucester; Earl of Hertford, Lord of Abergavenny and Caldicot.
1140-43. Green sulphur cast (cracked), circ., 58 mm.
Equestrian; Miles, in armour, on horseback to right, holding with his left hand a kite-shaped shield, in his right hand a banner flag with streamers.
+ SIGILLVM : MILONIS : DE GLOECESTRIA   (Late Rom.)
Acc. No: 25.384.   BM 6064.
D: Arch. XIV, 276, Pl. XLVII/4; XXI, 554-5; Brit. Arch. Inst. *Catal.* (Gloucester Mtng.) 32; *Gentl. Mag.* LXV, 737, Pl. 2/5; Williams (1982) 11 (No. 12).

W 287.   *Another Impression.* Green plaster cast (defaced).
Acc. No: 92.149H.

W 288.   WILLIAM, Earl of Gloucester, son of Robert Consul.
1147-83. Buff plaster cast, circ., 77 mm.
A lion statant guardant, turned to the right, the tail uplifted; in background, a conventional tree or lily.
+ SIGILLVM WIL...MI GLOENCESTRIE CONSVLIS·   (Rom.)
Acc. No: 01.11
E: NLW, Penrice and Margam Ch. 20 , 22, 23, 1943 (fine, with counter-seal), 1944, 1945, 1946; all cannot be dated precisely, and with the exception of 20 and 1943, are imperfect.
D: J.B.A.A. XXXI, 291-2; Matthews II (1900) 43, VI (1911) cxi.

W 289.   *Another Impression.* Yellow sulphur cast (chipped).
Acc. No: 25.384.

W 290.   ISABEL, Countess of Gloucester and Mortain, previously married to Prince John.
1200-16. Yellow sulphur cast (cracked), p.o., 83 x 51 mm.
The countess, draped in a long dress with long maunches hanging from her wrists, holding in the right hand a lily-flower, in the left a bird.
....ILLVM : ISABEL' : COMITIS.. GLOECESTRIE.... MORETV...   (Early Lom.)
Acc. No: 25.384.
E: NLW, Penrice and Margam Ch. 104 , (*cf.* 113 , of 1213-16), 113C (undated, imperfect), 2041 (of 1199-1215), 2042 (1216-19), 2043 (undated).
D: Birch (1897) 210, (1902) 65; Clark II (1910) 343, 351.

W 291.   GILBERT DE CLARE, 5th Earl of Gloucester.
Obverse.
1218-29. Buff plaster cast (fragmentary), circ., 62 mm.

Equestrian; to the right, a horse caparisoned; arms: three chevronels, DE CLARE. (Legend wanting).
Acc. No: 12.171.   BM 5834 Ø.
E: BL, Harl. Ch. 75 B.37 (1218), 75 B.38 (Undated, fragment). NLW, Penrice and Margam Ch. 131 (undated), 2045 (1218), 2046 (*ca.* 1220) which see for the reverse; 2047 and 2048 (both undated and imperfect).
D: Arch. LXXXIX, 4, Pl.VI (h); Williams (1982) 10 (No. 10), 20 (No 40).

W 292.   Privy Seal.
1218-29. Buff plaster cast, circ., 28 mm.
A shield: three chevrons, DE CLARE.
+ SIGILL' .... DE CLARA   (Lom.)
Acc. No: 12.174.   BM 5834 R.
E: NLW, Penrice and Margam Ch. 2048 (undated).

W 293.   RICHARD DE CLARE, 6th Earl of Gloucester.
Obverse.
1230-62. Buff plaster cast, circ., 68 mm.
Equestrian; the earl on horseback to the right, in armour with flat helmet, his sword in his right hand, his shield: three chevrons, DE CLARE, held in his right hand.
+ SIG..........................IE   (Lom.)
Acc. No: 12.173.   BM 5843 Ø.
E: BL, Add. Ch. 20,039 (Undated).
D: Arch. LXXXIX, 7, 14, Pl. IV(a), Pl. VII(a); Matthews VI (1911) cxii.

W 294.   *Another Impression* (with fuller legend).
Off-yellow sulphur cast (cracked), circ., 70 mm.
+ SIG................CLARE : C..MITIS : HERTFORDI..   (Lom.)
Acc. No: 25.384.   BM 5844 Ø.

W 295.   *Another Impression.* Buff plaster cast.
As W 294. Acc. No: 12.166.

W 296.   *Reverse.* Buff plaster cast, circ., 68 mm.
A shield: three chevronels, CLARE; supporters: *dext.* (missing), *sin.* a lion rampant; suspended by a strap.
+ SIG..................CLAR.................E   (Lom.)
Acc. No: 12.173. BM 5843 R.
E: BL, Add. Ch. 20,039 (Undated).

W 297.   *Another Impression* (with fuller device and legend). Buff plaster cast, circ., 71 mm.
+ SIGILLVM . RICARDI DE : CLA..........S : GLO.......E ·   (Lom.)
Acc. No: 12.166.   BM 5844 R.

W 298. GILBERT DE CLARE, 7th Earl of Gloucester.
Obverse.
1262-95. Off-white plaster cast, circ., 74 mm.
Equestrian; the earl in armour on horseback to left, flat helmet with
vizor closed, his sword held behind him in his left hand, his right grasps
his shield: three chevronels, DE CLARE.
SIGILL' GILEBERTI · DE · CLARE · COMITIS (: GLO)VERNIE   (Lom.)
Acc. No: 12.172.   BM 5836 Ø.
E: BL, Add. Ch. 20,398 (Undated), Cott. Ch. XVIII, 48 (fragment of
    1292); NLW, Penrice and Margam Ch. 4020 (detached).
D: Arch. LXXXIX, Pl. IV(b); *Arch. Jnl.* XCVII, 164, Pl. IX, c,d; Matthews
    VI (1911) cxli, cxiv; Williams (1982) 20 (No. 40) where wrongly
    described as the *reverse* of the seal of the the 5th Earl.

W 299. *Another Impression.* Buff plaster cast.
Acc. No: 12.167.

W 300. *Another Impression.* Green plaster cast.
Acc. No: 12.172.

W 301. *Reverse.* Cream plaster cast, circ., 74 mm.
Equestrian; the earl on horseback to right, flat helmet with vizor closed,
his sword in his right hand, shield : as W 298.
SIGIŁ : GILE..RTI : DE : CLARE : COMITIS : HERTFORDIE   (Lom.)
Acc. No: 12.172.   BM 5836 R.
E: As W 300.

W 302. *Another Impression.* Black plaster cast.
Acc. No: 25.384.

W 303. First Privy Seal.
In use 1276. Buff plaster cast, circ., 22 mm.
A shield: three chevronels, CLARE; suspended by a strap.
...SIGILLVM · SECRET..   (Lom.)
Acc. No: 12.168.   BM 8606.
D: Arch. LXXXIX, 4; Matthews VI (1911) cxii, cxiv.

W 304. Second Privy Seal.
Ca. 1290. Yellow sulphur cast, circ., 27 mm.
A shield: three chevronels, CLARE, suspended by a strap: supporters:
two lions rampant reguardant.
+ SECRETVM · GILEBERTI · DE · CLAR.   (Lom.)
Acc. No: 25.384.   *Cf.* BM 8607.
D: Matthews VI (1911) cxii-iv.

W 305. *Another Impression.* Buff plaster cast.
Acc. No: 12.168.

W 306. DE CLARE family, member of.
Obverse. Buff plaster cast, circ., 85 mm.
Equestrian; to right, head wanting; shield, and caparisons of horse:
three chevronels, CLARE. (Legend wanting also).
Acc. No: 12.170.   BM 5845 Ø.
D: Matthews VI (1911) cxiii, cxvi.

W 307. *Reverse.* Buff plaster cast, circ., 82 mm.
Armorial; a shield: three chevronels diaper, CLARE, with wavy scrolls of
foliage; background hatched, within a broad border of wavy scrolls of
foliage. (Legend wanting).
Acc. No: 12.170.   BM 5845 R.
(For the CLARE arms, see: Arch. Jnl. LI, 43-8).

W 308. WILLIAM and ELEANOR LA ZOUCHE.
Obverse.
1329-37. Buff plaster cast (cracked), circ., 79 mm.
Equestrian; William on horseback to right, his sword held aloft in his
right hand, his shield in his left; horse caparisoned, with fan plume;
arms on shield and caparisons: ten roundels, four, three, two, and one,
in pile, ZOUCHE; field diapered lozengy.
S' WILL'I : LA ZOVCHE DOMINI · DE GLAMORGAN   (Lom.)

Acc. No: 01.12.
E: NLW, Penrice and Margam Ch. 204 Ø(1329).
D: Birch (1897) 301, (1902) 107; Matthews II (1900) vi, cxiii, 47.

W 309. *Another Impression.* White plaster cast (defaced).
Acc. No: 92.150H.

W 310. *Reverse.* Buff plaster cast, circ., 79 mm.
The lady Eleanor standing on a carved corbel, wearing a long narrow
dress with flat head-dress; holding in each hand a shield: *dext.* three
lions guardant passant ENGLAND; *sin.* three chevronels, CLARE (her
ancestral arms); all within a carved gothic-type panel of eight cusps;
field diapered.
+ SIGILL.. WILLELMI LA ZOVCHE : DOMINI : DE GLAMORGAN   (Lom.)
Acc. No: 01.13.
E: NLW, Penrice and Margam Ch. 204 R (1329)

W 311. HUGH LE DESPENSER.
Reverse only.
1338-49. Yellow sulphur cast (broken), circ., 81 mm.
A shield: quarterly, 1. and 4. diapered, 2. and 3. a fret, over all a bend;
DESPENSER; between two trees, the whole within a gothic-type border,
eight-foiled, in the upper foil a lion passant guardant.
+ S' HVGONIS : LE : DESPENSER : D'NI : GLAMORGANCIE : ET
ET ....IE   (Lom.)
Acc. No: 25.384.
E: NLW, Penrice and Margam Ch. 212 R (1338), 221 (undated,
    imperfect).
D: J.B.A.A. LIII, 238; Birch (1897) 308, (1902) 131; Clark IV (1910)
    1218; Matthews I (1898) 22, VI (1911) cxiii.

W 312. EDWARD LE DESPENSER.
Obverse only.
1349-75 (copy of 1358 impression). Buff plaster cast, circ., 87 mm.
Equestrian; Edward on horseback to right, in armour, on his helmet a
griffin's head for crest; shield, and horse caparisons - arms of
DESPENSER *(as W 311)*; sword held obliquely in his right hand. (Note,
in the legend, the mid-14th cent. change from Lombardic Capitals to
Black Letter characters).
Sigillum : edwardi : le : despenser......morgan : z : morg::   (Bl.)
Acc. No: 01.14.
E: NLW, Penrice and Margam Ch. 229 Ø (1358), 230 (1358, imperfect).
D: Clark IV (1910) 1299, Matthews I (1898) 28, 48; VI (1911) cxiv.

W 313. THOMAS LE DESPENSER, 12th Earl of Gloucester.
1375-1400 (copy of impression of *ca.* 1397). Buff plaster cast, circ.,
51 mm.
A shield, DESPENSER *(as W 311)*, crest: a gryphon's head between two
wings erect, out of *(?)* a ducal coronet; between two trees on each,
suspended by a strap, a lozenge-shaped shield: *dext.* three chevrons,
CLARE; *sin.* a lion rampant queue fourchy, in a cusped quatrefoil,
BURGHESH.
· sigillum : thome : / : dn̄i : le : desp..ser :   (Bl.)
Acc. No: 01.19.   BM 9283.
                                                     PRO P. 1293.
E: PRO (Chancery Lane) DL. 27/217 (1398); *for a fragment of his
    equestrian seal, see:* NLW, Penrice and Margam Ch. 404 (1394).
D: Arch. LXXXIX, 15, Pl. XI-i; Clark IV (1910) 1417; Matthews II (1900)
    49, VI (1911) cxiv.

W 314. ELIZABETH LA DESPENSER.
In use 1401. Dark green plaster cast, circ., 37 mm.
A shield: *dext.* DESPENSER *(as W 311)* impaling *sin.* BURGHERSH *(as
W 313)*, ensigned with a griffin couchant; between the initials **E.S.**; all
within a gothic-type panel.
· le : Seal : elizabet : dame : la : despensere   (Bl.)
Acc. No: 25.384.   BM 9274-6.
E: BL, Harl. Ch. 56 D.30 (1401).
*(For the seal of Richard Beauchamp, Earl of Worcester and Lord of
Glamorgan and Morgan, see that appended in 1421 to Glamorgan*

Archives, Cowbridge Borough Charter: *Annual Report of the Glamorgan Archivist, 1983*).

W 315.   RICHARD DE BEAUCHAMP, 14th Earl of Warwick.
1423-39. Buff plaster cast, circ., 75 mm.
A shield: quarterly, 1. and 4. a fess between six crosses crosslet, BEAUCHAMP; 2. and 3. checky, a chevron Ermine, NEWBURGH; overall an inescutcheon of pretence, quarterly CLARE and DESPENSER (arms as W 313); crest: a swan's head and neck out of a ducal coronet; supporters: *dext.* a bear collared, muzzled, and chained; *sin.* a griffin collared; all within an ornamental gothic-type quatrefoil.
Richard.............mes · warrewici · et · albe · marlie ·
dn̄s . d'speser · et · de · in ......   **(Bl.)**
Acc. No: 12.169.   BM 7253 (where legend differs slightly).
E: BL, Add. Ch. 20,432 (1430), 2016 (fragment, 1435); Harl. Ch. (1431, imperfect).
D: *Arch. Jnl.* XXIX, 354; *J.B.A.A.* XXVIII, 165; Matthews II (1900) 51; VI (1911) cxiv-vi;

W 316.   *Another Impression.* Buff plaster cast (broken).
Acc. No: 09.16.

W 317.   RICHARD NEVILL, 16th Earl of Warwick.
Obverse.
1449-71. Green sulphur cast, circ., 90 mm.
Equestrian; the earl on horse galloping to right; his sword (pointing towards helmet and vizor closed) in his right hand, a shield in his left: a saltire, label of three points compony, NEVILLE; horse caparisons indistinct, but charged on the neck: quarterly, 1. and 4. an eagle displayed, MONTHERMER, 2. and 3. three fusils in fess, a label of as many points, MONTACUTE; on the flanks: quarterly, 1. and 4. quarterly, i. and iv. a fess between six crosses crosslet, BEAUCHAMP; ii. and iii. checky, a chevron, NEWBURGH; 2. and 3. quarterly, CLARE and DESPENSER (arms as W 313); on helm a coronet, and crest a swan's head and neck.
: sigillum : ricardi : neuil :: comitis : warwici : dn̄i : glamorgancie
et morgancie   **(Bl.)**
Acc. No: 25.384.   BM 6258 Ø.
E: NLW, Penrice and Margam Ch. 262-3 (1452).
D: *Arch. Camb.* 1872/35-6; Matthews II (1900) 51, VI (1911) cxv-cxiv; Cf. *Proc. Soc. Antiq.* 2nd Ser. XIX, 152-3.

W 318.   *Another Impression.* Buff plaster cast (cracked and imperfect).
Acc. No: 01.16.

W 319.   *Another Impression.* Brown plaster cast (chipped).
Acc. No: 92.151H/1.

W 320.   *Another Impression.* Brown plaster cast.
Acc. No: 92.151H/2.

W 321.   *Reverse.* Buff plaster cast (cracked), circ., 92 mm.
A shield: quarterly, CLARE and DESPENSER (as W 313), impaling: quarterly, 1. and 4. three fusils in fess, a label of as many points, MONTACUTE; 2. and 3. an eagle displayed, MONTHERMER; supporters: perhaps two rampant and chained bears (the head of one wanting); crests (defaced) perhaps: 1. out of a ducal coronet, a swan's head and neck, BEAUCHAMP; 2. out of a ducal coronet, a griffin statant, MONTACUTE.

...um : Ricardi .. neuil : comitis..........lamorgan.. et : morgan....   **(Bl.)**
Acc. No: 01.16.
(For the seal of the Duke of Clarence as Lord of Glamorgan, see: NLW, Penrice and Margam Ch. 266 (of 1471).

W 322.   RICHARD PLANTAGENET, 3rd Duke of Gloucester.
1477-85. Buff plaster cast, circ., 20 mm.
A shield: quarterly, 1. and 4. FRANCE (Modern); 2. and 3. ENGLAND; over all a label of three points; between three estoiles, within a carved panel. (No legend).
Acc. No: 01.17.   BM 12,715.
E: BL, Harl. Ch. 43 F.5 (1473).

W 323.   The Same, as Duke of Gloucester, and later as King Richard III.
Obverse.
In use 1484. Red wax, circ., 53 mm.
The duke on horseback to right, with raised sword; head, etc., wanting; arms of shield and caparisons as W 324 below; beneath the horse, a boar passant to right. (Legend wanting).
Acc. No: 73.13H (Gallery).
D: As W 324.

W 324.   *Reverse.* Red wax, circ., 53 mm.
A shield: *dext.* quarterly, 1. and 4. FRANCE (Modern), 2. and 3. ENGLAND, over all a label of three points (as Duke of Gloucester); impaling *sin.* per fess, 1. a fess charged with six crosses crosslet, BEAUCHAMP; 2. checky, a chevron Ermine charged with five leopards' heads jessant-de-lis chevronwise (for Cantelupe) NEUBURGH; for his wife, Anne Neville. Supporters, *dext.* a boar, *sin.* (lost); no crest. (Legend also wanting).
Acc. No: 73.13H.
D: *Arch. Camb.* 1873/79, Clark V (1910) 1724-5, Hopkin-James (1922) 145; Letter (12-6-89) from Mr. K. Underwood, Sedbury, Chepstow.

W 325.   HENRY VII as Lord of Glamorgan.
Obverse.
1495-1509 (copy of impression of 1503). Buff plaster cast, circ., 93 mm.
Equestrian; the king on horseback to right, over a rocky mount replenished with herbage, his shield *(arms as W 326)* flung over his right shoulder; horse bears a plume of three ostrich feathers.
Sig.........gis : henr.........erni......omin.... .glamo...........rga...   **(Bl.)**
Acc. No: 01.18.   BM 4788 Ø.
E: BL, Harl. Ch. 75 E.19 (1503).
D: Matthews II (1900) 53; VI (1911) cxvi.

W 326.   *Reverse.* Buff plaster cast, circ., 93 mm.
A shield: quarterly, 1. and 4. FRANCE (Modern); 2. and 3. ENGLAND; between sprigs of foliage, and encircled with the Garter and motto of that Order : **HONI SOIT QVI MAL Y PENSE**; crest: on a helmet a lion statant guardant crowned.
Sig..... .ancellari.................................nok   **(Bl.)**
Acc. No: 01.18.   BM 4788 R
E: BL, Harl. Ch. 75 E.19 (1503).
(For the seal of Henry VIII as Lord of Glamorgan, see: NLW, Penrice and Margam Ch. 2815 (of 1526).

PERSONAL SEALS (MEDIEVAL)

W 327.   Adam ap ....
? 12th - early 13th cent. Brown gutta-percha, circ., 40 mm.
Equestrian; armed figure of a knight on horseback to the right; an early date suggested by 'the long garments reaching below the feet of the rider, the "coiffe de mailles" without "heaume", and the absence of

hoardings on the horse'. Legend largely indistinct:
***?* + ...ADE FILII........RVAM**   **(? Lom.)**
From a matrix found (about 1882) at Little Vownog, Bersham, Clwyd.
Acc. No: 44.308.
D: *Mont. Collns.* XVII, 369-70.

W 328.   ADUVAR, John; possibly John ab Ivor.
Early 14th cent. White silicon rubber, circ., 25 mm.
See D 28. Acc. No: 58.153.

W 329.   *Another Impression.* Red wax (sent originally to Prof. Wm. Rees
for possible identification).
Acc. No: 92.152H.

**W 330.   BIGOD, Roger; Earl of Norfolk and Lord of Striguil
(Chepstow).**
As used in 1301. Red wax (cracked), circ., 24 mm.
A shield: a lion rampant.
· SIGILLVM · ROGERI · BIGOD   **(Lom.)**
Acc. No: 25.384.   BM 7471.
                                                                  PRO P 1037.
E: PRO (Chancery Lane) DL 25/2178, E 26/2/78A, E 213/185
    (1296).
D: Arch. XXI, 198-9.

W 331.   CHOT, Nicholas.
Early 14th cent. Dark blue silicon rubber, circ., 25 mm.
See D 29 *supra.* Acc. No: 87.27H.

W 332.   *Another Impression.* (Acc. No: 92.153H.). Dark blue silicon
rubber.

**W 333.   CLARE, Gilbert De, II or III; Earl of Pembroke and Lord of
Striguil (Chepstow).**
As used by 1148-52. Red plaster cast, circ., 80 mm.
The earl on horseback to right, with conical helmet and nasal; sword
held by his right hand, his long convex kite-shaped shield bears faint
traces of the CLARE arms (three chevronels). This seal bears a close
resemblance to the Second Seal of King Stephen.
........M · GV..........LE........   **(Rom.)**
Acc. No: 12.171.   BM 5833.
                                                                  PRO P. 1200.
E: PRO (Chancery Lane) DL 27/47 (1139-49).
D: Cf. J.B.A.A. X, 268, Pl. 25.

W 334.   CLARE, Richard De; 1st Earl of Hertford and Lord of Usk.
As used in 1130. Dark-orange plaster cast, circ., 62 mm.
The earl on horseback to right, his sword (held in his right hand)
pointing towards his helmet; details of helmet and shield obscured.
SIGILLVM · RICARDI · DE CLARE   **(Rom.)**
Acc. No: 25.384.

W 335.   CRESCERI, William.
Late 13th cent. Red-brown plasticine, circ., 25 mm.
A six-rayed star.
S' WILLI : CRESCERI   **(Lom.)**
From a lead matrix brought into the Museum (25-4-89) by Mr. E.R.
Mitchell of Pentwyn for examination.
Acc. No: 92.154H/1.

W 336.   *Another Impression.* (Acc. No: 92.154H/2). White silicon
rubber.

**W 337.   CRICKLADE, Alice (of Calne, Wilts; and of Llandough and
St. Marychurch, S. Glam).**
As used in 1456. Yellow sulphur cast, circ., 21 mm.
The initials: **A.C.** between two sprigs of foliage.
Acc. No: 25.384.
E: NLW, Penrice and Margam Ch. 411 (1456).
D: Clark V (1910) 1638.

W 338.   CYFEILIOG, Hawys of.
Late 13th cent. Red wax, p.o., 48 x 27 mm.
See D 32. Acc. No: 92.155H.

W 339.   *Another Impression.* Buff plaster cast.
Acc. No: 23.89/4.

W 340.   Uncertain.
Red-brown silicon rubber, circ., 18 mm.
See D 30. Acc. No: 92.240 H.

W 341.   David Llywelyn.
? Early 13th cent. Red silicon rubber, p.o., 36 x 22 mm.
An ornamental fleur-de-lis.
+ S' DAVIDI . LEWELINI   **(Early Lom.)**
From a lead matrix found by Mr. A Duncan (early in 1987) in a field of
Treleddyn Farm, St. David's, Dyfed (NGR uncertain, but presumably
close to SM: 731258). The matrix is now in Scolton Manor Museum, Nr.
Haverfordwest.
Acc. No: 92.156H.

**W 342.   David Tanat; perhaps of Abertanat, Llanyblodwel (Salop;
formerly Merionydd).**
As used in 1416. Yellowish-brown plaster cast, circ., 29 mm.
A shield, *couché:* a chevron between three pheons points down. Crest: on
a helm in profile with short mantling, a stag's head. Supporter: *sin.* a
demoiselle. Legend on a scroll:
Seel : david tanat   **(Bl.)**
Acc. No: 92.157H.
D: Siddons (1981) 542 (No. XVI), (1991a) 242 (Fig. 54).

W 343.   DIGBY, (?) Sir John
d. 1533. Grey-mauve silicon rubber, rectangular, 13 x 11 mm.
See D 31. Acc. No: 35.268.

W 344.   DWNN, Gruffydd; of Croesallgwn, Llangyndeirn, Dyfed.
As used in 1438. Yellowish-brown plaster cast, circ., 31 mm.
A shield, *couché:* a wolf salient. Crest: on a helm with mantling and
wreath, a gryphon's head.
Sigillum Galfridi donn armigeri   **(Bl.)**
Acc. No: 92.158H.
D: Siddons (1981) 534 (No. II/2); (1991a) 10 (Fig.9), 237 (Fig.47).

W 345.   *A Later Seal.*
As used in 1442. Yellowish-brown plaster cast, circ., 43 mm.
A shield, *couché:* as W 344 (but clearer impression) with different
arrangement of the mantling.
: Sigillum : galfridi : doun *(? donn)* **: armigeri**   **(Bl.)**
Acc. No: 92.159H.
D: Siddons (1981) 535 (No. II/4).

W 346.   *Another Impression.* Cream plaster cast.
Acc. No: 31.78/7.

W 347.   Eve, daughter of Kederid.
Later 13th cent. Red silicon rubber, circ., 27 mm.
An ornamental fleur-de-lis.
+ S' EVE' FIL' KEDERID   **(Lom.)**
From the lead-alloy matrix found by Mr Richard Jones of New Inn,
using a metal detector, at Llanfihangel Gobion, Gwent (NGR: *SO* 3495
0945) and presented to Newport Museum *(Acc. No: 92.24).*
Acc. No: 92.160H.
D: Letter from Mr Rodney Hudson, Newport Museum (20-11-91);
    Monm. Antiq. IX (1993).

W 348.   Eynon ab Iorwerth.
Late 13th cent. Red plaster (cracked), circ., 26 mm.
? Four heads of corn conjoined.
· S' · EYNON F' IORVER ·   **(Lom.)**
An impression sent by Mr C Cater of Wrexham (1988) from a matrix
found by a member of the Mold Historical Society at approx. NGR:
SJ 225623. . An Eynon, son of Iorwerth, had lands in Hope at this

period, but his seal shows an animal device (*Clwyd R.O. (Hawarden) D/PT 407*). One Eynon ab Iorwerth was a witness re lands in Gresford (*NLW, Plymouth Deed 324 (of 1337)*) and, using a different seal occurs as a land-owner (*Ibid. 366, of 1346*).
Acc. No: 92.161H.

W 349.   GALLES, Yvain de; (Owain ap Thomas ap Rhodri of Gwynedd).
As used in 1376. Yellowish-brown plaster cast, circ., 27 mm.
A shield, *couché*: quarterly (though divisions not seen), in each quarter a lion rampant. Crest: on a helm in profile, two curved (*?* bulls') horns (one missing on this impression). Field reticulated.
LE SEEL YVAIN DE *?* GA.....   **(Lom.)**
Acc. No: 92.164H.
D: Siddons (1981) 544 (No. XX/2); (1991a) 18, 283-4 (Figs. 85-88).

W 350.   GAM, Morgan; Lord of Afan, West Glam.
Ca. 1230-40. Yellow sulphur cast, p.o., 36 x 25 mm.
Morgan on horseback galloping to left, his sword held aloft with his left hand. The band at the base of the horse's neck is serrated at its lower edge. (An equestrian image is rare on pointed oval seals).
+ SIGILLVM · MORGANI · CAM   **(Lom.)**
Acc. No: 25,384.   BM 5783.
E: BL, Harl. Ch. 75 A. 25, and B. 40 (both of 1234); NLW, Penrice and Margam Ch. 1973 (undated). *For a variant seal, see:* Penrice and Margam Ch. 2035 (undated).
D: Clark VI (1910) 2300; *Cf.* III, 926; Birch (1897) 230, Siddons (1984) 299 (No. III/1), Williams (1982) 12 (No. 16); *for circular seals of Morgan, see: Arch. Camb.* 1867/20-22, 1868/183-84); Siddons (1984) 300 (No. III/2).

W 351.   GETHIN, Richard.
As used in 1435. Yellowish-brown plaster cast., circ., *ca.* 48 mm.
A shield, *couché*: a chevron between three crows, wings raised. Crest: on a helm in profile, part of a similar bird (rest missing). Supporters: *dext.* a stag, *sin.* a crow, wings raised. In field, above the supporters, two knotted cloths with what appear to be bats' wings.
? Richart ....   **(Bl.)**
Acc. No: 92.165H.
D: Siddons (1981) 535-36 (No. IV/1); (1991a) 58 (Fig. 29), 237 (Fig. 46).

W 352.   *A Later Seal.*
As used in 1438. Yellowish-brown plaster cast (fine impression), circ., 51 mm.
Shield, *couché*: as W 351, the chevron cross-hatched, and the crest complete: a crow, holding in its beak a scroll, upon which an inscription, perhaps: **de bdicone**, or **Duw a digon.** Instead of supporters, two knotted cloths with bats' wings - larger than in W 351.
Richart Gethyn   **(Bl.)**
Acc. No: 92.166H.
D: Siddons (1981) 536 (No. IV/2).

W 353.   GOREWI, Robert.
? Late 13th cent. Buff plasticine, circ., 23 mm.
A fleur-de-lys.
+ S' ROBERTI · GOREWI   **(Lom.)**
From a matrix found in excavations at Usk led by W. Manning in 1968, near medieval buildings. The surname of the original owner suggests a Herefordshire provenance.
Acc. No: 92.167H.

W 354.   GOUGH, Edward.
As used in 1415. Yellowish-brown plaster cast, circ., 30 mm.
A shield, *couché*: three wolves' heads erased, two and one. Crest: on a helm in profile with mantling, a winged dragon's head and neck. Foliage in field.
edw..... ..(*?*)th   **(Bl.)**
Acc. No: 92.168H.
D: Siddons (1981) 536 (No. 5).

W 355.   GOUGH, Matthew, of Hanmer, Co. Flint; ob. 1450.
As used in 1442. Yellowish-brown plaster cast, circ., 36 mm.
A shield, *couché*: three boars passant, two and one. Crest: on a helm with mantling, a panache of five ostrich feathers; five more on each side of the shield, tied together.
matheu Gothe   **(Bl.)**
Acc. No: 92.169H.
D: Siddons (1981) 537 (No. VI/3); (1991a) 58 (Fig. 30), 237 (Fig.45).

W 356.   GRAY, Henry; 2nd Earl of Tankerville and Tilly, lord of Powys, hereditary Chamberlain of Normandy.
As used in 1421-29. Yellow plaster cast, circ., 50 mm.
A shield, *couché*: quarterly, 1. and 4. a lion rampant within a bordure engrailed, GREY of HETON; 2. and 3. a lion rampant, POWYS WENWYNWYN; over all an escutcheon: TANKERVILLE. Crest, on a helm with mantling of foliage, a ram's head. Supporters: *dext.* a four-footed winged dragon; *sin.* a hind. (The bracketed portion of the legend is uncertain, and has never been satisfactorily deciphered:
S' henric' gray comitis d' tancarville de powys et tilly (chamberlain de comitatu normadie).   **(Bl.)**
Acc. No: 25.384.   BM 10,255.
D: J.B.A.A. II, 94; XVII, 64, 77-9 (where a variant legend; *Cf.* Siddons (1985) 239 (No. XXVIII), (1991a) 268 (Fig. 74).

W 357.   GRAY, Sir John, cousin of Henry.
As used in 1433. Yellowish-brown plaster cast, circ., *ca.* 44 mm.
A shield, *couché*: a lion rampant within a bordure engrailed, GREY of HEYTON. Crest: a ram's head and neck. Supporters: two winged dragons, collared and chained.
: Sigillum : iohan.... g....   **(Bl.)**
Acc. No: 92.170H.
D: Siddons (1985) 239-40.

W 358.   Gruffydd (or Griffin) Maredudd.
Mid-14th cent. Dark blue silicon rubber, circ., 25 mm.
Device indistinct, but perhaps a five-rayed sun with a small star between each ray. Legend indistinct, but possibly:
+ S' GRI : MER.........   **(Lom.)**
From a matrix found by Mr K Evans of Mathern, Gwent, in November 1988, at NGR, ST : 512925.
Acc. No: 92.171H/1.

W 359.   *Another Impression.* White silicon rubber.

W 360.   HANMER, John *or* Jenkin, of Hanmer, Co. Flint.
As used in 1404. Yellowish-brown plaster cast, circ., 28 mm.
A shield, *couché*: two lions passant guardant in pale. Crest: on a helm in profile, a lion sejant guardant. Branches on either side of the helmet.
Seel . Jehan *æ* ....mer   **(Bl.)**
Acc. No: 92.172H.
D: Siddons (1981) 539 No. IX), (1991a) 269 (Fig. 75).

W 361.   Hywel ap William.
See D 35 *supra*. Red wax, circ., 42 mm.
Acc. No: 67.155.

W 362.   *Another Impression.* (Acc. No: 92.173H). Dark-green plasticine.

W 363.   Ieuan Griffin.
As used in 1389. Yellowish-brown plaster cast, circ., 43 mm.
A tree eradicated, from which is hung on the left side a shield defaced. On right side, a crouching lion.
S' IE.......N....   **(Lom.)**
Acc. No: 92.174H.
D: Siddons (1981) 538 (No. VIII).

W 364.   *?*I.R. White silicon rubber, oval, 12 x 11 mm.
See D 33. Acc. No: 92.163H.

W 365.   Ieuan Wyn.
As used in 1373. Yellowish-brown plaster cast, circ., 25 mm.
A shield, *couché:* quarterly, in each quarter a lion rampant; over all a
bendlet. Crest: on a helmet in profile, a wolf's head. Supporters: *dext.* a
lion guardant, *sin.* a wolf.
SEEL IE.an W..   **(Late Lom.)**
Acc. No: 92.175H.
D: Siddons (1981) 542-3 (No. XVIII), (1991a) 284-5 (Figs. 89-90).

W 366.   Iorwerth Du.
Ca. 1280-1325. Red wax, circ., 27 mm.
Three shoots (*poss.* heads of corn) joined at centre point.
S' : IORVERth : DV   **(Lom.)**
From a matrix found in the Wepre area (between Shotton and
Connah's Quay, Clwyd), by a member of the Mold Historical Research
Society in 1990. (One Iorwerth du ap Llywelyn was a witness to a deed
at Whitford in 1327: *Clwyd (Hawarden) R.O. D/NA/245*).
Acc. No: 92.176H/1.

W 367.   *Another Impression.* (Acc. No: 92.176H/2). Red wax.

W 368.   Ithel ap Bleddyn.
Late 14th cent. Buff plaster cast, circ., 25 mm.
A shield, *couché:* Per pale two lions rampant addorsed, their tails
intertwined. Crest: on a helm, a human head between two *humogau* (a
kind of medieval lacrosse stick). In field, *dext.* two pierced cinquefoil
roses slipped; *sin.* one of the same. All within a carved and cusped
panel.
Sigillu : Ithel : ap : Bledyn   **(Bl.)**
An official of this name was Escheator of Flint about 1357. This
impression was presented by the Carmarthenshire Antiquarian Society.
Acc. No: 23.89/5.   BM 6859.
D: Arch. Camb. 1850/33; Tonnochy (1952) No. 340; Williams (1982) 12
(No. 19); Siddons (1991a) 235-6 (Fig. 44).

W 369.   *Another Impression.* (Acc. No: 92.177H). Red wax, en placard.
Presented in 1981 by Piers Langholt to the Museum of London, which
in turn donated it to the National Museum.

W 370.   Jordan, ...LEL.
? Mid-Late 13th cent. Red-brown silicon rubber, circ., 28 mm.
See D 38. Acc. No: 92.178H/1.

W 371.   *Another Impression.* Red-brown silicon rubber.
Acc. No: 92.178H/1.

W 372.   *Reverse of matrix.* Red-brown silicon rubber, circ., 28 mm.
Fleur-de-lis ornamentation.
Acc. No: 92.178H/3.

W 373.   Jordan, chaplain.
Ca. 1280-1330. Red-brown silicon rubber, p.o., 31 x 19 mm.
Two birds of prey on either side of a sheaf of corn. Beaded borders.
+ S' IOR · DANI : CAPELLANI :   **(Lom.)**
From the matrix found in excavations at Haverfordwest Priory in 1986,
and now in the custody of Cadw.
Acc. No: 92.177H.

W 374.   LAGELES, Thomas (of Laleston, W. Glam).
Ca. 1200-10. Yellow sulphur cast, circ., 39 mm.
A lion passant reguardant, contourny.
+ SIGILLVM : THOME : LAGLES :   **(Lom.)**
Acc. No: 25.384
E: NLW, Penrice and Margam Ch. 2008, *cf.* 2009 (both un-dated).

W 375.   Lleision ap Morgan, Lord of Afan, West Glam.
Second Seal.
As used *ca.* 1215. Yellow sulphur cast, oval (pointed at top), 40 x 38 mm.
Lleision in armour, riding on a horse galloping to the right; his right
arm extended with sword raised aloft.

+ SIGILL' LEISAN FIL' MORGANI   **(Lom.)**
Acc. No: 25.384.   *Cf.* BM 5980.
E: NLW, Penrice and Margam Ch. 109, 110a, 2027, 2030, 2031 (all undated); for his circular equestrian seal, see: BL, Harl. Ch. 75 C.35 (of
ca. 1220); NLW, Penrice and Margam Ch. 106 (un-dated), 107 and
108 (both of 1213); 149 (used in 1247 by his nephew); for a variant
non-heraldic seal, see: BL, Harl. Ch. 75 C.34 (of *ca.* 1220); NLW,
Penrice and Margam Ch. 110b, 111, 112 (all un-dated).
D: Arch. Camb. 1867/3-4; Clark III (1910) 930 (*cf.* II, 304); Birch (1897)
210, 226; Siddons (1984) 300 (No. IV/1); *for his circular seal, see:*
Siddons (1984) 300 (No. IV/2); Williams (1982) 22 (No. 43); *for his
non-heraldic seal, see:* Williams (1982) 22 (No. 45).

W 376.   LUVEL, Elymasu.
? Late 13th cent. Red plaster-cast, p.o., 31 x 21 mm.
Uncertain device: possibly a wolf (*cf.* No. W 377).
·:· S' ELYEMA (?) V LVVEL   **(Lom.)**
From an impression sent (1988) by Mr C Cater, taken from a matrix
found by a member of the Mold Historical Research Society at approx.
NGR: SJ 226643..
Acc. No: 92.180H.

W 377.   LUVEL, Walter (of Llangewydd, W. Glam.).
1202. Yellow sulphur cast, circ., 36 mm.
A little wolf (Fr. *'louve'*), as a rebus on the owner's name, passant to
right.
+ SIGILLVM : WALTERI : LVWEL :   **(Lom.)**
Acc. No: 25.384.
E: NLW, Penrice and Margam Ch. 80 (1202), 1975 (No.2; un-dated),
2058 (un-dated).
D: Clark II (1910) 265; Siddons (1991a) 260, Williams (1982) 14 (No.
29).

W 378.   Madog ap Knaytho, of the land of Afan-Kenfig, West Glam.
Ca. 1220-30. Yellow sulphur cast, p.o., 34 x 29 mm.
A fleur-de-lis.
+ SIGILL' : MADOCI : FILII : KANAITH'   **(Lom.)**
Acc. No: 25.384.
E: NLW, Penrice and Margam Ch. 1973 (un-dated); for a variant seal,
see: Ch. 1962 (No. 2; un-dated).
D: Clark VI (1910) 2300; Williams (1982) 15 (No. 33).

W 379.   Madog ap Madog.
Ca. 1300. Red wax, circ., 29 mm.
A sun or star of eight rays. (The initial **S** of the legend is reversed).
+ S' MADOCI F' MADOCI   **(Lom.)**
From a lead matrix found in 1988 by Mr C. Cater near Borras Hall,
Wrexham, Clwyd, in whose possession it remains. (One Madog Duy vap
Madog vap Adam, had property at Gresford in 1320: *Clwyd (Hawarden)
R.O. D/PT/178;* one Madog Vaghan ap Madog ap Thomas had land in
Hope *ca.* 1343: *D/PT/404 and 407*).
Acc. No: 92.181H/1.

W 380.   *Another Impression.* (Acc. No: 92.181H/2)   Red silicon rubber.

W 381.   MALHERBE, William.
? *Ca.* 1270-1300. Pale green plasticine, circ., 22 mm.
See D 34. Acc. No: 92.182H.

W 382.   Matthew of ....
As used in 1305. Yellow sulphur cast, hexagonal, 19 x 19 mm.
The *Agnus Dei,* with banner.
+ S' MATHEI · DE ....   **Lom.)**
Seal probably used by Robert de Cantelo.
Acc. No: 92.183H.
E: NLW, Penrice and Margam Ch. 191 (2nd seal).
D: Clark III (1910) 987; Williams (1989) 70 (No. 312).

W 383.   MORTIMER, Roger de; Lord of Wigmore and Maelienydd.
As used in 1250. Yellow-green sulphur cast, circ., 45 mm.

A shield: barry of six, on a chief two pallets between two gyrons, MORTIMER, over all an inescutcheon.
+ SIGILLVM : ROGERI : DE : MORTVOMARI   **(Lom.)**
Acc. No: 25.384.   BM 11,966.
D: Boutell (1905) 65, 173.

W 384.   **? NE(VE)LA, Stephen.**
? Ca. 1310-20. Dark blue silicon rubber, circ., 19 mm.
A lion passant, to right.
+ S! STEFANI NE..LA   **(Lom.)**
From a bronze matrix found in top-soil near Ewenny, S. Glam., at presumed site of Ewenny Fair, by Mr S Sell, in 1988. (Site No. 1812M, Find 047).
Acc. No: 92.184H/1.

W 385.   *Another Impression.* (Acc. No: 92.184H/2). Cream plaster cast.

W 386.   *A Replica Die* of same. (Acc.No: 92.184H/3). Dark-blue silicon rubber.

W 387.   **NOR...E., Florence.**
Late 13th cent. Red silicon rubber, p.o., 35 x 25 mm.
A double quatrefoil, with an estoile above and a crescent below.
+ S' FLORANCE NOR...?   **(Lom.)**
From the matrix found (in 1990) by Monmouth Archaeological Society in the fill of a defensive ditch back-filled in the late-thirteenth century, at 22-24 Monnow St., Monmouth. Monmouth Priory had a secondary dedication to St. Florent, and this may have influenced the choice of Christian name. The interpretation of the surname is open to question.
Acc. No: 92.185H.
D: Monm. Antiq. VIII (1992) 29 .

W 388.   **Philip ab Ieuan.**
? Early 14th cent. Red silicon rubber, circ., 25 mm.
A quatrefoil.
S' PHI · AP : IEVAN :   **(Lom.)**
From the lead matrix (now deposited in Torfaen Museum, Gwent) found by Mr R. Langley of Pontypool, nearly one metre deep below the water-line in Llandegfedd Reservoir at NGR 325005. There is a possibility that the seal was re-deposited from another part of the locality during the construction of the reservoir, and so the find-spot may not be its ultimate provenance. (One Philip Ieuan was active (in 1321-22) in a riot at Goldcliff Priory, and was one of several men to take the prior captive to Usk Castle.
Acc. No: 92.186H.
D: Williams and Hudson (1990) 57-8 (No. 10); *Cf.* Rees (1975) 103.

W 389.   **REDVNE, Iadda.**
? Late 13th cent. Red silicon rubber, circ., 15 mm.
A barbed star of six rays.
· S' IADA REDVNE   **(Lom.)** *(? for SI' ADA)*
From a matrix brought in by Mr S. Sell (Glamorgan-Gwent Arch. Trust), and found by Mr Chris Hughes, Bank Fm., Scurlage, W. Glam.
Acc. No: 92.187H/1.

W 390.   *Another Impression.* (Acc. No: 92.187H/2). Red silicon rubber.

W 391.   **Robert fitz Maurice.**
Ca. 1270-1320. Cream plaster cast, circ., 23 mm.
A quatrefoil.
·:· S' · ROB'TI · FIL' · MAVR'   **(Lom.)**
From a lead matrix in the collections of Tenby Museum, Dyfed, and found by the late Mr Michael Waugh, possibly in the Penally Hill area. The name of the seal's owner may suggest some-one of Anglo-Norman stock.
Acc. No: 189H/1.

W 392.   *Another Impression.* (Acc. No: 92.189H/2). White plaster cast.

W 393.   *Another Impression.* (Acc. No: 92.189H/3). Orange-red silicon rubber.

W 394.   *Another Impression.* (Acc. No: 92.189H/4). Dark-blue silicon rubber.

W 395.   *Another Impression.* (Acc. No: 92.189H/5). Dark-blue silicon rubber.

W 396.   **Robert fitz Thomas.**
? Early 14th cent. Red wax, circ., 28 mm.
A cross moline, between four decorative stops.
+ : S : ROBERTI : F : ThOM   **(Mostly Lom.)**
This is the *reverse* of W 408 *infra*, which see for notes.
Acc. No: 92.190H/1.
D: Williams (1982a) 139 (Pl. XVII).

W 397.   *Another Impression.* (Acc. No: 190H/2). Red wax.

W 398.   **R............. .**
? 16th cent. or earlier. Red silicon rubber, hexagonal, 14 x 10 mm.
A capital letter: **R**, between foliage.
From a signet ring found at Llanmadog, Gower, West Glam.
Acc. No: 92.191H.

W 399.   **ROTHELANE, William, probably of Rhuddlan, Clwyd.**
As used in 1426. Yellowish-brown plaster cast, circ., 29 mm.
A shield, *couché: ?* a lion passant, and a chief. Crest: on a helmet and mantling, indistinct (perhaps a griffin's head).
wylliame ...hlane   **(Bl.)**
Acc. No: 92.188H/1.
D: Siddons (1981) 541 (No. XIV).

W 400.   *Another Impression.* (Acc. No: 92.188H/2). Yellowish-brown plaster cast.

W 401.   **SCURLAGE, Richard (of Scurlagiscastle and Burry, W. Glam.).**
As used in 1361. Yellow sulphur cast, circ., 23 mm.
A shield: three bars; between two slipped flowers, and within a cusped gothic-type panel.
.. SIGILLVM : RICARDI SCVRLAG   **(Lom.)**
Acc. No: 25.384.
E: NLW, Penrice and Margam Ch. 398 (1361).
D: Clark IV (1910) 1307, Siddons (1991a) 261 (Fig. 64).

W 402.   **SENSIS, Peter.**
Ca. 1300. Cream plaster cast, circ., 19 mm.
A palm tree, and beneath its branches: *dext.* a sun, *sin.* a moon. The legend is debatable; one interpretation is:
* S' PETRVS : SENSIS   **(Lom.)**
assuming the **T** and **R** to be conjoined; could it refer to 'Peter of Sens'; another reading is: **SAPERO SENSIS**, but is less likely.
From a bronze matrix found by G. Gregory and reported by S Sell (Glamorgan-Gwent Arch. Trust) at the assumed location of Ewenny Fair, Mid-Glam., (Site No. 1812M, Find No. 020).
Acc. No: 92.192H/1.

W 403.   *Another Impression.* (Acc. No: 92.192H/2). Dark-blue silicon rubber.

W 404.   *Another Impression.* (Acc. No: 92.192H/3). Dark-blue silicon rubber.

W 405.   **STURMI, Geoffrey; of Stormy and Morgan, W. Glam.**
Ca. 1170. Yellow sulphur cast, p.o., 68 x 44 mm.
Geoffrey walking to right, in tunic with helmet, blowing a horn and holding a lance.

+ SIGILLVM · GALFRID... (ST)VRMI .   **(Late Rom.)**
Acc. No: 25.384.
E: NLW, Penrice and Margam Ch. 1978-9 (before 1207).
D: Clark I (1910) 150-1; Williams (1982) 14 (No. 26).

W 406.   **SULLY, Reymund de; of Sully, S. Glam.**
As used in 1230. Yellow sulphur cast (chipped), circ., 28 mm.
A shield: three bars, SULLY.
  + SIGILL' REIMVNDI · DE · S.....   **(Lom.)**
Acc. No: 25.384.   BM 13,773.
E: BL, Harl. Ch. 75 A.35 (1230; indistinct).
D: Clark II (1910) 472; Birch (1897) 241.

W 407.   **SUTTHUNE, Henry de (of Sutton, S. Glam.).**
As used *ca.* 1290. Yellow sulphur cast, circ., 29 mm.
A stag at speed, to the right.
+ S' HENRICI · DE · SVTTONE   **(Lom.)**
Acc. No: 25.384.
E: NLW, Penrice and Margam Ch. 119 (un-dated).
D: Clark III (1910) 870; Birch (1897) 126; Williams (1982) 14 (No. 27).

W 408.   **Thomas fitz Baldwin.**
? Early 14th cent. Red wax, circ., 28 mm.
An uncertain device, variously interpreted as a letter **M** (for Mary), as a pair of hands (at prayer), as a pair of wings, or an open ear of corn.
+ : S : ThOME : F : BALd :   **(Lom. mostly)**
This is an impression from the obverse of a stone matrix (the property of Mr and Mrs Kinsey, Churchstoke), presumably found in that area some time ago. The matrix appears to be a 'family seal', one perhaps used by both father and son, jointly or consecutively; e.g. on the father's entering into a property purchase or sale with his heir's consent, or, alternatively, his father's seal which the son, on his sire's death, employed for reasons of sentiment or convenience, engraving his name and device on the reverse. Thus, the obverse is the seal of Thomas, son of Baldwin; the reverse *(No. W 396)* is that of Robert, Thomas's son. No original impressions are as yet known.
Acc. No: 92.193H/1.
D: Williams (1982a) 139 (Pl. XVII).

W 409.   *Another Impression.* (Acc. No: 92.193H/2). Red wax.

W 410.   **Thomas ap William.**
? Early 14th cent. Cream plaster cast, circ., 22 mm.
A cross moline.
+ S' THOME · FILI · WILLI   **(Lom.)**
From a lead matrix found in a garden in Haverfordwest.
Acc. No: 80.57H.

W 411.   *Another Impression.* (Acc. No: 92.194H/1). Olive-green plasticine.

W 412.   *Reverse of matrix.* Cream plaster cast, circ., 22 mm.
Shows a fleur-de-lis by way of ornamentation, and also the mark of the handle.
Acc. No: 80.57H.

W 413.   *Another Impression.* (Acc. No: 92.194H/2). Grey plasticine.

W 414.   **TUDOR, Jasper; Earl of Pembroke.**
Reverse only.
As used in 1459. Greenish yellow sulphur cast, circ., 84 mm.
A shield, held by an angel with wings expanded: quarterly, 1. and 4. FRANCE (Modern), 2. and 3. ENGLAND, within a bordure charged

with fourteen martlets for Jasper Tudor; crest: wanting; supporters: two wolves sejeant ducally gorged and chained. Roses separate the words of the legend:
+ Sig..... domini : jasparis : comitis : penbrochie   **(Bl.)**
Acc. No: 25.384.   BM 6483 R.
E: BL, Sloane Ch. XXXII, 20 (1459).
    For original impressions of his later seal as Duke of Bedford and Lord of Abergavenny, see: Glam. Archives D/D. Xio, 1/1 (Und.); Gwent R.O. D.2.34 (1492); NLW, Badm. MS 1447 (1493); and casts: BL, LXXX, 77, 78; *for his privy seal,* see: PRO II, 107 (No. P 2152, of 1457).
D: Arch. LXXXIX, 12, Pl. X.b., Boutelle (1958) 175; for the later seal, see: Siddons VII (1991) 52 (No. 57/1); *for his seal as Lord of Abergavenny:* ibid. 52 (No. 57/2).

W 415.   **Walter ap Reginald.**
13th cent. Red wax, circ., 25 mm.
A lion tricoporate; (a lion with three bodies uniting in a common head); beaded borders.
S' WALTERI : FIL' : REGINALDI :   **(Lom.)**
Acc. No: 33.417/1.
From the matrix found (*?* *ca.* 1840) in the ford just below the bridge across the Wye at Hay-on-Wye, Powys; and brought in by the Rev. Canon W.E.T. Morgan of Cusop (Sept. 1933).

W 416.   **William Cogh (junior) of Kenfig, Mid-Glam.**
As used *ca.* 1267 (or before). Yellow sulphur cast, oval -pointed at base, 31 x 24 mm.
An inverted fleur-de-lis.
+ S' WILELMI · COGH'   **(Lom.)**
Acc. No: 25.384.
E: NLW, Penrice and Margam Ch. 184 (un-dated).
D: Birch (1897) 191-2; Clark II (1910) 469.

W 417.   **William David.**
As used in 1375-81. Yellowish-brown plaster cast, circ., 20 mm.
A shield: bendy, a chief charged with *?* lozenges; indistinct.
ELM.... DAVD...   **(Lom.)**
Acc. No: 92.195H.
D: Siddons (1985) 238 (No. XXIV, 1/2); (William may not have been a Welshman).

W 418.   **William James.**
As used in 1436. Yellowish-brown plaster cast, circ., *ca.* 26 mm.
A shield: on a fess between three stags passant, a leopard's face (indistinct).
S : Guillame ⟨ James   **(Bl.)**
Acc. No: 92.196H.
D: Siddons (1981) 539 (No. X); (William may not have been a Welshman).

W 419.   **W.............** Red wax, circ., 12 mm.
See D 37. Acc. No: 31.78/9.

W 420.   **YOUNG, Gruffydd, D.Cn.L; kinsman and chancellor of Owain Glyn Dŵr; later bishop of Bangor, of Ross (Scotland), and of Hippo.**
As used in 1404. Yellowish-brown plaster cast, circ., 24 mm.
A shield: a lion rampant (*?* guardant), in a bordure engrailed.
+ S! Griffin. ..nge decretoru : doctoris   **(Bl.)**
Acc. No: 92.198H.
D: Siddons (1981) 544 (No. XXI).

NON-ATTRIBUTABLE PERSONAL SEALS (MEDIEVAL)

W 421.   b. o. f.
? 14th-15th cent. White silicon rubber, hexagonal, 17 x 15 mm.
See D 44. Acc. No: 25.384.

W 422.   *Another Impression.* (Acc. No: 92.199H). Red wax.

W 423.   *?* Late 13th cent. Red plasticine, circ., 18 mm.
A one-masted sailing ship.
? S' VAWITRIV.   **(Lom.)**
From a matrix found by Mark Cooke of Bridgend, north of the A 48
road, at NGR: SS 97387562.
Acc. No: 88.167H.

W 424.   *Another Impression.* (Acc. No: 92.200H). Red plasticine.

W 425.   *Ca.* 1300. Blue silicon rubber, circ., 18 mm.
Two birds seemingly at rest. The upper (perhaps a crow or hawk) holds
in its beak a portion of food (possibly a smaller bird or rodent); it
appears to be perched, its claws gripping a twig or branch; the bird
beneath is lifting up its head, expectantly may-be, but its beak is closed.
• ALAS IE SV PRIS ⁀   **(Lom.)**
(*'Alas, je su pris'* : *'Alas, I am captured'*)
From the latten matrix found during excavations at Greyfriars,
Carmarthen, led by Mr T. James (1986; CGF 83/3486; Context 340)
Acc. No: 92.201H/1.
E: Cf. D 41 above.
D: Cf. Antiq. Jnl. LVII (1977) Pt. 2, 324-329, for examples of similar
      image and legend.

W 426.   *Another Impression.* (Acc. No: 92.210H/2). White silicon
rubber.

W 427.   *Another Impression.* (Acc. No: 92.201H/3). Blue silicon rubber.

W 428.   *?* Early 14th cent. White silicon rubber, circ., 16 mm.
See D 41. (The same legend with variant device).
Acc. No: 83.126H.

W 429.   *Another Impression.* (Acc. No: 92.202H). Blue silicon rubber.

W 430.   *Ca.* 1300. Dark blue silicon rubber, circ., 18 mm.
See D 40. Acc. No: 92.203H.

W 431.   *?* Early 14th cent. Blue silicon rubber, circ., 18 mm.
A dragon to the right. Beaded border.
? SIGIL' ROUAR(?)INS   **(Lom.)**
Found by Mr K Evans of Mathern, Gwent.
Acc. No: 92.204H.

W 432.   *? Ca.* 1300. White plaster cast, circ., 19 mm.
An eagle displayed. Beaded border. Legend mostly indecipherable.
• ....IS⁀⁀   **(Lom.)**
From a corroded bronze matrix deposited in Tenby Museum (1989) by
the late Mr M Waugh, and perhaps found in the Penally Hill area.
Acc. No: 92.205H/1.

W 433.   *Another Impression.* (Acc. No: 92.205H/2). Pale-blue silicon
rubber.

W 434.   *Another Impression.* (Acc. No: 92.205H/3). Red-brown
plasticine.

W 435.   *Another Impression.* (Acc. No: 92.205H/4). Blue silicon rubber.

W 436.   *Replica Die* of same. (Acc. No: 92.205H/5). Blue silicon rubber.

W 437.   *?* 16th cent. Red wax, oval, 15 x 14 mm.
A lion passant, double-queued.
From a brass matrix found in early 1987 by Llantrithyd Place (South
Glam.).
Acc. No: 87.36H.

W 438.   *Ca.* 1270-1310. White silicon rubber, circ., 16 mm.
A squirrel with a nut in its paws; beaded borders.
•   I CRAKE NOTIS   **(Lom.)**
(*ME: 'I crack nuts'*)
From a bronze seal matrix (now in Newport Museum) found by Mr K.L.
Morgan in the Llantarnam area of Gwent (at NGR 310929) on a site
being prepared for industrial development.
Acc. No: 92.206H.
D: Williams and Hudson (1990) 55, 57-8 (Nos. 7-9); *for similar seals, see:*
      Tonnochy (1952) No. 754; Wise (1985) 49 (Fig. 29); *Arch. Jnl.* XII,
      296, as also D 42 and W 439.

W 439.   13th-Early 14th cent. Red wax, circ., 16 mm.
See D 42. Acc. No: 31.78/7.

W 440.   Early 14th cent. Red wax, circ., 17 mm.
A cock and a hare looking into a cauldron. Beaded borders.
HER IS NA MARE BOTE COK POT HARE   **(Lom.)**
(*'Here is no more than cock, pot, hare'*)
Impression from a copper seal found at Caerleon, Gwent.
Acc. No: 25.384
D: Lee (1862) 119, Pl. XLVII-12.

W 441.   *?* Early 14th cent. Red wax, oval, 15 x 13 mm.
With D 43 *supra.* Acc. No: 24.520

W 442.   Love-seal.
Ca. 1300-30. Red wax (cracked) oval, 20 x 17 mm.
Set within an engraved onyx, a figure walking to left, *?* Satyr, or an
huntsman, holding a *?* lagobolon in left hand, a dish on the right
shoulder.
IE SVI SEL : DE : AMVR : LEL   **(Lom.)**
(*'Je suis seal d'amour leal'* : *'I am the seal of love loyal'*)
From a silver matrix found *?* in Gwent.
Acc. No: 31.78/5.
D: Notes and Queries, 2nd Ser. VI, 175; *for another example found in Gwent,*
      see: *Gentl. Mag.* LXXXI, 116, 617.
E: Such seals were tokens of good will, fidelity or love. Many other seals
      bore this legend, though not this device. They include, to name but
      a few instances:
      BL, Harl. Ch. 46.F.54 (1335), Harl. Chs. 47.G.47., 75.D.12., 83 G. 54
      (all undated); Detached Seal XLVII, 1144 (ascribed to 1292);
      Durham Seals (Cathedral) Misc. 3811, 4044/9, 4078/u (of 1324-6);
      see *Arch. Ael.* 3rd Ser. VII, 289, for their description. For numerous
      other references, see NMW, Card Index of Seals (at the former W
      314).

W 443.   Love-seal.
13th cent. Grey silicon rubber, p.o., 39 x 28 mm.
See D 39. Acc. No: 86.40.

W 444.   *Another Impression.* (Acc. No: 92.207H). Red wax.

W 445.   Trinity Star.
Early 14th cent. Blue silicon rubber, circ., 15 mm.
A Star of David, otherwise called the Trinity Star, lightly ornamented by
tracery or foliage. Within the centre of the star is a crouching animal,
facing front and probably dormant; it has a furry coat or mane, and a
quite long tail; it is perhaps intended for a lion at rest, though it might

be a squirrel or fox. It is possible that initials occur in field between the points of the Star. (No legend).

From the latten matrix found in excavations, led by Mr T. James, at Greyfriars, Carmarthen; (CGF 84/3452; Context 314).

Acc. No: 92.208H/1.

D: Cf. Arch. Cant. CVIII (1990) 291 (Fig. 4/3) for a similar seal found in Cobham Park, Kent; Norfolk Arch. XXXIX (1985) 220 (Pl. V) for another found at Thetford, Norfolk.

W 446. *Another Impression.* (Acc. No: 92.208H/2).Blue silicon rubber.

W 447. Merchant's Mark.
- - -   Red wax (cracked), oval, 16 x 14 mm.

Device: within a beaded border.

Impression from a signet ring found in soil at Llantwit, S. Glam., and now held in the British Museum (*Reg. No: 1852, 5-21,2*).

Acc. No: 35.683.

D: Cherry and Redknap (1991) 124.

W 448. *Another Impression.* (Acc. No: 92.209H). Red wax.

PERSONAL SEALS (MODERN)

W 449. AMBROSE, William.
19th cent. Red wax, oblong, 16 x 14 mm.
See D 66. Acc. No: 66.459.

W 450. *Another face* from the same matrix. Red wax, oblong, 17 x 14 mm.
See D 67. Acc. No: 66.459.

W 451. *Another seal,* with same motto. Red wax, rounded oblong, 17 x 14 mm.
See D 68. Acc. No: 66.459 (WFM).

W 452. *Another seal.* Red wax, rounded oblong, 17 x 13 mm.
See D 69. Acc. No: 66.459 (WFM).

W 453. B., O.H. Red wax, oval, 21 x 15 mm.
See D 70. Acc. No: 58.318 (WFM).

W 454. DAVIES, Dr. Joseph (of Bedwas, Gwent).
1793-1873. Red wax, circ., 19 mm.
Monogram of **J.D.**
MILDY AND FIRMLY   (Caps.)
Acc. No: 38.601/10 (WFM)

W 455. HERBERT, Thomas (of White Friars, Cardiff).
1735. Red wax, oval, *Ca.* 15 x 12 mm.
Indistinct, but seemingly equestrian to right.
Acc. No: 25.384.

W 456. I.H.T.
? 19th cent. Red wax, shield-shaped, 12 x 10 mm.
See D 89. Acc. No: 68.234/57.

W 457. KEMEYS-TYNTE, Charles.
1779. Red wax, oval, 23 x 21 mm.
A shield: a lion couchant guardant between six crosses crosslet; crest: an escallop (perhaps only decorative as there is no wreath). The first cross is obscured by a canton which may have borne the arms of KEMEYS : three pheons. Beaded borders, no motto.
D: Cf. Arch. Camb. 1918/118. Acc. No: 92.210H.

W 458. MANSEL, Sir Edward; Sheriff of Glamorgan (1575).
Ca. 1575-85. Yellow sulphur cast (broken), oval, 48 x 44 mm.
A shield: quarterly of ten: 1. a chevron between three maunches, MANSEL; 2. three bars, SCURLAGE; 3. a carbuncle, PENARD or PENNARDD; 4. three mullets, SCURLAGE or STACKPOLE; 5. per pale indented, PENRICE; 6. crusily a lion rampant (? de BRAOSE); 7. two lions passant guardant, DELAMERE; 8. a tower triple-towered (variant

of CYDIFOR ap DINAWAL, for JENKIN ap RHYS); 9. Ermine, a cross botonny or ? flory, semée of garbs (KYNE or KYME of Kent); 10. on a fess between two chevrons, ? three eagles displayed. Crest: a flame of fire.

· SIGILLVM · EDWARDI · M......   (Ren.)
Acc. No: 25.384.

D: Arch. Camb. 1864/124 (where 'Nearly every main quartering represents a manor in (*the Mansel's*) own county); Arch. Camb. 1867/209; Siddons, M.P., personal correspondence (8/92).

W 459. MANSEL, Sir Edward, of Margam.
Ca. 1703-06. Red wax (broken), oval, *ca.* 22 x 17 mm.
A shield: a chevron between three maunches, MANSEL; overall an inescutcheon, a hand (for baronetcy); crest: an eagle rising.
Acc. No: 92.211H/1.
E: NLW, Penrice and Margam Ch. 762 (1702), 765 (1705).

W 460. *Another Impression.* (Acc. No: 92.211H/2). Red wax (fragmentary).

W 461. MANSEL, Sir Thomas; Sheriff of Glamorgan (1701).
Ca. 1701-11. Red wax (cracked), oval, 32 x 29 mm.
A shield: quarterly, 1. a chevron between three maunches, MANSEL; 2. three bars, SCURLAGE; 3. crusily a lion rampant, de BRAOSE; 4. two lions passant quardant, DELAMERE; overall an inescutcheon: a hand (for baronetcy).
SI · THOMÆ · MANSEL · MILET · BARONETI · ·   (Ren.)
Acc. No: 92.212H.
E: BL, Detached Seal LXXXVII.   BM 11,574.

W 462. PRICE, Dr. William (of Llantrisant, Mid.-Glam.).
1800-93. Red wax, oblong, 14 x 12 mm.
See D 96 supra. Acc. No: 50.5/8 (WFM).

W 463. *Another Seal.* Red wax, oblong, 18 x 14 mm.
Out of a mural crown, a lion rampant reguardant.
Acc. No: 50.5/9 (WFM).

W 464. RACKETT, Thomas; (father of the Revd. T. Rackett, F.R.S., F.S.A., F.L.A).
1750. Red wax, oval, 24 x 20 mm.
A shield: a ragged staff upright between three fleurs-de-lis, in chief a ragged staff (for RACKETT) lying horizontal; crest: an eagle displayed.
Acc. No: 25.384.

W 465. WALDRON, James.
Mid-19th cent. Red wax, oval, 25 x 19 mm.
See D 101. Acc. No: 32.572/5 (WFM).

NON-ATTRIBUTABLE SEALS

W 466.   - - Red wax, oval, 6 x 4 mm.
A lion passant, to the right.
From a signet ring found in the parish of Pennant, N. Wales.
Acc. No: 92.213H.

W 467.   1582. Red wax, oval, 20 x 18 mm.
See D 105. Acc. No: 44.16.

W 468.   (? Merchant's Mark).
17th cent. Red wax, oval, 11 x 10 mm.
See D 106 above. Acc. No: 31.78/9.

W 469.   (? Bardic Seal).
19th cent. Red wax, circ., 15 mm.
A wild goat.
Acc. No: 50.5/10 (WFM).

W 470.   *Another Impression.* Red wax.
Acc. No: 50.5/11 (WFM).

W 471.   (? Bardic Seal).
19th cent. Red wax, circ., 12 mm.
A sheep. Acc. No: 50.5/12 (WFM).

W 472. 19th cent. White silicon rubber, rounded oblong, 15 x 12 mm.
See D 111. Acc. No: 79.95H.

W 473.   ? 18th-19th cent. Dark blue silicon rubber, circ., 18 mm.
Over the motto: **FREINDSHIP** *(sic)* **AND LOVE**, a lower arm supporting a
? cockerel to left, between two cherubs holding aloft a crown.
Taken from a copper alloy fob-seal found by Mr Cooke of Bridgend in
July 1988 west of Cowbridge (NGR: SS 975754).
Acc. No: 92.214H.

W 474.   As used in 1591. Red wax, oval, 10 x 9 mm.
Uncertain device; perhaps a plant with flowers.
From Llanrhystyd, Dyfed. Acc. No: 92.215H/1.

W 475.   *Another Impression.* (Acc. No: 92.215H/2). Red wax.

W 476.   *Another Impression.* (Acc. No: 92.215H/3). Red wax.

-   -   -   -   -

Small collections of personal seals occur, inter alia, in: NLW, Donald Jones
Deeds, Box 1: Bdle. 1 (of West Glamorgan area; including the seal of
Kingsmill Mackworth, 1741); NLW, Glansevern Deeds 13669 (mostly
seals of Montgomeryshire families; including the seals of Owen Owen,
sheriff in 1766; Viscount Clive, and A.D. Owen of Glansevern); and in
the Dept. of Maps and Prints, including impressions of the Fraternity of
the Holy Trinity, Cardiff.

SEAL MOULDS

W 477.   Replica of a stone block (cut in oolitic limestone) seemingly
for casting the *reverse* side of seal matrices; of date perhaps about 1270-
1340. The block makes provision for a circular seal, and for three oval
dies - two of them having a handle for suspension. All fit in well within
the general pattern of the lesser personal seal dies of the period.
Dimensions:
Stone block: 70 mm. x 50 mm. x 30 mm.
Circular mould: 25 mm. diameter; 6 mm. depth for suspension loop.
Pointed Oval moulds: 47 x 19 mm., 7 mm. depth for loop.
38 x 17 mm., 7 mm. depth for loop.
30 x 18 mm.
D: Mein (1992) 24-8. Acc. No: 92.216H. (found at Trostrey, Gwent).

WYNNE OF PENIARTH COLLECTION

A collection of original seal impressions.
(Acc. No: 21.24).

**W 478.   Courts of Great Sessions: Judicial Seal for the Counties of
Montgomery, Denbigh and Flint.**
Temp. Elizabeth I (1558-1603). Dark-green wax, circ., 69 mm.

Obverse: Equestrian (image faded).
............ANGLIE . FR................   **(Ren.)**

Reverse: Armorial (image faded).
.........**MERI DENBIGH**...............   **(Ren.)**

Personal Seals:

W 479.   Late 17th cent.-early 18th cent. Dark-red wax, o., 17 x 15 mm.
A lion rampant standing upon a rock, between the letters (arranged
borderwise) **O** and **PVC.** Beaded border.

W 480.   ? 17th cent. Cream wax, circ., 14 mm.
A cross-hatch.

W 481.   17th-18th cent. Red wax, circ., 13 mm.
A quadruped with greyhound featured head, standing on grass.

W 482. 17th-18th cent. Red wax, circ., 11 mm.
A bird facing left.

W 483. Late 17th-early 18th cent. Red wax, o., 17 x 15 mm.
The capital letters: **G.S.** within an ornate frame.

W 484. ? Late 17th cent. Red wax, o., 21 x 18 mm.
Venus seated supporting Cupid with her left hand, a spear held by her
right hand; Cupid pointing bow and arrow at her. All between the
capital letters: **T.B.**

W 485. ? 16th-17th cent. Brown wax; two like seals, each circ., 10 mm.
A cross-hatch.
E: A seal of similar design and size occurs in NLW, Peniarth Deeds
(2nd Schedule) 2038 (of 1566).

W 486. ? 16th cent. Brown wax, octagonal, 10 x 10 mm.
An uncertain device, possibly a rudimentary monogram.

W 487. Uncertain date; perhaps 16th-17th cent. Red wax, o.,
15 x 13 mm.
A heart pierced by two feathered arrows, points down.

W 488. ? 16th-17th cent. Red-brown wax, o., 21 x 17 mm.
A shield, quarterly: 1. two bars, in chief ?; 2. 3. and 6. indistinct; 4. a
chevron between three mullets; 5. ? an animal head, in chief two
lozenges.

W 489. ? 17th cent. Ochre wax, circ., 19 mm.
A heart, ensigned with a fleur-de-lis, between the capital letters: **T.M.**

W 490. Of uncertain date. Red-brown wax, circ., 13 mm.
The capital letter: **N.** with a sprig above and below.

W 491. Late 17th-early 18th cent. Red-brown wax, o., 15 x 14 mm.
A ship, with three masts and bowsprit, in full sail.
D: Personal communication of Dr. M. Redknap.

W 492. Griffin ap David
Ca. 1300. Plasticine impression (with Plaster of Paris replica of matrix),
circ., 27mm.
A conventional floral design.
+ **S' GRIFFINI : F. DAVYD**   **(Lom.)**

W 493. Of uncertain date. Red-brown wax, circ., 9 mm.
An uncertain symbol; possibly a merchant's mark.

W 494. Late medieval. Pale-red wax, circ., 14 mm.
The Crucified Christ, below whom two or three suppliant figures.

W 495. ? 16th cent. Two seals: both red-brown wax, circ., 13 mm.
(a). A septfoil, or star of seven broad rays.
(b). The capital letters: **L.G.** with ? a crown above.

W 496. ? 18th cent. Red wax (cracked), circ., 18 mm.
An uncertain figure, possibly standing by a tree.

W 497. ? Late medieval. Red-brown wax, circ., 14 mm.
A blank shield. Border lozenged.

W 498. Of uncertain date. Red-brown wax, o., 19 x 17 mm.
A monogram, including the letters: **T** and **E**; with a sprig above and
below.

GROUP B : PAPAL *BULLAE*

B 1. CLEMENT III; 1187-91.
Obverse. White plaster cast, circ., 40 mm.
Within a beaded border the name of the pontiff:

C L E
MENS
P͡P · I I I ·

Cast from a *bulla* found at Dover Castle. The original was (in 1881) in the possession of the Revd. J. Shrimpton of Cardiff.
Acc. No: 59.381.   BM 21,734 Ø.

B 2.   *Reverse.*
Within a beaded border, and set within beaded frames, *dext.* the head of St Paul, *sin.* that of St Peter, and between them a tall cross paty set on an orb or mound. In field above, the Roman initials:
S' PA S' PE.
Acc. No: 59.381.   BM 21,734 R.

B 3. HONORIUS III; 1216-27.
Obverse. Leaden *bulla*, oval, 36 x 40 mm., 50.0 gms.
As F 1, but inscribed:

HONO
R I V S
· P͡P · I I I ·

Reverse.
As F 2, with a pellet immediately surmounting the cross and within the arc below.
Found by Mr Griffith Hughes (of 11 Castle Tce., Dolwyddelan, Caerns.) about 1875, in the wood at the foot of Uchel-graig, Dolwyddelan Castle, when as a boy he fell from a tree on to a lot of small stones.
Acc. No: 38.422 (Gallery).   BM 21,746.

B 4.   *Another Example* (55.3 gms.).
Found at the site of Abbey Cwmhir, Radnorshire.
Acc. No: 92.61.

B 5.   *Another Example* (worn; 36.5 gms.).
Found at the site of Abbey Cwmhir, and presented by Lt. Col. J.L. Phillips.
Acc. No: 92.61.

B 6. GREGORY IX; 1227-41.
1st or 4th type (1228 or 1237). Lead (imperfect), circ., 36 mm., 36.7 gms.

Obverse.
Beaded border largely missing. The state of the *bulla* does not permit precise identification.

G R E
GORIVS
P͡P · V I I I I ·

Reverse. Usual arrangement; badly worn.
Presented by H.M. Office of Works.
Acc. No: 79.27/2.   BM 21,750 or 21,764.

B 7. GREGORY IX; 1227-41.
2nd type; 1230. Lead (imperfect), oval, *ca.* 45 x 39 mm., 35.4 gms.

Obverse.
As F 1, but inscribed:

G R E
GORIVS
P͡P · V I I I I

Reverse. Usual arrangement.
Given by L.F. Winks, in memory of his father, the Revd. W.E. Winks, F.R.A.S., Hon. Curator of Cardiff Museum, 1876-1914. Of unknown provenance.
Acc. No: 54.484.   BM 21,754.

B 8. ALEXANDER IV; 1254-61.
Later type; 1255- . Lead, circ., 36 mm., 50.9 gms.

Obverse.
Usual arrangement, but inscribed:

A L E
XANDER
· P͡P · I I I I ·

Reverse.
Usual arrangement.
Found during reparation work at Tintern Abbey, and presented by HM Office of Works.
Acc. No: 32.430/4.   BM 21,798.

B 9.   *Another Example* (42.5 gms.).
Found at Abbey Cwmhir, and presented by Lt. Col. J.F. Phillips.
Acc. No: 62.202 (Gallery).

B 10. URBAN IV; 1261-64.
Obverse. Lead (imperfect), orig. circ., 36 mm; 38.6 gms.
As F 1, but inscribed:

V R
BANVS
.... · I I I I ·

Reverse.
Usual arrangement.
Found at Cymer Abbey, Meirionydd, during reparation work, and presented by H.M. Office of Works on behalf of Maj.-Gen. J. Vaughan.
Acc. No: 32.432/2.   BM 21,808.

B 11. GREGORY XI; 1370-78.
Obverse. Lead, circ., 35 mm., 49.6 gms.
As F 1, but inscribed:

G R E
GORIUS
· P͡P · X I ·

Quatrefoils form the stops in the lower line.

Reverse.
Usual arrangement.
Found at Strata Florida Abbey, Ceredigion.
Acc. No: 92.219H   BM 21,886.

B 12. JULIUS II; 1503-13.
Obverse. Lead, circ., 36 mm., 42.2 gms.
As F 1, but inscribed:

· I V ·
LIVS
PAPA
· II ·

Small leaves or scallop shells form the beads of the border.

Reverse.

The heads of SS Paul and Peter, each set in an oval compartment and facing each other, between them a branch of three acorns slipped supporting a long cross paty (incomplete on this impression). Above, to either side of the cross:

S - S
P - P
A - E

The initials of St Paul are lacking on this impression. Borders formed by acorns, in allusion to the pontiff's family name: *Della Rovere*, an oak tree eradicated. The reverse has been cast on this *bulla* upside down in comparison to the obverse.

Bequeathed by Sir C. Thomas-Stanford.

Acc. No: 32.247.   *Cf.* BM 21,978; 21,982.

B 13.   CLEMENT VII; 1523-34.

Obverse. Lead (worn), orig. circ., 40 mm., 54.6 gms.

Badly worn, but inscribed:

C L E
M E N S
· P̄P̄ · V I I ·

Reverse. Badly worn.

Found in the garden of the Bishop's Palace, Llandaff.

Acc. No: 29.91.   *Cf.* BM 21,990.

B 14.   GREGORY XIII; 1572-85.

Obverse. Lead (with segment of cord attached), circ., 35 mms., 40.9 gms.

As F 12, but inscribed:

G R E
G O R I V S
P A P A
X I I I

Reverse.

Apparently from the same matrix used by Gregory XII (1406-15). Within two oval compartments the heads of SS Paul and Peter inclined towards each other. Between them a cross moline; above, in line with the limbs of the cross, the initials:

S S
P P
A E

Presented by H.M. Office of Works.

Acc. No: 79.27/1 (Gallery).   BM 22,007.

- - - - -

Other Papal *Bullae* known to exist in Wales:

Pontiff.	Location and Notes.
Celestine III. (1191-98).	Newport (Gwent) Museum. Found near site of Llantarnam Abbey. *Monm. Antiq.* VI (1990) 56-7; another found in 1992 in a field fronting Llanfaes Church (near Beaumaris, Anglesey) at NGR: SH

603779, and now in the possession of Mr. Peter Corbett, Benllech.

Innocent III. (1198-1216).	NLW, Penrice and Margam Charters 82, 83, 84 (all of 1203).
Gregory IX (1227-41).	Museum of Antiquities, Bangor (detached).
Innocent IV. (1243-54).	NLW, Penrice and Margam Ch. 141 (of 1244); Museum of Antiquities, Banog (detached). *Another example* found by metal detector to west of St Cattwg's Church, Cheriton, Gower; (S. Sell, Glam./Gwent Arch. Trust; letter of 4-12-90). In ownership of N. Phillips and S. Miller, Cheriton. For Innocent's *bulla*, see: *Rev. francaise d'heraldique et de sigillographie* XXI, No. 35 (1969) 4-6.
Alexander IV. (1254-61).	NLW, Penrice and Margam Ch. 171 (of 1260), 173 (1261), 4017 (detached); Newport Museum (detached); all of the pontiff's later type of *bulla*. *Monm. Antiq.* VI (1990) 56-7 (for the Gwent example, also found close to the site of Llantarnam Abbey); Museum of Antiquities, Bangor (detached).
Clement IV. (1265-68).	NLW, Penrice and Margam Ch. 185 (of 1268), 4018 (detached); Carmarthen Museum (detached - found at the site of Netley Abbey, Hants; Acc. No: 1976:3842).
Gregory X. (1271-76).	NLW, Penrice and Margam Ch. 4019 (detached).
Benedict XII. (1334-42).	Carmarthen Museum (detached; Acc. No: 1981:60). Found at site of Carmarthen Priory. *Arch. Camb.* CXXXIV (1985) 142-3; *Arch. in Wales* 19 (1979) 37 (No. 72).
Urban IV. (1378-89).	NLW, Penrice and Margam Ch. 236 (of 1383); Margam Abbey Church (detached).
Boniface IX. 1389-1404).	NLW, Penrice and Margam Ch. 238 (of 1394). Museum of Antiquities, Bangor (detached).
Martin V. (1417-31).	NLW, Penrice and Margam Ch. 245 (of 1423).

The Museum of Antiquities at Bangor also has detached examples of the *bullae* of the following pontiffs:

Sixtus IV (1471-84), Clement VII (1523-34), Paul V (1605-21), Clement XI (1700-21), Clement XII (1730-40), Benedict XIV (1740-58), and Pius IX (1846-78).

(Other examples of alien seals discovered in Wales occur throughout Volumes II and III of this Catalogue*).*

INDEX OF PRINICIPAL MOTIFS

The Plates: unless otherwise stated, the seals are reproduced at actual size.

D1

D3

D2

D4

D7

D10

D8

D12

D9

D13

D5

D14

D15

D17

D20

D21

D22

D18

D23

D24

D25

D26

D28

D29

D19

D27

D30

D31

D32

D33

D34

D35

D36

D37

D38

D39

D40 x 2

D41 x 2

D42 x 2

D43 x 2

D44 x 2

D45

D46 x 0.5

D47 x 0.5

D50

D49

D48

D51

D52

D56

D57

D58

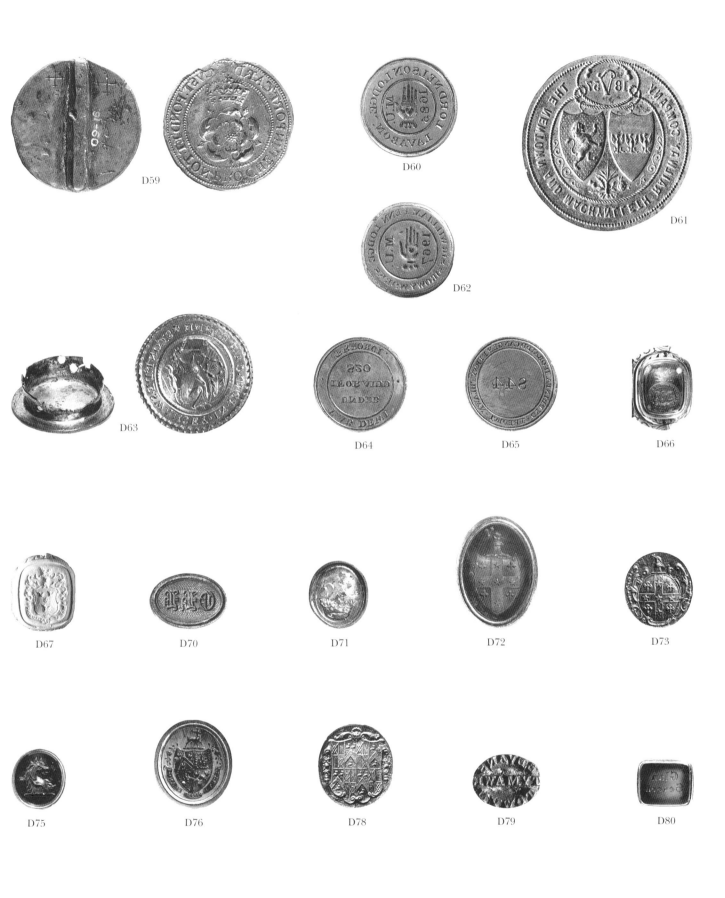

D59

D60

D61

D62

D63

D64

D65

D66

D67

D70

D71

D72

D73

D75

D76

D78

D79

D80

D81

D82

D84

D85

D86

D87

D88

D89

D90

D91

D92

D93

D94

D95

D96

D97

D98

D99

D100

D101

D103

D104

D105

D106

D107

D108

D109

D110

D111

D112

D113

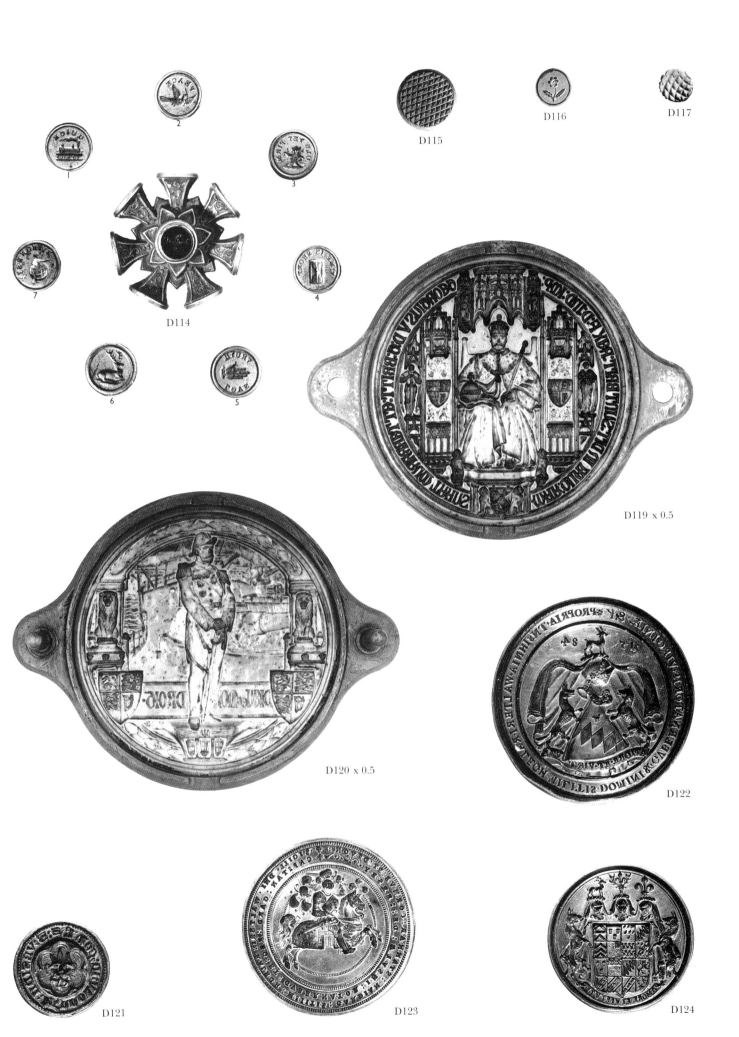

D115

D116

D117

2

1

3

D114

7

4

6

5

D119 x 0.5

D120 x 0.5

D122

D121

D123

D124

D125 x 2

D126

D128

D129

D127

W1

W3

W4

W5

W6

W7

W8

W20

W14

W26

W25

W27

W28

W29

W30

W33

W32

W31

W34

W35

W36

W37

W38

W40

W42

W43

W44

W54

W51

W53

W45

W46

W48

W47

W49

W56

W58

W62

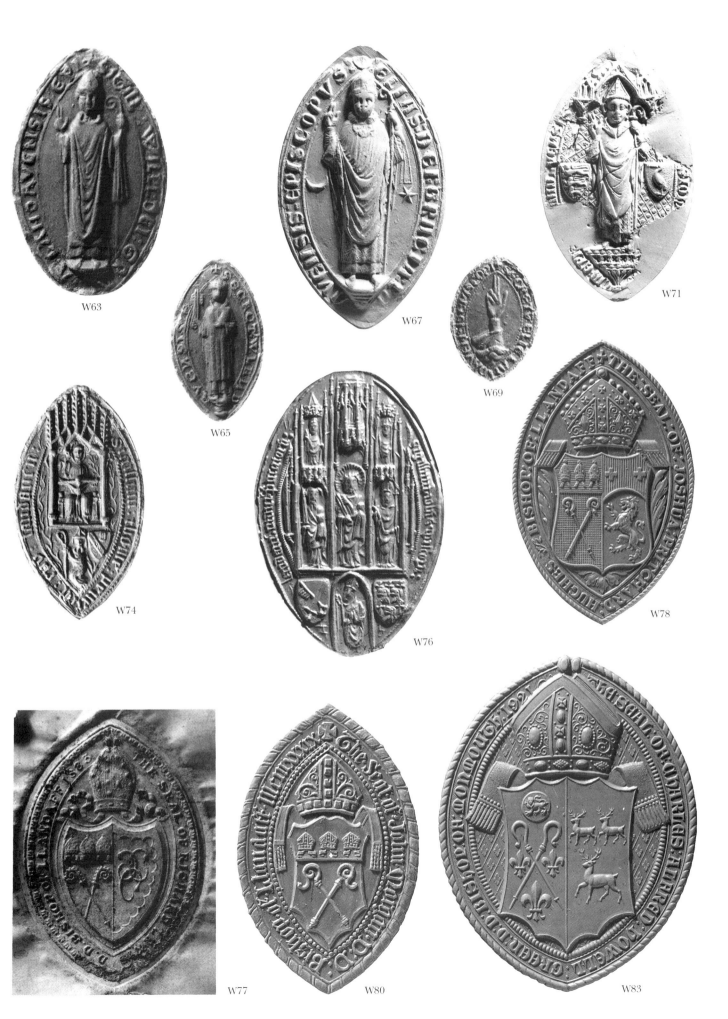

W63

W65

W67

W69

W71

W74

W76

W78

W77

W80

W83

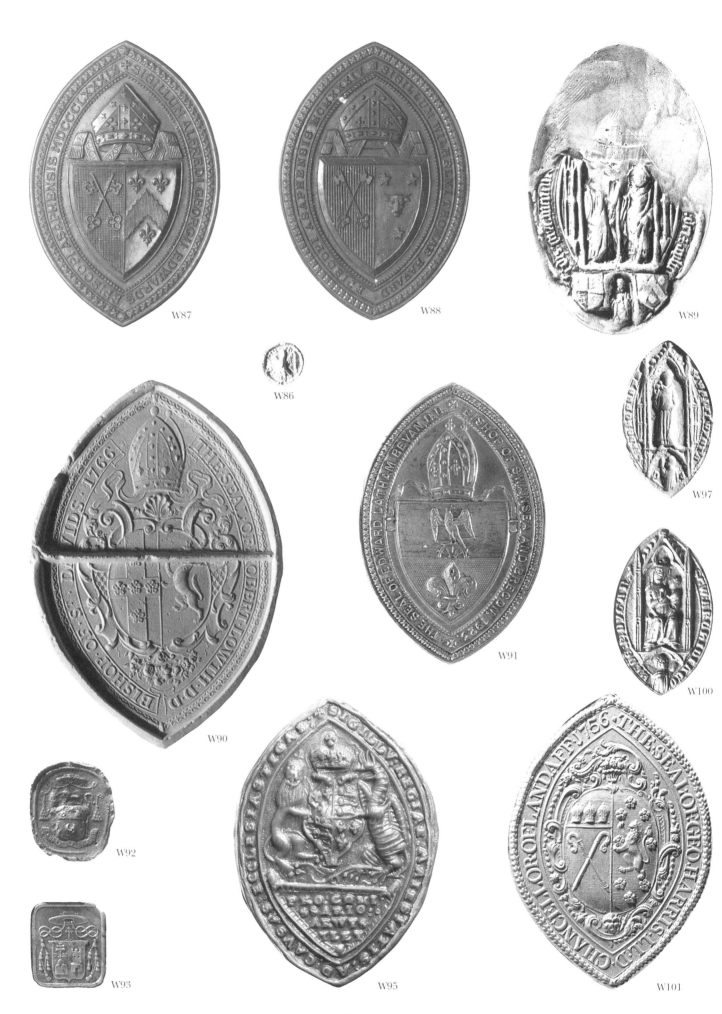

W87

W88

W89

W86

W90

W91

W97

W92

W100

W93

W95

W101

W102

W103

W104

W106

W107

W108

W109

W110

W111

W112

W113

W114

W115

W117

W119

W123

W124

W121

W125

W128

W129

W132

W133

W141

W142

W146

W143

W144

W147

W148

W150

W154

W149

W151

W165

W158

W159

W161

W163

W166

W167

W170

W171

W173

W175

W178

W184

W174

W186

W188

W189

W185

W194

W190

W191

W192

W195

W196

W197

W200

W207

W208

W201

W202

W216

W210

W213

W211

W214

W219

W220

W223

W228

W225

W227

W229

W230

W231

W234

W238

W239

W235

W236

W237

W240

W241

W251

W245

W243

W244

W249

W259

W261

W254

W250

W263

W264

W265

W266

W267

W268

W271

W270

W272

W273

W274

W277

W278

W279

W282

W284

W280

W283

W285

W286

W288

W292

W293

W290

W296

W294

W298

W297

W301

93

W306

W308

W303

W307

W310

W304

W311

W312

W313

W317

W321

W315

W314

W322

W323

W324

W325

W327

W328

W331

W330

W333

W326

W334

W335

W338

W337

W340

W341

W343

W342

W344

W345

W347

W348

W349

W352

W353

W351

W354

W350

W357

W356

W358

W364

W355

W363

W366

W360

W361

W365　W368

97

W370

W372

W373

W374

W375

W376

W377

W378

W379

W381

W382

W384

W383

W387

W388

W389

W391

W396

W398

W399

W401

W402 x 2

W405

W406

W407

W408 x 2

W412

W410

W414

W415

W417

W418

W416

W419 x 2

W421

W420

W423 x 2

W425 x 2

W428 x 2

W430 x 2

W431 x 2

W432 x 2

W437 x 2

W438 x 2

W439 x 2

W440 x 2

W441 x 2

W442 x 2

W443

W445

W449

W453

W447

W450

W454

W456

W457

W458

W461

W462

W465 x 0.5

W459

W464

W467

W463 x 2

W466 x 2

W468

W469

W470

W471

W472

W473

W474

W479

W478

W480

W481

W482

W483

W484

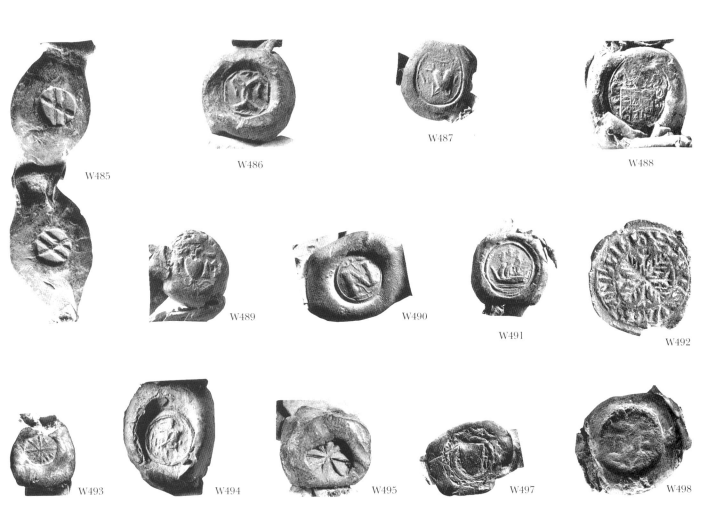

W485   W486   W487   W488

W489   W490   W491   W492

W493   W494   W495   W497   W498

W477

B1
B2

B3

B6

B7

B8

B10

B11

B12

B13

B14